JUNCTION BOOK ONE
DEFIANCE WORLD

BEAR ROSS

AETHON
BOOKS

DEFIANCE

©2019 BEAR ROSS

Print and eBook formatting, and cover design by Steve Beaulieu.

Published by Aethon Books LLC. 2019

In the gap between worlds, where the timeless present melds with both the past and future, there exists a place called Junctionworld. It is an interdimensional crossroads, a dark, disk-shaped city nearly one hundred miles across where thousands, perhaps millions, of distinct realities intersect via the Worldgates.

The Worldgates themselves are eight monolithic shapes, some formed like swirling vortexes, others like octagons or inverted triangles. Regardless of their configuration, each stands over a mile high and wide, and are spaced around the Junctionworld's urban perimeter. No written history can tell who built the towering interdimensional structures, only that they provide the pathways to invasion, conquest, trade, and terror.

Each Worldgate emits a different pattern of bright, swirling light, bathing the zones around them in their own distinct flavors of illumination. As distance from the gates increases, the colors fade away to the gray, swirling skies that loom over the rest of the dreary pocket dimension.

Control of these portals lies in the hands, if they can be called that, of the Gatekeepers. This powerful race of conquerors regulates and taxes all trade and traffic passing through the giant glowing gates.

The Gatekeepers, ruled by a council of eight GateLords, are polite to a fault, administering Junctionworld through adherence to their rigid, arcane laws known as the Old Code.

The armored overbeings keep the teeming masses of a thousand races pacified with mechanized blood-sports, catering to their baser needs in giant arenas of steel. The Gatekeepers pit sentient pilots against each other in hulking suits of walking armor known as mechs.

These gladiatorial battles, especially those fought to the death, are recorded by the Gatekeepers for broadcast. These transmissions flow back to Central Data, the mile-high tower standing at the hub of the wheel-shaped city. Central Data is the GateLords' palace and fortress, but also their network headquarters. From that bristling spire, the arena sportscasts are sent through the Worldgates as entertainment fodder for a million up-stream worlds.

When the arenas fail to keep the restless population distracted, the Gatekeepers send in their Enforcement Directorate troopers. These soldier-slaves, formed in giant, organic printers, are known by their ancient manufacturing brand, the Model Nines. The Nines are backed by their own combat mechs and armadas of hovering drones.

Should the Nines falter, though, the tower of Central Data stands ready as a final option, bristling in nuclear and conventional weaponry. Together, they stand ever-ready to crush rebel and invader alike in defense of the Gatekeepers.

The mech gladiators, even those that survive their first handful of matches, are taxed and levied to the point of near-slavery by the Gatekeepers. Their life-debt, the cost of rescuing them from danger in their old home dimensions, is used as leverage to keep the armor pilots fighting and producing content for the networks.

Only one being, a human named Solomon Kramer, has ever managed to win his liberty from the interdimensional overlords using his combat skills, raw determination, and the Gatekeepers' own tactics against them. If there is one thing the GateLords and their underlings will not tolerate, it is the embarrassment of being bested at their own game.

The Gatekeepers' thirst for dominance demands that they grind down Kramer and his family, while their Old Code restricts the manner in which they do it. Their goal is to extinguish the legacy of those that would dare defy them, lest it inspire others to question their power.

The irritating need for freedom must be crushed.

CHAPTER ONE_

Jered Kramer squinted as the harsh artificial sunlight poured through his walking armor's thick, semi-transparent canopy.

"All systems online, Jered," the mech's battle computer said. "My weapons and propulsion systems are nominal, and all secondary systems report in the green. I am ready to fight 'For Our Freedom, And Yours.'"

"Eh, that's my dad's old line, Judah," replied the mech's pilot, Jered Kramer. "Sounds good, though. You and I need to come up with something of our own. Confirm, diagnostics read green across the board. Let's go get some."

"Agreed, Pilot. Let's 'get some,'" the smooth robotic voice said, over-accentuating the words. "Your father also liked that phrase."

"Yeah, that's probably where I got it," Jared said as he flipped a bank of switches. "I kinda wish dad was here to see me, now, even if he hates this place."

"An understatement, pilot," Judah said. "The word 'hate' only begins to describe your father's opinion of Berva Proxima arena and the Gatekeeper charged with its management."

Jered and his walking armored mech, Judah, stepped through the grand archway of the arena. The roar of the teeming alien crowd swelled as the huge colosseum's lights focused on him and his towering armor.

"No doubt, Judah," Jered said, grinning at the thought of his angry father. "All the Gatekeepers hate Dad, but he and Mikralos seem to have something extra special going on between them."

"Agreed, pilot," Judah replied. "The particular fact that Honored Mikralos holds your contract of servitude, forcing you to defend this arena's status, must wound Solomon Kramer deeply."

"Whoa, easy on the guilt-trip, you're starting to sound like my mom," Jered said. "Hey, who is this guy, anyway?"

"Your opponent today is a fellow human," Judah answered. "Masamune Kyuzo, piloting a customized Bernex Systems K-17."

"Human, huh? Wait, did you say a K-17?" Jered asked, smirking to himself. "Custom or not, who the void still steps into the arena in one of those old things? This is going to be too easy."

"This is his first Hammer League fight and his first death match, apparently, pilot. I have evaluated his previous, lower-league shield-matches, however, and there is a—" the machine said before Jered interrupted.

"He's just another notch, Judah. Fresh meat," Jered said. "Don't bother me with the details. This will be over, soon enough."

Jered looked out the sides of his cockpit at the carved, shot-pocked stones next to him. Elaborate flourishes engraved into the entrance showed battle scenes and the portraits of fabled mech gladiators who once fought here. Jered hoped to add his name and visage to the laser-carved portal someday, even if the place was just a bottom-tier dump and slaughterhouse. Today's victory would mean that they were half-way to freedom. *Sorry, Masa-whatever-your-name-is. Nothing personal,* Jered thought to himself.

Jered finished his pre-fight ritual, tapping his chest straps four times and re-positioning the 2D photo of his two little sisters on the mech cockpit's dashboard. He ran his fingers over Judah's control yokes, flipping off his weapons' safeties as he eased Judah's giant armored bulk into a slow, thundering jog.

As quick as it started, the mech froze in its tracks, skidding to a halt. Frowning, he eased the control yokes forward again. Nothing.

His weapons display panel remained red and black, large slashes appearing over icons of his cannon and chainsword. The safeties weren't disengaging.

He hit them again, trying to bring the mech's weapons online. Judah's control displays blacked out, then "ERROR Control Module Compromised ERROR" began flashing over and over in his heads-up display.

Jered thumped the side of his cockpit's main electrical panel, jarring it open.

"Gate damn it, not now, Judah!" he said.

Without Kramer's say-so, retractable blast plates in his mech's hull emerged, assembling themselves in an angular, protective shell that followed the canopy's smooth shape. The interior of the command compartment grew dark, then lit up as the internal displays came online, mirroring the outside view through protected cameras. The extensive threat indicators and digital readout of the arena's interior came up, but the normal control icons failed to appear.

"Judah, what the void is going on?!" Jered yelled.

Only the sound of hissing static answered his shouted question. Suddenly, Jered collided with the side of his cockpit as Judah lurched, unbidden, into motion. The thousand-species crowd roared as the combination of stoic Judah and helpless Jered stormed through the carved arch.

Cursing, Jered Kramer smashed his fists bloody against the interior of the armored cockpit glass. He screamed his frustration to the dead control displays and the armored shell which prevented the arena's cameras from seeing his plight.

The mech continued its plodding gait to the starting circle, about half-way to the center of the cavernous auditorium. The lights in the arena's high ceiling turned down to minimum illumination. Small camera drones flew in strangled orbits around Jered's armor, and the main spotlight in the armored camera turret flooded over them from above.

The ring announcer's voice boomed an introduction in a number of alien tongues and data streams as Jered continued to thrash at Judah's controls to no avail.

Judah came to a lumbering stop in the floodlit ring of the engagement point, facing the maddened crowd. The walking armor was now in autonomous mode, but the external lights that normally would have signaled that condition were not flashing.

To Jered's horror, the mech drew its large chain-saw sword and pointed upwards in a salute to Gatekeeper Mikralos, the proprietor of Berva Proxima arena. The motorized close-combat weapon, the pride of his father's armory, was longer than a full-size hovercar and drew its brutal cutting power directly from the mech's fusion turbine.

The challenger, in a red and white mech bristling with cannon and missile launchers, did the same with the power claw on its left arm.

The Gatekeeper's viewing box, an armored bubble high

above the stadium seats, flashed answering lights in acknowledgment, returning the salutes.

A strobing white pulse from every light in the massive building signaled the start of the match. Jered pulled the ejection handles on either side of his headrest. Again, nothing. The artificial sunlight of the stadium returned to its normal illumination. Horns and sirens sounded the start of the death match, and Jered moaned, though no one could hear his dread.

Combat was now joined, and Kramer's screens flashed telltale alerts as the opposing pilot boosted his mech's jets hard for cover. The red mech shot behind one of the scattered clusters of large granite rocks dotting the mile-wide floor. Small exhaust plumes flowered bright yellow from launch tubes on the enemy mech's armored back as it made its initial move, each flash signaling the launch of a guided warhead.

Judah, still not under Jered's control, sidestepped behind hard cover the instant before impact. The missiles tracked into the face of the twenty-foot-tall wall barricades the towering mech sheltered behind. Sharp explosions thundered, their echoes cascading from the walls and audience shields. A half-dozen glowing spots appeared on the side of the wall facing him, the result of shaped charges that came just short of drilling through the two-foot-thick edifices.

Jered bellowed in fear and rage, yanking and bucking against his controls. The faithful armor which had borne his father into conflict for years continued to rebel. *The anti-sabotage checks were supposed to keep dung like this from happening,* he thought. *Prath, if I live through this, you're a dead ape.*

Crew Chief Prath would have to wait, though. Jered's hijacked mech popped exhaust nozzles from compartments in its lower legs, and Kramer could hear the microturbines begin to spool up in Judah's large backpack-like dorsal housing.

"No, no, Judah, what the void are you doing?" Jered cried.

"This is suicide! Hard boost this early? We'll be sitting puddle-flaps! This is a gate-damned nightmare!"

"Je-red... This. Not... not... Me... >*bzzt*< Interior Overri-" Judah's audio speaker managed to say in jerking tones between bursts of garbled electronic gibberish.

"Judah! Judah, initiate control system purge!" Jered said, screaming to his console. "Blow the main reactor manifold bolts! Vent it! Vent it all!"

Jered and Judah were now roaring across the steel deck of the Berva Proxima arena, dodging incoming bursts of auto-cannon fire and swirling missile volleys with graceful ease. The sports network's drone cameras were hard-pressed to keep up with the jinking and maneuvering, and the jolting acceleration forced Jered to push his arms back through his seat's restraints. The enemy mech loomed, the distance closing.

Judah's giant chainsword began spinning up, the whining keen adding to the flood of noise coming from the turbines. Jered felt the armor's weight shift, leaning in for a final assault. Reflex made him manipulate the dead controls, but it was to no avail. The massive combat robot's feet threw sparks as it slid across the arena's steel floor. Its feet caught momentary purchase, and the killing machine rolled into a headlong controlled tumble. With a fearful blur of movement, its giant sword was now arcing overhead, as if to cleave the opposing mech-gladiator's armor in two.

But the jets cut out short. Jered saw the distance was too far to engage in close combat. His armor began a stiff, overdone display of hacking and parrying at the air, fighting an opponent who was still far off, as it continued to charge on foot.

The enemy red and white mech brought its main gun to bear. There were no rocks, there was no barricade, no protective cover at all. *Fatal ground, as the old man would say,* Jered Kramer thought.

Time slowed. Jered could almost see down the cannon's barrel at the shell waiting to be fired. The muzzle looked like a water pipe a construction crew installed near the family compound when he was a kid. The picture on his dashboard, the one with his two kid sisters, rattled loose from all the maneuvering. His mech's furious, useless charge continued unabated.

He reached for the photo as it fell, trying to catch it. The cannon's muzzle flashed, highlighting the smiles of his sisters Jessica and Hannah.

Jered's world filled with bright pain as he bucked against the seat's restraints. He looked down at the new hole in his mech's control readouts, then further down, at his own midsection. Jered's lower body was now a shredded wreck, and flame and smoke curled up within Judah's control cabin. Something welled up in him as his breath slipped away, a cauldron of white-hot fury turning to cold. He gasped for air as one hand fumbled for the fallen picture of his sisters.

Kramer's vision closed in, and the last thing he saw was the red and white power claw breach through the blast shields, through the armored glass, through the display screens, and through what was left of his chest. Blackness swallowed him. The crowd roared, while Judah continued to jibber a mindless staccato into his dead ears.

notice it. She looked at the main viewer screen up on the wall, then checked to make sure Solomon Kramer was all the way upstairs before she took a quick drink from the bottle, wincing at the taste.

The screen showed a short biographical segment about her brother, narrating his life story. Jessica forgot about her sister and Tevren as the liquor took effect. She smirked at the network's melodramatic and carefully-edited portrayal of Jered Kramer, the 'Heir Apparent to the Kramer Legacy,' and stole another bitter sip from the container.

What the biographical blurb didn't tell the audience was that her older brother had screwed up, once again, at the casinos in the Fourth Gate Zone. Today's event was part of working his debt off by engaging in cut-rate death matches for a Gatekeeper. A Gatekeeper who her dad hated, hated even more than the rest of the gross little blobs that ruled Junctionworld.

"Mikralos," she blurted aloud, the booze loosening her young tongue. *Gatekeepers had the weirdest names*, she thought.

Jessica, being sixteen standard years, enjoyed her older brother's wild, reckless attitude and lifestyle, but she knew that her father was right: The Gatekeepers were looking for any excuse to subjugate and re-enslave Solomon Kramer, his legacy, and his family.

The interdimensional overlords plucked Kramer from his own time and planet because their scouts identified him as a fighter, a prime candidate for the arenas. If they had known then what they knew now, the Gatekeepers probably would have left him to his fate.

Those many decades ago, when they offered to rescue him from certain death, Solomon was fighting against incredible odds in the sewers of the Warsaw ghetto. He was a starving rebel in a futile uprising, outnumbered over a hundred-to-one by the Waffen-SS. Cornered and injured, still he fought on.

The Gatekeepers, though formal and domineering, love an underdog. Jessica's father said it helped them for marketing their broadcasts, to have a pilot with a valiant backstory. The overbeings brought him to Junctionworld and charged him for his renewed existence. The cost of their rescue was his inescapable servitude. They healed his wounds, trained him to pilot mechs, and the rest was history.

Solomon Kramer had been a thorn in the blobs' sides for years, now, ever since he won his freedom against all odds. It was an embarrassment to the Gatekeepers, one they had tried to correct many times, but her father was just too good, in and out of the arenas. His cagey ability to stay one step ahead of them came at a different cost, though.

Solomon's constant paranoia from living in this formal-yet-lethal pocket dimension had been justified too many times, already, by the machinations and plots of the alien overlords. The elder Kramer was convinced that Jered's selling of himself back into Mikralos's arena was part of some conspiracy by the Gatekeepers. Jered was a good pilot, nearly as good as her old man, but Jessica hoped nothing bad would happen to her brother. Not only might Jered get hurt, but it would prove her father, gripped by his madness, was right.

Like I don't hear Dad's conspiracies enough, she thought, letting out a sigh.

The warm-up to the upcoming death match on the viewing room's main screen droned on in the background. Two alien sportscasters chattered away, their pre-game banter blending into the background as musical fanfare played. Gingerly testing the hot parts, she found they were cool enough to be handled. Jessica test-fitted the parts of the heavy revolver together, the large, simplistic parts interlocking together with a bit of effort and hand fitting.

Jessica focused on getting the cylinder mated to the frame of the revolver, the four gaping mouths of the large chambers each lining up with the barrel as she cocked and dropped the hammer, rotating them through their firing cycle. Horns and flashing lights from the screen briefly strobed in the background, glinting off the sleek lines of the custom firearm. She reached for the bottle from its hidden spot, and took another swig.

She couldn't wait to show her Poppa the new revolver. She stared at it, turning the heavy chunk of printed and machined steel over in her hands to view it from all angles. She tried a few dummy cartridges in the cylinders, just to see if they fit, and could be extracted once fired. Everything worked perfectly.

A howling scream from upstairs filled the habitat. It was her mother. Alarmed, Jessica tucked the bottle away and looked up at the screen.

Judah, the Kramer family's brightly-colored gladiator mech, crumbled in the match's instant replay sub-screen, a cannon shot piercing through the main canopy's armor over and over again in excruciating detail from a variety of angles. Jessica's jaw and the pistol dropped.

Confused, Jessica rewound the sports network to the start. After the introductions and opening fanfare, Jered and Judah went from the starting ring into a suicide run at the opposing mech. It was surreal, watching her expert gladiator pilot of a brother charge into close range without a single scrap of cover. Next, the cannon hit. Then, a crushing blow in close combat that hollowed Jessica's heart.

She watched as the red and white mech slugged its heavy battle claw through the shattered cockpit, shoving the armored gauntlet's talons so far into Judah's hull that the sponsor's logos were no longer visible on the forearm. As the crowds roared, the other pilot ripped Jered's shattered corpse through the breach, throwing it to the ground. The red mech's jets flared, and the cameras caught every cinder as Jered was charred to pieces, her brother's body washing away in a torrent of reactor plasma. Judah, now a shattered husk of wrecked armor, toppled backwards to the arena floor.

There were wails of pain and anguish upstairs as Jered died over and over on the replays. Her mother's shrill voice became frantic, and her father's deeper tone came in response, but not distinct words. *Were they arguing? About what? She thought.*

Muffled shouts and angered cries flew between her parents upstairs, unseen by Jessica. Her father's voice yelled, and then a gunshot rang out through the habitat. Something heavy fell to the floor above her head with a thud.

Solomon Kramer's paranoia caused him to build or buy only the best security systems for his home and workplace. At the sound of the firearm's discharge, internal alarms blared, and blast doors slammed shut throughout the home's living spaces. Each room became its own stronghold and survival cell. Jessica was trapped in the living room, unable to assess the situation or reach her parents upstairs. The overhead illumination blinked out, and the only light in the sealed room came from the looped sportscast of her brother's grisly death.

"Mom? Poppa? What the void was that?" Jessica yelled towards the ceiling, booze-blurred fear causing her voice to crack in mid-question.

Even through the armored walls, Jessica could still hear the sound of her mother's crying, a soul-bruising sound which crescendoed into another scream. A second gunshot rang out. Then silence. Jessica gripped her newly-assembled revolver tight and at the ready, though she didn't have a single round of live ammunition to load in it.

Jessica strained with her blurred senses, hoping to hear any movement from upstairs. Only the silence of a graveyard met her ears. She could no longer look at Jered, dying over and over, on the view-screen. She threw the bottle of liquor at the image projector, shattering it. The living room was now pitch black.

Time passed. Sirens moaned in the distance, barely perceptible through the habitat's thick walls, growing louder as they approached. It was the Enforcement Directorate, the Gatekeeper's combination of armed forces and police. They were a brutal force, a mix of drones and bio-printed, blindly obedient, Model Nine troopers.

Blinding sparks and choking smoke flew from all four edges of the armored hatch connecting the hangar to the kitchen. The heavy security door clattered to the ground with a deep boom, crushing her mother's kitchen table. Jessica hid her revolver in the thigh cargo pocket of her utility coveralls, the heavy weapon bulging against the seams as she took cover behind the couch.

Past the ragged edges of the scorched kitchen hatch, Jessica saw her father's hangar, filled with a cloud of hovering security drones. A trooper's silhouette occupied the space once taken up by her father only minutes before, one hand holding a laser carbine, the other commanding her to come forward.

"Subject. Attention. Present empty manipulators. Step forward," the Enforcer said in the clipped tones used by the bioprinted soldiers. "Make no furtive movement. Approach. Deadly force may be utilized."

Her hands up, Jessica came around the edge of the couch into the blinding spotlights of the drones. The tall, lanky trooper pulled her into his iron grip, slapping her into restraints as she tried to voice her protests.

"Gate damn it, my parents are still in there," Jessica screamed, trying to pull away from the Enforcer. "They're stuck in there, and I think they're hurt. I don't know why. I need to get back in there! I have the access codes, just let me go, and I'll help!"

Unmoved, the Model Nine trooper passed her down a gathered line of identical armed and armored beings. The half-dozen Enforcers formed a stacked-up entry team. Each, in turn, searched her with mechanical precision, spinning and pushing her to the next in line once their assigned portion of her person was cleared. She tried to squawk her protests, but her intoxicated senses were hard-pressed to resist. Near the end of the stack, the soldier-being tasked with her lower body removed the revolver from her pocket. The last Enforcer placed the weapon in an evidence bag and scanned her hand with a digit-press reader. A hologram of her face and personal information appeared in midair. The base-line trooper handed the scanner to a nearby Model Ninety-Nine officer and stuffed her into a waiting Enforcer grav-vehicle.

"Process subject Kramer, Jessica, at Fourth Zone Barracks. Prep for intel scan, but do not execute until order sent. Stand by for further instructions," the advanced officer model told its subordinate, who nodded in acknowledgment.

"You venting blob-puppets, let me go!" Jessica said, raging at the unflinching, expressionless soldiers through the grav-car's window. "Let me go, you pinheaded, tank-bred meat-bots!" Tears now flowed down her face as the reality of the situation bore down on her.

The vehicle lifted off. Looking back through the window, Jessica heard the muffled explosions, and saw the eye-blistering flashes, as the Enforcers breached her family's home, door by door, room by room.

CHAPTER THREE_

"Ugh, Jev, can you turn that dung off, please?" Jessica Kramer said. She ran her hand through her dark hair, trying to avoid looking at the main viewing screen in the dank, robot-staffed bar.

"Apologies, Pilot Kramer," Jev, the bot-tender replied, sliding down a mechanical track behind the bar's counter. Jev's external lights pulsed, changing the channel. The mechanical server whirred back to where she was seated, head cameras at a slight bow. "This Unit should have been monitoring the transmission output. Next beverage is on the house."

A handful of shouted protests ensued from the crowd as the current program, a top ten review of the most brutal arena kills in the last ten years, flashed to one of the other hundreds of Gatekeeper-controlled sports feeds.

The new program was some live event with amateurs no one cared about in one of the lower-class arenas. The bar's mix of alien and human conversations lowered in volume, then went back to their normal hum. A dark laugh rose from one of the tables as one of the mechs on screen lost an arm to a rotary cannon burst.

Jessica Kramer sighed and accepted the beer. She was not in the mood for this cheap, sordid booze-shack. She was especially not in the mood for seeing her brother Jered die, once again, in a gate-damned 'best-of' show while surrounded by strangers.

Five painful years had passed since that day at Berva Proxima, but Jered Kramer's spectacular, pointless death inside Judah still made the retro-arena network feeds. Per Jered's old contract, part of the money from those broadcast residuals still went to her, his last living relative on Junctionworld. It wasn't much, just enough to get by in this miserable garden of mechanized slaughter.

The fact that Jessica Kramer paid her existence taxes, housing levies, and the dozens of other Gatekeeper fees with the money generated by their use of Jered's death footage was a bitter, ironic twist that made her want another beer. And another. And another, until her memory of that day went away in a black smear.

The years since the events of that day continued to haunt her, yet here she found herself, waiting for the next tap on the shoulder, the next inevitable ethyl-alcohol-soaked challenge by some lunkhead to see if he or she measured up to a Kramer. Jessica caught the wink and nod between two mech pilots as they looked in her direction and murmured a joke. She tried to ignore them, then decided she would probably break both of their jaws later, if she had time before her upcoming gladiator match.

Jessica seemed to catch too many people staring at her

before they averted their eyes. Maybe it was her father's paranoia, coming back to manifest in her. She took a deep drink from the new beer and tried to relax. With a subtle movement, she re-engaged the snap on her pistol's holster. The impulse to kill every being in the room definitely came from her mother.

The Fourth Gate Kramers. Five years ago, it was once a badge of honor, one that struck fear in the hearts of enemy pilots and Gatekeepers alike. It was a phrase that paid. *Feh.* Now, that name and a five-credit debitpress could barely get you a watered-down beer in a place like this. In a chipped glass, of course.

"Jev, another, please," Jessica said to the bot-tender.

"One moment, Mech Pilot Jessica Kramer," Jev answered in a robotic tone. "You advised This Unit that you are due for a match tonight at Red Iridium Arena. Your customer profile preferences indicate you are to be served only four beverages on days prior to an arena challenge. Do you wish to override?"

A holographic release form appeared in mid-air in front of the beverage bot.

"Yes, please. I'll be fine, Jev, thank you," Jessica said. She pressed her glowing thumb through the proffered image. She noticed the two jokers across the bar furrowing their brows in confusion when she thanked the bot-tender. It was easy to be rude to drones and bots, even though Jev's rudimentary AI appreciated the courtesy at some small level of semi-sentience. Being polite to a machine might be silly, but it showed humanity, which was a scarce quality in this ugly little pocket dimension called Junctionworld. She got that from her mother, too.

The beer glass filled from the bottom through a one-way valve. She watched the level rise in thirsty anticipation. *This was the last one*, she promised herself. *Well, maybe the one after this one...*

Jessica's back was to the door, but she felt something in the room shift. One hand accepted the beer, the other went back to the grip of the pistol on her rib cage.

"Sentients and sapients, I greet you in the Ways of the Old Code. May the illumination of the eight gates shine bright upon this establishment," said a smooth electronic voice from the doorway of the bar. A large metallic pod filled most of the portal, its gleaming body lined with low pulsing lines chasing each other. Two Model Nine bodyguards in heavy body armor stood on either side of the pod, their weapons pointed at the bar patrons.

"We wonder," the pod's voice said, almost like a purring coo, "if there are any among you gentlebeings from the house of Kramer, of the Fourth Gate? If so, we have a proposition of a business nature."

Jessica smirked, pulled her hand off the butt of her revolver, and looked over her shoulder to the Gatekeeper in his floating armored pod. Both of the bio-printed bodyguards trained their weapons on her.

"Mikralos, is that you, you payment-stretching, gate-damned pustule, after all these years?" Jessica said, lifting her fifth beer to her lips.

The Gatekeeper floated to her spot at the bar. His reinforced life chamber was a gleaming pink fishbowl shrouded by the rest of the protective silver chassis. Jessica continued to drink, suppressing a shudder at the sight of the grotesque little overlord.

The Gatekeepers were not an ancient race, not like the Szran->click< or the Redfolk, but they were a powerful one. They had conquered Junctionworld and its Eight Gates, after all. Mikralos and the rest of the Gatekeepers looked like fat, distorted babies in a traveling artificial womb, but they each packed more firepower and advanced shielding than a

Concordium main battle tank. The bodyguards were almost for show; a status symbol, of sorts.

"Ah, daughter of the Fourth Gate Kramers, Jessica," Mikralos said. "We greet you in—"

"In the Ways of the Old Code, yes, yes, Mikralos," Jessica said, twirling her hands in a rolling motion. "Spare me the Gatekeeper formalities and 'Old Code' crap. What do you want?"

"Very well. Direct and to the point. Very Human," Mikralos said. "As you may know, we are still in possession of your deceased sibling's combat armor. Well, what is left of it, such as it is. Collateral for his unpaid debts, of course."

Jessica bristled and turned her bar stool to face the hovering overlord. Mikralos's bodyguards flicked off the safeties of their weapons with an energy-charged whine.

"Yeah, you still own Judah, our old family ride, I know," Jessica said. "Jered's death ripped my world apart and busted the Kramers out of business. It's a sad story, sure. Get to the point." She tried to keep a nonchalant tone in her voice, but her knuckles were turning white around her beer.

"Not to mention the accompanying murder-suicide of your parents," Mikralos said. "Then insolvency collapsed your valiant and once-prosperous team, scattering them to the various gate paths. Much has transpired since then, according to our sources. A series of regrettable occurrences, indeed, Mech Pilot Kramer."

"We understand you're now piloting in the Light Exo Leagues? Limited Ordnance class, yes?" Mikralos said.

She nodded.

"How...quaint," the Gatekeeper said, faux pity dripping from his speaker's voice.

Jessica wasn't sure if the reminder of her parents' deaths or her diminished status in the minor leagues of the mech fighting organizations stung more. She began to stand up from the stool, and the bodyguard weapons edged closer as she rose.

"Why you encephalitic, atrophied waste of a—" Jessica said, her voice edged with intoxicated anger.

"Consider your next words carefully, mech pilot," the voice coming from the Gatekeeper's armored module said. "We have come to this base and loathsome place to conduct business, not to recount your tedious and pedestrian past miseries. Now, sit down, and consider this token."

A smooth metal claw emerged from the skin of the Gatekeeper's pod. It held a cylindrical object about the size of a thermos, scorched on one side, dented on the other. An array of wires and conduits stuck out of a small port on top of the battered object. A small red light glowed in the middle of the module's scorched patch when it dropped into her hands.

"You... you pulled Judah's control module out of the wreckage," she said, slumping to her stool as she ran her fingers over the blistered paint.

"Yes, pilot Kramer," Mikralos said, "though the damage was severe, our associates manage to recover the battle computer from your family's mech, 'Judah.' Arkathan circuitry, from a time before they were wiped out. A very handsome component in both structure and capability. 'They don't make them like that anymore,' we believe is the parlance of your father's homeworld."

"I know, trust me," Jessica said. "My current mech's control module can barely keep me walking and shooting at the same time. It's a basic machine-brain, but it's all I can afford. I haven't even bothered to name it—"

"We offer this to you, human, but not lightly," Mikralos said, cutting off her rambling. "Do you wish to entertain our terms?"

Jessica took a long drink from her beer glass, draining it. She looked over her shoulder to the bar bot.

"Jev, set me up another, please. Put it on the kind Gatekeeper's tab, here," she said.

She took the new glass and blew the foam off the top in the direction of the nearest Model Nine bodyguard.

"Let's hear it, Mikralos."

———

"No gate-damned way, blob. You want this done, you do it yourself," Jessica said. She stormed down the alleyway, away from the Gatekeeper and his bodyguards, towards the back door of Jev's bar.

"We would, Pilot Kramer, but appearances must be kept," Gatekeeper Mikralos said. "There is an order to how these things must proceed. Protocols must be followed. 'The Ways of the Old Code,' and such."

"You mean you get to clear the dark cloud hanging over your arena," Jessica said, her face turning flush as her volume became louder. "Using me to set up some disgusting, chintzy 'blood vengeance' match. That's low, even for a—"

"Again, you test us with your words, when we offer only benevolence and good will to you," Mikralos said, calling to her as she started to walk away. "Besides, we both have something to gain. We are being more than generous in placing the services of a very distinguished design and fabrication facility at your disposal. We both have lingering questions, Pilot Kramer, questions that can only be answered by the 'Judah' control module. A control module that only activates when in the presence of members of its controlling house." Jessica stopped and turned.

"Yeah, I noticed the red indicator light come on," Jessica said. "That's the first time Judah's woken up since Jered died, isn't it?" Mikralos's pod made an awkward bobble motion, and the lights on his pod's surface seemed to fidget and twitch.

"Well... yes and no," Mikralos said. "Your sister, Hannah, sought an audience with us after your brother's death, demanding to analyze and question the command module. Unfortunate missteps were made on her part during the negotiations. We... could not accommodate her requests. She departed Junctionworld soon after with her technical associate. 'Tevren,' we believe, was the second human's name."

"And good riddance to the both of them, too," Jessica said. "But let's call it for what it really was, Gatekeeper: you tried to extort Hannah to access the data in Judah's module, even though it might have shown what really happened, and cleared the reputation of your lame dung-pot of an arena. Before she left, Hannah told me you wanted half a million credits for your gate-damned 'accommodation.'" Jessica spit after mentioning her sister's name.

"It is not as simple as you say," Mikralos said, his pod's claws making a swirling gesture of embarrassment. "But, yes, that small detail of the occurrence is accurate. Let it be known that her offer and our financial requirements were at odds. Knowledge is power here in Junctionworld, and power costs credits, pilot."

"Even though the incident made your Berva Proxima a joke, and nearly put you in receivership?" Jessica said.

A jagged series of pulses ran along the ribbons of light carved into the Gatekeeper's carapace.

"Our financial matters at the time, and since then, are our own concern, pilot," Mikralos said, an edged grate now present in his pod's smooth voice. "You needn't occupy your feeble mind with pondering that which you do not understand. You need only remember your place."

"My *place*?" Jessica said, incredulous. "Oh, that's nice. Fine. So, what's changed? What's new, that this oh-so-generous offer is now on the table?"

"We have come into new information concerning your brother's death," Mikralos said. "Naturally, since his humiliating demise caused the gladiator sports media to cast aspersions on how our beloved Berva Proxima is operated, our ticket sales and subscriptions have suffered. The facilities are in disrepair. We have even had to resort to... to renting out the main arena floor for trade shows and sales conventions."

"Mmm... I've seen the commercials on the data webs," Jessica said, cocking her head. "You must be pretty desperate, since those ads run non-stop. That one about the 'Transdimensional Insurance Agent Convention' really cracks me up. Not exactly the high-profile, upper-crust stuff you're used to, is it, *Honored* Mikralos?"

"It is a slow, sordid ruination, Pilot Kramer. Tread carefully," Mikralos said.

Jessica took one last drink from her beer, then threw the glass to the ground, shattering the vessel on the alley's hard, filthy pavement.

"Oh, I'm sure life must just be *horrible* for you, Mister Gatekeeper, *sir*," Jessica said, taunting Mikralos as she wiped a dribble of beer from her lips. "You poor, *poor* thi—"

The lights tracing over the Gatekeeper's pod froze and turned to black. A silver claw was around her neck, pinning her against the wall, her boots kicking at the air. Her hands scrambled to hold onto the slippery liquid steel. Her vision grew dim around the edges. The blood vessels in her eyes pounded, and her lungs burned for air.

"We have been more than patient with your clumsy verbal jabs and snide remarks," the Gatekeeper's voice hissed, "but do not delude yourself into believing you can *mock* us, *underbeing. Ever.*"

Mikralos lowered her to the ground and hovered away. Jessica kept one arm on the alley wall where he dropped her, coughing and hacking for air. The other hand searched for her pistol. The holster was empty.

She looked up, sputtering through tears and snot. One of the bodyguards, the one she blew the beer foam at earlier in the bar, had her revolver in his hand.

The handgun's cylinder was empty, the pudgy 20mm cartridges dumped in the puddles of muck at his feet. The body-guard toyed with the weapon, bobbing it up and down as he offered it to her.

Still trying to catch her breath, Jessica reached for the pistol. The Model Nine trooper snapped the revolver's cylinder shut with the flick of a wrist and tossed it into a pile of trash bags ten feet away. The impact and noise sent a hidden den of octorats scurrying.

"Gate damn it, meat-bot, that pistol's *mine*," Jessica said, snarling through ragged breaths. "You wanna play, Niner? Okay, let's play."

She spit, clearing her throat, and snapped a knife out from a sheath in her boot. The hum of its high-frequency blade drilled a hole in the air. The second bodyguard's energy rifle, its muzzle glowing, rose. The vibro-blade's grip in her hand switched from hammer to icepick, the blade positioned along her forearm. She wiped her mouth with the back of her knife hand, and moved for her other blade.

"Enough!" Mikralos said, his speaker booming the words. "We have business to conclude, human. Control your savage impulses, or the deal is off. No command module. No vengeance death match. No answers to your questions."

Jessica stopped her advance and sneered at her opponent, switching the vibro-knife off. She spit at the feet of the Nine holding her at rifle point.

"It is regrettable that we had to lay our claws on you, Kramer," Mikralos said, his lights pulsing slower as his voice became more composed. "For the sake of our potential business dealings, we will overlook your impertinence. Walk with us, Mech Pilot. Our conveyance is in a holding pattern overhead. We are summoning it now."

The Gatekeeper's transport was a larger, sleeker version of his personal pod, a mix of limousine and anti-grav yacht. It, too, was a silver color with pathways of light embedded in its hull. It glided into the alley from far overhead, its shimmering shape descending from the flickering gray skies over Junctionworld without a sound.

A ramp flowed from the rear of the craft, and Mikralos moved up the freshly-materialized incline. His bodyguards followed, their weapons still trained on her. He gave a command to the crew waiting at the front of the craft, and then turned to Jessica waiting at the bottom of the ramp.

"Tomorrow, at this same time and locale, we will send this same transport unit for you," Mikralos said. "If you find the terms we offered acceptable, walk up the ramp, and you will be taken to a private fabrication facility, the best in Junctionworld. There, you will be equipped to fight the man who killed your brother. Together, Pilot, we might correct this long, torturous ordeal. May fortune smile on you, Mech Pilot Kramer, at your shield match tonight at Red Iridium."

Her head still hurt, a combination of the beer and the choke-out. She watched the craft spirit away on silent, glowing grav-drives. The octorats made another disturbance in the alley's trash piles. Jessica looked down at her watch.

Gate damn it, I'm running late, she cursed to herself, trying in vain to ignore her emerging hangover.

By the time Jessica found and reloaded her revolver, she was running even later for tonight's fight.

CHAPTER FOUR_

"Kramer! Kramer, you're late again, primate," Sgok, a Skevvian, said. He rose up on his main set of tentacles, peering over the edge of his desk as she tried to sneak by unnoticed. A holographic display of tonight's fight schedule hung in midair over the pit boss's podium, reds and blue denoting the duels about to happen and the various combatants' states of readiness. The column next to her name blinked red. Sgok's writhing appendages pulsed with chloroplasts that changed color according to his emotional state. Judging from the throbbing red and brown pattern, the mech arena's pit boss was not in a good mood.

"Uh, sorry, Sgok, I got held up dealing with a Gatekeeper. You know how it is. The mouthy little blobs take forever just to finish a sentence," Jessica said, trying to downplay the Skevvian's signals of indignation. Her hair kept falling out from under her helmet liner cap. She brushed it back into place as she poked at the command display next to her gladiator mech.

"I don't care if it was one of the GateLords, themselves, human," the pit boss said, clicking his hard beak in disgust. "The least you can do is show up to work on time."

"I, uh, got caught in traffic. There was a bad wreck on the hoverpath descending to the arena. My skimmer almost ran out of propellant. No, really, I swear," Jessica said, avoiding eye contact with the mottled, tentacled being.

"Yeah, sure. You and I both know you live right around the corner, over by that robo-bar. Lucky for you, I scrambled the matches around. Hold still while I buzz you in," Sgok said, raising a scanner in his left tentacle cluster.

"Oh, c'mon, Sgok, I'm running way late, you just said so yourself," Jessica protested, pulling her helmet on as she ran a quick series of boot-up checks for her mech's reactor core. "Just check me in manually and let the other guy know I'm ready to go, would ya?"

"You know the rules, Kramer," Sgok said. "You get bio-scanned in for enhancers and other drugs, just like every other fighter who isn't fighting in Unlimited status. I don't need the portable detector, though. I can smell the alcohol coming off you from here, vertebrate."

"It was just a few suds," Jessica said. "Just enough to take the edge off some pre-match jitters, Sgok, honest. Hey, cut me a break."

Sgok scowled, his colors showing his deepened resentment. He put the scanner away and pressed a button on his desk. The display status next to her name changed to a mint holographic green. Jessica pumped her fist in victory.

"Not so fast. I knew your folks, back in the day, Kramer," the pit boss said, his other tentacles twitching in annoyance. "They were good people. Your pops would have never dreamed of showing up to a match drunk. Void, even your wild-man of a brother, Jered, never went into the arena in your condition. You want some advice? Junctionworld is one big party, all fun and games, until it isn't. You'd better watch it, kid."

A large elevator descended from the killing floor above them, and the light and noise of the crowd flooded through.

"Sure, sure, Sgok," Jessica said, her mood suddenly cold. "Thanks for rubbing the old family legacy in my face right before a match. Really appreciate it."

She climbed the rungs welded to the side of her mech's hull, slammed the cockpit glass down over her, and made her mech suit jump up to the elevator with a small flare of jets. Papers and empty beverage containers flew from Sgok's cluttered desk.

"No gate-damned jets in the pits, Kramer!" Sgok yelled, pointing his tentacles at a prominent warning sign. "It says so, right there!"

Jessica made her mech shrug its shoulders in an exaggerated non-apology, mimicking the movement with her own body. She waved goodbye with the armor's large hands as she disappeared up the elevator shaft.

"Gate-damned bone-squid," she said under her breath as her combat armor came online.

The spotlights of Red Iridium focused on her as she and her mech rose through the horizontal elevator portal. She burped, breathing out beer fumes, and tapped her consoles and panels to check her main systems' readiness. The weapons and power reports flickered, then presented themselves slowly. She frowned at the sluggish combat computer's less-than-stellar response time.

"You're definitely no 'Judah,' are you, you nameless thing?" she said into her helmet's microphone. The mech's computer burbled a muted response as it struggled to compute an answer to the query.

"Cancel question," Jessica said before the simple command

module tangled its pathways up trying to evaluate her sarcasm. *Gates, I need to buy an upgrade.*

"Nameless... nameless... heh. 'NoName.' I like that," she said, grinning to herself. "Computer, change ident to 'NoName.' Give me a readout on the opponent mech after you've updated your self-cog files."

A pulse and whirring sound, and tonight's challenger mech revolved on one of the holographic displays in front of her. A RevShock Series Five. Light biped armor, fitted for close combat. Decent, but nothing spectacular. Three single-shot missiles to her two. Her blades were nastier, though.

"Who the void picks a vibro-spear for their main weapon, anyway?" she said. "Who's the pilot?"

The mid-air image of the mech faded, and her control computer showed a light purple humanoid's face and short biography, along with a kill-knockout-disabled-spared record of zero, three, two, and one. No kills yet, since his only battles had been shield matches like this one. The other pilot was aged and scarred, with dark purple burns mottled along one side of his face, head, and neck.

"A little late to be getting in the fights, old man," Jessica said as she continued to read. "Ah. A Fifth Gate refugee. He came through with those other purple-skinned bipeds a few years ago, before the blobs nuked the whole damned zone. Stupid venter must think he can just show up and be a pilot. No drugs, no implants, just raw meat," she said.

NoName's visual indicators pulsed as the computer tried to interpret her musings as a data request.

"Zerren Beff... Beff," she said to herself as she scanned the scarred man's details. "Where have I heard that name before?"

A rippling ring of fireworks cascaded from the top of the dome above, interrupting her recollection process. The air around her crackled, but it wasn't due to the fireworks. She sneered as her mech's league-required internal force field blinked on, a dancing nimbus forming just outside her cockpit glass.

Gate-damned rookie shields. They're just going to slow me down, she thought.

The sparse crowd cheered and clapped behind their own protective shielding, even though the overhead display was just a hologram. A place like this, in a bottom-rung fighting league, couldn't afford real pyrotechnics.

This was Limited Ordnance, Light Exo Class, and a Shield Match, to boot. Most matches weren't to the death, unless something went really wrong with the flickering force fields that surrounded both mech's cockpits. There was nothing really at stake, no real jeopardy. This was the equivalent of padded power armor, or wearing a grav-harness when learning to ride a skim-racer. Jessica Kramer hated being lumped in with has-been slugs on their way down or shiny rookies trying to make their way up. *This place doesn't deserve me. Mikralos's offer was proof of that,* she thought.

As the firework holograms faded away, Zerren Beff's cockpit armor slid from concealed panels in the hull, large scales forming protective interlocking plates over his command module. Now, he was protected by both armor and force fields.

He raised his mech's main weapon overhead, showing off for the crowd as he activated the vibro-blade-tipped spear. The spearhead sparked and blurred as it achieved its ideal cutting frequency.

Jessica's own protective armor came together in a similar fashion, a double-cocoon of metal and force fields enveloping her in sickening security. She rigged her mech to strobe its running lights as each piece of cockpit armor slammed into place. With each beat of light, gleaming blades slid farther and farther out of each forearm of her mech suit, until both cutting weapons were at full extension. It was a stunt, a minor crowd-pleaser, but it gave her mech a tiny bit of style.

"Skill keeps a pilot alive in the arena," her father, Solomon, used to say to her. "Style, though, is what keeps the Gatekeepers booking you for matches, and gives you more chances to beat them in the long run."

Through the booze, her thoughts drifted from the match ahead to memories of her father. She felt for a metal container in her jumpsuit's chest pocket, above her holstered weapon, and tapped it twice for good luck.

Her internal displays glowed bright within the now-enclosed cockpit. A side video feed showed the sports network cameras' view of her and her mech, its twin blades held aloft.

Her light mech was a converted industrial unit, scavenged and parted together, with a lobotomized control computer. Like her opponent, she was equipped only with single-shot missiles. League rules said she was allowed to substitute a light cannon with limited reloads instead of the missiles, but the stop-off at Jev's bar cut into her wrench time.

The crowd produced muted applause when the house announcer introduced her opponent, Beff. When her own name came over the speakers, NoName's external microphones heard louder applause, assorted jeers, and a faint, but distinct, hooting call. Her ears pricked up at the familiar sound. It came from someone close to one of the camera turrets. She turned her mech's sensors to scan the crowd in their armored enclosure. An Ascended, similar in build to an oversized, evolved orangutan, held a hand-drawn sign over his head, his height making him stand out among the crowd. 'House Of Kramer' was scrawled in large letters.

She laughed in surprise as she recognized her father's and brother's old crew chief, Prath. She pointed her mech's right arm towards him in recognition and salute, and he pointed a big brown hand back. He flipped the sign, and 'For Our Freedom, And Yours' was written on the back of it. She smiled and touched the screen, blinking away the tears before they could start.

Oh my gates, it's Prath, after all these years. What was he doing here? She thought. Memories of Jered rose up, but she beat them down, hard and cold. *Time to focus on the fight, girl.*

Red Iridium Arena's floor tonight was a Stygus-pattern layout, named for the first Gatekeeper to come up with the design. A tall, X-shaped structure formed the center of the kill ring, blocking direct fire between the combatants from their floor-level elevator entrance platforms. The layout called for rings of smaller x-barricades interspersed around the arena. None were large enough to hide a complete mech behind. The design forced the match's action to the center where the mech-gladiators either slugged it out, or one party picked the other apart while they tried to seek inadequate protection.

A giant four-sided hologram counted down from eight to zero, and the Gatekeeper word for 'fight' appeared. Jessica launched her mech into a run to the left, trying to find a flanking shot around the center obstacle. The exterior feeds from the house cameras cut out, since they were banned from in-cockpit use by the gladiators. Red Iridium's floor was more than a mile wide, but the two light mechs moved fast, even faster when they engaged their jets. Jessica pushed her armor forward, seeking the inadequate protection of the nearest small barricade while she evaluated the situation. The internal shielding provided a sluggish gyroscopic effect on her mech's movement, robbing power and momentum as its refresh rate struggled to keep up with the rapid movement of her giant armored suit. *Gates, I hate Shield Matches*, she thought.

"Between the beer and the shields, it feels like I'm fighting in a lead overcoat, NoName," she said to her battle computer, which made another puzzled attempt to interpret her meaning.

Beff's mech wasn't in sight, yet. He must have made a mad dash straight for the... yup, there he was, vaulting over the top of the center X-barricade with a flash of his jets. His mech held the giant vibro-spear in both armored hands, its blade a smeared visual blur. His mech pivoted to face her, the large pole-arm at the ready. He pulled back hard behind the center X's nearest wall, but not before firing a missile at her. The launching charge spit the rocket out with a dull puff, then the main motor engaged with a flash.

The unguided rocket scorched past her armor, missing it by a wide margin. She flicked on power to her own forearm blades, and they began to glow. A small channel of super-heated plasma raced in a magnetic groove where the cutting blade would be, fed from her mech's reactor.

Jessica continued her attack run towards the central X-barricade, arcing into the far side from Beff. She hoped to catch him flat-footed on the ground by storming in from behind. If she poured enough power on to her jets, she could tear him a new—damn, there he was, already, up high. The beer was making her sloppy.

Beff's red and purple mech arced up over the barricade again, his jets flaring as he made a meteoric jump. His second rocket flashed as it launched, and Jessica put up one arm by reflex to block the shot. She was in too close. She grunted in pain and shock as the rocket hit.

The concussion of the shaped charge warhead stunned her, even through the armor and protective shielding, and the right forearm of her mech fell away in a billow of smoke and tattered metal. Alarms screamed in her helmet and interior displays, and NoName started overloading her with damage reports.

Right arm was gone, and the blade with it; just a smoking

wreck from the elbow down. It was a rookie mistake, or he was just lucky, or she was hung over from mid-day drinking. Or all three. The crowd's sudden roar when the rocket hit added to the swirl of stimuli, and she chewed back the urge to puke from the impact. *Can't stand still, assessing the damage, girl. Gotta move!* She thought.

She hammered her jets while dashing to the side. She caught the sight of him mid-air, coming right at her. He landed hard, the twenty-foot-long vibro-spear spiking into the arena floor where she had been seconds before.

She fired one of her rockets, but he was too close, and the warhead's proximity safety didn't disengage. The missile skipped off Beff's cockpit armor with a shower of sparks, corkscrewing away. It then detonated forty feet up in the air. Shrapnel spattered them both, but Jessica's ringing ears paid the metallic rain no mind.

NoName displayed an attack vector for her, and gave the ready signal from her jets. She hit them hard, and her intact left arm swung in as she hurtled towards Beff's mech. The fool was still trying to wrestle his spear from the floor plates when he saw her attack begin. He tried to backhand her with his mech's arm, but she dodged, slashing the back of one of his armor's legs in the same fluid motion. Flaming hydraulic fluid erupted from the strike of the plasma blade. Another spinning backhand from Beff's armored fist rang off her cockpit, sending her tumbling. The crowd roared its bloodlust-filled approval.

"Dad always said to go for the hips on RevShock armors, NoName," she said. The computer burbled agreement.

Jessica shook off the thump from the glancing punch. She set up another pass at Beff's damaged armor, her jets flaring as she made her move. Her opponent stood, waiting for her, favoring his mech's damaged leg. As she homed in for the kill, Beff's armor staggered and flowed into a feint. He pivoted on the flaming limb and the spear shaft, then executed a backwards roundhouse kick with the other leg.

The back of his mech's foot caught her armor high in the torso, ripping off a bank of booster jets. The unexpected impact sent her mech sprawling to the floor, spitting parts, and the crowd shrieked and cheered at the sight of the two armored titans whirling at each other like colliding buzzsaws.

Beff's own computer had staunched the damage, and the flames slowed to a trickle as he took short, limping jet-hops away from her. *Away from her? Gate-damn it.* He was trying to open the distance and use his last rocket to full effect.

She tried shaking off the sudden rolling impact, shaking her head inside her helmet.

"Old guy's got some tricky moves, huh?" Jessica said to herself. NoName shut off the fuel flow to her damaged jets and gave her a new combat assessment of her mobility. It didn't look good.

She tried to bring her mech up from its prone position, but the lack of an arm and a damaged rack of jets hindered her. NoName burbled an electronic warning and flashed a series of red pulses. Beff was now out of proximity safety range, and his last warhead was armed. She still couldn't right her machine. The deployed forearm blade was of no help, hindering her efforts to get back up.

Her mech continued to flail, kicking up sand and sparks. The armored cover of Zerren Beff's third missile pod flipped open, and she found herself looking directly down the distant launch tube. His mech's hull disappeared behind the flash as the main rocket motor engaged.

Jessica kicked the legs of her mech sideways and slammed the controls to the right. Beff's third rocket struck, and her mech's right foot was gone in another *"krumf"* of soot and flame.

She screamed in frustration from the damage and helplessness. Her mech flopped on its side, smoke billowing from the elbow and ankle stumps underneath it. Beff charged in, his giant spear held high to skewer her. Tonight's crowd expected a minor match. They were getting one void of a show, and their cheers and applause thundered through the cavernous building.

"NoName, kill the left blade and shunt the plasma to whatever jets we have left!" she yelled to her computer. Beff's charge at her crippled mech continued as NoName ticked off the closing distance, the sight his blurred spear-tip filling Jessica with dread.

NoName's targeting features demanded she fire immediately at Beff's cockpit. She canceled the command with the stab of a finger against a display.

"No! Wait for it, then put it here!" she said, pointing at the oncoming enemy mech on another touchscreen.

Her remaining blade retracted and powered off, and she popped her armor up to a sitting position with a tiny, jarring flash of jets. Her footless leg folded underneath her, and she launched her last rocket just before her opponent entered the safety interlock distance. The projectile caught Beff's armor in the side, just above the hip.

The already-damaged leg flew off in a fury of pieces and parts. A chain of small explosions stitched up from the hips to the spine and shoulders of the opposing mech. With a loud groan, Beff's momentum carried him forward. The shattered armor stumbled and crashed to the ground, flames riding its back all the way down. The vibro-spear clattered to the deck, sliding and hissing past her as it dug a furrow through the scattered patches of sand and exposed metal.

Light Exo league rules dictated once all distance weapons were expended, canopy armors were to retract to enhance the close combat and up the danger factor, even though shielding was still in place. After Jessica fired her last rocket, her own cockpit armor withdrew back in mechanical stages with machined precision, and she took in the direct view of Red Iridium. It was amazing.

She saw her own image on the display screens, her name written in flashing Gatekeeper letters, and took in the jubilation of the crowd. The match was over, they were just waiting for the official decision by the officials in their armored booths. She gave a thumbs-up to the cameras zoomed in on her, and started to look for Prath in the stands.

The friendly crowd's cheers turned to screams, and she turned to see Zerren Beff's burning mech.

The mandatory cockpit shields could protect against incoming weaponry, and provided some resistance to most close combat weaponry, but they did nothing against fire. Mech gladiators, whether they were organic or machine, didn't fear cannons or cutting lasers, but burning to death was a demise dreaded by all.

Beff's shattered cockpit armor was jammed, his main hull blazing from the missile strike and internal detonations. One side of the control module's shell peeled back like her own, but the other half was a tangled mess. Jessica saw that Beff was panicking, his compartment filled with a swirling orange-gray mix of smoke, flames, and fire extinguisher discharge.

Automated crash bots emerged from armored doors in the stadium's walls, but they weren't going to make it in time. Kramer cursed, silently urging her opponent to focus, to fight the pain of the flames, to pull the ejection lever.

Zerren Beff's armor sparked, and the damaged cockpit armor and transparent canopy soared off at an awkward angle. A red and yellow ball flew from the flaming compartment. It was a protective airbag containing the pilot, ejection seat, and a small rocket motor.

Arcing through the air on a tiny jet of flame, it landed with a wounded thump on the arena floor. The crowd cheered, and Jessica sighed in relief.

Zerren Beff kicked his way out of the inflated rescue cushions. He flopped around like a fish in a frying pan, beating the last of the flames out on his pilot coveralls and harness. Disgusted and angry, he tore off his helmet and threw it as hard as he could. It hit a bare patch of floor and bounced into the path of a portly ambulance vehicle bot arriving late to the party. The rescue bot's tank-like treads flattened the helmet. The infuriated Beff turned an even darker shade of purple. Jessica suppressed a laugh, and watched the crash crew bots fight the rising flames of Zerren's shattered mech as he stormed back to the mech pit entrance on foot.

Jessica watched, amused, as the recovery bots approach her own shattered mech. A whole new foot would need to be printed, machined, and fitted. This was not going to be a fun repair bill, even with her doing most of the labor.

But, if this job for Mikralos paid off, the invoice would be small change, a pittance compared to what awaited her in the Hammer Leagues. She was moving up to where the Gatekeepers and their networks dished out real credits, and in real quantities. Sponsorships, endorsement deals, and near-bottomless gear budgets. A med-bot poked a sensor antenna at her, chirping to inquire if she needed medical attention. Kramer waved it off, and undid the snaps to her helmet.

"Thanks, but no thanks, med-bot," Jessica said. "I couldn't afford the fees for a check-up, even if I needed it. I think Beff might need some burn cream, though. If you hurry, you can catch him before he gets back to the pits."

She smiled as the repair bots attached grav pods to her immobilized mech. Once secured, the long, pontoon-like pods glowed to life, buoying the damaged machine up to a low hover. She jostled in the cockpit as the bots towed her to the pits.

Jessica Kramer imagined how she was going to spend the money of tonight's fight, after the Gatekeepers took their fees and taxes out of it. She would start with that nice pair of red boots she saw last gate-week at the Third Gate megamall. She would treat herself to some premium ammo for her pistol, something explosive-tipped. *Ooh!* Maybe a week at a low-gravity spa, with a tall, dark-eyed masseur with strong hands. *Hmmm... nice.*

CHAPTER FIVE_

"Nice save out there, Kramer," the deep, metallic voice of a sentient combat machine said. "For a meatbag, I mean."

A hovering repair drone squawked as the last bead of lasered weld cooled on her mech's new ankle joint. Jessica turned from the repair, hit the small switch that made her darkened welding visor transparent, and looked up. She dismissed the drone with an idle wave. Her eyes focused on the giant, angular figure leaning against the rusted industrial framing of the Red Iridium's repair pits.

"Why, Green Four, to what do I owe this pleasure?" Jessica said to the towering steel figure. Green Four was a member of mechanical beings that came from deep within the First Worldgate's network of worlds. "You, abasing your 'Unlimited' self to talk to a 'Limited Ordnance' lightweight like me? Should I bow, or curtsy?"

The combat machine playfully held up a giant pair of hands

in a pleading motion of surrender, though his steel fingers were tipped with claws that could slice through the side of a tank. Green Four was the size of Jessica's light exo rig, but there was no provision for a cockpit in him. He was his own pilot.

"Whoa, whoa, easy, there, Kramer," the living machine said. "I don't want you to do another cheap missile shot on me like you did that Beff guy, there." A deep chuckle rumbled through his speaker.

"Ha ha, very funny, you walking, talking junkheap," Jessica said, flipping her welding visor back. "He came damn close to running me through with that spear. Even with your speed, you would have been a big metal pincushion. That, out there, was all skill, baby. Meatbags rule, and you know it."

"I gotta admit," Green-Four said, "your targeting computer was really on his game. Even for a lobotomized semi-sentient processor, he pulled your fat out of the fire. You should thank him, you know, show some appreciation. Maybe a nice ultrasonic bath for his pathways, get his signals firing a few nanoseconds faster," The metallic gladiator clicked his right optical sensor cover with a quick wink.

Jessica put her hand to her chest, feigning outrage as she clutched at non-existent pearls.

"Why, Mister Self-Aware Killing Machine, sir," Jessica said, grinning, "what a wonderful backhanded compliment."

"Hey, I just call 'em like I see 'em, Kramer," Green-Four said. "Seriously, though, you ran a good match out there. I mean, even if—"

"Don't even, Greenie," Jessica said, holding up the laser torch as a pretend warning.

"—you are just—"

The laser torch began to glow, and Green Four grinned.

"—a meatbag," he said.

"You know what, that's it," Jessica said, grabbing a piece of twisted armor as she fired up the welder. "I'm going to make you pretty, Green Four. *Real* pretty. I've got some extra bits here that I'm going to weld on your hide for jewelry. You're going to be my fancy new war-doll."

"Alright, alright, I'm going," Green Four said, laughing. "Just get away from me with that scrap, you upright gut-pile! I've got a match tonight!" The armored goliath's heavy footsteps retreated further down pit row to his own cavernous repair stall.

"You wait until I go 'Unlimited,' Greenie!" Jessica called after him. "I'll be full of cybernetic implants and loaded up on combat drugs, and then we'll tussle! You'll see!"

"Your father never needed those loathsome injections or implants to get the job done, you know," a voice said from behind her. "His skill, combined with Judah, was more than enough."

Startled, Jessica wheeled around, the laser torch at the ready. She dropped it when she recognized the large brown and orange figure standing in front of her. He was a member of the Ascended race. More specifically, this Ascended was Prath. He was still as tall as she remembered, an evolved orangutan standing over seven feet tall with a technician's vest full of tools. He held a hand-painted sign in front of him. It was the same one she had seen on her cameras, just before the match with Zerren Beff.

"Hello, little human," he said.

"*Prath!* Oh, my Gates! That *was* you in the stands, you big, beautiful ape!" she squealed, throwing herself around him.

The old crew chief held her for a long moment as she sobbed against him. Jessica pulled back from the embrace, wiping grease from her gloves on to her face as she brushed away the tears. The tall Ascended wiped away the ones she missed with a large, leathery hand, and started to groom her scalp as he smiled down at her. He gently kissed her forehead, pulling her back to his chest. She continued to sniffle and cry, but she smiled up at him.

"What... what are you doing here, Prath?" Jessica said as she tried to regain her composure. "How many years has it been? After everything happened, I heard you went back to Devro-Tech Combatives, but I went there, and you had already moved on, but then I didn't hear anything for the longest time—"

"Hush, Jessica, hush, it's all right, now, I'm here, now," Prath said, interrupting her. "I'm sorry for the intervening years, but after the tragedy of Jered and then your parents..."

Prath grew silent, his large brown eyes glistening with their own tears.

"I was so alone, Prath," Jessica said. "After mom and dad died, the Gatekeepers seized everything, and the Enforcers threw me in juvenile processing. And then, after I busted out of there, everyone was gone. I had to make my own way."

"I know, love," Prath said, patting her back.

"And then I couldn't go home, and the habitat and compound were sealed," Jessica continued, her voice breaking from time to time. "It's like they just let the place rot. Dad said they wanted to humiliate us. Maybe that was their plan."

"I tried to get back, as well, little human," Prath said. "They threatened to kill or imprison me numerous times."

"Me, too," Jessica said. "And then, everyone just disappeared, went their own ways... I only had enough to... I mean, there was a little money coming in from the network, showing Dad's and Jered's fights on highlight reels—" She began to choke up again, and Prath held her by the elbows, looking down into her watering eyes.

"It wasn't easy for any of us, Jessica, dear, believe me," Prath said. "The years have been hard, what with Jered, your parents, the collapse of the Eighth Gate, along with a fistful of other unmentionable events... life on Junctionworld has been harrowing for everyone."

"What about the others?" she said. "Did they go with you?"

Prath shook his head, hugged her, then let her go.

"Remember little Corbin, my assistant?" the tall ape said. "Dead. He was caught in the suppression nukes four years ago, when the Fifth Gate almost fell to those giant tentacled beings. Rigella committed suicide around the same time, popped herself through the processor with an EMP round. NK-Five was killed in his first match in some underground, back-alley match put on by the Burella Boys. Most of the old team are gone, dead, or worse."

"And... and Tevren? Is he...?" Jessica said. Prath's orange brow settled in a scowl as he shook his head and grunted in disgust.

"I heard Tevren was somewhere behind the Eighth Gate when it was sealed off," Prath said, his large brown hands enveloping hers. "And... and Hannah was with him, too."

"Gate damn it."

Jessica's face hardened at the mention of her sister, and she wiped the last of her tears with the back of her glove.

Prath traced the grease and tears down one side of her face, looking at her with pride.

"Language, Jessica," he said. "You know we don't speak in such base vulgarities."

"Sorry, Prath, it's just—"

"It's never so bad that we lower ourselves with uttering the profane," Prath said. "Ah, look at me, falling back into lecture mode like it was still yesterday." Jessica giggled and wiped a tear away.

"Yeah, you always were more like a professor than a tech, Prath," she said. "I remember, this one time, you and dad were installing a new arm on Judah. You were working a power wrench with one foot, an electric meter in the other foot, you were hanging off Judah's shoulder hardpoint with one hand, and even then, you were pointing and fussing at Jered and me about something—"

"'Jered and me,'" Prath said. "I remember that. You and your brother were throwing a missile warhead between you like it was a game of egg toss. Yes, I remember it well, little human. Those were good days, before, well, you know..."

He trailed off, and a sad grin covered his face as the memories seemed to come back in force. They spent another uncomfortable moment of silence together, and then Prath's focus turned to the mech behind her. After a moment of evaluation, his face turned to a scowl.

"Is that... I couldn't make out the details from my seat during the match," he said, incredulous. "You're piloting *that?*"

"Huh? Oh, yeah, that's the new ride," Jessica said, beaming with pride. "I haven't named him, yet. Well, I might call him 'NoName.' We'll see. I've only been at it for a few gate-months, or so, in Light Exo. My record so far is—"

"No kills, none officially, yet, anyway. Seven knockouts, counting tonight, and you haven't been disabled or spared, yet," he said. "Yes, I know your stats, love."

"Oh, you know about the underground stuff, huh?" Jessica said.

"I kept tabs on you, little human," Prath said with a cool tone. "Even when you were slugging it out in the unsanctioned fights, I was watching. Not too close, of course. I didn't want to draw attention before the time was right."

"What?" she said, confused.

"Later," the Ascended said, raising a hand to quiet her.

"Back to your mech: I thought it moved like a TC-400 series cargo handler! How did you manage to pull that off? Are those... BelterTech jets you've got on there?" The tall primate walked around the battered mech propped up in its repair rack.

"For more maneuverability up top, yeah," she said. "A couple pairs of Wyvern boosters on the legs, too, for more thrust out in the open. It wasn't easy, but I remembered a few tricks from my time in your shop. I picked up the basic frame from a surplus auction at the Third Gate loading docks. It was worn out as all void—"

"Language."

"Prath," Jessica said, putting a hand on her hip, "I'm a grown woman wrenching on my own mech, in my own repair bay. I'll swear if I damned-well please, you big, beautiful ape. Now, like I was saying, basic frame at auction, right? I did a teensy-weensy little bit of underground brawling, and used those winnings to get this rig up and running. TC-400s are just civilian versions of the Gatekeeper Enforcement Directorate mechs."

"Hmm, yes, about as much as a mule is like a racehorse, you mean," Prath said.

"Well, yeah, exactly, if you think about it. This thing is slower and stronger, it's built to take more abuse, and it has lower maintenance downtime. That means I can pack on more armor, take more punishment, haul more ammo, and spare parts are easy to get. Sgok takes care of me, and throws some spare parts my way, sometimes. Gaskets, power relays, adapters, stuff like that. Light Exo Limited Ordnance is a big pile of—um, it's for the birds, though. I hate it," Jessica said.

"You aspire to higher status matches, one assumes?" Prath said.

"One *assumes* correctly, yeah. I have something in the works," she said, a sly grin on her face.

"You mean the match that Mikralos is putting together. The

vengeance bit against Masamune Kyuzo. 'The Desecrator,' I believe the networks call him," Prath said, making a minor tweak to one of her mech's jet nozzles. Jessica looked up in alarm, her eyes wide.

"How... how did you know about that?" Jessica asked.

Prath finished the adjustment, put the tool away in the crash cart, and shut the drawer. He put both hands on top of the toolbox and sighed.

"Little human, what do you know of Solomon Kramer's legacy?" Prath asked. "I mean, your father's real, enduring legacy, not just the pulp churned up by the network marketing departments to make beings watch old reruns?"

"He... Poppa was one of the first mech gladiators to live long enough to pay off the life-debt, and then he built—"

"Solomon beat the Gatekeepers at their own game, Jessica, here in their own little pocket dimension," Prath said, "and he did it so well, they couldn't do a thing about it. Well, not in public, at least. Their Old Code forbids it, and they are so *very* conscious of maintaining appearances when it comes to their code. They never forgave him for that."

"Prath, this is coming out of nowhere. I'm confused. What does that have to do with—"

"They had to destroy him, Jessica," he said. "They had to make an example of your father. Of your brother Jered. Of your entire family, if they could. This is what they felt they had to do, to maintain their control of this place. This is what my years of watching, of listening, of putting the pieces together, led me to conclude. And now that you're fighting in the public eye, you're next," Prath said.

He pointed down at her repair cart. "Your tools are a mess, by the way. Is this what I taught you?"

"No, I... wait," she stammered, trying to take it all in. "What do you mean? You said you've been busy, that you lost contact with me. But you also said you've been keeping track of me. What gives?"

"I had to protect you, Jessica," Prath said. "The best way to do that was to find out where the next attack was coming from, and to shift their attention from you to me. The DevroTech job was just an excuse to operate in plain sight, keeping them fixated on me while I kept my eyes on the arenas and you. I paid off Jev, too, to feed me audio and video data streams when you're in the bar. You drink like a fish, by the way."

"Prath, that's—" she tried to say, before he held up a large hand.

"The name Kramer began showing up again on the winner boards," he said, "and that drew the attention of beings who hold on to grudges for centuries. You started fighting, with your mish-mash mech, there, and I started to see old wheels begin to turn again, the same players from before starting to exert themselves. The Gatekeepers have their sights on you. It was time to come back."

"What, so now, you just show up, and drop this all on me, after all the gate-damned—"

"Young lady," Prath said, frowning.

"—after all this grief, and confusion, and struggle," she said. "Why come back now, Prath? Something stinks."

"Yes, something does stink. It's your attitude, and your situational awareness," Prath said. "*Think*, girl. Why is Mikralos seeking you out, now, after all these years? How can he, a lower-level owner of a second-rate grindhouse arena, a mere foot soldier in the Gatekeeper hierarchy, offer such a magnificent prize and the ability to use an elite fabrication and repair shop? Why is he waving this juicy morsel under your nose? You're a good pilot, dear, but let's be honest, you're not *that* good. You're being led to the slaughter, in a public execution that will be a lesson in Junctionworld."

"Lesson? What lesson, Prath?" Jessica said, scowling. "And, damn it, I am that good!"

"Pilot, *think* about it," the Ascended crew chief said, holding up one of his feet in a frustrated clench. "I was here years before your father arrived and started winning. They threw everything they could at the Fourth Gate Kramers. Your father trounced them and their champions, and made money doing so. It disrupted their 'Old Code.' More importantly, it started costing them power over those they held in indentured servitude. There was talk surrounding your father of a 'New Code.' Solomon Kramer was a nail that stuck up, and the Gatekeepers needed him hammered down."

"So, they wanted Dad to look bad. So, what?" Jessica said. "That doesn't explain Jered, Prath."

"Your brother, gates rest his soul, was in over his head outside of the arenas," Prath said. "He was in deep to a number of gambling houses, especially Dionoles over at the Celestial Kingdom. It played right into the manipulator claws of the Gatekeepers."

"That casino over by the Fourth Gate?"

"The same, love. Jered had a nasty gambling habit, and was atrocious at Pistols and Sevens."

Jessica winced at the mention of the Gatekeeper casino table game that mixed cards and firearms. Her brother Jered was obsessed with it. His losses were staggering, to the point that he sold himself back into servitude as an obligated fighter. His "borrowing" of Judah, without their father's permission, resulted in a family fight that was still one of her worst memories.

"Oh, so you know how tough that game is?" Prath said, raising his eyebrows in surprise. "Jered stunk at it, but the Gate-keepers kept feeding him cocktails and credit advances. The game demands a great deal of focus and attention, and not just at drinking and gunplay."

"And? C'mon, bottom line it for me, ape," she said, feeling herself getting angry and frustrated with all this information suddenly dumped on her.

"And, the Gatekeepers used your brother as a weapon against your father, as a way to reassert their control over the arenas, and Junctionworld as a whole," Prath said. "They planted rumors in the sports media, vicious, nasty untruths that nearly drove your parents apart. It was insidious, and they weren't subtle about it. I remember, once, when Dionoles and Mikralos both showed up at your father's home."

"Yeah, I remember that, too." Jessica said, searching back through her painful memories. "That was right before Jered died."

"Two Gatekeepers in the house of a freed slave, at the same time? Unheard of!" Prath said. "They met behind closed doors in the front reception hall. There was a huge argument, an epic conflagration, and your father made them both leave at gunpoint. That was right before your brother was murdered," Prath said, his large canine teeth bared in agitated reflex.

"Wait, Prath, Jered died at Berva Proxima, fair and square," Jessica protested. "It was a stupid death, but no one 'murdered' him. You make it sound like it was some kind of conspiracy, with all this 'Old Code Gatekeeper vendetta' dung."

"Language. That's exactly what I think it was, little human. What it is, even now," Prath said. He was still upset, but his fangs were no longer visible.

"Well, then, why did they wait so long to come back for me?" Jessica said. "I've been on my own for years. I mean, why didn't they just take me out, like, with some assassin, or make my death look like an accident?"

"Because it's a long game, Jessica," Prath answered, "one that results in the utter destruction of everything associated with the House of Kramer, including you. You're no good to them dead in some back alley, an anonymous corpse fed into the void like trash. They want you crushed in the arena, humiliated and beaten down. They want a message sent. That's why we're going to take Mikralos up on his offer. We're going to have an insider's view of how deep this rotten contagion goes."

Jessica pulled a beer from a small cooler in her tool chest and stared in contemplation. Prath continued to straighten her tools.

"Uh, Prath, what do you mean, we?"

"We, as in you and I, little unorganized human," Prath said. "We're going to get to the bottom of this."

As Prath's statement sunk in, He snatched the beer from her hand. Raising it to his lips, he drank it in one long, slow chug. He looked at the label in disgust and threw the bottle over his shoulder without a look. It landed in a trash receptacle across the repair bay with a crash of glass.

"The GateLords are looking to grind down the last vestiges of your family, and using Mikralos and his arena to get you to agree to the setup," Prath said, breathing out a small burp. "Mikralos waves Judah and the Hammer Leagues under your nose, and you agree like a drunk reaching for a free beer. Oh, incidentally, your taste in brands is atrocious."

"It's all Jev has on tap that I like, that little robot snitch," Jessica said. "Well, that's biocoded for 'human,' anyway."

"Well, I would say you like it a bit too much, love," Prath said, trying to rub the taste out of his mouth. "And stick with poisons tailored to your own species, for future reference. You're in training for a vengeance match that's probably rigged, now, Mech Pilot Kramer."

"So... you're going to help me?"

He nodded. She beamed at his decision, and reached for another beer.

"That also means you're on the wagon," Prath continued. "We need you sharp. No more booze for you."

"No booze? But—"

He raised a calloused brown finger as a warning before she could roll her eyes.

"Ugh... fine," she said.

CHAPTER SIX_

Jessica walked up the silvery boarding ramp of Mikralos's floating sky-car, or yacht, or whatever the void it was. It was big, bigger than she remembered yesterday, its interior decorated in rich, understated luxury.

A conveyance crewman stood at the top of the ramp waiting for her. It was a bio-print, a synthetic humanoid, and it motioned her to a kidney-shaped couch forward in the craft, up by the pilot and copilot control chairs. The crewman was from the same product line as Mikralos's two bodyguards, but it was a specialty model with features oriented more to a pilot's duties. Enlarged forehead, slender build, and dexterous hands stood out to her as the main differences.

Like most Gatekeepers, Mikralos utilized the classic "Model Nine" line of bioprinted humanoid as soldiers, servants, and technicians. Jessica always found them creepy due to their skewed proportions and features. Something was just off about them, and it gave her the willies. They were everywhere, though, so it was often easier just to tune them out, to see right through them.

She handed the Nine a printed slip of plastic. He read it, a blank look on his smooth face.

"Data received. Purpose?" the Nine said in that choppy, abbreviated diction they all seemed to use.

"That's the location of my mech, meat-bot," Jessica said, cocking her head to the side. "Red Iridium Arena, in the maintenance pits. The head honcho down there is a Skevvian named Sgok. Contact Mikralos and have my mech and my tool boxes delivered to our destination. Also, my crew chief will be waiting there, too. He's an Ascended. Big orange ape. Can't miss him. His name's Prath. He comes, too."

The crewman looked at a blinking wrist computer display, and nodded. Mikralos had them on remote, and answered the crewman's question before it was even asked.

"Good," she said, smiling.

The craft gained altitude without effort or the feeling of acceleration, and they were soon high above Junctionworld. Jessica looked down through the viewport and saw Jev's bar shrink into obscurity among the clutter and squalor of Maro Point, the lower-class slum where she lived. *Used to live, hopefully, if this paid off,* she thought.

Maro Point was halfway between the glowing red ring of the Second Gate and the pulsing, spiraling towers of the Third. It was just a place to stay. It wasn't home. Except for Jev's, she wasn't going to miss it in the least.

Jessica watched through the window as freight ground-trains, floating grav-barges, and sleek airborne craft laden with passengers transited through the massive, glowing interdimensional portals. The ripples from the dozens of entry and exit points spread across the vast face of the Worldgates at various altitudes and frequencies like waves of light on an electric sea.

They were mile-wide windows into other skies, crackling and pulsing with unknown and terrifying energies.

The vehicles passing through the gates flashed in and out of existence like it was no unusual occurrence, because, beyond the constantly-changing light show, it really wasn't too strange, once you got used to it.

This place, Junctionworld, was an exchange point for travel and trade, no different than a crossroads or harbor. What made Junctionworld unique was its placement as an intersection between worlds and realms of existence, not just cities or towns.

She sniffed as she thought about all the money and commercial goods that passed through the Gatekeepers' flabby little hands, how they skimmed from every transaction between a million worlds, and it still wasn't enough for them.

Money wasn't enough. They wanted control, too. Their gate-damned 'Ways of the Old Code' were justification for centuries of enslavement, conquest, and exploitation. They were just too polite to use those exact terms.

If what Prath said was true back in the mech pit, there were soon going to be two less silver-podded blobs in existence. She didn't know how, but she was going to make them pay.

She waved off an offered drink from one of the craft's other crew-beings, and continued to stare as the neon grid of Junctionworld scrolled beneath her.

Soaring towers outlined in lights, abject slums framed in darkness, and gray, flickering skies above all of them. Arenas, hovels, and the ever-present glow of the gates. Except for scattered commercial and manufacturing districts, there wasn't much else in between.

She looked into the distance. In the center of Junctionworld's disk shape was the fortress tower called Central Data, where the GateLords compiled and broadcast their arena entertainments to millions of planets on the other sides of the

Worldgates. It was a swooping, cone-shaped structure as imposing as any of the eight gates, its gleaming ebony surface studded with cannon turrets and missile hatches larger than the craft she was in.

The population of Junctionworld might live in the glow of the gates, but they also existed under the guns, nuclear and otherwise, of Central Data. Every square inch of J-world was sighted in, laid out in pre-measured defense zones. Between the tower's weaponry and the Gatekeepers' Nine soldiery, rebellion by the populace or invasion through the gates was near-impossible.

The slowly-recovering nuclear wasteland of the Fifth Gate Zone was testament to the blobs' willingness to sacrifice the civilian population to prevent takeover from beyond the portals. When those giant tentacled things tried to come through a few years ago, the GateLords had nuked the place down to bare Shine, the weird foundation material that was the indestructible bedrock of this place.

The craft skirted past Central Data, and they were now in the Sixth Gate Zone. In the distance, she could see the maddened purple swirl of the Eighth Gate. The vast majority of the pocket dimension was alive and lit with the bustling lights of traffic, civilization, and commerce. Not the Eighth Gate Zone, though.

In stark contrast, the long wedge of Junctionworld dominated by the Eighth Gate was dark and lifeless, its gloom interrupted only by the lights of armored weapon towers and patrolling mechs assigned to the containment zone.

Jessica's brow furrowed as she remembered Prath's mention of Tevren trapped behind the Eighth Gate. Well, there were millions, maybe billions of beings trapped behind the gate when the GateLords shut it down without explanation three years ago. Tevren was the focus of her thoughts, though, at the moment.

Something welled up in her, and she tried to push it back down. Her memory wandered to his eyes, his lips, his hands... and why he could possibly be there with her bitch of an older sister, Hannah.

Jessica Kramer turned from the window, one hand brushing a tear away before it could form, the other tight on her revolver's pistol grip. Mikralos's grav-craft was angling in for a landing, sleek and smooth, and not a moment too soon.

Gate damn you, Hannah, she thought.

CHAPTER SEVEN_

"You're not bringing that pile of scrap into my facility, mech pilot. I don't care how big your monkey is," the short, scale-covered Myoshan said to Jessica. She towered over him, Prath even more so, but he appeared unconcerned by that fact. The squat, reptilian being crossed his arms and jutted his fang-filled lower jaw out in a defiant pout. One set of eyes, the pair facing them, were scowling slits. Prath and Jessica could not see the rear pair of eyes that all Myoshans possessed.

Myoshans were stubborn little cusses, as a rule, but they were damn good mechanics and fabricators. Jessica noted that this place had a dozen or so of them scurrying about. *This little spud's claws and clothes were clean. That must make him the boss,* she thought. She took a look at her old friend, and her own two eyes grew wide. *Uh oh...*

Prath's large teeth came into view at the Myoshan's opening statement. The Ascended crew chief's mottled lips pulled back into a full threat display upon hearing "monkey." The small shop supervisor took a step back at the sight of Prath's fanged agitation.

"Try 'Ape,' or 'Ascended,'" Jessica said, placing her hand on the tall orange-and-brown primate's shoulder. "It'll get you a lot further with him. Trust me."

"What's he going to do," the Myoshan retorted, "throw dung at me if I don't use his preferred forms of self-reference? Hmmm? I think I need to speak to the client. I mean, just look at this wreck you showed up with, human. Is that a TC-400, for gate's sake? A... a gate-blessed *cargo loader?*"

"We had a match last night at Red Iridium, shopkeep, so, yeah, NoName's a little scuffed up," Jessica said. "Nothing that a little tape and stickers won't cover. I had to hang a Disable on a rookie's record. You might have seen it on the recap video feeds."

"I don't watch junior leagues at bottom-tier arenas, mech pilot," the Myoshan said. "We cater towards a more... *select* clientele here at Vervor's Foundry Works. As a rule, we service those elite few at the top of their game, not charity cases with their walking junkpiles."

"Why, you sawed-off little spud," she said, surging towards the Myoshan, "I ought to—"

It was now Prath's turn to try and hold back Jessica. A bright glow from the direction of the loading dock distracted them from their discord.

"Forgive the interruption and the lack of physical presence, gentlebeings," the voice and image of Mikralos said. "As always, we greet you in the Ways of the Old Code."

A Nine from the Gatekeeper's transport crew held a projector the size of a large medallion. A hologram of Mikralos's fleshy face floated in mid-air, regarding all of them in turn.

"Master Vervor, owner of this fine establishment," the Gatekeeper said, "are we to understand that there is a complication with the work we have commissioned from you?"

The Myoshan knitted his short, clawed hands together, making his scales rasp.

"No, no complications, Honored Mikralos," the Myoshan said. "This human and her... *ape*, seem to have stumbled into the wrong fabrication and training facility, and have brought in a semi-salvaged conglomeration of parts that they seem to call a fighting mech."

"Ah, then, we see the root of the problem, Master Vervor," Mikralos said. "These two beings you see before you are indeed the same subjects we notified you earlier to expect. The current appearances of their selves and their machine may be cause for alarm, an understandable condition, but rest assured the remedy to its unsightliness is the reason we commissioned your services. Please extend every courtesy and resource to Mech Pilot Kramer, and itemize the expenses accordingly."

Vervor nodded at the Gatekeeper's admonition. The mention of her last name also made him change his orientation.

"I... I had no idea, sentients," Vervor said, his tone now full of deference. "We are a specialty shop. The majority of our clients are non-bipedal, or different biocodes from standard hominids. Forgive me, mech pilot, did you say 'Kramer?' As in the Fourth Ga—"

"Yeah, one and the same, spud," Jessica said, narrowing her eyes while putting her hand up. "Don't think you can suddenly be nice to me because of the family handle."

"Mech Pilot Kramer," the image of Mikralos said, "you and Master Technician Prath will have autonomy in all purchasing, fabrication, and training decisions, within the bounds of our arrangement, naturally, but you will not besmirch our reputation with Master Vervor or his business. We expect cooperation between the two parties. Any deviation from this requirement may result in revocation of the contract, and the Judah computer, its host armor, and any upgrades to the 'semi-salvaged conglomeration,' as you say, will be forfeit. Is this understood?"

Jessica mumbled her agreement. Vervor and Prath bowed with a single appendage held in front of them, palm up. The Nine returned the gesture on behalf of his master.

"Very well," Mikralos said. "Let us turn our collective efforts towards our mutual goal: victory in the glorious halls of our beloved Berva Proxima arena. We will forward research materials on the opponent via courier in a few hours. We understand he also has a match scheduled, soon, so it would behoove you to study him. In the meantime, Master Vervor, we leave you to it."

The image of Mikralos faded out. The Nine holding the holographic projector gave a stilted, awkward bow and stepped away. It boarded the waiting craft, which boosted off in silence.

The three of them spent a moment regarding each other. Prath crossed his arms and glowered at the shorter Myoshan. Vervor's scaled shoulders gave a small shrug, but his jaw stayed fixed and defiant. Jessica spit on the floor.

"Hmmph. My shop has a reputation to keep up," Vervor said. "The sight of your dilapidated cargo loader was unsettling, to say the least. Besides, how was I to know you were the daughter of the great Solomo-"

"Not a prudent idea at this time, good sir," Prath said as Jessica stormed away, slamming the shop's front door behind her.

CHAPTER EIGHT_

Once the angry human departed in her prominent and noisy way, the mech fabrication shop became quiet as a church. The faint sound of a Myoshan crew member rummaging through a tool bin came from somewhere in the back storage area. The rest of the shop's technicians wisely decided to find themselves elsewhere in the establishment, leaving the large front room to its two remaining occupants.

Prath, the tall, orange Ascended, and Vervor, the short Myoshan shop owner, stood opposite each other in the open bay, both avoiding eye contact. Neither one was willing to be the first to break the awkward silence. A short series of alternating sighs followed. Vervor scanned the door with his rear set of eyes, the addressed the hominid.

"Aren't you going to go after her?" Vervor asked.

"She'll manage to take care of herself, I'm sure," Prath said. "If she's anything like I remember, she'll be back. You might actually want to lock the front door."

The Myoshan rattled his fangs together with a slight clicking noise, the equivalent of an amused smirk, and snorted.

The tension broken, the Ascended stopped brooding and uncrossed his hairy arms. He extended his hand out, palm up, in a greeting from the Old Code.

"Erm, allow me to re-introduce myself, Honorable Myoshan," the ape said. "I am Prath, Master Technician. As you can see with your forward-facing set of eyes, the obvious lack of a tail shows me to be an ape, not a... a monkey. If you must know, it is a grave insult to my kind. We... we do not react well to the 'm-word.'"

"Duly noted. I am Vervor, Fabricator and Proprietor. I welcome you to my humble shop, Honorable... Ape," the Myoshan said through half-gritted fangs. A smile returned to Prath's face.

"Well, now that the small item of protocol has been settled," Prath said, "allow me to say, I have been an admirer of your work and reputation for some time. Would you please be so good as to give me a short tour of this beautiful fabrication facility? Is that a NeuHaas I see in the rear of the shop?"

"It is," the Myoshan said, his small chest now swelling with pride. "A state-of-the-art titanium foam printer and machining module. I even had the client pay for the object-scan option. My staff just installed it last gate-week."

"Wonderful," Prath said, clapping his leathery hands together. "Let's start there, if we can, Master Vervor. We have a tremendous task ahead of us, and only a short time to accomplish it."

"I can imagine," Vervor said, chuckling. "Your human. She really is quite the claw-full, isn't she?"

"I helped raise her, but that was years ago," Prath said. "Her father—"

"*The* Solomon Kramer, yes?" Vervor asked.

"Yes, the same," Prath answered, a distant look overtaking his face. "Solomon was a dear friend of mine, not just an employer. The Kramers were like family. I feel obligated to help the girl, even though she's a bit prickly. Ooh, what's this?"

Vervor handed the tall ape a machined piece of foamed metal with intricate undercuts and deep internal radii. It was the same shape and surface texture of a sliced-open ghostmelon, complete with machined seeds, and filled the Ascended's large hand.

"A sample part from the vendor," Vervor said, "to demonstrate the NeuHaas's capabilities. A trinket, really, but it's among the beginner files included in the machine's tutorials. My lead technician, you'll meet him later, has spent some time with the design program. Here's his first original piece."

Vervor pulled another machined part from the rack where the metallic fruit originally rested. Prath's dark eyes lit up when he recognized the shape.

"Is that?"

"Indeed, it is," Vervor said.

"I... I never thought I would see another left-hand wrist linkage assembly for a Slaughterbot 7," Prath said, holding the articulated part like he would a newborn baby.

"When we lost our supply chain behind the Eighth Gate," Vervor said, his claws reaching for another part, "the price on all remaining stock went through the roof. The aftermarket offerings were insufficient. The only reproduction parts on the market were severely lacking. We had to convince our clients with Slaughterbots to lose their mechs' hands, and substitute distance weapons for the entire arm."

"Such a brilliant design," Prath said, turning the metal object in his hands, "yet, such a fragile part. I knew of teams that went through them like clockwork, one per match."

"Hours of tear-down time to replace one, too. The Slaughterbots could pick up an egg from the nest, but that control came at the cost of delicate parts," Vervor said.

"My record was three and a half," Prath said, pride in his voice.

"I'm impressed," Vervor said, clacking his fangs in approval. "My technician was able to scan our last remaining unit in to the new titanium printer. A few clicks later, he's not only captured the shape, but he actually improved on the design. Notice the—"

"The gusseting and extra supports, yes," Prath said, admiration in his voice. "I like how he handled the bracket transitions, too."

"My tech is a Niff, and thus, a bit skittish," the Myoshan shop owner said, "but very proficient. We're going to start vending them on the Merc Web."

"They should sell well," Prath said.

"Let's hope," Vervor said, gesturing for them to move on.

The two seasoned veterans of the mech repair industry ambled about the large shop. Vervor would point out various tools or bits of heavy equipment, and Prath would compliment him on his impeccable tastes in hardware brands.

The facility tour ended after a few minutes, and Vervor invited Prath into his office. The tall hominid was wary of entering the Myoshan-sized space. He breathed a sigh of relief when a hidden larger door, surrounding the smaller visible door, opened.

Vervor took a seat behind his industrial desk, and motioned with a claw for Prath to take a seat, as well.

"No, I'll stand, Master Vervor, thank you," the Ascended said.

"As you wish, Master Prath," Vervor said. He propped his clawed feet up on the desk, his rear set of eyes scanning a bank of security monitors arrayed behind him.

"Tell me, Prath," Vervor asked, "what type of match are we gearing your pilot and her... curious machine towards?"

"I'm not sure the terms have been settled, yet," Prath said, his eyes downcast, "but our young Jessica Kramer will ultimately be taking part in a vengeance match at Berva Proxima."

"Vengeance match? The last Kramer to fight at Berva Proxima was..." Vervor trailed off, then bolted up in his small, luxurious chair.

"Yes, Jered Kramer and Masamune Kyuzo," Prath said. "The fight they always show on the best-of collections."

"She's going up against Masamune Kyuzo?" Vervor said. "The human? *The Desecrator?*"

"Sadly, yes," Prath said. "There's a bit more to it than just that—"

"But, she'll... she'll be slaughtered!" the short, scaly Myoshan interrupted. "She'll end up as ashes on the arena floor!"

"Well, your concern is admirable, Master Vervor, but—"

"No offense, Master Prath," Vervor said, reaching for his comm line, "but concern be damned! I need to contact the client again, and make sure I get paid up front!"

CHAPTER NINE

SEVENTH GATE ZONE
FERRO FORTRESS ARENA

"Master Mech Pilot Masamune," a random journalist yelled up at him from the repair pit floor, "how do you respond to the newest wave of reports, that your impressive kill streak is only due to your illegal use of electronic warfare jamming units, and possibly even nanites, which the Gatekeepers have strictly forbidden for centuries?"

Kyuzo looked down from his cockpit at the reporters clustered around his mech's feet. If he were a more expressive human, the hard, placid look on his face would actually be a mix of snarl and sneer. Hearing the questions shouted up at him, he had to make a conscious effort not to disengage his weapon safeties in the arena pits. Composing himself, he addressed them in a stern, formal tone.

"I'll address those baseless allegations, and the others," Master Mech Pilot Masamune Kyuzo said, staring into the sea of cameras pointed at him, "after I finish grinding my next opponent into the stadium floorplates. For the record, I categorically deny any involvement in the accusations against me, and look forward to clearing my name. This press conference is over."

Masamune donned his helmet as he closed the cockpit glass over himself. The correspondents gathered at the feet of his armored vehicle continued to yelp questions up at him, their drone cameras and manipulator-held holographic recorders hoping to capture his reaction to the more outrageous and loaded inquiries. His crew chief, Hepsah, pushed them back, aided by the rest of his ground personnel.

She turned to him as his mech's armored segments slammed together over the clear glass, giving him a thumbs-up. Masamune returned the gesture with his prosthetic hand, the black plastic reflecting the last of the camera flashes as the protective leaves formed an interlocking cocoon around his cockpit. He contemplated the deep thudding of the extra armor's formation as his manual controls retracted. Cables snaked from the back of his headrest into ports in his neck and arm, and the command-and-control meshing began.

Masamune Kyuzo tasted the bitter electronic buzz, beginning in the back of his teeth, and felt the grating sensation spread through his skull. The surge of his connection to his mech came in waves, and he kept his tongue high and centered in his mouth. Streaming blood from his mouth like a madman made for good ratings on the in-cockpit camera, but a bitten tongue was painful and annoying.

His command computer increased the digital overlap to his nervous system, and he felt his mind and mech merge as one. The phantom numbness took over his organic body, like the elusive moment one felt just before falling asleep. Kyuzo closed his natural eyes, and the mech's camera inputs took over, feeding the images of the outside world and targeting displays to the control implants in his brain.

The mech pits and staging areas in Ferro Fortress Arena

were different from most fighting establishments. Instead of emerging from underneath or the sides of the combat floor, fighters dropped in from portals carved in the giant building's armored ceiling, their booster jets screaming as they impacted in front of the maddened crowds.

Masamune looked from his perch at the stadium's seats filled with frothing, bloodthirsty sentients. Tonight's event was a Black-Box Death Match, Hammer Class, Full Weaponry, meaning neither combatant knew the others' identity in advance, there were no protective fields around the cockpits, and there were no rules or regulations applied when it came to what they pulled out of their armories.

Kyuzo disliked the gimmicky nature of the fight arrangement, but it also added a hint of anticipation. Kyuzo was now undefeated in his last thirty-three death matches, all of them kills in his now-trademarked style. It was a spectacular record, but he was bored, and feared he was losing his edge. The public relations war the press waged on him did not help. Perhaps tonight would be an unexpected challenge.

The arena pit boss's voice came over his communications input.

"Desecrator, you're on deck. Profile introductions are winding down. Move your mech forward, to the lip, and good hunting," she said.

"My thanks. All systems are go. Standing by," Masamune said.

Spotlights and cameras converged on his mech's hull, bathing him in light and attention high above the throng. His sensors gave him an exact count of the thousands of lenses focused on him, including the personal capture-cams of the audience. He felt his natural face grin.

One last systems check. Feel the body breathing, then put it away. Let the electricity coursing through the mech's pathways and motors take over for his normal sensations. Flare the jets and double-check the ammunition feeds. His sword checked and double-checked, still clamped to his hull by magnetic locks. Focus on the engagement signal lights.

Green... yellow... red. Attack!

The electronically-blended combination of Masamune and mech vaulted from his ready pad into the pulsing air of the arena, and the crowd roared. The floor setup, like his opponent, was unknown until this moment. It was a "king-of-the-hill" arrangement, his sensors alerted him, complete with minefields in large patterns radiating from the center's low peak. Some were active, their red lights blinking through the dirt, others were inactive, for now.

His plummet from the launch pad slowed on a column of plasma from his jets, and he rotated in mid-air as he descended to catch a view of his opponent. Gorth! It was Gorth! *Well, void, it's been a while*, he thought. He opened a comm channel.

"It's going to be tough killing you, Gorth," he said.

"You said it, double-legger. Come get wrapped up," the Skevvian said.

Most sentient species construct mechs to resemble their own bodies, both for familiarity and psychological purposes. Every mech pilot, regardless of origin, wants to be a walking armored nightmare. It added visual shock value, and helped drive the ratings. Gorth's mech was no exception.

The Skevvian's chassis mimicked his natural form, only armored, weaponized, and over twenty feet tall. Its black and orange hull dripped with thick steel tentacles and bristled with weaponry. A heavy snapping beak protruded from under the enclosed cockpit. All Custom. *The Bone-squid has style*, Kyuzo thought.

Signals blared in his mind, and two missiles launched from the enemy mech. Masamune cut his jets, free-falling, looking for a mine-free landing zone that offered some cover. He located a cluster of barricades off to his right, and pushed his mental controls hard to get behind them as he fell. He flared his jets at the last second, landing hard. The missiles overshot him and slammed into the arena wall, exploding just under the jubilant, protected crowd.

Gorth's squidmech landed on the far side of the central hill, jets glowing from its clawed tentacle tips and a set of main boosters under the central hull pod, and disappeared from Kyuzo's sight. Masamune looked around, evaluating the arenascape.

His sensors told him his jets needed to cool down from the taxing descent from the pits above. He popped a sensor tower over the barricades, saw the coast was clear, and moved out on foot.

The barricades he left were adjacent to a blinking red mine-field. Still on the run towards the center hill, he scooped up a large rock and tossed it into the array of crimson dots. An explosion erupted from the field, sending the stone hurling into the stands. It bounced off the protective fields with a shimmering flash of charged particles. *Yup, they were real mines.*

A holographic counter appeared overhead, ticking down to zero. The once-active minefield beside him blinked out, and Masamune found his mech's feet now surrounded by red dots. His jets weren't cool enough to boost out of here, and he froze his armored vehicle in its tracks. An explosion sounded from the far side of the hill, and the crowd roared. *Gorth was down a tentacle or two. Good.*

Masamune deployed his mech's autocannon from its left hull hardpoint and engaged the trigger. The rifled cannon chugged two dozen high-velocity shells into the ground, deto-nating the mines buried between him and the red blinking field's edge. The dust settled, and he stepped on the craters with a few giant strides, leaping the last stretch to clear an undetonated explosive device.

The network drone cameras orbiting around him shifted to his rear, and his sensors alerted to two more missiles coming in. His battle computer identified them as impalers, armor-piercing with no warhead. They were meant to pin down a target without destroying it. Gorth wanted an in-close kill. Masamune grinned.

Kyuzo saw his jets were cool enough for a boosted dodge. He laid down a suppressive burst from his autocannon as the missiles bored in on him. The barricades the missiles came from erupted in small puffs as his cannon rounds impacted, and he hammered his jets to the right. The rockets scorched past him, skipping off the arena floor and into the stadium walls.

"Gorth, you keep missing like that, and Hepholios is going to take the repair bill out on your corpse," Masamune said.

"There's only one corpse in this conversation, human," Gorth answered back over the comm channel.

"Come out from behind that barricade, bone-squid, and let me see your pretty face."

"I'll show you 'pretty,' primate. Enjoy the sparkly lightshow."

The whine of a rotary cannon spooling up came to Kyuzo's external sensors, followed by the muzzle flash and tracer streaks of hundreds of rounds arcing at him. Masamune threw his mech to the ground, trying to get under the incoming hail of fire. Rounds stitched across his hull and armored cockpit. It was like being in a tin shed during a depleted uranium hailstorm. Damage reports flashed in his brain, but he ignored them.

"Incoming, Gorth," Masamune said, raising his mech's right arm. A bulky compartment's hatch slid open, and a rocket-propelled bunker-buster emerged from below the forearm. With a loud *thoonk* sound, he sent the awkward cylinder spiraling through the air. It was big and slow enough to track with the naked eye, and Masamune heard the crowd's applause build as it soared across the arena floor.

Arching high over the direct stream of Gorth's gatling fire, the heavy demolition charge hit the distant barricade cluster dead center with a *krumpf*. The surrounding area disappeared in a brief flash of explosive. A roiling cloud of dirt and barrier fragments swallowed the spark of light, the spherical shockwave caught by his cameras for his personal highlight reel. *Nice shot*, he thought.

His battle computer butted into his musings. The main jet boosters on his mech's back were torn to shreds by Gorth's fusillade. He had leg jets only. A series of loud pops from the site of the explosion ended his damage self-assessment. Black smoke billowed from the shattered structures that once hid the squidmech. *Was he knocked out? Was his ammo cooking off?*

No. The black mech streaked out of the cloud of even darker smoke, sparks and burning parts trailing as he jetted back around the hill. It was a smokescreen. From a quick glimpse through his sensors, the rotary gun's barrels were ripped off, and his missile racks looked empty.

Masamune urged his mech into a run, his autocannon pursuing the squidmech with fire. Two rounds found their target deep in the side of the enemy, and plasma gouted from the metallic wound. Gorth tumbled out of the line of fire, his tentacles flailing to maintain control. A turbine hit! They were both now without main jets.

The overhead counter flashed into holographic existence again, and the undamaged portions of the arena floor began to blink red. Masamune paid the mines no mind. The channel carved by Gorth's gatling fire formed a long, straight path to the ruined barricade and the edge of the central hill. Kyuzo's mech charged up the narrow, beaten zone of cleared explosives. The area all around the long scar turned to blinking red, but Masamune's agile handling brought him through the danger zone unscathed.

The Skevvian's mech clambered to the top of the arena's central hill. Gorth activated plasma blades that slid from the tips of two of his front tentacles. Masamune saw the unsteady stance of his opponent. The black and orange monstrosity made small corrective jolts, compensatory measures for two tentacles damaged earlier by the mines.

Masamune raised his mech's autocannon.

"I could drill a hole clean through your cockpit from here, you know," he said.

The two glowing plasma blades beckoned him up the hill.

"You could. Your rep says you like it up close, though. Unbutton, and let's finish this," Gorth said.

"Close is where I do my best work. You're about to find out," Masamune said. He slammed the retraction button, and his cockpit armor began to come apart and stow itself away. As his mech set its giant metal foot on the base of the hill, the entirety of the arena's flat plains turned to red blinking minefields, all armed, all active.

"I still owe you, you know, for that match at Topaz Narrows Arena. Do you remember it?" Gorth said as his cockpit armor pulled back to match Kyuzo's. The glass underneath was spiderwebbed and cracked from the demolition charge's concussion, but Masamune could still see the Skevvian. He was wounded. Burned. The damaged plasma turbine must have blown back into the cabin.

"Not off hand. Topaz Narrows? Was that our draw?" Masamune said, his mech's autocannon flipping and folding back into its stowed position. He unlocked his sword, and brought it into his mech's armored right hand. He redirected plasma from his remaining jets to the blade, and it began to glow.

"It was a draw, but only because you pulled a cheap move," the Skevvian said, his voice full of venom. "It was a coward's play. You feigned dead until I came within range, and then you did one of these—"

The sinister metal beak on Gorth's mech opened, and another pair of impaler missiles presented themselves like fangs. Masamune was halfway up the hill, exposed, and Gorth had the high ground. Dual flashes signaled the missile launches, one after the other. Kyuzo's battle computer was pulling his mech to the side, discharging what plasma it could spare from the sword. Masamune read the path of the incoming missiles, staggered half a step, drove a jet to meltdown just in time, and avoided the first missile's strike. The other, however, slammed through his cockpit glass. The blow was deafening, and the rocket's solid shaft and solid fuel motor embedded itself next to Masamune's neck and through his seat's headrest.

The physical pain of the hot rocket motor next to him jolted Masamune's real eyes open, breaking his control. His mech spun and staggered down the side of the hill, its left arm trying to pull the burning spike out of the cockpit. The crowd jumped to their feet and flippers, the roar of their thousands of voices drowning out his own cries of pain. Gorth's projectile ran deep through his circuits, and Kyuzo's vision swam with doubled inputs from the mech's sensors and his own eyes.

Gorth leaped from the top of the hill, his two plasma blades slashing and angling for the exposed cockpit of Masamune's stricken mech. The impaler missile's shaft pulled free from the cockpit with a shriek of metal, a thick streak of Masamune's blood running down the side of the spike. Kyuzo clamped his eyes shut, trying to ratchet down on the pain, to regain his connection with the mech's computer. Gorth was damn close.

Masamune felt primal fear and adrenaline pull his shoulder blades together, and the battle computer shielded the shattered cockpit with the right arm's sword and forearm.

Gorth's claws and tentacles were all over him as the two mechs slammed together. The Skevvian sank both plasma blades deep into the protective forearm, carving molten chunks from the composite armor. Sparks and heat rained down on Kyuzo, and he yelled in frustration again as the pain threatened to break his fragile control connection.

The momentum of the collision sent both mechs tumbling down the hill in a whirling pile of limbs, tentacles, and shredded, slagged armor. Masamune's mech was still wrapped up by Gorth's, the armored limbs of the Skevvian knotted around him, slashing at any available targets of opportunity. Kyuzo could hear Gorth screaming and laughing as the snapping beak of the enemy mech tore horrific bites from the top of Masamune's hull. Their mutual tumble came to a rest on the edge of the minefield, the Skevvian mech trying to snare, strangle, and stab the human's machine as it tried to right itself and protect its vulnerable pilot.

Gorth disengaged. He could no longer see through his canopy, and it ejected with the short bark of explosive bolts. Pulling back a short distance, he charged again for a leaping attack, his tentacles whipping, probing for openings. Masamune's computer found an opening of its own. Kyuzo agreed, initiating the attack. He reached his mech's scarred and slashed left arm through the swarm of tentacles, crushing the hull connection socket of one of the plasma-blade limbs. The blade powered down just before it could sever the right wrist and sword hand of his mech, and the blow glanced off the armored gauntlet.

Masamune pushed through the pain of his physical body, retaining the punishing grip on the underside of Gorth's mech.

He shoved the seething black and orange squidmech out to arm's length, holding it there while his plasma blade glowed to life. Gorth continued his maddened ranting, his remaining plasma tentacle stabbing white-hot holes in the side of Masamune's mech over and over again.

Masamune Kyuzo smashed the front of Gorth's mech with the pommel of his blade, three blows landing in rapid succession. The final impact ripped the beak from the hull, stunning the Skevvian as his helmet bounced off the forward control panel of his cockpit. Gorth's battle computer continued to flail the mech's tentacles in an attempt to attack, but a brutal pair of slashes by the glowing blade's edge peeled them off, one by one. A charred tentacle exploded as it fell into the minefield, its metallic coils sent flying in a spray of armored rings and conduits.

The roar from the crowd filled Masamune's mechanical and organic senses. Flash strobes washed over him as he held his helpless opponent in mid-air, its few remaining tentacles making only limp, feeble attempts to attack. A chant began to build from the stadium's seats, slow and steady from a multitude of different throats and communication systems.

"Dese-crate... Dese-crate... Dese-Crate..."

"DESE-Crate... DESE-CRATE... *DESE-CRATE!!!*"

The rolling tide of the arena-wide call for blood flooded over him. The crowd whipped itself into a frenzy, chanting over and over until it was a blurred cacophony of madness. Gorth came to his senses, awakened from his knockout by the tumultuous din of the mob. Kyuzo's own natural eyes opened as he severed his command link with the mech's battle computer. The manual control yokes reemerged from the cockpit's side panels, filling his blistered hands. He glared at his enemy, cold hate streaming from his scorched and bloodied face.

"Masamune, please, I beg you!" Gorth said, his burned and battered tentacles spread in an appeal for mercy.

"I remember Topaz Narrows, now, Gorth. I was knocked out, on automatic controls. I came out of it and disabled you. It was ruled a draw. It was nothing like the dung you just pulled," Masamune said.

"You're right. I'm sorry. Please, please spare me."

"'An insidious gambit shall not go unanswered.' That's the Old Code. You know that," Masamune said. "Besides... we have an obligation as gladiators to our audience." He motioned to the frenzied masses chanting for death.

"NO! No-no-no-NOOOO!" Gorth's voice shrieked as Masamune's mech held up the dismembered enemy hull like a prized decapitated head, displaying it for the rabid throng. The crowd's noise swelled as Kyuzo dropped his mech to one knee, spiking his opponent cockpit-first into the minefield. The explosions sliced through the armor, pressure waves and fragmentation tearing the pleading Skevvian to pieces. Secondary explosions rang Masamune's ears as parts from the mech flew in different directions, detonating their own mines.

The crowd chanted "desecrate" louder and louder as the victorious mech stood upright and placed an armored boot on the shattered remains of Gorth's mech. Masamune braced his mech's stance to counter the upcoming acceleration, and flipped off a safety on the manual controls. His tired plasma turbines spun up, and he dilated the focus of the leg's jet nozzles wide open. The plasma cascaded over the broken Skevvian mech, bathing it in flames. Armor softened, structures bent, and Gorth's body peeled away to cinders under the star-hot assault. The crowd filled the arena with the sound of delirious insanity.

Master Mech Pilot Masamune Kyuzo shambled his damaged mech back to the main elevator, passing through a partition under the audience stands. The arena ground crew guided him on to the platform, signaling to stop when he was centered in the round lift pad. As the edges of the elevator glowed, they rose. He leaned back in his damaged seat, his fingers feeling over his shoulder at the edges of the hole torn by the impaler missile. A thousand feet higher, they reached their destination: Ferro Fortress's mech pits.

A bottle of water fell into his lap, breaking his aching daydream. His crew chief waited on the mech pit's main floor, her arms crossed. Hepholios, the Gatekeeper who owned the arena, floated alongside her. A wall of armored Nines with rifles was in the background, staged in a skirmish line behind his packed-up tool boxes and other equipment. *What the void is going on here?*

Kyuzo, moving slow from the pain of the recent fight, climbed down from his cockpit. Hepsah and his crew usually gathered around him in celebration after a kill. None dared move while under the guns of the Nines.

"Well done, Desecrator, well done, indeed. We greet you in the Ways of the Old Code," the Gatekeeper's voice speaker said.

"Honored Hepholios, it is not often that you visit the mech pits at your own arena," Masamune said, taking a deep pull from the water bottle. "To what do I owe the pleasure of this personal visit?".

"Well, as they say, 'life is change,' Desecrator," Hepholios said. "We are rather fond of you, of your ability to generate revenue and ratings, so we wanted to give you the news in person, being to being."

"And what news is that?" Masamune asked.

"In light of the recent unpleasantness, we regret to inform you that your contract with us is canceled," the Gatekeeper said.

"Your sponsorships, your endorsements, your exclusivity with this house, all are terminated."

"Terminated?!!? What the void is this? I just—"

Weapons safeties clicked off from the squad of bioprinted troopers. Hepholios held up a claw from his chassis, ordering them to hold their fire.

"Do not interrupt, Master Pilot Masamune," the Gatekeeper said. "We understand this may be upsetting, but it is merely business, and your business here, unfortunately, is at an end. You and your crew have twenty minutes to remove your belongings from the mech pits here at Ferro Fortress Arena."

"Oh, and there is the matter of this..." The Gatekeeper gestured another claw towards a thin sheet of plastic being held up by Masamune's livid crew chief, Hepsah.

"Oh, come now, such pouting, such visible discontent, Hepholios said, his pod's running lights pulsing gold and orange. "Not all is grim and doom, gentlebeings. These are your new instructions."

"Instructions?" Masamune said, his voice edged with cold rage. "Instructions from whom, since I am now cut loose? If our contract is over and done with, I answer to no one."

"Oh, that is precious, underbeing, it truly is," Hepholios said with a cool purr in his voice. "No, do not presume you are loose, adrift, or masterless, Master Mech Pilot. You are simply... *reallocated.*"

Enraged at the thought of being reduced to property, Kyuzo felt his prosthetic arm reach for a holstered pistol that was not there. It took all he had to keep focused on the mincing Gatekeeper's condescending words.

"These commands are from your new contract holder, and they are to be obeyed," Hepholios continued. "Tend to your wounds. Ensure your people and property are moved. Then, report to the address written there within the hour."

"We bid you farewell, Master Mech Pilot," the Gatekeeper called back, pulling behind the line of Nines. The gunline of troopers kept their weapons at the ready.

Hepsah handed the plastic sheet to Kyuzo. He scanned it briefly, then threw his helmet against a toolbox, bellowing in pain and anger.

CHAPTER TEN

SIXTH GATE ZONE
BERVA PROXIMA ARENA

Masamune eyed the leather couch, the polished furniture, the chandelier made of intertwined, over-stylized alien nymphs floating above him. The two Model Ninety-Nine guards on either side of the thick armored door remained motionless. He picked up his glass of cold water from its ornate coaster, took a sip, and set it down on the glowing glass of the tabletop. A servant bot emerged from the side of the table, refilled the vessel, and placed it back on the coaster, chirping a small electronic fuss at him.

Masamune smirked, ran his hand over the new patch of skin printed onto his neck, and put his tired feet up on the couch. Before the domestic appliance could re-emerge to scold him, the large doors to the Gatekeeper's office opened.

"We welcome you, Masamune Kyuzo, Master Mech Pilot, in the Ways of the Old Code," Mikralos said. Another Gatekeeper hovered behind the arena master. Masamune remained stone-faced. The address Hepholios gave him was to Berva Proxima Arena, so Mikralos was an expected encounter. The second overbeing, though, he recognized as Dionoles, owner of the Celestial Kingdom casino. *It's been a few years. What brilliant cluster-copulation do these two have in mind, now?* He thought.

Masamune Kyuzo bowed after he crossed into the spacious but spartan room, a decided contrast to the luxurious and gaudy waiting area. Screens filled the concrete walls, some frozen as artwork, others showing current or past mech gladiator contests in looped replay. A large rusted chainsword dominated the back wall of the office, behind what Masamune presumed was a combination of desk and armored pillbox. The gnarled and battered combat implement was the length of a passenger car and covered in faded alien emblems that Masamune did not recognize.

"We have asked you here, Master Mech Pilot, because we have an offer," Mikralos said. "Allow us to skip the normal pleasantries, and come directly to business. What is the remaining balance of your life-debt, and do you know who currently carries the note?"

Masamune felt his jaw and remaining organic hand clench. He relaxed, and said, "Honored Mikralos, I no longer, personally, carry the life-debt. My balance was paid in full some time ago. I thought this was common knowledge, and rather well-known."

Mikralos waved a pudgy, dismissive hand inside his armored fishbowl. Bubbles trailed in the thick liquid behind the gesture. "Yes, yes, Master Mech Pilot, we are aware of that particular line item. The reconstruction debts from your wounds in the arena, though, what of them? The breeding tax on your offspring with your pair-mate, her transdimensional extraction fee, your mech's operational costs now that we have peeled your sponsorships away. These debts accumulate, and still force you to work in the arenas. We wonder if you know the sum total?"

"The exact number on my debt ledger escapes me at this moment, Honored Mikralos," Masamune said. "I am a fighter, not an accountant. Wait. Did... did you say you've *removed* my sponsors? NeuroCyber and Titan Finance both dropped me... because of you? You were involved in that? The rumors of the cheating, the electronic jamming, the nanites?"

"Of *course,* the smear campaign and subsequent dropping of your sponsorships were baseless," Mikralos said. "We created it, after all. It was effective in separating you from your previous contracts, and brought you to our service. As to the financial particulars, pay them no mind. You'll be happy to know that the exact number is known to us, since we are now the holders of your note."

A credit number in the low seven figures flashed on one of the screens in the room. It was the sum value of everyone and everything he loved, reduced to mere digits.

"We also purchased your exclusivity contract from Ferro Fortress Arena," the other Gatekeeper, Dionoles, said. His voice speaker emitted a higher and more anxious tone. "A not inconsiderable expenditure, despite your recent scandals. We created the tumult, and now that we have purchased you at a discount price, we will also make it go away. For this, you may thank us."

The figure on the wall screen nearly doubled. Masamune's eyes narrowed, and his fists, flesh and synthetic, tightened in silent rage. He breathed in, forced himself to relax, and faced the two overlords.

"Honored beings, I must make something perfectly clear before there are any misunderstandings," Masamune said, his tone deliberate and measured. "I know what is happening here.

I have never thrown a fight, and I never will. I live and die by your Old Code, as I have sworn. Since you have gone to great pains to bring me here, you should know this."

"Oh, noble 'Desecrator,'" Mikralos said, "we would never imagine of asking a fighter of your stature and record to engage in inappropriate dealings in or out of the arena, despite your freshly-spoiled public record. This meeting serves only to introduce you to the fact we are now your patrons in the endeavor to redeem your soiled reputation."

"'Patrons?'" Masamune said.

"Well, patrons, benefactors... owners," Mikralos said, the trace lights on his chassis flowing in a magma-like pattern of black, red, and orange. "However you wish to frame it. Regardless of the context you choose, you belong to us, now, and we have a small assignment that benefits all involved."

"Never mind the 'reputation' babble from our esteemed colleague, Master Pilot, we can also make this happen," Dionoles said. The floating credit number flashed, then dwindled to zero.

Masamune scowled. Dealing with Gatekeepers was a sordid, ugly business. Even when glimmers of hope appeared, the goalposts moved, the rules changed, and the counter-attacks came at you from all directions. They held all the cards in a rigged game.

"Let's hear it, then, *honored* sentients," Kyuzo said.

"Ah, be mindful of your tone," Mikralos said, holding up a pod claw in caution. "Reach back in your memory, Master Mech Pilot. Do you remember the name Jered Kramer?"

"I do," Masamune said. "One of my first matches in the Hammer Leagues, after I made the move up from Light Exo. Pitiful, for such a feared opponent. His reputation far exceeded his performance."

"Well, there is more to it than just that, Masamune Kyuzo. Allow us to explain," Mikralos said. Dionoles's running lights shifted to a yellow and purple pattern, and the armored door to the office closed with a grinding thump.

CHAPTER ELEVEN_

SIXTH GATE ZONE
VERVOR'S FABRICATION WORKS

"What in the name of the Eight Gates do you think you're doing, Niff?" Jessica Kramer said, her 20mm revolver pointed at the furry, multi-armed blue being hunched over the workbench. At the harsh sound of her voice, the Niff technician looked up from the jumbled control components of her mech splayed before him.

He startled as he focused on the huge muzzle. His pupils dilated, and magnified by the opti-visor on his face, they appeared to be the size of fists. He cringed, his four hands pulling back from his work on the electronics test bench.

She probably should not have snuck up on the squirrel-like being, but she was not in the mood for niceties. Her Prath-imposed dry spell, and ethyl-alc withdrawal, was making her miserable.

His species, the Niff, had a disgusting way of dealing with potential attackers. His body's defenses kicked in before he could rein in the reflex.

"Please, gentlebeing, I-I mean no harm. I-I am Kitos, Combat Systems Technician, a simple worker in this place of trade," he said.

Jessica pulled the hammer back on the giant revolver. Her eyes started to water as the scent hit her.

"Master-Vervor-assigned-I-I-to-this-work-for-gate's-sake-don't-shoot," the four-armed, lemur-like being with the huge eyes cried.

"Vervor!" Jessica called, her voice carrying down to the shop master's office with the waist-high door. The Myoshan peeked his scaly head out, his main set of eyes pointing at her and the Niff.

"What is it now, mech pilot—what in the gray void do you think you are doing, pointing that primitive weapon at my technician?" Master Vervor said.

Kramer decocked the pistol and holstered it in one smooth motion. She covered her nose from the acrid smell now in the air.

"Okay, just checking," Jessica said. "Nothing personal, there, drippy. Void, that stinks." The technician excused himself, a blue puddle of ichor trailing him to the relief facilities.

"You were much easier to deal with when you were drinking, human," Vervor said.

"Blame Prath. He's the one making me go without," Jessica said, picking up Judah's dented control casing while avoiding the puddle she scared out of Kitos.

"Blame Prath for what?" an Ascended's voice said as a large shadow filled the doorway. Prath had a beverage carrier with a foursome of stimulant drinks in it. He surveyed the situation, saw Vervor's agitation with Jessica, and the blue trail of slime. He traced the trail to the restrooms, and looked back at Jessica.

"You didn't," he said.

"She did," Vervor said.

Prath sighed and set the coffees on the bench.

"You can't keep doing this, you know, little human," Prath said, looking at Jessica. She blanched, looking down at her feet while stroking the butt of her gun.

"'You will not besmirch our reputation with Master Vervor,' my dear Ascended," Vervor said, his fangs jutting out in defiance. "Those were the same exact words we both heard from the hologram. This is not the first incident of such a nature, you know. You and your 'little human,' here, are proving to be menaces to my shop and staff. We should weld a muzzle into that junk-mech's cockpit, for our own safety!"

Jessica's posture stiffened and her eyes narrowed. The fingers on her draw hand flexed.

"Why, you—" she started, before Prath cut her off.

"Not. Now. Jessica. Compose yourself. You're a Kramer. Act like it," Prath said in a deep, forceful tone that echoed through the cavernous mech bay.

Jessica flushed, the look she gave Vervor now shifting to Prath.

"This is burdenbeast dung, and you know it, Prath," she said, her eyes narrowed to slits. "How the void was I supposed to know who the tech was? All I saw was he was working on the one key we have to solving—"

"He is named Kitos," Prath said, interrupting, "and he's one of the best mech techs in this gate zone, and a natural with Arkathan circuitry, even damaged items. He's going to blend your current battle computer with what we can salvage from Judah. You would have known that, if you hadn't stormed off yesterday in an unprofessional huff, pilot. Now, go get a shop towel and clean up the mess you made."

Jessica's expression turned from anger to disgust, and her freckled nose wrinkled.

"The mess *I* made? There's no gate-damned way I'm—"

"You'll do it and like it, or I walk," Prath said, his fangs now half-bared. "You can use your charming personality, and find a way to get your beat-to-void cargo mech back to Red Iridium."

Jessica's mouth was a snarl, paralyzed with fury, and she sought for the right crippling retort.

Vervor turned his back on the two of them as Kitos emerged from the multi-species toilets, but his rear-facing eyes kept them both in view. Kitos pulled a mopping machine out of a nearby closet, making a loud racket as other cleaning supplies fell off the shelves.

"That won't be necessary, Kitos, thank you," Prath said. "Our humble pilot was just about to give you a heartfelt apology and clean up for you, *weren't you*, Jessica Kramer, of the Fourth Gate Kramers?"

Jessica's fists were clenched tight, and her eyes full of daggers for everyone in the room. She snatched the control pad for the mopping machine from Kitos and started to punch the buttons with short, stabbing motions.

The mopping machine powered up, hovering on a glowing field. Jessica sent it racing over Kitos's slime trail, sucking the noxious mess up with an array of scrubbers and vacuum inlets. Miniature arms and hoses emerged from its stained shell, cleaning the work bench without disturbing any of the delicate instruments or work pieces. She cleaned the seat last, restoring it to factory-new condition.

The operation was over in a minute, including the flight back into the tight storage closet, and she tossed the control pad back to Kitos.

"Sorry," she said in a low growl. Kitos caught the tablet and looked to Prath and Vervor.

"There, you see, you're a natural, little human," Prath said.

Perhaps we should start a new arena sport for piloting cleaner bots. You'd be a star."

"Not funny," Jessica said, her arms crossed.

"No, not at all, when you think about it. These beings are here to help us, and you should keep that in mind. By the way, you dropped something," Prath said, motioning to something by her feet. She looked down, and found nothing.

"What?"

"It's your attitude. Pick it up, and straighten it out."

Vervor tried to disguise his sudden laugh by coughing. It didn't work.

"Here. Take the sting out of your crabbiness and ethyl-alc withdrawals. Have a cup," Prath said, passing out the drinks he brought. "We have to figure out a way to up-armor your mech's legs and re-route the plasma blade lines to the reactor so they're not so exposed."

"After that," the Ascended continued, "I want the command module from the old chassis implanted directly into the CR-400's control board. I designed those adapters myself, years ago, and they'll help with the interface. So, drink up and look alive. Our first conditioning match is in four days."

CHAPTER TWELVE_

Skreeb Fourth-Hatched's cybernetic eyes whirred as they focused, searching for the target.

"He's in there, huh, Skreeb? Whattaya see? Can we go, yet?" the Skevvian asked.

Skreeb ran a metallic hand across the top of his head, smoothing down his finned crest. He was a Shasarr, from a race of large, reptilian warriors. A few rough-and-tumble years on the mean streets of Junctionworld had resulted in him replacing a few parts.

"Yeah. That's what my info guy says, Velsh," Skreeb said to his partner. "The boss wants this guy brought in. He's late on his loan payments. Either he covers the balance, or we start sending pieces of him back through the Worldgates to his loved ones."

Master Vervor's mech shop was across the street, its windows and retracted blast shields lit by the blinking neon lights of the bar down the street. No sign of their mark, yet, but he did see something that made him grit his fangs. A dozen Myoshan techs clambered on a framework of scaffolding and movable repair decks, all of them busy installing parts on to a shrouded mech chassis.

"Oh, great," the Shasarr said.

"What?" Velsh asked.

"Myoshans. I hate those damned spuds," Skreeb answered.

"Oh yeah? Why's that? 'Cause folks is always gettin' Myoshans and Shasarr mixed up?" Velsh said.

"Yeah, that's part of it," Skreeb said. "We're nothing alike. Just because we have scales, morons think we're related, or somethin'. Completely different species."

"And another thing, Skreeb," the Skevvian said, "how come they're always called 'spuds?'"

"'Spuds.' You know... little, brown, lots of eyes..."

Velsh returned Skreeb's explanation with a blank look.

"I don't get it."

"'Spuds,' like potatoes."

"What's a 'potato?'"

"Forget it, Velsh."

An exhaust fan kicked on, startling him and his tentacled partner. The alley filled with a hot draft that pushed at him, making his concealed weapon visible to anyone passing by. He looked around, self-conscious, and ruffled his coat, breaking up the outline of the heavy laser carbine hidden beneath it.

He looked up with his camera eyes, and ducked into a shadow, pulling Velsh along with him. An Enforcement Directorate drone flew high overhead, its red running lights blinking bright against the dark Junctionworld sky.

They waited, neither being making a sound. Once Skreeb saw the drone wasn't coming back for him, he took a long puff on the vaporizer implant in his forearm, breathing the fumes out of his gills.

"Skreeb, what the void are we doing here?" Velsh said. "You

know this is the Sixth Gate Zone. It's the *Headhunter's* turf, for gate's sake. Is the boss trying to start a war, or somethin'?"

"The boss says it, and we do it, faster than you can... can..." Skreeb trailed off, at a loss for words.

"Can what?" his partner asked.

"Don't worry, Velsh. You just do it, do it quick, and when I say so," Skreeb said. "I'm the shot-caller, here. You worry about the job, not the ventin' Headhunter."

"What's in the vape? More of that stuff Monfra sells?" Velsh said.

"Yeah. I don't know what the void it is, but it's smooth," Skreeb said, releasing another smokescreen of fumes.

"You shouldn't be getting all clouded up, Skreeb," Velsh said, worried. "We're kinda hangin' our breedin' appendages out in the wind, here. I mean, what if one of the Headhunter's heavy hitters or snitches spots us here, out of our own territory?" His tentacles wrapped and unwrapped around his small pistol with a nervous fidget.

"If you're scared, go hide yourself up in the transport pod and change your color to match the back seat. I'm staying put until we know we've got our mark," Skreeb said, his head crest rising in irritation. The vape was smooth, yes, but Velsh's whining was damaging his inhaled calm.

A target indicator blinked inside his head, forming a target in his vision. Skreeb's cybernetic eyes notified him that the desired target was inside the shop. He grinned, turning to Velsh.

"There, now, shush your little beak, Velshie," Skreeb said. "My shiny eyes just picked him up in that repair bay over there. Our tip paid off."

"Good. Now, we know where he is, and we can get the void out of here, and get back to the Fifth Gate Zone where we belong," Velsh said, a colored pulse of relief flowing across his skin. "We gotta go get some more clothes, a lot of gloves, cover-alls, drop cloths, you name it."

"Why? We know he's here. I say we just snatch him up," Skreeb said, his claws pulling back his coat to bring the laser to bear.

"You ever try to snatch up a Niff, Skreeb? They spray and splatter this nasty stuff all over the place as a defense mecha... mech..."

"Mechanism," Skreeb said.

"Yeah, mechanism. We need something like an isolation tank or a coffin to put 'im in. At least a big garbage bag. Niffs are like feces-bombs, ready to let go at the slightest spook. And the smell," Velsh said, shuddering.

Skreeb's head crest laid flat in annoyance.

"You sure you're not just dunging me 'cause you're skittered by the Headhunter?" he said.

"That crazy damned cyborg is one thing," Velsh said, raising a tentacle in a stabbing motion to make a point. "Grabbing a Niff covered in its own filth and slamming it into the back of my ride is another."

"Which reminds me," the Skevvian continued, "I need to install a liner in the trunk, something we can hose out, or rip out and burn. Damn, this is gonna be a nasty job. Why'd it have to be a Niff?"

Skreeb took another deep hit from his vaporizer, looked around to see that they weren't observed, and motioned with his head to go back to the ride.

"It's always somethin'," he said, a purple haze streaming from his mouth and gills. "Doesn't have to be right now, though. Like you said, we need supplies. Alright, we'll come back later. Let's get something to eat, first."

Skreeb's blunted senses failed to notice the previous Enforcement Directorate drone after it doubled back. It hovered in silence, tucked under an awning a few blocks away. Once the two beings departed in Velsh's air car, the drone's telephoto lenses and microphone turret retracted back into its main hull. With a whining whir of ducted fans, it flew off to report to its maintenance stable.

CHAPTER THIRTEEN

SIXTH GATE ZONE
BERVA PROXIMA ARENA

The two parties face each other in the dark bunker, the only light coming from the glowing negotiation table between them. On one side, a pair of Gatekeepers. On the other, a human female and her Ascended crew chief.

"These are our last, best, and final terms, Mech Pilot Kramer," Mikralos said, his running lights edging from light gray to black. "Should you find them lacking, you are free to ambulate back through the portal and consider our accord sundered. All property involved will default to its true and rightful owners."

"Yes, well, as we have stated before," Prath said, "the terms are nearly acceptable, Honored Mikralos, it's just that we—"

"Master Technician Prath, as we have stated numerous times before," Mikralos said, cutting the Ascended crew chief off. "We are in direct negotiations with Mech Pilot Jessica Kramer. We understand you are here in an advisory capacity, but protocol demands that you are to follow the established negotiation protocols. The last statement was intended for the Primary, Mech Pilot Kramer. She is to address the demand, or these proceedings will be considered adjourned." Yellow, red, and black pulses ran along Mikralos's chassis lines, indicating his annoyance with the tall ape. Dionoles, the casino operator Gatekeeper floating beside him, murmured something to the Berva Proxima arena master.

Jessica chewed her lip as she shifted in the plush chair. The upholstered seat was now far less comfortable than when they started negotiations two hours ago. The black-edged screen of the glass table separating the two sides was a cluttered display of 2-D images, documents, and diagrams covering the broad legal and financial spectrum of contract negotiations between Gatekeepers and their fighters. *Mom used to handle all this for Dad, and made it look so easy,* she thought to herself.

"It's a 'Gatekeeper's Cross,'" Prath whispered in her ear. "A classic underhanded ploy of theirs, building you up just to drop you, with a minimum of evidence. Walk away. We'll have other ways, little human, other opportunities." Jessica leaned over, covering her mouth as she whispered back to him.

"He invoked 'last, best, and final,' ape," Jessica said. "We have to do something, or it's all over. It's their damned Code. I have one last play, I think. Watch." She cracked her knuckles, one by one, and spread her palms on the table.

"Point of order, Mikralos," Jessica said, "on the matter Prath was trying to bring up. They're stickers, Mikralos. Endorsements. Visual indicators of Gatekeeper confidence in the fighter they've paid so many credits to equip and train. Why is the Celestial Kingdom putting up the money to front this endeavor, but won't authorize their logo on my mech?"

"Our concerns are our own, Pilot Kramer," Mikralos said, "as we have continued to state for the better part of the last two hours."

"I call burden-beast dung on that, Honored Mikralos," she said, raising her voice. "These concerns of yours should be shared between both parties. What is this whole thing, a set-up? A distraction from a larger issue? Or am I being used as part of some old vendetta? And why isn't the other fighter, this 'Masamune' character, here?"

Mikralos's running lights turned a cold blue at the mention of the word 'vendetta.'

"We invoke Internecine Parley, retaining all rights, and so forth," Mikralos said. Jessica held up a hand in acknowledgment before the Gatekeeper drowned her in 'Old Code' negotiation babble. Dionoles, the Gatekeeper entrusted with the Celestial Kingdom casino, hovered close to his fellow overlord. The flicker of an anti-surveillance bubble blurred them both from view as they huddled together to consult.

She turned to Prath.

"First time they've done that, and we've been at it a while. I must have hit a nerve. They... they can't hear us, either, right, Prath?"

"Correct," Prath said, "but they may still have recording devices in the room, and will probably play back any side conversations for later listening."

"But it's a neutral room," Jessica said.

"Nothing is neutral with the Gatekeepers, you know that," Prath answered.

"Fine. 'Screw you, Mikralos,' for the record," Jessica said in a louder voice.

"Childish, but not unwarranted, little human," Prath said.

"So, you still think this might be a Gatekeeper's Cross?"

"A classic one," Prath said. "If they fund you, and don't slather you in their logos, they're betting against you, or setting you up. The fix is in. Fortunately, we knew that going into this. They might know that we know, too. This all might be a charade, a front to provoke you into the final match. The preliminary matches they want to put on are just to build hype for the final death match with Masamune. This 'Desecrator' is no being to take idly, love."

"Wait, what do you mean, 'a charade?' So, am I wasting my time here?" Jessica said, her eyes flashing with frustration and anger. "I just want them to admit it, damn it."

"Admit what, little human?" Prath said, his hand gestures wide and questioning. "The negotiating table is not the place to pry facts or admissions out of them, or try to make them squirm. This is their arena, of sorts. This is where they do some of their best work. You've held them off for an hour, Jessica, and I commend you, but this is getting us nowhere. Their words are one thing. Their actions are another. Follow the actions, and be ready."

"Remind me why are we intentionally putting our head in this noose, again?"

"Jered," Prath said softly.

"Jered. Right."

The bubble surrounding the two Gatekeepers strobed and dropped out of sight. Both hovering alien overlords were now at the negotiating table.

"Two lead-up fights and a main event, yes? We agree to one inconspicuous Celestial Kingdom logo with sponsorship mention during the announcements for the first fight, five small logos if you make the second event, and full corporate regalia for the main event. Do not embarrass us, human. The changes have been made in the relevant clauses," Dionoles said. The casino operator's small claws, more suited to counting currency and shuffling paperwork, downloaded a scroll of modified conditions and clauses to the negotiating table's screen.

Prath frowned at the new terms worked into the contract, and started to raise his hand.

"Fair and done," Jessica said without even looking down. Her lack of instant disagreement, which had characterized the last two hours, made both Gatekeepers look at each other in muted surprise.

"Then... then, though it is quite sudden, we are bound in agreement," Mikralos said, a silvery claw extending from his carrier hull. "Excellent. All parties and witnesses will now place their manipulators on the table for scanning, and these proceedings will be recorded with Junctionworld Central Data."

She slapped her hand down on the table to be scanned, and turned to Prath.

"Well, ape, into the noose we go," she said.

"You were too quick to agree, little human," Prath said, placing his hand, palm-down, on the witness pad to be recorded. "However, sometimes it's the best way to give the hangman one last kick in the balls."

CHAPTER FOURTEEN

JUNCTIONWORLD CENTRAL ZONE
CENTRAL DATA TOWER

Gatekeeper Mikralos hated these meetings with his superior, GateLord Novalos. The being had once been his commanding officer, and, after years of scheming, maneuvering, and backstabbing politics, now ruled the entire Sixth Gate Zone. Novalos demanded constant updates on the Kramer situation, and the GateLord made it his personal quest to see the family ground under heel. *Well, to claim the glory for it, anyway,* Mikralos thought.

Like his previous life, centuries ago, Novalos had once again 'volunteered' Mikralos for a mission. This time, instead of conquest, the GateLord tasked Mikralos with arranging the downfall of the Last Kramer, but only in strict adherence to the Old Code. Arranging the complicated parts of enacting the vendetta had not been easy. The effort was a huge credit and time soak, requiring his close attention. The distraction made his already-suffering arena business lurch even further towards receivership.

Nevertheless, Mikralos did as he was ordered. He and Solomon had years of bad blood between them. If the plan resulted in the extinguishment of the Kramer lineage, he was happy to do it.

Mikralos's grav-yacht cruised in on flight approach to the foreboding mass of Central Data, its slick black skin pocked with massive turrets and launchers. Mikralos borrowed the sensory feed from the craft's sensors, channeling the data into his own vision.

He scanned the barrels of the many cannons studding the surface of the network headquarters, but paid them little mind. He had already seen what they were capable of. The nuclear-devastated wastes of the Fifth Gate Zone, and the accompanying millions of dead, were testament to the damage they could cause.

Mikralos's craft continued on its carefully-chosen path through the aerial defenses of the Central Zone. Below them, thousands of feet below, he passed over the blinking lights of that garish mercenary gathering place known as Captain York's. It was a notorious mega-bar, a rancid pit of ethyl-alcohol consumption, a place where mercenary mech pilots and their arena-based gladiator counterparts could meet for companionship and new job offerings.

Mikralos hated the eyesore, and wished he could personally drop a cluster-grip of pressure nukes on the miserable location. He knew, though, that it was a vital intelligence-gathering tool for the Gatekeepers, giving them a centralized location where they could monitor conversations and keep tabs on the brutal, vicious fighters they "employed" to keep the viewing masses tamed.

His craft glided, smooth and silent, into one of the gaping

hangar decks of the Central Data tower. His flight crew stayed with the craft while Mikralos hovered down the rear ramp.

"We greet you, Mikralos, Master of Berva Proxima Arena," a Gatekeeper's voice said as he left the ramp. A trio of other Gatekeepers, their armored conveyances all gleaming and spotless, waited for him on the hangar floor. The center being was the one who greeted him. Mikralos extended a claw in response.

"Ah, Ketrius, Lead Director of Arena Network Programming, we greet you in the Ways of the Old Code," Mikralos said. "Actually, if we may correct you, our full title under the Old Code included the additional clauses of 'Champion of the Conquest and Bearer of the Blazing Sword Cluster, Fourth Award.' Alas, we regret we cannot tarry. We have an appointment with Honored Novalos."

Mikralos kept a polite, formal poise in his claw arrangements and carapace body language. *We trust you as far as we can hurl your carcass, backbiter,* Mikralos thought.

"The war was a long time ago, Mikralos," Ketrius said. "Life after battle is not always as glorious. Some beings never reach those rapturous heights again. We understand such was the case with yourself."

The two Gatekeepers by Ketrius's side exchanged looks, reveling in the subtle snark directed at the arena master by their fellow executive.

"What brings you to our lovely Central Data tower, this beautiful day, Mikralos?" Ketrius said, his invective sickly sweet. "Have you come to beg for more support funds? Has that rusting arena dome of yours finally collapsed? We do not recall broadcasting an event feed from your establishment for some time. Oh, do tell us, how goes the convention business?"

The pair of junior network Gatekeepers continued to chitter, their running lights showing their amusement at the senior executive's wordplay. Mikralos suppressed his first impulse to stitch a line of plasma bolts across the threesome.

"It warms our circulatory system's main pump," Mikralos said, feigning a smile, "To see the GateLords' precious pets being so well taken care of, here in the hallowed halls of Central Data. We have not seen such gleaming, unsullied sets of armor in quite a while."

"A regrettable consequence of living in the distant, forlorn Gate Zones, no doubt," Ketrius said, now defensive at Mikralos's insinuation, "Do not blame us if you cannot find, or afford, a sufficiently-proficient bot to keep your chassis in immaculate condition. Some of us care about our appearance and visual professionalism, Mikralos."

"Ah, Ketrius, ever the dandy," Mikralos said, his lights pulsing red and black. "We doubt you would have lasted more than a few minutes in actual combat, during the invasion of Junctionworld. Remind us, again, where were you stationed during the campaign to take this place?"

Ketrius started to sputter and back up, his companions no longer sharing in their laughter.

"Ah, never mind, the memory comes to us, now," Mikralos said, savoring the sudden tension as the decorated combat veteran berated the executive. "Ketrius, we recall you were a staff officer for that fool over the Fourth Corps. What was his name..."

"Favarius," Ketrius said, a snarl finding its way into his voice. "Lord Favarius, to his subordinates, like yourself."

"Yes, yes, 'Lord and Corps Commander Favarius,'" Mikralos said, a wicked glint in his eye. "Was he not killed by a Ja-Prenn assassin drone in the middle of his dormant cycle? Are... are junior staff officers not charged with the sworn duty of protecting their commanders at all times? It has been several centuries, so you must forgive us, as we were never assigned to a comfortable headquarters command billet. We, as you may recall, were at the front lines, tearing apart brood queens and warrior drones with our armor's chain-blade."

Every Gatekeeper fought against the biomechanical Ja-Prenn during the prolonged battle to wrest the pocket dimension from their control. Few front-line warriors survived contact with the nexus units of the hives, the brood queens and their colossal protection drones. Though three hundred years had passed since the conquest, all Gatekeepers wore their combat status as a badge of honor, and Mikralos was no exception. He may not be a shrewd arena operator, but he was a verifiable death dealer at the controls of a main battle armor.

"Well, we would love to continue reminiscing of times past," Mikralos said, "but we must not keep Honored Novalos waiting. We look forward to exchanging pleasantries again, Ketrius. Farewell."

———

Mikralos made his way past the dispirited trio of network executives to the hangar level's elevators. He confirmed his upstairs appointment at an armored desk staffed by a combat team of elite Model Ninety-Nine guards, and entered the mile-tall lifter. The vertical journey took only seconds, the grav-compensators under the elevator's deck plates shedding the effects of the heavy acceleration and deceleration with ease.

The elevator doors opened, and Mikralos made his way through the decorated halls of the GateLords' upper levels of the Central Data tower. His superior, GateLord Novalos, awaited him in ornate office chambers trimmed in neon green and gold. *Well, there is certainly no accounting for taste,* he thought. He paused before continuing into Novalos's executive suite. *Damnation, that sounds like something Ketrius would say.*

"Mikralos, our faithful subordinate," GateLord Novalos said, skipping the formal title greeting. "Come, come, join us."

What an impolite, decrepit old toad, Mikralos thought, masking his ire at the elder statesbeing's informality. *This will be our office, some day. After some redecorating, of course.*

"Tell us, young one, how goes the Kramer affair?" the older Gatekeeper asked, beckoning him forward with a vintage-model claw.

"GateLord Novalos, GateLord of the Sixth Gate Zone, Supreme Planner of the Invasion," Mikralos said, adhering to custom, "we greet you in the ways of the Old Code."

"Yes, yes, the Old Code," Novalos said, settling into his combination of command docket and respiratory assistance module. "Do not belabor us with protocol. Update us on the situation."

Mikralos sighed inside. *You are just going to forget,* he thought, *then lapse into stories of glories of yesteryear. Still, here we are...*

"The plan to eliminate the Kramer name is proceeding at its normal, strategic pace, Lord," Mikralos said.

"Heh. Glacial pace, you mean," Novalos said, scoffing.

"Lord Novalos, we believe we are on the cusp of drawing the Kramer daughter into the arena, and to her humiliating death," Mikralos said. "The trap has taken years to spring, as we have waited for her to re-emerge into view. We believe that time is soon."

"'Soon,'" Novalos said with a gentle, mocking tone. "If we had a credit for every time we heard the word 'soon' come out of your speakers, dear Mikralos, we could build another Central Data tower. You were a superb warrior, but long-term plots such as these require a more subtle touch. Perhaps we erred in tasking you with heading up this endeavor?"

"Lord Novalos, we assure you," Mikralos said, bobbling his

chassis in embarrassment, "we are confident the plan will come to fruition. All we require is a small infusion of—"

"Ah, here it comes, at last," Novalos said, interrupting. "More funds?"

Mikralos hovered in silent shame.

"We will, once again, transfer a few million more credits to you," Novalos said, boredom in his gravelly voice. "We assume the normal arrangement, through your confederate at the Heavenly Palace Casino?"

"Through Dionoles, yes, Lord," Mikralos said, lowering his chassis. "It is only to obfuscate the source of the funds, so none may dare question our direct involvement in her eventual fate."

"As the Old Code requires, of course," Novalos said, his running lights pulsing blue and purple. "It will be done."

The old GateLord stared ahead in contemplation, bubbles slowly streaming from his additional life support hookups.

"There are few regrets we have in this life, Mikralos," Novalos said. "One of those regrets is ever hearing the name 'Kramer.'"

"We will destroy her for you, Lord Novalos," Mikralos said, trying to salvage his pride. "We request your permission to reassemble our original combat triad. The funding will assist in securing the assistance of our old comrade, the Fifth Gate Zone Recovery Specialist, Beliphres."

The GateLord dismissed the notion with a claw-flick.

"Do not bore us with details, Mikralos," Novalos said, "when our greater meaning seems to escape you. No, we speak not of the offspring, Arena Master. The daughter is but a symptom of the original disease. No, we speak of the patriarch, Solomon Kramer. If we had known then, what we know now, we should have left him to die where the scout teams found him. We should have known, based on his last-ditch resistance to his genocidal enemies, he would be a stubborn, stiff-necked prospect. Little did we know at the time, eh, Mikralos?"

"We agree, GateLord Novalos," Mikralos said. "Though our reasons for hating the Kramer clan are our own."

"Ah, yes," Novalos said, "that sordid arrangement the two of you had, where the battle slave tricked you into his absolving his life-debts and other taxes in perpetuity. We remember that match. A disappointing affair."

Mikralos grounded his chassis in shame, his running lights off.

"We will make our amends, Lord," Mikralos said. "Of this, we can pledge our solemn word and honor."

"Pledge what you will, just see that it happens, Mikralos," GateLord Novalos said, extending a claw in warning and dismissal, "for your own sake, and the lives of your comrades."

CHAPTER FIFTEEN

SIXTH GATE ZONE
VERVOR'S FABRICATION WORKS

"What the void is that supposed to be?" Jessica Kramer said, looking at the weapon suspended overhead in a pair of rigging slings. "I'm a blade fighter, not a hammer-dragger. What venting idiot thought this was a good idea?"

Kitos, the blue Niff technician, was ready for her this time, and kept his internal fluids internal. Master Vervor turned from the controls of the shop's gantry crane. His lower fangs jutted out at her, a counter to her bluster.

"The contract was forwarded to us after you signed it, human," the Myoshan said. "Your first bout is classified as a Multi-Combatant Brawl, Modified Shield Match, Close Combat Only. You're going to need more than blades. Besides, it's what you agreed to."

"Prath? Prath!" she said.

Prath poked his head up, turning his attention from the holographic news display at a nearby workbench.

"The fine print, little human," the sitting Ascended said. "You were so busy doing your inquisition bit on the Gatekeepers, you forgot to read the fine print. The second Gatekeeper changed the first shield match from a Light Exo Class, All Ordnance, Single Combat to something much nastier, and on a much more crowded arena floor. There will be four combatants, to be exact. You agreed before I could bring it to your attention."

"A *slug-brawl?* Seriously?" she said, stomping her foot. "Why a mallet, though? I didn't really sign up for that dung, did I?"

Prath changed his holograph projector from the news to the contract. A few manipulations, and the fight agreement floated in front of them, the section in question outlined in garish red print. Jessica's brow wrinkled as she read it.

"Oh, void," she said.

"I told you, love, the negotiating table is their arena," Prath said. "'One corporate logo for the Celestial Kingdom Casino, tasteful and inconspicuous in nature, to be mounted on the face of a hammer/cudgel/kinetic impact device, sufficient to be held with both of the specified mech's manipulator hands.' It's right there, in the contract you signed with such confidence and gusto."

"You were supposed to be watching my back in there, ape!"

"How could I," Prath asked, "when you agreed right away to a last-second concession made by Gatekeepers? They *never* fully agree to something. There's always a poison pill in their negotiating tactics, some clause or condition that must be pried out, like a rock in a piece of candy."

"Well, void. This is some dung, gate damn it."

"Language."

Jessica huffed and blew her hair out of her face. She stared at the hammer, trying to melt it with her gaze.

"Well, it looks like a wonderful kinetic impact weapon, regardless of our pilot's eager zeal to sign documents," Prath said, dimming his news hologram. "Master Vervor, what is it called? I don't think I've seen a skull-thumper that big used in any of matches before."

"It's a BGDH-1," Vervor said, his small chest puffing with pride. "One of my own designs. I put it in the fabricator to run as soon as I received the contract."

"What does that acronym stand for?" Prath said.

"'Big Gate-Damned—'" Vervor started.

"'Hammer One,' I get it," Jessica said, smirking.

"I-I thought hammer name was clever," Kitos the technician said.

"I didn't ask, *Squirty*," Jessica said. Kitos's four shoulders slumped, and he looked down to return to his work. Prath shot her a look which she tried to ignore, but couldn't.

"Ugh. Okay, there's some potential, there, I'll give you that," Jessica said. "I like the spikes on the opposite face of the hammer surface and the pommel on the shaft. I need some heat, though. I really wish I could go back to my blades." She stared up at the hammer, then over at her mech NoName's original plasma-edged weapons. They were still in pieces after the match with Zerren Beff at Red Iridium.

"Contract doesn't say we can't modify it, right?" Jessica said, raising an eyebrow.

"Nope," Prath said, rebooting his news hologram.

"Well, then," she said, "let's get to it. I have an idea, Squir—"

Prath made a loud, fake cough, rippling the air flowing through his floating sports and news hologram. Jessica rolled her eyes at him, then turned to the meek and frightened four-armed being.

"Ugh... Kitos, *dear technician*, I would like to discuss with you a possible modification to Master Vervor's wondrous design," Jessica said, batting her eyelashes at both the Niff and his Myoshan boss, making sure her crew chief saw her exaggerated display.

"Better. Keep working on it," Prath said from behind his news hologram.

CHAPTER SIXTEEN

FIFTH GATE ZONE
VOID'S EDGE REFUSE DISPOSAL COMPLEX

Beliphres had many claws contained in the hull of his carrier chassis. He had always been a more practical Gatekeeper, more at home on the battlefield or the streets than command bunkers or network offices. This particular manipulator was crude in form and function, a leftover from a previous generation of Gatekeeper war-chassis. It was heavier and stronger than current models, though, able to crush and tear armored hulls in close combat. He had others, of course, smoother and sleeker, but when this battle claw emerged from his hull, its brutal shape sent a message: he meant business.

"Very well, Cleeg," Beliphres said, gesturing with the heavy implement. "You have refused to answer our questions to our satisfaction, and have exhausted the last of our good will. You sleep in the void, tonight. Farewell."

He starting the machine up with the large mechanical claw. Cleeg burbled and wept as the monstrous garbage compactor spooled up. Its blade-covered drum turned faster and faster, preparing to shred Cleeg's exoskeleton to chitinous chunks and splinters.

Gatekeeper Beliphres's dark eyes maintained their cold gaze as Cleeg moved down the processor's conveyor belt. A large bag of trash, rancid and bulging with drippings and sludge, burst when it hit the whirling blades of the compactor. The putrid smell of rotten meat and sour milk filled the loading dock. Cleeg screamed, pleading, as his turn came up next.

"Honored Beliphres, I swear, I swear, on the life and love of my spawnlings—"

"Hmm, yes, there is that unattended matter, too," Beliphres said, stopping the machine. "How many?"

"How... how many what, Beliphres?" the insectoid being asked.

"Spawnlings, Cleeg. How many?" Beliphres said.

"My mate and I have a brood of seven," Cleeg said, desperation in his voice. "Seven, Honored Gatekeeper, seven little sets of mandibles to feed, seven little hearts that need me to come home. Please, I, I had no idea that my business partner was up to something. He skimmed the set-aside accounts, Beliphres, not me! I'm just the financier, a fellow victim of that idiot's plan. I'll gladly pay you back, double, triple, just please don't—"

"Double? Triple?" Beliphres said. "The time for the negotiation of monetary compensation, dear Cleeg, is in the past. We are now in the executive phase of our transaction."

The Gatekeeper started the machine up again, but dialed down the speed of the conveyor belt. Cleeg's feet became a green blur of shell and splattered blood, and the loading dock was filled with chittering screams.

"You see, Cleeg," Beliphres said, pontificating, "a business partnership is a joining of resources and wills, an agreement to shoulder the pain and profit of a venture."

Cleeg's four knees went next. They burst like ripe fruit-bulbs, yellow fluid gushing as the blades split them.

"Your partner, Tophor, thought keeping three sets of books would go unnoticed by us," the Gatekeeper said. "He paid for that last night, but was kind enough to enlighten us to your location after some... unpleasant persuasion. You, Cleeg, knew the character and demeanor of your partner. Even if you claim ignorance to Tophor's transgressions, you cannot claim to be surprised. You chose this being to join on your business journey, and in doing so, you chose your current plight."

The tugging, cutting motion of the processor's drum blade ripped Cleeg's translucent wings from their sockets, filling the air with glittering bits.

"Your own poor judgment is the cause of this present consternation, Cleeg," Beliphres said. "We are merely the logical consequence of the choice you made when you began this misadventure."

The gore-splashed blades sang a deeper note as Cleeg's head and torso were pulled into the garbage processor.

"Congratulations, gentlebeing, you have arrived at your chosen destination," Beliphres said. A smirk formed on his distorted features. "No more tears, Cleeg, only dreams."

"Gates, I love those speeches you give when they get fed in the chipper, boss," Skreeb Fourth-Hatched said. His vaporizer inlet glowed, and he pulled a gill-full into his system. His Skevvian partner, Velsh, nodded in avid agreement next to him.

"We Gatekeepers were conquering poets, once, young Skreeb," Beliphres said. "Our subjugation of this place," he waved the heavy battle claw around, motioning at the whole of Junctionworld, "was recorded in song and verse, our deeds and methodologies formalized and enshrined in the oft-mentioned Old Code. Our race never excelled with the brush or chisel. We were warrior wordsmiths, talented with both plume and plasma cannons."

"Uh, 'plume,' boss?" the Skevvian asked.

"'Plume,' young Velsh," Beliphres said. "The shaft of a bird's feather, sharpened, dipped in ink. It was for extracting thoughts from the mind and placing them on parchment."

"Uh, boss... 'parchment?'" Skreeb, the tall, reptilian cyborg asked. "And, uh, how did the extraction process work? Did it, you know... did it hurt?"

Small bubbles streamed in Beliphres's carrier sphere in a silent sigh.

"Forgive us, dutiful, shopworn Skreeb," the Gatekeeper said. "We know you are unburdened with an excess of vocabulary or intellect."

Both beings looked at the Gatekeeper with blank expressions on their faces.

"Never mind," Beliphres said. "Find this insect's family hive and make sure his progeny, seven plus a broodmate, we believe he said, are snug and secure inside. Then, torch it."

"Torch it. Right, boss," Skreeb said.

"These Khalixx like to build in hexagonal patterns, like honeybuzzers," the Gatekeeper said. "Make sure the six hives around it are immolated, as well, but leave a smattering of survivors to tell the tale. You did the same with Tophor's residence and family, one presumes?"

"Yeah, boss, we poured that incendiary goop down their throats and lit it, just like you said," Skreeb said, his head's crest rising from the joy of the memory. "It was fireworks city. I captured the vid on my eye cameras. Pour, light, then poof!"

The Shasarr cyborg continued to stare with his unblinking eye implants at the Gatekeeper. Beliphres glared at both of them, annoyed as the moment dragged on.

"And? Yes?" the Gatekeeper said.

Velsh poked Skreeb with one of his tentacles, breaking his momentary stupor.

"Huh? Oh, we also found the debt-runner, boss," Skreeb said. "But, there's a hitch, though. Our tip-off gave us the name of where he works. 'Vervor's Foundry Works.' Real high-end mech shop over by Berva Proxima arena. He's in there, but we wasn't sure how to go about..."

"You were surprisingly wise to not extract him, Skreeb," Beliphres said. "Vervor's establishment is in the Sixth Gate Zone, and that is the Headhunter's territory, is it not?"

"Yeah, boss," Skreeb said.

"Were you seen? No challenges to your presence?" the Gatekeeper asked.

"No, boss, we was careful," Velsh said. The memory of the overhead Enforcement Directorate drone ran a chill through his nervous system, and his tentacles clutched and unclutched.

A light signaled on the interior of Beliphres's protective bubble, followed by a quick scrawl of text. After reading it, Beliphres pointed the heavy claw at one of his armored Nines standing on the perimeter of the loading dock. "Summon our transport."

The bioprinted guardsman saluted his acknowledgment, running to secure the nearby landing pad as he opened comms with the Gatekeeper's grav-yacht orbiting overhead. Beliphres turned back to his Skevvian and Shasarr associates.

"Download the video feed from your eyes to our craft's internal computers, Skreeb," Beliphres said. "We wish for some in-flight entertainment while we travel to Honored Mikralos's abode."

CHAPTER SEVENTEEN

SIXTH GATE ZONE
ENFORCEMENT DIRECTORATE BARRACKS

Model Ninety-Nine Drone Technician 83556-A, known as "Blues" to his squadmates because of his eclectic musical tastes, checklisted the outgoing shift of Airborne Enforcement Drones before they launched. After running quick pre-flight checks on each of them, he sent them out on their patrols. Once they were gone, he turned his attention to the returned drones hanging in their racks.

Airborne Enforcement Drone 6-44 waited at its retrieval station, its red indicator light blinking in contrast to the solid yellow lights shown by its eight other compatriots in the local Directorate station's hangar. 6-44 was the last to be lubricated, maintained, and have its files downloaded.

Blues reviewed the video feed from the drone on his forearm computer, skipping ahead to the segment highlighted by the drone's computer for evaluation. The images of an air car, a Skevvian, and a Shasarr cyborg flashed across the drone's patrol report, along with data summaries of their criminal records and mug shots.

The Skevvian was named Velsh. The Shasarr was Skreeb Fourth-Hatched. No unusual activity was reported, but their past records and presence was cause for monitoring.

Under normal circumstances, Blues would forward the matter to Intel section, where fellow Model Ninety-Nine who earned the rank of detective and would compile and follow up on the report. That report would possibly flow to the One-Oh-Nine Lead Enforcer or Centurion farther up the chain in the Enforcement Directorate, where a decision would be made about further action.

Blues knew who these two beings were, though, and had other plans. Someone important, someone outside the normal channels, needed to see this.

He dropped the video log chip from Drone 6-44 into a small pocket concealed in his maintenance coveralls. His shift report noted that the memory device in 6-44 was corrupted, and replaced with a fresh blank one.

Blues ended his work shift and checked out of the Nine barracks with the Lead Enforcer on duty. Regulations allowed him only two hours outside of the hive-like building for personal time. He hustled to cross the Sixth Gate Zone to his destination on foot, checking often to see he wasn't being followed or drawing undue attention. He wore a hooded jacket and reflective visor to conceal his black eyes and softened Niner features. Since he maintained similar systems, he knew how to slip past the endless array of scanners and cameras studding the crowded streets of the dilapidated housing districts and commercial broadways.

Blues arrived at the run-down neighborhood of Sebyus with half of his time gone. Sebyus was a mix of refugee camp and high-rise ghetto, packed full of sentients still homeless from the

Fifth Gate nuclear strikes. Graffiti in a dozen languages covered the walls and trash filled the streets. No malevolent Gatekeeper schemes uncoiled here. No valiant mech-gladiators did battle, except on tattered posters and blinking hologram displays. Here, like in most of Junctionworld, there was only misery.

He turned down an alley, arriving at an off-list checkpoint. The Nines manning the post wore standard Enforcement Directorate uniforms, but their gear was augmented, far more potent than arsenal-issued weaponry. An initial challenge at muzzle-point was met with a short counter-phrase.

"The Future, The Way," Blues said. The Nines at the checkpoint acknowledged him, but did not scan him, and he passed with barely any notice.

A ruined factory two blocks past the checkpoint was his final waypoint. As he drew nearer, rubble and cannon impacts became more prominent on the sides of the building, along with piles of rusted shell casings and the smell of decaying carcasses. In front of the factory a pair of Enforcement Directorate mechs sat toppled, their hulls shattered and burned. They were trophies of the building's owner from a battle fought years before, and neither the Sixth Gate Zone's Enforcement Directorate commander or even the GateLord dared order their recovery or retrieval.

Older, scarred Nines guarded the charred entrances of the factory. They were vintage combat models, pulled from service due to excessive damage or age. Many bore cybernetic replacement parts. They were "Recykes," renegade Nines who were off the books, extracted from the reprocessors before they were scheduled for destruction or broken up for parts. They, like this place, did not exist on any official map of ledger.

One older Nine at the gate recognized Blues and raised a prosthetic hand. He held a big-bore projectile weapon, similar to Enforcement Directorate carbines, but customized. A large ammunition drum jutted from the side, and it was trained on Blues' bioprinted sternum.

"Greet," the older Nine said.

"Confirm. Data. Boss optics. Solo," Blues answered in the chopped language used by Nines.

"Priority?" the Recyke asked.

"Utmost," Blues said.

"Stand by, Blues. Access req inbound."

After a pause and a small burst of radio transmission, the Recyke guard opened the heavy door, his aim shifting from Blues to its prior direction down the street.

Another checkpoint, this one an armored teller's window flanked by another pair of veteran guards, awaited him inside the building. The booth and walls around it were festooned with the severed heads of every race of sentient and sapient found in Junctionworld. Some were bare skulls, others in various states of rot. Some were separated only a short time beforehand, their dark clotting trails running down the walls. The chamber reeked of death, but a Nine was not moved by such things.

The Model Ninety-Nine in the teller booth put down his computer tablet and regarded him with equally black eyes.

"Blues, long time. Welcome. Query: visitation purpose?" the Ninety-Nine said. Model Ninety-Nines like the teller and himself did not have to communicate in the short, clipped speech of the more basic Nines, and non-essential words could slip into their conversation. Things were still curt. This was important.

"Greet, Nolo. Data. Potential intrusion. Priority utmost," Blues said, holding up the small memory device he carried.

"No doubt. Boss standing by. See Blues now. Proceed after search. Transport pending after briefing," the Ninety-Nine said.

"Acknowledged. Grateful," Blues said.

Blues held his hands and the data-chip out to his sides. One of the guard Nines covered him with a weapon while the other searched him with a scanner device. They switched search and weapons positions and repeated the process. Redundancy was built in to the Nines. The boss could handle anything that came at him, short of a nuke, but it was the way things were done.

Blues proceeded down the large, shot-out hallway. Skulls with lights mounted in them lit the former industrial concourse with a faint glow. Human, Myoshan, Redfolk, even Nines were represented. Most were unknown to Blues. He was gene-formed as a drone mechanic, not a xeno-biologist.

The hallway led to a large, pitch-black room with a single beam of light emanating from the ceiling. Blues stood in the pool of the spotlight. Something big rustled and whirred in the darkness.

"Blues, I'm told you have something for me? Something Utmost?" the smooth mechanical voice asked.

"Affirm, Boss," Blues said. "Selfsame unit pulled vid feed off drone after patrol. Data alerts intruder, two times, plus softskin vehicle. Known subordinates, Beliphres. Location, Berva Proxima area, Sixth Gate Zone. Data offered, solo copy."

Blues held the data-chip up into the light. Large, vibroblade-tipped fingers, each the size of Blues' forearm, reached out from the darkness. The giant red hand plucked it from Blues's outstretched palm with deft precision. The flat piece loaded into a slot on the claw's main wrist with the help of subordinate serpentine tentacles. A pair of black, glittering eyes, the same color and size as his own, opened in the darkness. The soft glow of a screen illuminated the room, showing off the Headhunter's menacing form and surroundings.

The giant red cyborg had started life as an experimental type of Nine, but that was where the similarity between him and the average bioprinted trooper ended. The rumors at the barracks said he was actually a special type of One-Oh-Nine. He had been a Centurion, once, a combat adviser and bodyguard to the GateLords themselves. They turned him into this, and he escaped, setting up his own dark kingdom in the Sixth Gate Zone.

Parts of the Headhunter were still Niner. His face, brain, spine, and other assorted bits of reinforced meat were original, though enhanced. The remainder was custom-fabricated, unstoppable killing machine. His body was like an Unlimited mech from the arenas, a pulsing, writhing conglomeration of red armored plates, weapons components, and armored sinew. Multiple types of weapons, claws, launchers, and scything blades covered his armored hull, making him a lethal threat at any distance, near or far.

Blues was genetically conditioned to know no fear, yet still he shivered at the sight of the renegade crime lord. If Nines could feel primal panic, the Headhunter would be the thing that inspired it.

"Let's just see what you've got here, Blues," the Headhunter said, going over the data in front of him. "Oh, that's interesting. Skreeb and Velsh seem to have lost their map and sense of direction. Maybe even their minds, trolling around in my sector of control."

"Selfsame cogged you lay optics on first, boss," Blues said. "Selfsame cogged priority utmost."

"And you thought right, Blues," the cyborg said, his metal body shifting in his oversized seat. "I really did need to see this, right away."

"I used to patrol that area when I was just a rookie Enforcer, before they modded me," the Headhunter said. "Old Vervor's mech shop is across the street. Looks like they're scoping it out for something."

His steel muscles coiled and reconfigured as he spoke. The

charging station he sat on was shaped like a nightmarish throne. Its black-chromed surface was covered, like most of his décor, in skulls. Most prominent among the trophies were two pink glass spheres, their ruined flesh-and-bone contents settled to the bottom of the liquid-filled containers in ragged piles. The sight of them always troubled Blues. It was not easy seeing Gatekeepers, the supposed apex beings of their civilization, mounted like trophies. He pushed the uneasiness aside.

Imprinted doubts. Mass-produced lies. Loyalty to Sameself's own unit-type first and utmost, Blues thought. The Headhunter was the future of Junctionworld. The Headhunter was going to lead them to freedom.

The data feed reached its end. The being known as "Headhunter, Centurion and Warlord," if one subscribed to the Ways of the Old Code, flicked off the holo display.

"My thanks, Blues," the cyborg said. "Please let Nolo, up front, know that I need him back here."

One of the Headhunter's lower set of arms raised a hand in salute to the drone technician, who returned it as he bowed. Blues turned and made his way to the teller booth, accepting the credit stick Nolo offered him. He exchanged a nod with the Ninety-Nine adjutant, and stepped into the hover car waiting out front.

CHAPTER EIGHTEEN

SIXTH GATE ZONE

THE HEADHUNTER'S LAIR

"Beliphres, you loathsome blob, what are we going to do with you?" the Headhunter said aloud to no one in particular. "I suppose the hardest part will be finding room for a third trophy mount without throwing off the design flow of the room."

The red cyborg accessed the data and images again. They poured from an emitter in one of his hands. The pictures projected against the far skull-covered wall like a lumpy-screened cinema.

Nolo, the rebel Headhunter's adjutant and an advanced Model Ninety-Nine trooper, appeared at the entrance to the chamber.

"Wanted to comm with Selfsame, boss?" Nolo said.

"Nolo, we're going to send a message," the Headhunter said, one set of his giant claws flexing. "I know Beliphres's territory in the Fifth Gate Zone is nuked, but it looks like his boys are looking for greener fields in our little patch of heaven. Find me a list of targets."

"Oh, and pull what we've got on Vervor's mech shop," the Headhunter said before Nolo could turn to leave. "I'm going to pay a visit. How's he doing on his protection payments?"

"Selfsame will prep transport, and brief Boss en route," Nolo said.

CHAPTER NINETEEN

SIXTH GATE ZONE

VERVOR'S FABRICATION WORKS

The impact of the mech's hammer striking the reinforced target shook the entirety of Master Vervor's shop, even through the insulated, force-field-protected testing booth.

The data fed into a computer station, where his large, orange body stood over the Niff technician, Kitos. Master Technician Prath skimmed the input displays, stroking his chin as he evaluated the wide spectrum of information.

"That left arm is just a touch out of synch on the downstroke," Prath said. "And the torso twist needs more follow-through. Adjust the acceleration and voltage up by half a percent for that combo. Specifically, these actuators here, and here."

The tall Ascended reached a large, brown hand over the shoulders of the Niff technician, pointing out signal points on the display's readout. The data spikes and graphs streamed in from Jessica's mech's internal sensors, and NoName verified the changes via the shop's hardwired link. They wouldn't be able to do this once the upcoming match started. Unlike mech racing or team sports events, there were no maintenance or adjustment pit stops in the arena. It was just an all-out brawl.

Prath nodded after Kitos confirmed the recalibrated settings. He keyed the microphone on his headset, looking up at the angry little human in the mech's cockpit.

"Again," he said.

"Prath, I hate using pre-set hit combos," Jessica Kramer said over the comm link, disgust and boredom dripping from her voice. "You, of all beings, know they're just blind, clumsy routines that can get you killed."

"It's going to be ugly out there, Jessica," Prath said. "There will be all manner of mech-sized swords, flails, and fists flying everywhere. You've never fought a match like this before. We're just entering these combinations in case you are incapacitated. The control components we've implanted from Judah into your NoName computer will be able to compensate if you're staggered and dopey. Now run it again, half speed. Just air, this time. I don't think that strike plate in the booth can take much more."

Jessica sighed over the radio and gave the command to her mech to run the sequence. Her armored machine ran through the paces of a pre-programmed hammer attack, one composed of an overhead slam, a hooking slash with the claw on the back of the hammer's head, and then a stab with the spiked base of the handle. The mech's slow pantomime of an attack hit only air.

The chassis' new armor, enhanced components, and fresh paint job impressed the small group of Myoshan techs assembled outside of the test booth. They watched the mech move through its paces, enraptured. It was slow-motion mechanical poetry, the result of days of hard, tough work under Vervor's and Prath's intense supervision. Too bad it wouldn't last past the first few seconds in the arena. Such was a mech tech's life.

Prath reviewed the new data, and turned to Kitos.

"Perfect, Kitos. Good work," Prath said to the Niff.

He turned his headset on again.

"Garbage, pilot, pure garbage," Prath said. "Are you even trying, up there? Run it again, once more, with feeling."

Kitos blinked his large eyes in confusion. Jessica yelled out in frustration over the radio.

"I-I does not understand, Master Technician Prath," Kitos said, trying to keep his voice low. "I-I made the correct adjustments as you wished."

"I know that, and you know that, Kitos," Prath said, his lips peeling back from his fangs in a smile. "But you know pilots. They can't be told how wonderful they're doing. Their egos are horrific enough in normal situations. If we let her know she's doing well, there'll be no dealing with her once she gets out of the cockpit."

"I heard that," Jessica said over the comm. Kitos cowered.

"Only because we let you. Remember that," Prath said.

He clicked off the link and turned to Kitos. He arched a large orange eyebrow.

"You think we're ready for a full speed test?" Prath asked. "Powered and un-powered?" Kitos gulped and nodded.

"I-I believe so. Systems are showing optimal," Kitos said, wringing his two pairs of hands together.

"Jessica, we're going to run a full speed test, now," Prath said. "We're up against the deadline for reporting to the pits."

"Master Vervor!" Prath said, calling down the hall to the shop proprietor.

"Yes," said the Myoshan business owner, his voice grating through his small office door.

"Your attention and approval are requested, please," Prath said.

Grumbling, the short, reptilian shop owner stalked towards

the back of the large fabrication facility. Jessica's modified mech filled the giant testing booth. The transparent armor and flickering force fields of the testing chamber were expensive, but necessary.

The once-homely mech stood ready. Vervor's crew modified it to such an extent, its resemblance to what first came into the shop was superficial, at best. Prath had to admit, the Myoshan proprietor and his staff knew their stuff. Kitos proved to be an expert in grafting Judah's hardware into the NoName computer. Jessica's choice for a base mech, a cargo unit which shared a number of systems with the Enforcement Directorate's armored police units, also proved to be a wise choice. *This had come together nicely,* he thought.

"Come, have a look, Master Vervor," Prath said. He keyed up his headset, "Little human, full speed run, kinetic only. Engage."

"Roger, Prath," Jessica said.

Jessica engaged the subroutine, and her mech became a blur. Three resounding clangs of the aptly-named BGDH-1 thundered throughout the shop, passing, once again, through the test box's armor and soundproofing. The hammer sent deep gouges into the test booth's metal strike plates, the circular logo of the Celestial Kingdom casino driven deep into their armored surfaces.

Vervor took a step back at the unexpected thunderstrikes. Prath clapped. Kitos clenched, his pupils dilated in alarm.

Recovering, Vervor's fangs jutted out in satisfaction, and both set of eyes, forward and back, squinted.

"Satisfactory. And energized?" Vervor said.

"First, your Technician Kitos is to be commended," Prath said. "Running the plasma channels from the reactor through the arms, and making the power coupling flush with the palms of the hands was a stroke of genius. His craftsmanship is brilliant, especially considering the time limitations."

"Master Prath, I know how good Kitos is," Vervor answered. "He wouldn't be here, otherwise."

Prath smirked, and keyed his microphone again.

"Energized test run, pilot. Full speed. Try not to slice through the test chamber. Engage," Prath said.

"Not likely, Master Ape," Vervor remarked. "My testing booth's shields are rated stronger than most arena crowd-protection fields."

Jessica looked at her wrist watch and swore. Prath sympathized with his pilot. They were cutting things close, and the transport vehicle hadn't even arrived yet. One last test. She flicked off the safeties and felt the mech's reactor keen higher in pitch.

"NoName, 'Firehammer' sequence, engage," Jessica Kramer said, and braced herself.

Her mech's two large arms rotated back over her, the large weapon now superheated with plasma vented from her engine. Then, a swirl of motion and a deep boom as the full-strength blow pulverized the first strike plate. The BGDH-1 rotated in the mech's hands, and the glowing claw on the back of the warhammer's head tore through the side of the strike plate with a thick, hissing noise.

The mech pulled back through the claw strike like a man trying to reel in an oversized fish. When it was leaning on its back foot, the grip on the hammer switched. The heated bottom spike of the hammer's handle now became a short spear, one mech hand holding the middle of the shaft like a chisel, the other driving force through the hammer's head like an awl through leather.

The scorching spike sank through the strike plate and jutted through the entirety of the thick steel. With a quick jerk, the

mech pulled back again into a defensive crouch, hammer at the
ready. A white-hot hole was left through not just the plate, but
the wall of the test chamber. Master Vervor didn't know
whether to jump for joy or strangle Prath.

A large shadow darkened the open loading dock bay at the
rear of the warehouse-sized building. An enormous transport
vehicle, armored and utilitarian in design, backed up to the
shop's mech-sized rear entrance.

"Ah, Honored Mikralos's transport must be here from Berva
Proxima," Prath said. He took off his headset and began to roll
up his tools. Kitos put a pair of hands across the Ascended's
forearm, a gesture of caution.

"Master Prath, I-I don't think that's the Berva Proxima transport vehicle," Kitos said. His golden eyes were wide in alarm.

"No, it's not," Vervor said, balling his small clawed fists.

Jessica climbed down from the mech's cockpit and hit the
button to open the test chamber's large transparent door. A
squad of well-armed, patch-armored Nines spilled from the
back of the vehicle, their weapons covering every angle of the
shop. Jessica's revolver was out, but a fistful of 20mm Mattis
rounds were no match for a half-dozen heavy weapons pointed
back at her. She decocked the weapon and held it over her head.
The Nines kept her targeted, but made no move to disarm her.

A series of thumping footsteps came down the ramp of the
transport. A crimson, multi-armed titan the size of a small mech
emerged from the shadowed rear of the vehicle, his organic face
thrown out of proportion compared to the rest of his monstrous
cybernetic body.

"Master Vervor, I see you have guests," the Headhunter
said, his smaller weapons and appendages curled back by his
sides, his main close-combat arms wide in greeting. "Forgive my
sudden arrival. I won't be long, but there is something important
I think we need to discuss."

CHAPTER TWENTY

SIXTH GATE ZONE

VERVOR'S FABRICATION WORKS

"I thought that blob Mikralos ran this sector?" Jessica Kramer said, holstering her weapon. She placed her hands on her hips. Prath held up one hand and called to her in a voice laden with caution.

"Jessica, dear, maybe this isn't the right—" Prath said.

"No, no, Ascended," the Headhunter said, cutting him off. "She is within her rights to ask. I am, pilot, the local... 'protector,' for lack of a better word. I'm the being who gets things done. I run things here on the ground level. Mikralos just runs the arena. Badly, I might add."

"So, you're the local crime lord," Jessica said. Prath started to speak, but an upheld secondary claw from the cyborg stopped him short.

"Well... yeah, you could say that," the Headhunter said, a small grin forming on his face. "Another way to say it is... I provide an alternative to the Gatekeepers' little slave-games of life-debts and dirty deals. Sentients need goods and services without the blobs being involved, and I provide them."

"So, you're a *benevolent* crime lord," Jessica said. "Heart of gold, and all that. Got it. I've still never heard of you." Prath covered his forehead with his hand.

"Well, that's kinda the point, human," the Headhunter said, an intrigued look on his face, his claws flexing like they had lives of their own.

"Hmmph. Whatever," Jessica said, unimpressed. "So, is this going to take long? I have a match tonight."

"I've heard of you, sir," Prath said, stepping forward. "Or should I say, Headhunter, Centurion and Warlord?"

"Really? How formal. Do tell, Ascended," the cyborg's black eyes were full of delight, having been addressed by his full, formal title under the Old Code.

"Don't let my youthful good looks fool you, sir," Prath said. "I have been around the arena a time or two, so to speak. He gestured to Jessica. "Please forgive Mech Pilot Kramer. She doesn't know the stories they tell of the former Enforcer who protects an underground kingdom that the Gatekeepers refuse to acknowledge even exists, lest it wound their pride and reputation. Word is, your reach is extending past the Sixth Gate Zone, now. Most impressive, sir."

The Headhunter shrugged, smiling.

"I must admit, I'm... flattered, Master Ape. Amused, even. May you never find yourself on my wall," the red cyborg said, clicking one of his sets of vibroclaws like a giant pair of scissors.

The Headhunter turned his sleek armored body to face Jessica. "Kramer, eh? I see the resemblance, now. I knew your-"

"Everyone knew my old man," Jessica said, her flat voice cutting him off.

"Huh. Well, of course," the Headhunter said. "Nolo, take her name down. I think I might want to keep up with her arena career." Nolo, his right-hand Ninety-Nine, duly noted her name on the tablet he carried.

"Now, to business," the Headhunter said, his mood and weapons arms shifting. "Master Vervor, I am led to believe that your technician... Kitos, is it? Is he here?"

Kitos's already-quivering fur laid down, and he tried to become smaller, to shrink from the sight of the red cyborg.

"Kitos, you seem to have had an awful patch of bad luck, lately, betting on the back-alley mech matches," the crimson titan said, a tinge of sympathy in his voice. "Word is that you're into debt to Honored Beliphres for more than a hundred thousand credits."

A small squeak of defense fluid peeped out of Kitos. Prath and Vervor both took a small step away from him.

"'Beliphres.' Where do I know that name from?" Prath said, under his breath to Vervor.

"One of the lower-status Gatekeepers," Vervor said, trying to be discreet. "He's made trouble for us in the past. The Gate-Lords put him in charge of rebuilding the Fifth Gate Zone, but he's a bit of a rogue. Fancies himself an underworld heavy hitter, of sorts."

"Fortunately," the red cyborg continued, ignoring the whispering duo, "you and Master Vervor's shop are on my side of the line, Niff. As long as you're here, you're under my protection."

"Very noble of you," Jessica said. The cyborg caught the sarcasm in her remark, and grinned. She returned the look with a smirk. The Myoshan shop owner raised a small, scaly claw.

"And Beliphres, Honored Headhunter?" Vervor said. "I assume if you found Kitos, the Gatekeeper is also aware of his location."

"If Beliphres crosses that line, well," the Headhunter said, turning back to Vervor, "I just might need to kickstart the next stage of my expansion plans a bit early."

"'If?' 'Might?'" Jessica said, a sardonic, mocking tone in her voice. "I'm hearing a lot of 'maybe,' here, Headhunter."

"You've got fire, human. I like that," the Headhunter said. He pointed a large set of claws at Prath. "Keep the Ascended, over there, close to you, though. I can tell you like playing the tough loner, but you're going to need beings you can trust around you when things get rough. Fire only gets you so far."

"Oh, and one more thing, pilot," the giant cyborg said.

"Yeah?" she answered.

"I did some looking into things, called up a few old friends," the Headhunter said. "You're being set up by Mikralos, but you probably already know that. There's even money on you going into tonight's big brawl, but my numbers guy says things are looking pretty bad when you get put up against Masamune Kyuzo. Even the Celestial Kingdom, your own sponsor, is taking heavy wagers against you. You're not even in long-shot territory. Watch yourself. It looks like a—"

"—Like a Gatekeeper's Cross. Right. Got it, Mister Headhunter, sir," she said, giving him a sarcastic impersonation of a salute.

"There's that fire, again," the Headhunter said. "I don't know if it's fake tough or crazy brave, but I like it."

The Headhunter turned to Nolo, who held his tablet in hand.

"Put a half-million credits on her for tonight's match," he said to his Model Ninety-Nine adjutant. "I'm going to keep my sensors on you, Kramer. Don't let me down."

The Headhunter pulled back into the transport vehicle, his steps thudding through the shop's mech bay as he went up the ramp. The Recyke Nines withdrew, falling back in overwatching pairs, their weapons still targeted in every direction. The hovering armored truck's rear door closed with a hiss, and they were gone.

"Mech Pilot Jessica Kramer, a moment of your time, please," Prath said, a thick brown finger curling for her to come near. Jessica rolled her eyes, dreading the incoming lecture. *Great,* she thought.

The heavy mech-carrier to Berva Proxima hovered up to the loading doors just as the Headhunter's transport left. Vervor began barking orders to the shop's other Myoshan technicians and fabricators in his native tongue, and prepped the modified CR-400 mech for transport to the arena.

CHAPTER TWENTY-ONE

SIXTH GATE ZONE
BERVA PROXIMA ARENA

The summons from Gatekeeper Mikralos was ill-timed, and Masamune Kyuzo did not enjoy being searched or kept waiting. Kenji, his oldest child, was sick in bed at the habitat pod. The boy always managed to bring home a new affliction or ailment from the local neighborhood's learning center. Little Miko, his daughter, wasn't ill, yet. However, she tended to come down with whatever malady her big brother caught, given enough time and exposure.

Junctionworld was a whirling dervish of diseases that could wreak havoc on young immune systems, human and otherwise. Pathogens from millions of dimensions kept the autodoc databases busy.

Masamune fumed. He should be at his mech garage, repairing the damage from the Gorth match, or tuning his battle computer for the upcoming event, or helping his wife Anora at home with the children.

Instead, he stood in the upper spectator section of Berva

Proxima arena, sharing an antechamber with a Skevvian and a hacked-up reptilian cyborg.

What were those beings called? They weren't Myoshans. Too tall, and not enough eyes. Skasar? Shasarr? No matter, he thought.

The area was more cramped than Mikralos's main office on the lower levels of the arena, where he last saw the arena master and Dionoles, the Gatekeeper casino owner. The tall being in front of him insisted on sucking on a foul-smelling vaporizer implanted into its forearm, filling the small room with the exhaust from its gills.

The exhaled fumes made Kyuzo's eyes twitch and burn. The crested sentient seemed to take delight in blowing in his direction.

Is this moron trying to provoke me? He thought.

Masamune's pistols were checked with the two Ninety-Nine bodyguards at the previous door, but from the looks of these two, the guns wouldn't be necessary.

Masamune made the calculations. He would take out the bone-squid first when the lizard took his next puff. A round-house kick to cave in the side of its skull would be a nice start. He then imagined himself strangling the crested lizard-thing with the Skevvian's tentacles until those acrid little clouds stopped coming out of the Shasarr's gills. The idle daydream took his mind off the pain from his irritated eyes.

The two sentients murmured to themselves, their voices low. Their attention turned to the entrance of Mikralos's office and viewing pod. A Gatekeeper who Masamune did not know floated out from the metal-curtained archway, his protective vessel stopping halfway through the partition. His hull was different, less gaudy and ornate than most. It wasn't chromed and gleaming, more matte and subdued. The unfamiliar overlord called back through the curtain.

"We are grateful for your trust and remembrance of us, Mikralos," the Gatekeeper said to Mikralos, who Kyuzo could not see. "This assignment reminds us of the heady days of our conquest of this place. It pleases us to have the old combat triumvirate reunited, again. We shall proceed, with your permission. Farewell."

Pivoting into the waiting room, the Gatekeeper paid Masamune no mind, as if he were just another piece of furniture.

"Come, Skreeb and Velsh, we must attend to other matters," the Gatekeeper said to the two other beings in the antechamber. "Time is of the essence. Let us depart this place." The crested reptilian with the cybernetic eyes gave one last deliberate, derisive puff in Kyuzo's direction. The Shasarr and the Skevvian followed their master out through the antechamber's main door.

"Master Mech Pilot Masamune Kyuzo, we will see you now," the smooth voice of Mikralos called from the interior of the viewing pod.

Kyuzo parted the curtain of chains leading into the private viewing bubble. He bowed to Mikralos, whose back was to him.

"Honored Mikralos, I hope I am not interrupting," Masamune said, now standing up straight. The view of the Berva Proxima arena's interior from the armored bubble was all-encompassing. Smaller oval holographic screens blistered the interior of the transparent armored pod. Feeds from different sports networks and arena drones played on them. One display had Masamune's own publicity picture on it, a rotating profile of him from all angles while listing his fight record and mech stats.

"Masamune Kyuzo, Master Mech Pilot, ah, a delight to cast our gaze upon you," Mikralos cooed. "No, no interruption, just some pressing business that concerns the upcoming match. Honored Beliphres is an old friend, and was just leaving. He was part of our combat team, along with Dionoles, in days of yore. We conquered this sector of Junctionworld together, many, many centuries ago. Help yourself to any intoxicants at the bar that are code-compatible to you." The running lights on the Gatekeeper's chromed carrier chassis were a slow-running blue and white pattern.

"Thank you, but I cannot indulge," Masamune said. "My match with Kramer is less than two weeks away."

"Ever-focused, as always, eh, Masamune? Well, no matter," Mikralos said. "Would you care to sit with us to view Pilot Kramer's next match? Tonight's preliminary Light Exo fights are done. Our staff is resetting the arena for the main event."

"Will Honored Dionoles be joining us?" Masamune asked.

"No, unfortunately, Dionoles must to tend to other matters at his casino," Mikralos said. "The spectacle of arena combat was never really his object of fascination. He would rather review his revenue tallies, the house's wins and losses, and audit his staff's bookkeeping. He lives for contests of finance, not the clash of arms."

"Hmmm," Masamune said, feigning interest.

Silence passed between the two beings as advertisements flicked across the interior of the arena in both two and three dimensions. He caught his name in Gatekeeper spelling, dancing in holographic flames with what he assumed was Kramer's name in a mid-air commercial.

"How is it you came to Junctionworld, by the way, Master Mech Pilot?" Mikralos said, breaking the silence. "We are sure you have told us before, but indulge us." A wry grin came over Masamune's face.

"The usual story. Almost a Junctionworld cliché, to be honest," Kyuzo said. "I was scouted by a talent team. The drone and hologram message showed up at the right time, just before my death. I accepted the deal, terms unread. Now, here I am, working off a debt that can't be—"

"Yes, yes, but *before*," the Gatekeeper said, waving a dismissive claw. "Your occupation before the standard offer. What exactly did you do?"

"Oh, well," Masamune said, biting his tongue. "I was the offensive weapons officer on a Kaiju Buster, the Panzer Rex. It was a Devilbreaker-class mobile fortress. A much larger version of the mechs in the arenas. Much more powerful, but slower. My world had undergone a terrible war, an invasion, and we were defenders of one of the last of our cities."

"It sounds lovely," Mikralos said.

"Yes, well, it was home. When the offer was made," Kyuzo continued, "we had gone up against this vicious armored thing, hundreds of feet tall, with tusks the size of city buses. It emerged from the wastelands, and it beat us to pieces. For an animal so large, it was incredibly agile and strong."

"Larger or smaller than the creatures that emerged through the Fifth Gate? Those tentacled monstrosities that were nuked by Central Data?" Mikralos said.

"Much larger, and much more resilient," Kyuzo said. "It seemed to soak up the damage and become stronger. We had compact nuclear weapons, pressure nukes, able to create a fission reaction with a minimum of material by using an internal force field."

"Yes, we are familiar with them," Mikralos said. "We developed our own version. Quite handy in urban areas. So, back to your story."

"This thing shrugged them off, and came back us stronger," Masamune said, his eyes looking past the holographic ads as his memory of that day returned. "We were defeated. The crew were all dead, save for myself. The talent scout drone must have decided that our defense of the city was worthy, even though we failed. I dragged myself through the portal, and here I am.

Sometimes, though, I wish I had just stayed and burned with the rest of my crew."

"Hmm. Yes, most compelling, pilot," Mikralos said, his attention already drawn elsewhere. "We now recall having seen the scout team's footage in your back-story montage Central Data enjoys inflicting on the audience. Most sponsors must slurp up that drivel. Ah, speaking of drivel, they are about to begin the pilot introductions for the main match. Here's our 'Last of the Kramers,' now."

Masamune Kyuzo's brow wrinkled, and he stood up. He walked to the hemispheric front of the viewing pod, placing his forehead against the cool armored glass.

"Mikralos, begging your pardon, but why have I really been summoned here?" Masamune said, his voice edged with dreariness. "Is something happening that I should be aware of?"

"Why, our dear Master Mech Pilot, of course not," Mikralos said. "We would never dare to imagine changing our arrangement. You did well in the negotiations. Dionoles was most impressed, despite your shortcomings as a human."

"You brought me up here, just to tell me that?" Masamune said.

"Oh, well, perhaps not just that..." the Gatekeeper said, a coy edge in his tone. "There is the matter of one of the terms of our contract. Tell us, how go the repairs on your mech?"

"My armor is damaged, but the repairs are well underway," Masamune said. "The boosters took a lot of fire, and there was extensive damage to my command console. Rest assured, though, my team will be ready for the match."

"Yes, well, speaking of assured," Mikralos said, his running lights shifting to orange pulses. "We are exercising the 'Assuredness In Armament' clause of our agreement." A hologram of the agreement Masamune signed with the two Gatekeepers flashed into midair, a blinking clause in small print highlighted for his attention.

Masamune turned from the glass, his fists clenched. A vein pulsed on the side of his temple. The two bodyguards appeared at the entrance to the viewing pod, their weapons ready.

"Your legendary discipline is slipping, Master Pilot," Mikralos said, motioning to a human-sized chair. "Do sit down. You cannot make money for us or exact our revenge if our Nines fill you with holes."

Masamune, his face flushed, sat in the offered chair. His hands held the sides and back of his head, his flesh and plastic fingers meshed through his close-cropped hair.

"Your match with the son of Solomon Kramer... Jered," Mikralos said.

"Jered Kramer, yes," Masamune said through gritted teeth.

"Do you still have the power claw you used in that kill?" Mikralos said. Masamune shook his head.

"I've retired that weapon from my inventory, Honored Mikralos," Masamune said. "That claw was my last sponsor's idea, not mine. It has been five years, and I have moved on to the sword, as you may have seen during my last match. A plasma-edged blade is what I do my best work with, now."

"Ah, how unfortunate," Mikralos said, his menacing coo returning. "It would be a delicious bit of irony, killing both Kramer offspring with the same implement. We think you should bring it back, perhaps augment it, somehow. We know you do most of your own work with your own fabrication team, and we mean them no disrespect, but we suggest you consult Master Vervor at his shop. See if he can add his expertise in refurbishing and modifying the weapon for the match with the Kramer girl."

"Honored Mikralos, as I said before, I've become much more proficient with—"

"It is not a request, Master Pilot," the Gatekeeper said sharply. "There must be a certain poetry, a symmetric finality, to this match. The last Kramer deserves an ugly and punitive end, a fitting extinguishment to the blood line which has caused us so much pain and embarrassment."

Masamune Kyuzo stewed. The Nines in the doorway did not shift their aim from his brain stem and spine.

"I've viewed the recordings of her matches," Kyuzo said, sighing. "She's a brawling amateur, unworthy of her family name. She's not ready for the Hammer Leagues, her mech is a scrap heap with a veneer of new parts on top of it, and this feels like an execution, not a death match, Honored Mikralos. I did not sign up—"

"No, you did not *sign up* for anything, Pilot, you were *bought*," Mikralos said, his tone even sharper. "Bought and paid for, to fight for us, and fight for us, you shall. You are an instrument, an extension of our will, and, on the lives of your children, you will perform as we demand. You will lance this last boil on the reputation of this arena, and you will cleanse the last Kramer-produced stain from the foundation of this society. Kramer is to be dispatched in the arena, and you will make it brutal, and you will make it something to remember. A message must be sent. Do you understand?"

A live image of Masamune's wife and children flashed up on one of the screens. His wife, Anora, nursed their boy with a spoonful of broth while their daughter played beside her with a toy mech. The view was from a hijacked camera from Masamune's own interior security system. The threat was more than implied. Masamune drew a measured breath, sneered at the Nines' weapons pointed at him from the doorway, and addressed the floating overlord.

"Oh, I understand, all too well," the mech pilot said. "You should understand this, too: there will come a day when accounts of all types will be settled, Honored Mikralos. This sad excuse for an arena, this dump, this whole system, this will all rain down on your head, someday, and I hope to be there when it happens."

Mikralos's running lights turned black and solid.

"Your tantrum is noted, and we are less than amused," the Gatekeeper said. "Were there not already other wheels in motion, human, we would gladly burn you down where you stand. Be mindful of that, Kyuzo, for your family's sake, before you engage in further outbursts."

"We were going to allow you to stay and watch the upcoming match with us, from our observation point," Mikralos continued. "That invitation is now rescinded. We are done, here, Pilot, and you are expected at Master Vervor's fabrication facility."

"You are dismissed," Mikralos said with the wave of a snake-like metal tentacle. The four-way match began in the arena below, the crowd's cheers and roars reaching all the way up to the high vantage point.

Masamune snorted, beaming contempt as best he could towards the overbeing, then stormed out of the room.

"Get out of my way, you venting meat-bots, and fetch my pistols," Kyuzo said, throwing his shoulder into one of the Nines as he passed between them.

CHAPTER TWENTY-TWO

SIXTH GATE ZONE
BERVA PROXIMA ARENA

Jessica was bored with the arena official's pre-match safety lecture, and wanted another drink. Sighing, she adjusted the object in the front pocket of her jumpsuit. She avoided Prath's persistent stare, and pretended to pay attention to the end of the briefing. She quickly lost interest in hearing the same old routine, and looked around at the other fighters gathered in the ready room.

Two of the other mech pilots, an augmented human wearing far too much purple, and the other, a short, squat member of the High Thirdgate folk, stole occasional looks at her. The fourth pilot, a golden representative of the Wardancer android race, would not even acknowledge her existence, looking past and through her.

Gate-damned Wardancers make me sick. Such snobs, Jessica thought.

"Pilots, you have all been made aware of the arena arrangement and match rules," the pit boss for Berva Proxima said.

"Again, all close combat weapons are in play, and cockpit fields will be in effect."

"Yeah, if Sixthson can stay on the field, and not turn tail again," the human in purple said, high-fiving his crew chief after the snide remark. The dwarf's crew chief held him back as the stumpy, powerful humanoid tried to launch himself at the taller human.

"You'll find out, Melino, you ventin' drug addict," Flevver Sixthson answered.

"Hey, better living through chemistry, spud," Melino said, twisting the combat-drug intakes in his neck for effect.

"I'm no spud, ya purple worm. We Thirdgate folk are short, like Myoshans, but I'm as primate as you. Better, even," the seething little man said. Sixthson's crew chief tried to keep the squat, powerful humanoid from going for the pistol on his belt.

The Berva Proxima pit boss pulled out a large automatic pistol and aimed it at the ceiling. The room settled down.

"Save it for the arena, fighters," the pit boss said, re-holstering once he knew he had their attention. "Honored Mikralos expects greatness in the arena tonight. If there are no questions, then confer with your crew chiefs. You have five minutes. Take the transports to your mechs at their respective entry portals, and let's come out fighting."

Jessica Kramer stood up and turned to her Ascended friend and crew chief, Prath.

"Did you see the size of that thing?" Jessica said to the large orange-and-brown sentient. "It was probably bigger than him."

"Indeed," Prath mused. "A Partlow Arms Juggernaut. One does not see many, this side of the Third Gate Zone."

"Oh, I've gotta use the little human's room, real quick, Prath," Jessica said, giving the primate an embarrassed grin. "Pre-match jitters and tiny bladder. Bad combo."

Prath scowled as she walked away to find biologically-compatible relief facilities. He saw her zip open her suit's front pocket as she closed the door, reaching inside it for a rectangular object.

When she emerged, Prath was there, filling the hatchway. Before she could protest, his primal strength locked her in his arms. He lifted Jessica by the elbows, bringing her face up to his with ease. He took a deep breath, bared his fangs at the result, and set her down abruptly.

"Prath, what the void are you doing? I washed my face and hands," she said, bringing her hand up to her face.

"You're gargling with soap and water," Prath said, "but it doesn't quite cover the smell of the booze. Pathetic, Kramer. You really do have a problem. How long have you been sneaking liquid intoxicants?"

Jessica's face flushed, and she bared her teeth back.

"What's it to you?" she snarled. "I have been putting up with getting pushed around and ordered about like some... some child, long enough, Prath. If I want a stiff belt before a match, I'll damn well have one."

"Hand it over," Prath said, his long fingers outstretched.

She pulled a flask, engraved with an ornamental six-sided star, from her front pocket.

"No, Prath, it was Dad's," she said, protesting, "and... and it's my good luck charm, gate-damn it."

She unscrewed the top and made a show of pouring out the dark red liquor inside.

"There, it's empty, see?" she said. "Problem solved."

He beckoned, still.

"No. You can't have it," Jessica said as she stormed off to the electric cart. "Besides, I have a match to fight. Now, get out of my way."

He didn't move. She had to go around his large frame. As she passed him, his hand shot out to hers.

"Prath! What the—"

He pulled her in close to him, one arm around her like a vise. Her face pressed into his technician's tool vest. His other hand alternated between drumming his fingers on her head and running them through her hair.

"Gates envelop us, Kramer," Prath said, trying to contemplate through his anger and disappointment. "What are we to do with you? The mind boggles at your hard-headedness. Just... just don't do anything stupid in the arena, little human. We're going to talk about this, later."

"What are you talking about, Prath, I don't even need... this is just... you know, you're not my fath—" Jessica sputtered.

"No. Stop. Don't even say it," Prath said. "Just go. Fight. For Our Freedom, And Yours."

Prath released her. Jessica stood there, stunned, trying to mentally kick herself into gear, to somehow lash out at the big Ascended, to distract from her shame of being caught. Prath was the only being who gave a damn about her in all of Junctionworld, but she wanted to rip into him, to show him how bad she hurt, and she couldn't even do that right. To top it off, Prath used her dad's old motto to drive the point home, which stung even more. *Damn it!*

"Pilot Kramer, there's too much to say, and not enough time to say it," Prath said, his eyes still sad as he gently pushed her away with his long arms. "Go. Now."

She looked back, trying to inflict some other type of verbal barb, then closed her mouth when nothing came to her lips. Fighting back tears of rage, and a bit of shame, she turned to the cart without saying another word.

Jessica stewed on the short, bumpy ride to her starting gate. She pulled her helmet on, thumped it twice, thumped the empty flask over her heart twice, and climbed up her mech's armored legs to the open cockpit.

"What the void's wrong with me?" she said to herself as NoName's systems checked off in front of her, its muted electronic tones ticking off with each component reporting ready to fight. The arena's owner, Mikralos, perhaps by accident, more likely on purpose, assigned her to walk her mech through the same gate that Jered went through on his final match.

The solid blast shields over her cockpit weren't going to be used in this four-way close-combat brawl, so she had a fine view of the gate's carvings and projectile strikes. She saw the small memorial relief bust of Jered's face in profile. She touched the interior of her cockpit glass trying to reach for it. Her moping mood turned to grim fury, and her knuckles turned white as she grasped the controls.

"Never mind what's wrong with me, NoName," she said. "It's too long a list. It's time to go get some."

The enhanced control computer's visual feedback lights swirled, showing it was processing.

"*Get some.* Agreed, pilot," a familiar robotic voice said from her console.

Her eyes went wide at the unexpected sound. *What the void?*

The cockpit's mandatory force field shimmered around her as it engaged. The floodlights of the arena shone down on all four entry gates, bathing her and her fellow combatants' mechs in pools of light.

The arena's giant floating countdown display began ticking, mid-air holographic digits the size of mechs marching down to zero. The floodlights cut out just as rings of light around the edges of the stadium flashed, and the starting siren howled.

CHAPTER TWENTY-THREE

SIXTH GATE ZONE
BERVA PROXIMA ARENA

"Did... did you just say something, NoName?" Jessica said, wide-eyed and startled. "Or... is that *you*, Judah?"

Her hands pulled back from the control yokes in surprise, causing the mech to lurch and slow down. The cockpit force fields reduced her mech's speed to a plod, the gyroscopic-like effect of the protective shields sapping the momentum from the gigantic machine.

The three other pilots' mechs emerged from their entrance gates to rousing applause. Each of the three opponents screamed in on their jets to their arena start points, though their movements were slurred and slowed by their own cockpit force fields. All three turned to face her, watching her and her mech take their sweet time arriving at the fourth glowing circle.

"Identifier 'Judah' is not applicable to This Unit," the speakers in her helmet said. "Excessive hybridization violates Arkathan circuitry purity protocols. 'NoName' will continue to suffice for familiarity purposes."

"You kinda sound like Judah," Jessica said. "Well, only if someone performed a drunken lobotomy on him. Why the void is this just happening now?"

"Prath!" She shouted into her communications link, calling for her crew chief. Jessica stabbed the microphone button off in disgust when the line buzzed back a harsh triple-tone of noncompliance. Comms between the pits and pilots were forbidden during matches once the horn sounded. She was now own her own, her only companion a freshly formatted battle computer.

"Self-diagnostics and integration verification were ongoing after installation at Master Vervor's," NoName's new voice said. "This Unit is still only 87% capable of full function. However, that diminished capacity exceeds prior performance by 338%, Pilot."

"Eighty-seven? Great. Just great," Kramer said. "Your performance might be better, but your timing stinks. I'm going to skin that Niff tech who put you together for not warning me about this."

"Understood. There are a number of ways to approach the task of skinning a Niff. First—"

"Gate damn it, NoName," Jessica said, interrupting, "I've got three mechs waiting to bash my cockpit in, can't you see that? Get your head in the arena. Look, just shut up and help me fight. Give me some boost, but don't fire up the plasma lines to the hammer yet."

Kramer put a rubber mouth guard over her upper teeth and shook her head inside its helmet, trying to push away the effects of the alcohol that were now creeping up on her. *Prath, that arrogant ape, trying to tell me not to have a quick sip before a match,* she thought.

She engaged her thrusters, arcing into the edge of her

circular start pad. They couldn't start the four-way free-for-all until she entered her circle.

Jessica hovered NoName at the edge of the ring of floor lights. She pointed the mech's huge BGDH-1 warhammer at the sinewy black, gold, and purple mech on her right, about one hundred yards away.

"Melino, you're first, you juiced-up fop," she said, engaging her exterior speakers.

The chemically-augmented human's mech shivered in response to the challenge, its two segmented arms shaking and drooping with a mechanical jitter. The two appendages elongated into spiked, armored whips, tipped with vicious claws.

Jessica had seen set-ups like this before, but never fought against them. The long, tentacle-like appendages brushed the arena floor, small golden claws flexing at the ends. A light mounted in each chunky segment blinked an angry violet, and vibrospikes emerged from the side of each module. The purple mech now bristled with blades.

Melino raised his gloved hands from his controls, beckoning her to bring it on. He made a vulgar gesture, then strobed his cockpit lights. *Nice effect, for a guy in a purple jumpsuit*, Jessica thought, smirking.

Jessica flared one last pulse on her mech's jets, and dropped into the engagement pad. The match began.

The crowd roared as she and the purple mech flew at each other like a rocket-propelled magnet to steel. NoName issued a collision warning through her headphones, then highlighted an incoming metal whip-arm vectoring in at her. *Damn, those things could stretch*, she thought.

She made a short shift as the distance closed, cursing because the force fields slowed down her maneuver. The long, spiked arm sailed by her mech's thigh, ripping into the armor. Taking the hit for a chance to get in close, Jessica brought her hammer up, then slammed the large weapon into the upper shoulder of the whip-mech. The Melino's dilated eyes went even wider, his mouth agape, and she saw the heavy shock rattle him against his restraints.

She shoved the enemy mech away with the top of the hammer, spinning it into the middle of the four circles. The crowd roared as the spike on the back of the weapon caught a piece of hull, tearing off a black panel from the purple mech. Melino, stunned, landed in a twisted jumble of his own armored arms.

Jessica checked NoName's damage report from the thigh. *Superficial. Good.*

Her opponent's mech came to its feet and squared off with her.

NoName's summary reports on Melino told her that he was good with those whip-arms from a distance, but vulnerable close in. The newly-awakened computer plotted multiple attack paths on her cockpit interior to take advantage of the new strategy. Time to close the gap. *But the damn force fields are making me clumsy as a burden-beast,* she thought.

"Pilot," NoName spoke.

"What?"

"Data evaluation and proposal," the computer said.

"Now?" she asked, incredulous.

"This Unit can increase the refraction rate of the interior cockpit fields," NoName said. "Combined with counter-resonance—"

"Bottom line it for me, damn it," she said, talking over the computer's droning info-dump. Melino's mech braced to charge, and his jets flared. The menacing claws at the ends of the tentacle-like arms flexed.

"—of the power output, the debilitating gyroscopic effect could be mitigated," NoName said, in summary.

"You can smooth out the bumps. Got it. So, do it," Jessica snapped.

Behind Melino's oncoming mech, Jessica saw the match's two other combatants circling each other in a lethal coupling. One was a sleek, lethal mech which emulated the shape of its beautiful, snobby Wardancer pilot, Kierra. She had a pair of short plasma swords that Jessica envied. The other mech was a dilapidated, hodge-podge conglomeration of parts that made NoName look like a showroom model. That walking pile of scrap, piloted by Flevver Sixthson, the angry little High Thirdgater, looked to be armed with a pair of heavy, rusty claws.

The Wardancer's usual grace was disrupted by her cockpit shielding, and a combination of pirouette and double slash only managed to nick a piece of dented armor off of Flevver's junkmech. As Kierra set up another blade attack, a crude motor-ized saw emerged from a hatch on the portly, trashcan-shaped mech's cylindrical upper hull.

The rusty buzzsaw bit into the upper arm of its sleeker white and pink target, sending a stream of sparks flying. Pivot-ing, the slim Wardancer mech answered by puncturing the dwarf pilot's lower hull with her pair of short plasma blades. Sixthson tried to swing a heavy claw at the long legs of the Wardancer mech, but missed.

Jessica's direct opponent, Melino, charged her, surrounded by a halo of rocket flame. She turned her attention from the other locked-up pair of fighters as the purple mech bore down on her.

Another whip arm shot out at her and NoName. Before she could react, the interior and hull lights signaling autopilot control blinked on. NoName blocked the incoming attack with the shaft of her warhammer. The claws on the tip of the arm clamped on to her weapon, and she could feel herself being pulled forward, off-balance. Jessica pulled back hard on her control yokes, regaining her stance, as the auto lights blinked off.

"NoName, what the void are you doing? Back off and let me fight!" Jessica said, slapping the console.

"Pilot Kramer, This Units is charged with your protection," the Arkathan battle computer said. "You were not reacting in a sufficient manner. Increasing power to thrusters. Prepare for acceleration."

Dodging another long stab from a whipsaw arm, Jessica rotated her mech's torso. She forced NoName to hold on to the hammer with just one arm, disengaging the grip of her other armored hand. She wrapped up the second extended whip arm before Melino could retract it.

"I *am* reacting, you stupid bot! Give me the controls!"

Jessica locked Melino's long, segmented limb under her own, and felt the hum of its vibroblades chatter against her hull. She continued her twist at the waist, pulling him closer.

"Now, stomp it! Give me some thrust, and light him up!" she shouted.

"Inquiry. Stomp what?" NoName asked.

"The jets, gate-damn-it, the jets!" Jessica raved. "Burn this guy's arm off with the back jets while I have him tangled up!"

"Colloquialism understood. Engaging," NoName said.

"Oh, tell me this is not happening," Jessica said. NoName overheated the turbine's output, and a third of the captured arm melted and fell as Jessica's jets went through it like a blowtorch through a worm.

The drone cameras surrounding the two mechs all flicked their camera flashes in synch, capturing the attack for the replay feeds.

"Now we reel him in. Slip our free arm up his burned-off tentacle, and pull. That's right, NoName, keep pulling and twisting," Jessica said. "Get ready. We're going to spike him."

The burning remainder of Melino's arm flailed, slapping against her cockpit glass before disappearing from view. Jessica ignored it, concentrating on her system of incremental twists and pulls. She brought the black and purple mech in closer.

"Pilot," NoName said. Damage signals flared from her legs and back.

"Not now, damn it," Jessica said through gritted teeth. "Prepare to reroute plasma to the hammer."

"Pilot, there's—"

"Stand by, I said!" she shouted. "Ready..."

Melino's mech was fighting it, but NoName's heavier construction helped pull the enemy mech in closer. Jessica started to rotate the hammer, edging the sharp end of the shaft towards the enemy's Lower hull. If she did it right, she could run him through, puncturing his reactor.

The purple mech edged closer, its jets glowing, thrusting hard to maintain the distance, trying to avoid the hammer's spiked pommel. She grinned, ready to skewer her opponent.

Without warning, Jessica's autopilot lights came on, then her hammer wasn't there at all. Melino's good arm, which still held her BGDH-1, retracted, sending her battle implement sailing over his shoulder. The crowds erupted in bellowing surprise.

"NoName!" Jessica said. "You... just let go of our only weapon, you stupid, idiotic... chip-for-brains!"

"Enemy mech's damaged arm's exterior vibrospikes were still functional, pilot," NoName said, "and were inflicting mounting injury to This Unit as proximity increased. Calculations determined—"

"Shut up, NoName, or Judah, or whoever the void you are," she said. "Stand down! I'm calling the gate-damned shots, here." She slammed an override button on her console. NoName's voice muted with a subdued chirp, but his targeting displays and indicators still registered on her cockpit's interior screens.

Both of Melino's arms shot out at her, trying to stab her as she charged in. She dodged the damaged stub, but the maneuver put her into the path of the longer, claw-tipped appendage. It raked across the top of her hull, carving a groove into the side of her transparent canopy armor. She and Melino locked eyes. A maddened, rictus grin was on his face as he worked the controls in a frenzy. She could see the combat drugs streaming into his system from neon-lit lines.

She trapped the damaged arm again, yanking his mech into her. She initiated a spinning back kick, the jets in that leg adding their power to the movement. The arena's audience streaked across her field of view as the rotating acceleration crushed her back into her seat.

NoName's heavy heel sank into the target mech's chest armor, ripping off the damaged arm at the shoulder. The purple mech toppled again, charred parts of the segmented arm scattering across the floor. He landed with a long, tumbling skid, and his own autopilot lights came on. If this had been a one-on-one death match, now would be the time to deliver the killing blow. This was just a fancy Light Exo match, though, and there were two more mechs to face. Melino was stunned, and could wait. She needed that hammer back.

A pulse of jets carried her over to the weapon, where it lay on the arena's steel floor. There were four grooves gnawed into the handle from Melino's vibroclaws, but the plasma lines to the hook and spike appeared intact. *Damned half-brained computer and its 'calculations,'* she thought, hefting the warhammer in her mech's giant hands.

Melino's shattered, shell-shocked chassis attempted to right itself, its autopilot lights still engaged. An explosion and roar of the crowd drew her attention to the Wardancer and Sixthson.

The battle was not going well for Flevver and his trashcan mech. Vicious gouges from Kierra's plasma blades covered the squat mech's patched hull. Mech parts littered the area around the two walking combat vehicles, most of them Flevver's. Flaming stumps from a pair of cut-off arms billowed flame, and the little green mech wobbled on its thick, slashed-up legs.

The Wardancer pulled her mech back into a crouch as the crowd cheered, the two plasma blades crossed in front of her. Jessica's external microphones picked up a thumping battle remix of a popular First Gate dance song coming from the Wardancer's speakers. The pink and white mech sprang forward, lopping off the last weapon arm from the junkmech with surgical precision. The buzzsaw fell to the floor of the arena, joining the rest of its fellow smoking components, and the audience roared.

Ugh. Wardancers. Always thinking they were the stars of their own music hologram show, complete with soundtrack, she thought. Jessica flipped a toggle, engaging her own external speakers, and pulled out her protective mouthpiece.

"Quit toying with him, fancy-pants," she said, her words echoing across the arena. "Just get it over with, already."

The Wardancer finished the follow-through of her leaping assault, landing in a crouch. The android mech pilot turned her attention, and blades, to Jessica.

Cockpit shields didn't prevent a pilot from cooking to death, trapped in a paralyzed wreck. Flevver Sixthson did not waste the distraction Jessica provided, and punched out of his burning mech before the Wardancer could set up a final attack run. The dwarf humanoid's splintered cockpit glass blew out with a muffled pop, and his dented ejection pod rocketed him to relative safety. Jessica and the Wardancer both watched the capsule corkscrew across the arena floor towards the crowd.

The Wardancer, Kierra, raised one of her mech's plasma blades towards Jessica. A foreboding song played from the lithe mech's speakers, some grating revenge ballad Jessica never heard before.

"Someone in this arena owes me a kill. You just took his spot, Kramer," Kierra said.

"You'll have to wait your turn, *tiny dancer*," Jessica said. Melino's my knockout. I'm going to finish off floppy arms, over there."

"Not today, *daddy's girl*," Kierra said. The Wardancer charged up one of her blades, dumping extra power into it. Performing a vertical double spin, the tall mech hurled the energized weapon.

Jessica hit her jets as Kierra released the blade, strafing to the left of the glowing short sword as it flew... far to her right?

Jessica tracked the flying blade's laser-straight path... right through the torso of Melino's black and purple mech. The crowd roared as the autopilot lights blinked out, and the swaying mech crumpled. Kierra's plasma blade did the same thing Jessica had intended for her own attack. Flames and dissipating plasma blew out of the back of the mech as its containment fields failed. Melino's cockpit fell, with him still knocked unconscious, into the inferno.

"Thanks for setting up my win," Kierra said. "Maybe they'll give you an assist on your feeble stats. Care to join him, *Jessie?*" The Wardancer's music changed to a Skevvian track with a deep bass beat. It was brawling music. Jessica felt like obliging her. The roar of the crowd turned to calamity as flames and camera drones surrounded Melino.

"Gate damn it," Jessica said, pangs of conscience hitting her. "NoName, give me full power to the jets."

Kramer slammed on her thrusters as she boosted to Melino's burning mech. She cocked back the massive hammer in NoName's hands, swinging the weapon to and through the side of the burning wreckage.

The arena's crowd roared its approval as a glimmering egg shape soared from the flames at the massive impact, carrying the helpless Melino to safety. His blackened cockpit assembly trailed fiery debris as it bounced and slid across the mile-wide arena. It tumbled and skid to a rest against the far wall. There, a small squadron of crashbots surrounded it, pulling the human pilot to safety.

Jessica used the claw end of the hammer's head to pull Kierra's giant-sized plasma blade from the wreckage, scattering it far behind her.

"Pretty stupid, Kierra," Jessica said, turning to face the beautiful android, "throwing away half of your—"

The Wardancer's mech vaulted at Jessica, her jets burning hard. Before Kramer could bring her hammer to bear, a soaring leap carried Kierra's sleek machine up and over Kramer's stout, up-armored cargo mech. The pink killing machine continued its jet-propelled sprint past her and the burning wreck, scooping up the plasma blade from the arena floor.

Great, she thought. Jessica put her mouth guard back in, switched off her external speakers, and re-engaged NoName.

"Hey, NoName," Jessica said. "Think you can behave? Think you can let me be the pilot for a change?"

"Adaptive behavioral circuits have been monitoring the combat situation during the shutdown," NoName said. "This Unit theorizes it can assist without overriding pilot, except during extenuating—"

"Yeah, OK, sure, just shut up, already," Jessica said. "I need you focused, here, bot, not tugging at my elbow or quoting the thesaurus. Promise?"

The battle computer signaled its acceptance with a double flash of the console panels.

"Affirmative, Pilot," NoName said.

Kierra's mech paced back and forth in the distance, then she bent her mech into another attack crouch. The cloud of camera drones around her strobed their approval at the lithe pose. The Wardancer's external music changed as another song blended into the sparring music. It was some Third Gate teeny-bopper crap from a few months ago that always forced Jessica to change her audio data-feed. Kierra must be trying to kill her with disgust.

"Ok. Give me seventy-five percent power to the hammer," Jessica said. "I want that thing glowing, but I still need some jets." Her reactor stepped up its output, a deep whine spooling up behind her. She flicked on her speakers.

"Kierra, that song's as old as your dance moves," Kramer said.

"Such a petty, ugly remark," the Wardancer answered. "Just like you, Kramer."

Jessica pulled back from Melino's fallen armor, edging her mech closer to the scattered wreckage of Flevver's jalopy. Her external cameras showed her mech's foot was next to the amputated chopsaw from Sixthson's mech.

"I'll show you petty," Jessica said, "you worn-out excuse for a pleasure doll."

The Wardancers were a proud and lethal warrior cult, but they did not like being reminded they were originally created on Junctionworld as purpose-built comfort hosts. Long before the Gatekeepers took control, the Wardancer Rebellion ended with mass castrations of their overthrown enslavers, the K'Narr. Preserved containers filled with the offending members of that race still turned up from time to time in excavations and refurbished buildings, much to the consternation of the males in the construction crews.

The poise and grace of the sleek mech's posture faded, and a blazing display of overpowered jets told Jessica that her verbal goading had worked. Screaming something incoherent and machine-like over her loudspeakers, Kierra charged, her plasma-edged swords swinging in wild loops.

Kramer's mech shifted its weight from side to side, its glowing warhammer waiting for the incoming assault. As the distance closed, Jessica kicked up the foot next to the buzzsaw, sending it flying at Kierra's machine.

The Wardancer sliced the buzzsaw clean in two, one of the fragments tearing a small rip into her hull. The improvised distraction kept her from putting both blades into Jessica, but Kierra still carved a furrow up the left forearm of Kramer's mech.

"I think we touched a nerve, NoName," Jessica said.

"Agreed, Pilot," the computer responded.

Wasting no time to recover, Kierra charged again. Jessica blocked a flying kick from the Wardancer, raking the warhammer's energized claw across the back of the attacking mech's leg. The pink mech's momentum carried it into another kick, spinning and smashing into Jessica's hip. Another reversal, and Kierra brought both plasma blades overhead, trying to skewer Jessica through her cockpit. Kramer brought her hammer up, blocking the twin thrusts. The two mech pilots grappled, cockpit to cockpit, neither one gaining the advantage, as plasma weaponry sizzled all around them.

NoName threw an alert on the screen, showing Jessica a view from the lower abdomen's camera. Vicious spikes emerged from behind the Wardancer mech's shin covers. Despite the internal force fields, Jessica's feet felt the impacts through the floor of her cockpit. *Oh, void...*

Kierra hammered the undercarriage of NoName with repeated, close-in knee strikes, spearing and puncturing the hull with brutal force and frequency. Each fearsome blow made NoName's hull sing, and the glowing force fields around her flickered.

"NoName, what are those venting spikes doing?" Jessica demanded. "What's up with the fields?"

Before the computer could answer, Jessica felt a hot streak shoot up her own leg as a mech-sized spike entered the bottom of her cockpit, ripping the limb open from ankle to knee.

Crying out in pain, she pivoted the mech's hull, trying to shield its punctured guts and her own skin. The BGDH-1's plasma spike pivoted as well, lopping off one of the Wardancer's mech hands with it. The charged plasma blade hit the arena deck plating, sizzling and sinking in halfway to the hilt, the severed pink manipulator still gripping it.

NoName flashed a suggestion to turn the emergency rotation into a hip throw, and Jessica, pushing aside the pain, executed the plan. She sent the Wardancer to the ground using its own momentum, and the pink mech bounced a short distance away.

Jessica reached down to her torn boot. Her fingers came back dark with blood. She could see the arena deck plates through her cockpit floor. She gritted her teeth against the mouth guard.

"Oh, you're going to pay, you venting bi—"

Kierra anticipated NoName's charge, and rolled and boosted her mech to the side before the giant hammer came down. The thunderous strike echoed through the arena interior, its sound matched only by the crowd. Another rained down. Then, another. The Wardancer's force fields slowed her down, but her speed and grace helped her to keep evading the furious hammer-falls.

Jessica was losing blood. The hammer's impacts were getting sloppy. She wished her flask was still full, so she could drain it.

"Hold still, you gate-damned—"

The Wardancer mech, still scrambling, boosted its jets to

gain some distance, carrying her away from Jessica and NoName in a long arc. Kramer's vision closed in, her headlight from blood loss as the adrenaline subsided. Her hands trembled around the control yokes.

"Pilot?" her battle computer said.

"Ye... yeah, NoName?"

"The day. What day is it? Answer immediately," NoName said.

"Day? Isss... Third... no," Jessica said, slurring and on the verge of blacking out. "Seventh Gate Day? Dunno. Sleepy."

"Determination: Cognitive functions impaired," NoName said. "Override engaged."

The mech's autopilot lights came on, but Jessica found herself in a dream state, unable to focus. There was an audible gasp from the crowd as the exterior running lights signaled NoName's takeover, then a roar of outrage as NoName began maneuvering in a matter far more advanced than a regular command module.

The hooting and cat-calls of the mob slid over her, and she sneered at the noise. Jessica tasted rubber in her mouth, and spit out the guard. Her eyes rolled back, and things turned surreal.

She saw NoName point the BGDH-1's head towards Kierra again, mimicking Jessica's gesture to Melino at the beginning of the match. The Wardancer matched the visual challenge with her remaining blade. Limping, his leg damaged and trailing smoke, NoName twirled the hammer like a baton, bidding the warrior woman to come forth with his other hand. Kierra obliged, her jets blazing. The crowd roared, part elation, part outrage, as the blinding flash of drive plasma devoured the distance between them.

The Wardancer tried to arc again over the cargo mech's cockpit, this time leading with her blade. NoName evaluated, crouched, then shot out with the hammerhead's rear blade, catching her in midair like a gaffed fish.

Kierra's mech landed hard, bouncing against the arena floor, but NoName maintained control, refusing to let her get away. The computer punctured the plasma-charged hammer's rear beak into the captured mech's back. The slicing, slithering motion of the glowing claw ripped away Kierra's main jets, grounding her. Cheers erupted as flames and debris flew from the Wardancer mech's damaged shoulders.

The pink mech rolled to the side before NoName could land another blow. Kierra's machine tried a sweeping kick to the solid, sturdy mech's leg, to no avail. An air of desperation seemed to surge through the Wardancer's movements, and the crowd's initial howls of outrage turned to cheers as Kierra regained her feet.

The jarring motion of the fierce combat roused Jessica to her senses, as if out of a dream. The blur of the last few moments swam before her eyes.

"Run... fire... hammer..." she said before the darkness consumed her.

"Acknowledged, Pilot," NoName said. "Executing."

SIXTH GATE ZONE
BERVA PROXIMA ARENA

The shame and anger of Kyuzo's interaction with Mikralos still stung. He had to calm himself, to focus on the long-range goal of freeing himself from the grasp of the Gatekeepers. Their moving of the goalposts was not unexpected, but infuriating, nonetheless.

Storming from the blob's observation bubble, he found himself in the back hallways of the arena's infrastructure. Though he should have headed home, the roars of the crowd in the arena's stands brought him to a secluded area of the shielded bleachers, where there were no Nine guards about, and only a sparse number of spectators.

The match, while awkward at times because of the baby-shields, had been interesting. Kyuzo knew Flevver Sixthson by reputation, and was surprised the bellicose little man had lasted as long as he did before punching his eject button. Melino's rescue by Jessica Kramer, by way of hammer-strike, was another point of amusement.

She's a thug, rough and unprofessional. But, she's unpredictable, and that makes her dangerous, Kyuzo thought.

Now, the match had dwindled to the Wardancer, Kierra, and Kramer, his upcoming opponent. Kierra fought true to form, but the converted cargo mech was holding its own, despite the golden android's speed and skill.

The knee spikes were a nice touch, though. Very nasty. Masamune pondered about installing similar units on his own armored mech. He would have to see how the Wardancer managed to punch through the inner shields so easily. These things were known to happen, but still, it bore more investigating.

Now, the Kramer mech was under its own control, but its moves and tactics were far superior to anything he had seen or heard of before. The autonomous lights were on, but the machine tore Kierra apart like a seasoned pro. *Interesting... ah, here's the end,* he thought.

There was no fitting music playing from the Wardancer's speakers. There was no belaboring the killing blow to appeal to the bloodlust of the crowd. The final movement was surgical, and finished in the blink of an eye.

Kierra's mech charged, trying a spinning roundhouse that concealed a last-minute stab with her remaining plasma blade. Kramer's mech caught her in mid-maneuver, deflecting the attack while slamming the charging mech to its knees.

Here it comes. Beautiful.

The brutal hammer came up... and smashed down through an upthrust arm and blade, making a mockery of it, like it wasn't even there. The reversed blade movement severed the pink mech's remaining hand and sword at the wrist, sending it flying.

The energized weapon reversed, and the pointed tip of the shaft speared through the lower cockpit of the pink mech.

Before the audience could react, the match was over with a shudder and a twist.

In a growing swell, the crowd began to boo. Pandemonium reigned in the stands and spectators around him shouted to each other. Some defended her, others voiced their opinions that the Kramer girl had cheated, somehow, by using some unknown, advanced battle AI.

"The shields shoulda stopped that gate-damned hammer! Human musta cheated!" one being cried, spilling his meal of blood-grubs in his outrage.

"Blasted knee spikes of yon Wardancer were likewise undeclared advantage!" another sentient yelled back, pointing its claws in an accusatory manner at the first being.

The two beings tried to make their way to each other, to come to grips. Their clumsy efforts caused a tumult among the audience members around them. Kyuzo ignored them, focusing instead on the aftermath happening on the arena floor.

Kramer's victorious orange and blue mech powered down, kneeling in a controlled topple. Its cockpit dropped and lurched to ground level as the crashbots raced in from the sides of the arena.

The sports network drone cameras circled, their flashing cameras drinking in the individual scenes of mayhem. Images flashed up on the large displays all around Berva Proxima's pockmarked interior.

Masamune saw the Wardancer's mech was a total loss, run through by the vicious finishing blow. The hammer's final skewering attack severed Kierra's android legs. The plasma cauterized most of the wounds, leaving the beautiful android charred and legless. Golden, honey-like fluids poured from where the plasma hadn't sealed the damage. Bio-mechanic repairbots worked furiously to staunch the flow. It was ugly, but Kyuzo had seen the elite warrior femdroids survive worse.

Well, he thought, a dark smile crossing his face, *The K'Narr built those Wardancers to take a pounding...*

More poignant than Kierra's situation was the image of Jessica Kramer, her skin now gray from blood loss, her eyes rolled back. Despite her reputation for bravado, here she was on display for all of Junctionworld, saved at the last minute by her mysteriously-controlled machine.

The arena's crowd gave tepid cheers as both critically-wounded pilots were extracted from their mechs.

A draw. Not bad. Masamune Kyuzo pulled back from the bleachers, making his way down a stadium corridor, back to the back hallways of Berva Proxima. His eyes narrowed in satisfaction, his original hand clenched around his artificial fist in contemplation.

This rookie, Kramer, might not be a worthy challenge, but her mech's computer had spirit. *This might be a good match, yet.*

CHAPTER TWENTY-FIVE

SIXTH GATE ZONE

VERVOR'S FABRICATION WORKS

Jessica Kramer was furious as she paced back and forth in front of the assembled Myoshans of Vervor's shop staff. The dozen Myoshan crew members kept their dual pairs of eyes rigid and fixed, looking both directly ahead and behind. Myoshans, as a rule, maintained a military rigor in their behavior, and showed no waver in the face of the tall, obnoxious mammal currently bawling them out.

Kitos, the Niff technician responsible for grafting the old Judah command module into her mech, NoName, avoided looking at her. He used one pair of arms to shield his large, golden eyes from her view. The other pair of arms he held crossed in front of his blue, furry body.

Prath, her Ascended crew chief, also held a weary hand over his eyes. Master Vervor, the owner of the shop, chuckled at the sight of her tirade. As her rant increased in volume, the Myoshan crossed his arms, sticking his needle teeth out in firm defiance.

"Could somebody, anybody, please explain to me why my gate-damned mech went rogue?" Jessica shouted. "Why it decided to win my premier big-time match without me? Anyone? No?" She held a wrench, stabbing it in the assembled crew's direction, then threw it hard against the leg of her mech. It bounced with a clang through the silent, dread-filled shop.

Jessica hobbled back and forth on a custom healing cast. The printed arrangement around her cut and swollen limb looked like a plastic combination of honeycomb and spiderweb. The deep lacerations were healing, but the Wardancer's spikes had almost cost her a leg.

"You and your mech won the match, pilot," Master Vervor said, "even if you only scored a couple Disabled points."

"The damage is extensive, yes," the Myoshan shop owner continued, "to both you and your machine, but you won. What more do you want? You're being irrational, and I and my crew don't have to put up with your tantrums. You lot, get back to it. We have someone showing up this afternoon, another big, custom job."

Master Vervor dismissed his fellow Myoshans and they turned back to tackle the heavy work of putting NoName back into fighting shape. The short shopkeeper walked back to his office, shutting the door as the sound of work returned to the facility.

Kitos tried to join them, but stopped when Jessica speared an accusatory finger at him.

"Not you!" she said, making the technician freeze in his tracks. "You sit your blue butt down! I want answers, Niff!"

"Little human, screaming is not going to make this better," Prath said, trying to calm her down. "You've made your point, and we have a multitude of repairs to figure out. I think that's enough—"

"Don't 'little human,' me, Prath," Jessica said, whirling

towards the Ascended. "This drippy dungbag sent me out into the arena with an Arkathan computer that *suddenly, magically* came online the same time the match started, and started over-riding my controls in the middle of a four-way fight. I was up against a *Wardancer*, out there, for Gates's sake! It even gave my hammer away! Just opened up its hand, and gave it away, like a gate-damned bouquet of flowers, ape. How did he not know? I thought you were the *expert*, Kitos?" Kitos cowered, his ears folded flat, one set of arms over his head, the other wrapped around his body.

"I-I tried to graft command module from the damaged unit into the current computer," Kitos said, cringing. "Preliminary function tests were nominal. Master Prath said so!"

"The Judah module was self-healing," Prath said. "Most Arkathan circuitry is. It must have grown past the junction grafts. Again, that's enough, Jessica."

"Yes," Kitos said, agreeing feverishly. "Arkathan circuits can self-heal. They must have been still re-making pathways after the booth tests. I-I not know the extent of—"

"I don't want to hear any more excuses, you slime-squirter!" Jessica said, her volume high and full of menace.

"I-I thought Pilot Kramer wanted answers—" Kitos said.

"I almost *died* out there, Niff!" Jessica said, turning red. "The damn controls weren't responding. Is Mikralos paying you to help kill me, too, or something?"

"I *said*, I. Think. That's. *Enough.*'" Prath's eyes were hard, no longer covered due to his embarrassment at Jessica's outburst. The stern edge in his voice shut Kramer up in mid-rant. Prath's long fingers reached out to steady the Niff's repetitive rocking in his seat.

"Kitos," Prath said, a firm, soothing tone in his voice, "please take the Judah module, the NoName control computer, and the adapters, and set them up on the test bench. We will join you shortly." The blue ball of tension unwound, and the Niff gathered the components and left. Prath turned to the seething human pilot.

"You... you are really starting to test the limits of my good nature, Pilot Kramer," Prath said, his patience at an end. "Take your flask, or wherever else you're hiding your booze, and leave the shop. Wait for me at the bar on the corner. I will be along, shortly, once I have calmed down Kitos and apologized to Master Vervor for your behavior. We are going to have that talk."

Jessica's brow furrowed in confusion and she took a short step back.

"You're... telling me to go *to* the bar? Even though—"

"Ah, yes, *even though*," Prath said, interrupting her, "Even though I told you not to drink anymore? Even though I told you it would ruin your focus and endanger you in the arena? I think we both know how good you are at listening to my suggestions. You have a new souvenir to show for it, after all." He motioned to her cast.

"I wasn't drunk, Prath," Jessica said. "It was just a quick belt, and it was Dad's old flask. It was just, like, a good luck thing. It's no big deal."

"'No big deal' ended up with you comatose and nearly dead in front of thousands," the tall, orange ape said, his lips pulling back from his fangs and dark gums. "In addition, you gave away the surprise advantage of your onboard Arkathan computer! I *hope* it was the booze that let you allow a Wardancer in that close, where they are most dangerous. She tore you and your mech to shreds, in case you didn't notice. Not to mention, you should have closed in with your first opponent, the whip-sword pilot. Maintaining your distance only let Melino rip you pieces at his leisure. If you had more than a dozen matches under your belt, you'd have known that! So, in summary, I sincerely do *hope* you were drunk, because if you were sober, I can only think that it was a result of pure *incompetence*, pilot."

He was shocked at his own volume and display of anger. Prath held his hand to the side of his head and hid his fangs.

"Now, if you'll excuse me," Prath said, "I must look after Kitos and the diagnostics. Go to the bar, like I asked. I will come for you later."

"Fine," Jessica said. She stormed off, as best she could on a bum leg, out of the shop. She hit the main entrance door's exit button at the maximum extent of her wounded stride. It didn't release, and she bumped face-first into the thick plastic. The Myoshans watching her through their rear sets of eyes all had to suppress fang-clicks of laughter.

"Vervor! Your door! What's the void's wrong with this thing? Let me out of here," she yelled at the establishment's proprietor, shaking the unresponsive handle while slamming the button again.

The Myoshan proprietor emerged from his small office door carrying a remote control. He pressed the button, and a buzzer signaled the door's release.

"Security measure," Master Vervor said, a growl in his voice. "I'd rather not have a repeat of the Headhunter's last unscheduled visit. Besides, you've made enemies of the Wardancers, and I don't need any vengeance oaths being fulfilled on my shop floor. Oh, and mind the gentlebeing coming in, too. He has an appointment."

Jessica Kramer turned to the unlocked door's open frame to see it now occupied. Her eyes went wide with recognition, sending her hand to her pistol's grip. The human male produced something from between his outstretched prosthetic fingers.

"Mech Pilot Jessica Kramer, I am Masamune Kyuzo. My card."

CHAPTER TWENTY-SIX_

SIXTH GATE ZONE

VERVOR'S FABRICATION WORKS

Masamune Kyuzo was angry. Angry at Mikralos for forcing him to seek the services of this outside shop when he had his own fabrication capabilities. Angry at having to do unnecessary modifications to his mech. Angry for being manipulated and helpless in the face of the Gatekeepers' contract and Old Code.

He was nowhere near as angry, however, as the human he was now facing in the shop's doorway. Jessica Kramer pulled the door open with a livid fury that doubled when she recognized him. He remained stone-faced upon meeting her in person. Although his first instinct was to reach for one of his pistols, his honor demanded he offer his outstretched business card, first.

"You... you octorat-faced bastard," Kramer said, spitting at his feet. "I can tell you where to stick that card. I don't have a gate-damned thing to say to you."

He continued to hold the card out to her. It seemed to infuriate her more.

"I am not surprised at your reaction, Pilot Kramer," Kyuzo

said, "but I must admit, I am disappointed. I hoped we could meet as professionals outside of the arena, as fellow gladiators, since we're both being forced to use Vervor's services."

"'Professionals?' 'Fellow gladiators?'" Jessica said, seething. "What the void is this, some pre-match head game? Or did you come to gloat? When's the last time you saw what's left of the family mech, by the way, from your match with my brother? We've got most of the parts in the back bay, you know, including the *cockpit*."

Master Vervor's head poked through the door, besides Jessica's waist, evaluating the situation.

"Yes, the incident from many years ago," Kyuzo said, his arms tucked behind him. "Your brother's death was not my proudest moment."

"Gee, I really hope that's not an excuse or an apology, *'Desecrator.'*" Kramer said.

"Pilot Kramer, you were just leaving," Vervor said, trying to wedge between the two taller humans. "Please do so, now, and stop making a nuisance of yourself to my next appointment. I sincerely hope she isn't bothering you, Master Pilot Masamune."

"Thank you, Master Vervor, but it is no bother," he said, turning to her. "I'm addressing my fellow pilot. It's not an excuse or apology, Pilot Kramer, nor do I owe you one. Your brother died in the arena at my hand, yes, but it was an honorable death."

"Honor? I've only had a few years of hypno-surge history from my Dad's homeworld," Jessica said, fury in her words, "but you're no Fourth Gate samurai, honor-bound by a higher purpose, Masamune. You're just an assassin on a string, just a... a *puppet* of the blobs. What do the Gatekeepers have on you, that they're sending you out for my head?"

Masamune Kyuzo arched an eyebrow, the slight smirk now gone from his face.

"Pilot Kramer!" Vervor said, trying to push Kramer away with his small, scaled arms. She did not budge, and continued to talk above him. "You are out of line, addressing the Master Pilot in such a manner!"

"I know you're probably not used to hearing this, but this isn't all about you, Kramer," Kyuzo said. "No, I'm not Samurai. On my world, they died out six hundred years before I was born. I fight by this place's Old Code, though, for my own reasons. Despite what you may have heard, recently, there is no shame in how I conduct myself in the arena. Some of us have more at stake than... than just finding excuses for a fallen family member's dismal flash-and-crash." Masamune's prosthetic hand curled into a fist. The underside of his elbow ran over the grip of one of his holstered pistols, unsnapping its release.

"Ooh, cute remark, there, patchwork pilot," Jessica said. Her constant sarcasm was becoming tiresome to Kyuzo. "I guess if I screwed up as bad as you did a few years ago, I would be wearing metal parts, too. Hey, how did that whole scandal thing work out with Ferro Fortress, anyway? Didn't your sponsors cut you loose, floater? Is that what this is? You just trying to pay the bills, trying to keep your numbers covered?" Masamune's expression turned from cold and formal to hard and mean.

"You really don't know what—"

"Outrageous, Kramer! Stifle!" Vervor said, indignant at Kramer's accusations. "I need your crew chief up here to put a muzzle on you, Pilot. Never in all my days have I heard such disrespect, such insolence. I will be right back with her ape, Master Masamune." The Myoshan ducked back inside.

"Listen, I'm sure you're a wonderful guy outside of the arena," Kramer said, changing her tone to sickly sweet, "and not the sicko, thrill-killer, errand boy of the Gatekeepers that everyone plays you up to be. Maybe... maybe it's *me* who's really got things sideways, here."

She called back through the door at the retreating Myoshan.

"Vervor, make sure this octorat stays away from my mech, and tell Prath I'm getting a beer," Kramer said. "Oh, your peashooter's little snap is undone, by the way, *Desecrator.* Careful with that. Someone might get hurt." She put one defiant hand on her hip, the other on her rib cage next to her own bulky revolver's grip.

Masamune re-engaged the catch on his pistol with a scowl. She turned, a saccharin smile on her face. She made an obscene gesture in the air, holding it over her head as she limped in the direction of the corner bar.

Kyuzo watched her go, surprised by the anger she brought out in him with mere words. *She is a vicious one, no doubt about that,* he thought.

He remembered the cockpit recordings of her exchange with the Wardancer, how she unhinged the disciplined android warrior into making a reckless charge. He would have to guard against that.

Masamune focused, tamping down his anger to conduct himself in a more business-like manner. He entered Vervor's to discuss refurbishing his old battle claw, shaking his head as Kramer's words soaked in.

Good Gates, I hope my children don't turn out like her if I get killed in the arena, he thought.

CHAPTER TWENTY-SEVEN

SIXTH GATE ZONE
SERAPH'S ALC-SOAK BAR AND GRILL

She had only been in the bar twenty minutes, but Jessica Kramer was already on her fifth beer. A lilting cacophony of a song played on the bar's speakers, something in the Redfolk language, with its offset rhythms and shrieking strings, but at least the volume was low. The bartender here at Seraph's was a flesh-and-blood humanoid, not a bot, who kept himself busy slinging drinks to the mixed clientele of the working-class Sixth Gate Zone neighborhood. Prath took a seat on the barstool next to her with a sigh.

"Masamune's business at the shop is concluded," Prath said. "Have you calmed down, yet?"

She stiffened at the words 'calmed down,' then forced herself to relax. There were fewer words in the Universal language that she hated to hear more. *It's Prath, damn it. Hear what he has to say*, she had to tell herself.

"We're ready for you back at the test bench," the Ascended continued. "We need your bio-code to access the Arkathan software and memory nodes of the Judah control module, and I've given Kitos my personal assurance that you'll behave. Best to avoid Master Vervor, though."

He looked at the four empty glasses in front of her, and the full beverage in her hand.

"How many have you had, little human, including that one?" The Ascended asked.

"Still on my second one, ape, honest," Jessica said, lying as she buried her nose in the beer's head of foam. "Those other glasses were here already. It's not the cleanest of ethyl-alc joints. It almost makes Jev's place in Maro Point look respectable."

After a deep drink, she put the half-empty vessel on the bar top. Prath brushed the bubbles off her face with a long brown finger. She grinned at the gesture. He didn't.

"That Kierra woman nearly killed you," Prath said, his eyes sad and serious. "You know that, right?"

"Just because they're shaped like women, ape, doesn't make it so," Jessica said.

"I'm not here to debate the finer points of android physiology with you, little human," the Ascended said. "This is about your performance at Berva Proxima. We almost lost you. *I* almost lost you."

"You really think I was sloppy, ape? Honestly?"

"Yes, but it wasn't incompetence," Prath said. "I'm sorry for saying that, back in the shop. However, I think you have a lot to learn. Lesson number one: don't let Wardancers in close." He smiled with pulled-back lips.

"Lesson learned, trust me," Jessica said, knocking her knuckles on the side of the printed leg cast.

"Oh, you've got an abundance of lessons in front of you, love," Prath said. "Unfortunately, we don't have an abundance of time for you to learn them. These Gatekeepers aren't going to just wait for you to play catch-up. That's why we need to stay on top of our game."

"Yeah," she said, her tone flat as she contemplated her beer.

They sat in silence for a few moments, then she murmured something in a pained voice. The Redfolk music masked her words.

"What's that? I didn't quite hear you," Prath said.

"I said 'I'm sorry, ape,'" Jessica said in a low, resigned voice.

Prath pulled her against him. She felt him start to groom her hair, and she smiled. She stayed in his huge, firm embrace for a few moments, then tapped him to let her go. She downed the remainder of the beer in front of her, then ordered another.

"I've only been back in your life two gate-weeks, Jessica," Prath said, shaking his head slowly, "and I've seen you engage in more self-destructive behavior in the space of sixteen days than I did in sixteen years of watching you grow up."

"Yeah, well, I'm not a little girl, anymore, ape," she said. "I had to get by on my own while you were gone, and Junction-world's an ugly place. Plus, I was a screw-up when I was a kid. Everyone was just too busy to notice."

"Little human, please, we're getting along well, here. Let's not—"

"No, no, hear me out, Prath," Jessica said, her buzz loosening her tongue. "I promise, I really do. I promise that I'll try and do better. I know what you're saying, I just... I just get so gate-damned angry, sometimes."

"Well, you've been through a lot, like you told me," Prath said, putting a large hand on her shoulder in consolation.

"Maybe it's this place," she said, motioning around. "Not just the bar, though. What I mean is, J-World's a hundred-mile-wide den of filth, surrounded by the all-devouring void, pierced by eight gates that allow all sorts of evil to crawl in and out. It's a... a... 'an infernal, blood-soaked void-hole, ruled by egomaniacal little bastards.' That's what Dad called this place, in that book of his.'"

"Solomon did have a way with words," Prath said, a wry grin on his face as he remembered his old friend and team leader. "His autobiography still sells quite well. I'm surprised the Gate-keepers still allow it to be published."

"Who knows, but all the mech-jockeys still eat that stuff up. That's probably the money I'm drinking with, right now," she said, her words slurring. "And he and mom raised me, and my brother, and my sister, right in the venting middle of it. And then, 'poof,' they were all dead or gone, and I was alone in the middle of this ugly little dimensional crossroads. I think, all things considered, I'm doing okay."

She was pleased with her sudden alc-induced epiphany, and started to speak louder.

"And the Sixth Gate Zone, let me tell ya," Jessica said, raising her glass to Prath, "I thought the Fourth Gate Zone where I grew up was bad. This whole dung-pit is just a junk pile. It's where all of Junctionworld's reprocessing and recycling is done, stuff that's barely good enough to not be pushed off into the void. I mean, look at this grip of lunkheads in here. Refugees. Scrappers. Trash pickers. And their local arena, Berva Proxima, isn't even second-tier—"

Her words carried over the music, turning several sets of ears to them.

"Jessica, love, it's best you tone down the rhetoric," Prath said, scanning the multiple angry glances now being cast in their direction. "We're not at Maro Point, and these beings may not know you're joking."

"Who's joking, ape? This place is garbage," she said, gulping down more beer. "Just... pure garbage. Hey, you wanna hear a joke? I got a joke for ya. There was this saying, carved in one of Jev's bathroom stalls back in Maro Point. You wanna know what it was? 'Flush twice, it's a long way to the Sixth Gate.' Oh, man, that's a good one." She slapped the weathered plating of the bar top. She picked up the beer, downing most of it.

"Barkeep, another, please," Jessica said, holding her finger up to simulate a digitpress.

"It's on me, Morz," a voice said over her shoulder.

Jessica finished the last of her drink, and turned to see the voice's owner. He was a standard human, tall, well-built, with nice eyes and straight teeth. A little dirty, but this was an industrial sector after all. The shift must be ending at some local factory, from the look of all the similar working uniforms in the place.

He was cute enough, though, and the beers had her feeling good. Something... something about him reminded her of Tevren. That cocky smile. Her humorous mood went away at the memory of the tech who once worked for her father. She thought of her former infatuation trapped behind the Eighth Gate with her conniving sister, of what they might be up to, and she went cold.

"Whoa, what's that look for?" the young man said.

"Pass. I buy my own drinks. Vent off," Jessica said, her tone now serious.

"C'mon, we're laughing, having fun, right?" the young man said. "It's just a drink, you know, just between us humans? Hey, my name's Jeremy. Jeremy Collins. I don't bite."

Prath pulled back and leaned his elbow on the bar, amused at the scene.

"I mean no disrespect with the 'humans' stuff, Master Ascended," the young male added.

"None taken, Collins," Prath said, motioning to Jessica. "Watch yourself, though. This one does bite."

"'Just between us humans,' huh?" Jessica said, bristling. "What, you think you can buy me a brew or two? Maybe get a little friendly later? Maybe help propagate the species? Get out of my face, Collins." She turned her back on him and accepted the fresh beer from the bartender. Her other hand reached down for one of her knives. Her hands brushed only spider-webbed cast. *Damn, wrong boot.*

"C'mon, don't be that way. I'm just trying to have a conversation with a pretty girl, here," Collins said. "It's not often a guy gets to see such a beauti—"

"Like I said before, vent off," she said, cutting him off. "I'm not interested in some grease-plug in dirty coveralls who's just looking to dump some pressure."

The young man's expression flushed red, his initial advance left burning in flames. Laughter erupted from his coworkers at a nearby table. Looking over to them, his posture shifted. He looked her up and down, a sneer on his face as he searched for a retort.

"What's the matter," Collins said, "Too good for us 'scrappers and trash pickers?' You got some fancy, uptown slick, somewhere? Huh? Some pretty-boy with soft hands?"

"Go away, Collins," she said. "I'm trying to come up with a reason not to kill you."

"You talk big, I'll give you that," Collins said, pressing his verbal attack. "Hey, what about a sister? Got one of those, you little breed-tease? Maybe she'd be a little more friendly."

"Oh, dear," Prath said, slapping his hand over his brow.

Jessica continued to look straight ahead. She cocked her head to the side, popped her jaw, and considered denting the bar top with Collins' forehead. The impulse was strong. Instead, she pulled out her revolver, placing it next to her new beer with a heavy thunk.

"What'd you say?" Jessica said, scowling as she looked him in the eye.

The Redfolk tune on the bar's sound system cut out, and a

racking shotgun resounded through the establishment. Morz, the bartender, pointed his weapon's gaping muzzle at a sign on the wall. It read in seven common languages, "Keep it holstered."

She flicked her jaw in acknowledgment to the armed bartender, then turned to the young, human male, who was now backing up, his hands in the air. The look on his face conveyed he was no longer interested in the prospect of getting to know her better.

"You listen to me, Collins," Jessica said, her voice full of measured menace, "you greasy little... no, never-mind. We'll do this instead: You ever speak to me again, you even say 'hello,' and I'll forget all about how I just promised my friend Prath, here, that I'm trying to do better. You understand me?"

The human nodded, eager to end his encounter with Jessica, his eyes shifting between the revolver on the counter and the shotgun in the bartender's hands.

"Good," she said, putting the large pistol away. "I'm outta here. Enjoy the beer, Collins. You bought it, after all."

She wobbled towards the silent bar's front door on her wounded leg, heading back to Master Vervor's shop. The barkeep put his exotic scatter-gun away, and rang up a thin, paper-like plastic receipt from a glowing cash register. Morz handed the bill to the Ascended crew chief as he stood up to follow her.

The music and conversation resumed. Jeremy Collins, his pride wounded, returned to his table of workmates. They clapped him on the back and laughed with him, exchanging their own stories of similar encounters in the past.

Prath's brow wrinkled as he read the tally of her drinking streak.

"Six? Six beers? You were here for just... Gates bless it, Jessica," the orange ape said.

CHAPTER TWENTY-EIGHT

SIXTH GATE ZONE

SERAPH'S ALC-SOAK BAR AND GRILL

"Mammals," Skreeb said, watching the semi-dramatic silliness unfold in front of him at the bar. The Shasarr cyborg watched the human female limp out of the bar, followed by her orange primate companion. At the table next to him and his partner, Velsh, a raucous party of factory workers laughed and crowed as one of their number returned to them, embarrassed and forlorn.

Skreeb didn't see what the problem was. Shasarr courtships often utilized weaponry and death threats. *Such simple creatures*, he thought.

At the table the two beings shared, his Skevvian partner contemplated the slow-rising bubbles in a bottle of purple fluid in front of him. Skreeb Fourth-Hatched, the Shasarr cyborg, took a deep puff off of the vaporizer embedded in his arm, blowing the cloud of chemical exhaust up into intakes in the ceiling.

"Ready to do this thing, Velsh?" the enhanced reptilian asked his tentacled table mate.

"One more shot, Skreeb, then we'll do it," the Skevvian answered, his tone flat and sullen. "I still gotta pull the aircar around, and I keep thinking the Headhunter's going to pop out of nowhere and add us to his wall. I'm tellin' ya, I don't like this part of town one bit."

"Cheer up, Velshie," Skreeb said. "We've been in this place for hours, and the Headhunter ain't shown his big red self, yet, him or his Niner boys. Finish your drink, and we'll snatch up the boss's little Niff."

The Skevvian wrapped one set of tentacles around the bottle and its purple contents, pouring the carbonated syrup into a smaller glass. He tilted the shot back, letting it flow into his open beak. He shivered as the poisons hit his nervous system, then slammed the glass back on to the table.

"Okay, Skreeb. Let's do it," the being said.

CHAPTER TWENTY-NINE

SIXTH GATE ZONE

VERVOR'S FABRICATION WORKS

Vervor had just settled in, his Myoshan-sized office door closed and the staff instructed not to bother him. The bothersome human pilot, Kramer, and her ape were gone. To where, he hadn't the slightest care.

He kicked his small, clawed feet up on the desk, taking care not to press any buttons or touchpads built into the desktop. He closed both sets of eyes, and began to indulge.

Then the front door's bell rang. Again. And again. He sighed, remembering that he had the only remote for the security system. The buzzing alarm from the main entrance ruined Master Vervor's favorite activity: his mid-afternoon nap.

"Crumbling gates, hold on, I'm coming, I'm coming," the scaled Myoshan said, his momentary bliss now gone. He opened his office to see who was at the front door, his security remote clutched like a weapon in his claws. He clenched his fangs, hoping it was not that thrice-damned renegade pilot returning.

Damnation. It was her. Her, and her coddling, enabling,

emotion-blinded Ascended crew chief, Prath. *Hard to believe she's the spawn of Solomon Kramer*, he thought. *Greatness must have skipped a generation.*

They were arguing on the sidewalk outside his shop. Of course, they were always arguing. This time, though, their words did not carry through the thick plastic of the windows and walls. Master Vervor enjoyed the moment, trying to make the silence stretch as long as he could before letting them back in.

The smaller human vocalized in an angry manner at the tall, orange ape, her body bobbing and swaying as she heaped muted abuse on him. It could be the damaged limb altering her balance. It was more likely the ethyl-alc concoctions from the bar down the street. He asked his ancestor spirits for patience, and lifted the remote. As he pressed the access button to the security system, the door's magnetic lock popped with a loud buzz.

"C'mon, Prath! I told you I was going to do better. You *told* me to go the bar and drink a couple beers—", Jessica Kramer said, pulling the door open.

"Six, Jessica," Prath said, holding his fingers up. "I told you to go cool off, not drink the bar dry, and mislead me about it."

"Fine, *six* beers, of which, I only got to drink *five*, by the way," Kramer said. "So, I hurt some guy's feelings. I didn't pull my gun *on* him, I just pulled it out. He got the message. You heard the nasty things he said to me. Any other day of the week, and I would have broken his neck."

"He was trying to court you," Prath said. "The conversation didn't turn abusive until you initiated hostilities. 'Dirty grease-plug,' I believe was the phrase you used. And stop avoiding the fact you lied to me. You promised you were going to try and do better."

"Ah, gates, Prath, I didn't kill him," Kramer said, feigning exasperation. "So, I have that going for me, at least, right? Besides, you didn't even step in to defend me!"

"I have every faith and confidence," Prath said, reaching into his pocket, "in your ability to handle one unarmed male of your fragile species. Your behavior under the influence of your chosen toxins is the matter at hand. Alas, I knew it would come to this. Look here, please."

Her Ascended friend held up a small spray bottle in his large hand close to her head. Vervor knew the shape of the aerosol, and clacked his fangs in joyous anticipation.

Jessica's eyes crossed as she tried to focus on the dispenser. She recoiled as a mist hit her face, rubbing her nose in tingling pain.

"Prath, what the void was that?" Kramer said. "Are you trying to—"

She stopped mid-sentence. Her sinuses became inflamed, and she snorted. She bobbed her head from side to side, trying to shake off the sensation, then glared at Prath.

"Buzzkill," Kramer said, a shocked look on her face. "You used Buzzkill on me? Really?"

Prath pushed the door to Vervor's shop open, walking past her. She entered, still rubbing her nose and wiping her eyes, which were now starting to stream.

"I thought I could trust you to stay sober," Prath said, "but you proved me wrong before the last match. So, while you were recovering from your leg wound, I had the drone docs synthesize an antidote tailored to your particular system and addiction. If you wish to sneak around and be a drunk on the sly, well, I can counter the effect with... *minimum* side effects."

Vervor chuckled in the background, his hands on his hips. Prath handed her a shop towel from a nearby bench, and she cleared her inflamed sinuses and tear ducts from the booze neutralizer.

"Oh, ape, that's gross," Jessica said, throwing the soaked towel at Prath's feet. "I hate this. This feels like my head's on fire!"

Vervor recoiled, and motioned for a Myoshan staff member to fetch the floor cleaning drone. The short reptilian saluted, then ran to carry out the shop owner's unspoken orders.

"I hope it does," Prath said. "I want you to remember that, the next time you try and sneak in a drink or two, or *six*, for good luck. You took a stupid risk at Berva Proxima, and it nearly got you killed."

"Prath, I thought we worked this out at the bar? I thought we were okay?"

"We did," Prath said, "until I found out that even as you promised me you were going to do better, you were lying about the number of beers you were drinking right in front of me. I'm done being your doormat, love."

Kitos the technician appeared from behind a row of benches. He was eager to speak, and his four arms gestured in exhilaration. Prath motioned him to wait while he continued to talk to Jessica.

"So, from now on," Prath said, shaking the spray dispenser, "you can drink as much as you want, pilot. I've got Mister Buzzkill, here, to help me keep you in line before a match, or around the shop. Otherwise, it's your life to drink away. I'm just the dumb, gullible ape trying to save it, to try and help you, for Jered's sake."

Jessica's burning eyes narrowed.

"Are you sure you're trying to help me," Kramer said, new venom in her voice, "or are you just trying to make yourself feel better? Huh, Prath? Are...are you sure you're not just trying to compensate for sending my brother out to his death in a malfunctioning mech? You sure disappeared from the scene, real quick, after Jered died, huh?"

Kitos's fur and ears fell flat at the accusation. Prath looked wounded. Even jaded Master Vervor was surprised by the hate and pain the human female wove into her words. She was looking to dish out some pain, even if the target was Prath. Vervor could see from the Ascended's shocked, traumatized face that her words found their mark.

Prath rolled up his scattered tools and walked past her without another word, without even looking at her. The Ascended told Kitos farewell, thanked Vervor for his time and effort, and headed towards the shop's front security door.

Jessica stood, fuming, staring straight ahead while her crew chief gathered his things and left. Vervor buzzed the Ascended out, and the door closed quietly behind him.

Moments of strained silence passed. Kitos, still trying to catch her eye with one of his four hands, started to speak.

"Pilot, I-I have—" he said.

"Well, you certainly have a way with words, human," Vervor said, talking over him.

"Just... just don't talk to me, right now, spud," Kramer said, using the soft slur for Vervor's kind. "Just... leave me alone."

"Pilot?" Kitos said, trying to get her attention.

"Don't trouble yourself on that account, softskin," Vervor snapped. "You just pushed away the only being who gave a damn about you on all of Junctionworld. I'm obligated to fix your armor, not be your cheerful companion or straighten out your wreck of a life."

"Pilot Kramer, Master Vervor, there is something I-I think you both should see," Kitos said, trying to interject between them.

"He'll be back," she said softly, her jaw tightening.

"Oh, I doubt that," Vervor said, clicking his fangs. "Congratulations. I thought *I* was a crusty old thump, but I can see I still have a few things to learn."

Kitos began hopping, trying to create a break in their conversation.

"Gate bless it, Niff, *what?*" Jessica said. Despite the harsh words, she wasn't her normal, furious self, Vervor noted.

"I-I, oh, how does one say it," the technician stammered, shocked that they both were now listening to him. "I-I may have found—"

"Family gods preserve us, Kitos, get to the root of it," Vervor said, his two sets of eyes rolling, his arms crossed in impatience.

"I-I performed some initial tests on the new circuit growths, Master Vervor," the Niff said. "Access was possible because new junctions are not coded to any specific gene-lock. I-I was able to access a security log sub-directory, and—"

"There'd better be a point to this," Kramer said in a cold voice, pulling her humming vibroblade out of its boot scabbard. She pointed it at him more like an instructor's baton than a knife. He gulped at the sight of the weapon, but continued.

"Before the match, Pilot Kramer," Kitos said, his voice now sped up. "Your sibling, ident Pilot Jered Kramer. He was not the last being to access the Judah module. Internal service log shows Master Prath did pre-match checks right. Someone... someone else accessed the circuits after them both, though. It was masked in logs, but I-I was able to access through sub-directory. Not so."

Kitos's eyes bulged in fear at the vibroknife still in the upset human's hand.

"And? Who?" she said sternly.

The Niff gulped hard, his ears flattened against his skull.

"I-I identified the bio-access code of..." Kitos said, giddy fear in his voice, "of previous pilot of Judah logged into service directory of Arkathan battle computer, right before match. Bio-access code of... Solomon Kramer."

The high-frequency knife chirped as it hit the shop floor.

CHAPTER THIRTY_

"Solomon Kramer," Jessica Kramer repeated her father's name back to Kitos. "My dad. You're saying he... he was the last one to access Judah? But... but, Jered stole Judah from Poppa. He...?"

Her face was gray, as gray as when they pulled her from the cockpit after the last match.

The Niff technician, Kitos, swallowed hard and nodded, the nervous joy in his huge eyes now replaced by fear. The vibroknife continued to rattle and dance on the floor next to them. His glance tried to stay fixed on her, but kept darting to the jittering blade.

"I-I make no conclusions, only wish to inform, Pilot Kramer," Kitos said, "especially when agitated emotional state and weaponry are present. I-I only report findings from data. More information is required to form solid report." The blue, four-armed being wrapped his lower pair of appendages around his midsection.

"I'm not going to kill you, Niff," Jessica said. "I need to

know. What's it going to take?"

"It's going to take a circuit dive, Pilot Kramer," the shop owner, Vervor, said as he cleared his throat. "You're the bio-coded key to the Arkathan module. If you want more answers, you'll have to do it yourself. After you pick that up."

Master Vervor clicked off her dancing vibroblade with the deft touch of a toe claw, and kicked it over to her.

Jessica, still reeling from the effect of the anti-intoxicant spray, sniffed and rubbed her nose.

"I'm... sorry about before. I'm sorry I called you 'spud.' I just—"

"No need to explain, pilot," Vervor said. "Just get done what you need to, to bring the command module up to speed."

The Myoshan's fangs clicked against each other at a rapid beat as they intermeshed, his signal for being deep in thought. Vervor gave his technician Kitos a hard look with his forward set of eyes.

"Solomon Kramer was the ident key on the log?" the short reptilian asked. "*The* Solomon Kramer? You're positive?"

"The records synch with previous entries," Kitos said. "Service log entries go back for decades, Master Vervor. Last entry was blurred, but trace signals corresponded to previous entries. I-I checked and triple-checked. I-I wanted to make sure before I-I brought this up to Master Prath, but he... he left."

Vervor's hard look shifted to Jessica.

"Hmmm... yes. That was not unexpected, but it happened sooner than I wished," the Myoshan shop owner said. "The Ascended are a very patient race of sapients, but even they must have their limits."

Jessica heaved an exaggerated sigh at his inference as she stooped to pick up her vibroblade. Vervor's small, claw-tipped forefinger shot out when they were at eye level.

"*Don't*," Master Vervor said. "I've dealt with human body

language before, primate. Master Prath tolerated your disrespect because of your past together. The situation has changed. You're a guest in my shop, at the behest of a valued client. You're here to do business, not act like a petulant *choovah* in its death throes."

"Oh, yeah? What's a choovah?" Jessica asked. "It had better be something nice, something adorable." A defiant look crossed her face as she snapped her blade back into its boot sheath.

"I don't have time to give you a lesson in Myoshan zoology, pilot," Vervor said. "It's what you're acting like. Stop it. It's simple enough. Self-evaluate and fix it."

"I'm going to do this circuit dive with the Niff," she said, "and then I'm going to put 'choovah' in my data-search app, and I better like what I find, shopkeep."

"Oh," Master Vervor said, a prickly edge in his voice, "I'm sure, when you do, you'll be your usual fountain-of-joy self, human. You and choovahs are both very much alike in disposition. Either way, your feelings are the least of my concerns. I have a battle claw to work on for Masamune. Now, get to it, you two."

"Actually, Pilot Kramer, choovah is small, fuzzy—" the blue technician started to say.

Vervor's clacking fangs and short snarl cut the Niff short. He shrunk away from the shop owner.

"I-I understand, Master Vervor," Kitos said. "Please follow back to the test bench, Pilot Kramer."

———

"So, what's a choovah, Niff?" she said, making sure Vervor wasn't in earshot.

"I-I think we should concentrate on the task at hand, Pilot Kramer," Kitos said.

"He called me a choovah," she said. "Now, what's a choovah?"

"Hold still, please," Kitos said, trying to ignore the question. "Please take seat. I-I need to calibrate this sensor ring to your skull shape, pilot."

She laid back in a tattered, reclining chair next to the bench. The technician made adjustments to the array of instruments on the bench with one set of hands while he placed a large visor with the other pair. The wide, hood-like carapace covered her eyes and ears, and was a tangle of chords and wires.

"Ow, Kitos, this damn thing's pulling my hair," she said, reaching up to grab the ponderous headset from the Niff's slender blue fingers. "Here, give me the—"

"Caution, pilot," he tried to warn her. "Do not jostle against contacts on neuro-link. I-I already have Arkathan battle computer's module inputs engaged—"

Jessica's vision drained away, the sensation of her hair being pulled faded to nothing, and she blacked out.

Her eyes snapped open. She now stood in a small, gray room with a black border running around it at shoulder height. She couldn't breathe. Panic took hold of her as she clawed at nothing, fighting for air that didn't seem to be there.

"Biological interface synched. Stand by, Pilot Kramer," said an ethereal version of Kitos's voice from somewhere overhead.

She gasped, like her lungs were unlocked and allowed to function. Her chest wasn't burning from oxygen deprivation, like back in the alley with Mikralos. It was like the act of breathing never happened before, until now. She checked her wrist. No pulse, either. *Weird.*

Jessica looked down. She was dressed in her fire-resistant pilot suit, but there was no helmet. Her cast was gone, and she was unarmed.

"What the void is this, Kitos?" She yelled at the smooth,

featureless ceiling. There was no echo.

"Stand by, pilot," Kitos said from somewhere far up above. "I-I am also making circuit dive."

She must still be able to hear with her real, flesh-and-blood ears, but the sound was muffled, like a radio with the volume turned down to bare minimum.

Kitos materialized next to her, a shimmering composition of ones and zeros that shifted into solid form, blue fur and all. He was in his working coveralls.

"Apologies, pilot," the Niff said. "You entered Arkathan maintenance interface before I-I could make final connections. Buffer calibration between physical body in the shop and mental processes in here was not complete. You did not suffocate long, I-I hope?"

"Long enough. That... that was not fun, Niff," Jessica said. "A little warning would have been nice."

"Next time, pilot," Kitos said, "do not grab neuro-link from hands until I-I say so. Touchy contacts. Must fix."

"Yeah, well, let's get this over with," she said, "and hopefully there won't be a next time."

"I-I agree. Double dives can be tricky," Kitos said, "especially with rookie minds."

"Rookie minds? Just wait a—"

He smiled, gestured with one of his lower hands, and a seat flowed up from the floor under Jessica. She dropped, surprised, onto the form-fitting chair.

A section of the floor in front of Kitos turned to a silvery pool, then it, too, began to flow and form into the shape of a contoured work bench covered with displays.

"Pilot has her arena, I-I have mind, here," Kitos said. "Niffs and Arkathans must have shared common ancestor. I-I do few things well. This one of them." His large eyes were confident, devoid of their usual fear.

His four hands performed flicks and gestures with formations of lights around them, his gaze captured by whatever was scrolling in front of him on his workbench's digital surface. The gray walls of the small room brightened to white, then a swirling globe of holographic light appeared in front of them. It matched the console interface in her cockpit.

"No... NoName?" Jessica asked.

"Yes, This Unit is here, pilot," the battle computer's voice said. "Or, rather, you are here with This Unit. Bio-code recognized. Welcome, Jessica Kramer, of the Fourth-Gate Kramers."

"Wow," Jessica said.

"Yes, *wow*, indeed. Are the repairs on This Unit's chassis going well? The damage was quite extensive from the last match. This Unit has a list of itemized suggestions—"

"Actually, NoName," she said, a slight hesitation in her normally-confident voice. "I need help."

"Help?" NoName asked. Even digitally, she blushed.

"Yeah," Jessica responded. "I have... some questions. About the access logs. Kitos said I needed to be here to access the files behind the log entries, so... here I am."

NoName's globe of light blinked orange, then went back to its normal swirl.

"This Unit evaluated Technician Kitos's inquiries during his previous dive," the computer's voice said. "Now that Pilot Kramer's presence is verified, This Unit's access to the full-service logs is unlocked. Suggestion: Jessica Kramer should curtail pursuit of this line of inquiry. Per previous instructions: some questions are better left... unasked."

A loud, hollow thump echoed through the detail-less ceiling above them. Kitos and Jessica looked at each other, both puzzled by the sound. The digital avatar of Kitos shrugged at her with both sets of shoulders, then turned back to the swirling globe.

"I-I have a question, computer," the Niff said. "Readings on digital display show 87% nominal performance, per Arkathan standards. I-I now have internal diagnostics readout access. Readings show only seven of eight main command nodes are present. Were you aware of this?"

"Confirmed," NoName said.

"Function of missing node?" Kitos asked.

"Missing node's auxiliary controls: fine motor tuning and logic functions," NoName said. "Primary controls: main weapons."

Jessica pressed her hand along the side of her head. *Oh, gates, no*, she thought. *Jered.*

"Location of missing module?" Kitos said, scanning through the virtual data whirling in front of his large golden eyes.

"This Unit's missing node is located here, in Junction-world," NoName said, "but remote contact is not possible at this time. Remote node is on minimum subsistence power. Exact location unavailable at this time."

"I-I might be able to refine search, pilot," Kitos said, turning to her, "given more time. Will not be easy."

"See what you can do, Niff," Jessica said. "NoName, when was the chunk of your module taken out?" Another deep boom sounded from the ceiling above them, accompanied by the faint sound of Myoshans shouting in their native language.

"Five years ago, Pilot Jessica Kramer," NoName said. "Prior to scheduled death match at Berva Proxima Arena."

Jessica took a deep digital breath, bracing herself.

"Who did it, Judah, er, I mean, NoName?" she said. "Ident of previous user? Was it Dad?"

NoName's light globe pulsed orange again.

"Repeating, per previous instructions," NoName said. "Emphasis added: 'Some questions are better left unasked... bubelah.'"

"*Bubelah?*' *Oh*, no... no, no, *no*," Jessica said, standing up from the chair, which faded away to digits, then nothing.

"Problem, pilot?" Kitos said. "Is 'bubelah' some password? I-I do not understand."

"Nobody calls me that, Kitos. Not anymore, anyway," Jessica said. "NoName, I need to hear it from you, and quit playing games. Give me the user ident from five years ago at Berva Proxima."

"Repeating per previous instructions," the computer's voice said. "'Some questions are better left unasked, bubelah.'"

"NoName, IDENT, now, *gate-damn-it!*" she demanded.

The swirling lights of NoName's interface froze, and a shockwave rippled through them like a seizure. Above Kitos's and Jessica's heads, the faint sound of a security system alert could be heard, then a muffled sizzle. *That sounded like an industrial laser cutter operating in the shop. Vervor's shop didn't have a laser cutter, did it?* She thought.

Another Myoshan voice called out in alarm, but the sound was muted and distant because of the circuit-dive interface. Kitos was too immersed in the figures and data streaming in front of him to notice.

The lights of NoName's globe became unstuck, and resumed their normal ebbs and flows. A black doorway appeared on the far white wall.

"Ident manifestation processing," NoName said. "Stand by."

"Pilot!" Kitos said, turning to her in alarm as his readouts flashed new information.

The digital door opened without a sound. The scarred digital visage of Solomon Kramer limped through the portal, that playful, psychotic twinkle still in his eyes.

"Hey, baby girl," her father said.

CHAPTER THIRTY-ONE

VERVOR'S FABRICATION WORKS
ARKATHAN DIGITAL INTERFACE

Jessica Kramer was in the depths of her own digital hell. Each of NoName's cryptic answers, combined with Kitos's inquiries, caused the dread to well up in the pit of her stomach. She didn't know how she was going to react if she saw him. She was dreading the possibility of something like this. Now, 'this' was here, happening right in front her, in virtual form: her father had just stepped out of the memory banks of her mech's battle computer.

"Dad?" she said. She could feel digital tears forming.

"You shouldn't be here, baby girl," the image of Solomon Kramer said. "I don't know why you're circuit-diving into Judah, but you need to turn around, right now, and unplug. Go. Schnell."

"Dad, I have some questions. I—" Jessica said, her voice cracking from emotion.

The elder Kramer quieted her by holding up a hand. It was still callused, still strong. Jessica's throat started to tighten. The last five years of loneliness and pain surged to the forefront. She pushed it down, fighting to listen to her father's voice.

"I know there's a lot of things going on," Solomon Kramer said, "but now is not the time. Now, enough. Do as I say. Unplug."

At her father's words, she slapped her hand down to the side of her leg in protest, and caught herself doing it. She thought, *I haven't done that since I was, what, five?*

"Poppa, I need to know," Jessica said. "Did you sabotage Judah?"

"Why would I do that?" Solomon Kramer asked.

"Dad, you removed the weapons node from Judah, didn't you?" Jessica said. "Did you... did you know you probably killed Jered?"

The visage of Solomon Kramer put one hand on the back of his thick neck, the other waved the question away.

"I don't know what you're talking about," the old bull of a man said. "That's crazy talk. Look, I'm not answering any more questions. You've heard me already. Go."

"But, Poppa, I'm... I'm in trouble," Jessica said, pleading. "I'm in big trouble, actually, and I've been stupid, and pissed off Prath, and I'm mixed up in some bad things, and I'm so, so gate-damned *alone*, Dad. *Please*, I just need you to listen. Please listen? I really need your help. Poppa, I—"

Jessica stopped her own words, her face confused.

The visage of Solomon Kramer put one hand on the back of his thick neck, the other waved the question away.

"I don't know what you're talking about. That's crazy talk. Look, I'm not answering any more questions. You've heard me already. Go."

She reached out with digital fingers to touch his face. He seemed to look through her, not acknowledging her approach from the left side. She pushed her hand through the hologram's upper arm. The image of her father rippled, then froze. He disappeared.

Something rebooted, and he was limping through the black door again, a loop from the first time.

"Hello, baby girl," Solomon Kramer said, once more.

It wasn't him. Of course, it wasn't him. It was a defensive barrier programmed to keep her, or her dead brother Jered, or even her gate-damned sister Hannah, out. He must have foreseen the possibility that one of them would circuit-dive deeper into the remnants of Judah's Arkathan brain if things went wrong. *He was just trying to cover his tracks,* she thought, anger flooding through her.

She whirled, her face a mask of fury, pointing at Kitos's avatar at his artificial control panel.

"What the void is going on, here, Niff?" she yelled at him. "Where's the—"

A snarling sound, followed by a pair of gunshots thundered through the smooth ceiling of the control interface room. Automatic weapons fire answered the weapons discharges. The dying calls of Myoshans were no longer distant echoes.

Kitos's ears folded flat, his confident eyes now full of fear, just like in the normal world. He looked to his control display, then to the ceiling. NoName's globular interface strobed in red light.

"Proximity alert. Proximity alert. Prox—" NoName said.

The computer's voice cut out, and Kitos looked at her.

"Pilo—"

The Niff's digital body collapsed in a tumbling cascade of three-dimensional cubes, fading as they scattered across the floor. His control panel disintegrated in a similar manner. She turned to the simulation of Solomon Kramer.

"Poppa?" she said, reaching out.

The ceiling above her reverberated with the crashing sound

of tools hitting the deck. A Myoshan voice was calling out, full of pain. Kitos's cries of pain could also be heard, accompanied by rough laughter.

The image of her father regarded the noises coming from the ceiling of the digital interface room, then looked at her.

"Sounds like it's time to go. Take care, bubelah. We'll talk again, soon," Solomon's image said, the computer-generated eyes not quite making contact with her own.

Then, he vanished with a flash. The white walls faded to the gray with the black stripe, the same default configuration from when she dived in alone.

"Dad? Kitos? NoName?" she said, calling out to the silent ceiling. "What the... what the void just happened? What's going on out there? How do I get out of this thing? Kitos! Kitos, you slime-squirter, answer me!"

She could feel tears welling up. She tried to choke them down, to push them back, to convince herself that they weren't real, just like this little room wasn't real. It didn't matter that this was a digital construct, a hollow maintenance interface between synapses and circuit boards. The tears came anyway.

"No. No! No!!!" she howled, running to the digital wall where her father's image emerged before. Frantic, she ran her fingers over the smooth surface, pleading for him to return. There was no door, no seam. She beat the wall with her fists. Nothing.

She held her hands to her side, screaming and raging, the pain pouring out of her digital voice. Something shook, something broke loose in her, and she stopped screaming. She wept.

Deep sobs wracked her body, and she leaned against the gray wall, her palms and head up against the black stripe.

The stripe pulsed to life, a flat, iridescent ripples appearing on the screen where she touched it.

"Judah?" she said, choking back sobs.

A red strobe pulsed around the room.

"Negative. Selfsame Ident: NoName," the computer's voice said. "Interrogative: Challenge. Ident."

"*My* ident? It's... it's me, you moron," she said, wiping away bitter tears. "Jess... Jessica Kramer."

"Control interface malfunction," NoName said. "Password?"

Jessica lowered her head and took a deep breath.

"For Our Freedom..." she whispered, "And Yours."

"Password accepted," the lobotomized battle computer said. The swirling interface returned, hovering in the middle of the room. "Do you wish to review a menu of commands?"

"Just get me out of this venting box," she said, regaining control over her voice, "and back in the real world."

"Command accepted," the digital voice said. "Brace yourself, Pilot Jessica Kramer."

She closed her eyes in the digital program, opening them again to see only blackness. She was back. She pulled the heavy headset from her brow and sat up in the chair. She wiped away her real sweat and tears, and blinked as she adjusted to the bright lights of the shop. After her vision cleared, she gasped at what she saw.

Kitos's chair and circuit-dive hood next to her were smashed. Bullet and laser impacts scored the walls. Dead and dying Myoshans surrounded her and the ruined test bench. Some were scattered on the open shop floor, along with their weapons and blown-off extremities.

After the imagery hit her, the stink was next. She wrinkled her nose and gagged at the all-too-familiar smell. Kitos's trail of self-defense fluid, thick and pungent, led all the way to the laser-cut and explosion-warped front door.

Vervor lay near, crumpled behind an overturned tool cart.

He held a clawed hand out to her. A horrific wound breached the right side of his little torso.

"Pilot..." he rasped. "They took Kitos. You... must go... Headhunter."

The little Myoshan shop owner passed out, blood weeping from his side.

A mixed swarm of Enforcement Directorate Nines and airborne drones poured through the frame of the building's breached door. Their weapons searched for targets without a spoken word, the only noise coming from their hover fans and jostling gear as they flowed through the building. Emergency lights filled the windows and walls with scattered flashes.

Looks like the Headhunter's gonna have to wait, she thought.

CHAPTER THIRTY-TWO

SIXTH GATE ZONE

BERVA PROXIMA ARENA

Mikralos, nestled up in his observation bubble several stories above them, watched the two Gatekeepers gathered in his conference office on camera. He took smug satisfaction in making his old combat companions wait for him. They were not talking, which was typical, considering their long history. When they began showing signs of impatience, he smiled to himself. It was a minor power play, but necessary. Dismissing his Nine guards, he proceeded through the back hallways of Berva Proxima to join them.

The first Gatekeeper, Dionoles, hovered around the perimeter of the concrete room, his gaze deliberately held by the graphic images on the walls so as to avoid Beliphres.

Upon his entrance, Beliphres gave Mikralos a formal greeting in the Ways of the Old Code. His tone and diction were forced, and Mikralos could tell he was both nervous and irked. *You know you vented things up royally. Playing nice will not help you ooze your way out of this one, old friend,* Mikralos thought.

Around them, scenes from Vervor's Fabrication Works' security cameras played on repeated loops. The video showing Skreeb's and Velsh's fierce and fluid assault played on the most prominent of the holoscreens. It was almost a textbook example of forced entry, threat neutralization, and target retrieval. Despite his embarrassment, Beliphres seemed quite pleased with himself and his hench-beings.

Mikralos put aside his admiration for the martial poetry of the breach and subsequent kidnapping of the Niff. The unwanted attention this generated had to be addressed.

"The extent of your expedition into Master Vervor's shop far exceeded the scope of your permission, brother," Mikralos said. "You assured us, quite profusely, that your debtor, the Niff, was the primary objective, and all other considerations were secondary. You neglected to mention you would turn our preferred mech fabrication shop into a house of slaughter."

Mikralos gestured a claw to the carnage-filled screens around them. Dionoles continued to bobble around the room, muttering to himself.

"Our business associates are nothing if not enthusiastic, Mikralos," Beliphres said, a small smile on his face. "We admit, mistakes *may* have been made, but... these things tend to happen in such an... unpredictable field of work. Besides, your human pilot was left unharmed, as you stipulated. We are led to believe the Myoshan shopkeeper will recover from his wounds, as well. He will have to do some replacement hiring, of course." The gangster Gatekeeper's protective chassis' lights formed the equivalent of a chuckling shrug.

The higher-pitched voice of the third Gatekeeper, Dionoles, joined the other two.

"It is as we spoke to you earlier, Mikralos," Dionoles said, his speaker's voice steeped in indignation. "He does not take our quest seriously, nor its implementation. He proves, once again, his uncouth, baser nature. You were foolish to involve this reckless, unprincipled street thug in the plan. One wonders why Honored Novalos even deigned to allow him—"

A charged plasma cannon emerged from Beliphres's chassis, its muzzle spinning, glowing in its eagerness to fire. Dionoles reeled from the sight of the heavy weapon now pointed at him, but there was nowhere to flee in the enclosed concrete bunker of an office. His carapace settled to the floor, now surrounded by a wispy ghost of a force-field.

"Do not invoke the name of the GateLord to us, you sniveling, craven worm," Beliphres snarled at the cowering Dionoles. "Do not *dare* to presume you are better than us, simply because all you can be trusted to supervise is a house of stacked probabilities and misfortune. This is not your precious, sterile casino with its rigged parlor games, Dionoles, this—"

Beliphres pointed a claw to the monitors showing Vervor's Myoshan shop workers dying under the guns of his operatives.

"This is how work is accomplished in the face of struggle and strife, on the ground level!"Beliphres said, his running lights black and fixed. Dionoles covered his head with tiny appendages inside his bubble, a useless gesture before the might of the directed energy weapon.

"We are not running dual sets of accounting ledgers," Beliphres continued, seething, "or cheating drunkards out their pay, or skimming credits off the books. We leave those things to you, you pusillanimous skulker."

"Instead, we are bringing a nuked-out sector back to life" Beliphres continued, "using whatever means are necessary, all while trying to cover our own tribute payments to Central Data. This, this… *minor* ripple that concerns you oh-so-much was part of a contracted arrangement between ourself and Mikralos, two brothers, born of combat and conquest. What would a... a *fiscal* expert like yourself know of such things?" Dionoles refused to meet the furious Beliphres's gaze.

Mikralos laid a soft metallic claw on Beliphres's weapon, lowering the glowing muzzle with a gentle touch.

"You need not remind Dionoles of his unbecoming conduct during the conquest of this place, brother," Mikralos said. "It has been centuries since that event. He bears the burden of it, still, and his current station is a consequence of that disagreeable time." Beliphres's plasma weapon powered down, but remained deployed outside his carrier chassis.

"However, Beliphres, it is you who have placed us in this precarious position," Mikralos said," and your seeming lack of remorse troubles us. We involved you in this plan in order to enhance your status with Honored Novalos, that you might secure more resources in your rebuilding of the Fifth Gate Zone. When you accepted, we were pleased, because you bring considerable unconventional resources to bear." Mikralos gestured to the video feeds of the shop's crime scene again.

"Thus, when you approached us for permission to retrieve a debtor in our own assigned sector, we agreed. We thought both of us could benefit. We wonder, though, if your underbeings'... excessive action actions may have placed our arrangement in jeopardy."

"Oh, we freely admit, Mikralos," Beliphres said, "our hired lads may have been a bit vigorous in their prosecution of the debtor's apprehension. Honestly, though, one must admit that one Myoshan is about the same as the next, is it not? They are not exactly a scarce breed. Indeed, some portions of Junction-world seem to be overrun with the tiny, pugnacious things."

"Be that as it may—" Dionoles started to say. The muzzle of Beliphres's plasma weapon began to glow again. Dionoles controlled his shaking, and continued, "—Beliphres, you have placed all of us in an unbalanced, unsettling position. The plan was to eliminate the Kramer pilot in the arena, in public, so the humiliation of her family of human upstarts is complete and unquestionable. Your trigger-happy hench-beings almost perforated her in a mech chop-shop, and now the Enforcement Directorate is involved. This attention has placed the entire operation in jeopardy. The expenditures for the medical care for the surviving Myoshans will not be insignificant, nor the repairs of Master Vervor's shop. Someone must be held responsible. There must be an accounting." Dionoles seemed to shrink behind his semi-transparent energy shields even more as his tone became more accusatory.

"Spoken like a true trembler," Beliphres sneered. "The Enforcement Directorate? Is this a jest? We own them! We own them, down to the very chromosomes! They are our foot soldiers, our mindless meat-bots, ready and willing to do our bidding, are they not? If they refuse, we cull the agitators, and print more. Mikralos, you control this sector. Guide the Nine investigators elsewhere, or simply order them to suspend the case. The three of us are not interested in finding the culprits in this caper, after all. We know who did this. We did. We answer only to the GateLords, to the Council of Eight." He waved a tentacled claw in disregard.

"We fool ourselves with the illusion that we control the Nines, brother," Mikralos said. "Yes, we are their masters, but we suspect that even the Eight GateLords do not know the full extent of the... tenacity of our bioprinted soldiers and servants. None dare address it, but our grip on them is unstable, tenuous, at best. We Gatekeepers have given them too much control over the mundane operations of our society in our quest for greater power. None of us dare face the ugly, growing truth. Why, even in our own realm of 'control,' the vexing matter of the Head—"

"Do not say his name!" Beliphres and Dionoles said at the same time.

"*Headhunter,*" Mikralos said, a sly grin on his face. "He is not the phantom of some childhood nightmare, you skittish little cheesebeasts. He is only a rebellious experiment, a Nine gone rogue. Is he enhanced? Yes. Would addressing the problem be monumentally embarrassing for all involved? Again, yes. But, is he still mortal? The answer, battle brothers, is the same. He will be dealt with, much like the Kramer whelp. You two... you two are genuinely amusing. One would think we were about to unleash what is behind the Eighth Gate down on your heads."

"Do not speak of them, either, Mikralos. To do so is to tempt misfortune," Dionoles said. Even Beliphres was uncomfortable with the subject, his running lights pulsing in an uneasy pattern.

"Very well," Mikralos said. "Let us put the matter of Vervor's shop to the side, and move to the business of the daughter of Solomon Kramer. While Masamune Kyuzo is quite proficient in his craft, he is also quite human, and thus, subject to frailty and failure. An alternative plan must be formalized, one which we now wish to propose."

"We now call attention to those unconventional assets we spoke of, earlier, Beliphres," Mikralos said, beaming confidence. "Pray tell, do any of your enthusiastic trigger pullers have access to a heavy sniper rifle?"

CHAPTER THIRTY-THREE

SIXTH GATE ZONE
VERVOR'S FABRICATION WORKS

Jessica Kramer remained still, her arms folded, not making eye contact or presenting a threat as the Enforcement Directorate troops milled about Vervor's shop. The responding units of Nine troopers secured the area and staunched the bleeding of the few Myoshan mech-techs still alive, including Master Vervor.

This whole scene reminds me of my hab-pod, five years ago, she thought.

They were Enforcement Directorate troops, equipped to deal with both criminal response and military defense. Once they assessed that there was no imminent threat, the majority of them left, returning to their readiness outposts scattered throughout the Sixth Gate Zone. Now, it was just a matter of mopping up the multicolored blood and gore.

"Greet. Hostilities ceased. Area secured," one of the uniformed troopers said to her in their truncated version of speech. "Injuries to self? Mobility impaired?"

The Model Nine trooper's gear configuration marked him as

a combat medic. He gestured at her leg cast with a mobile scanner. Jessica shook her head, waving him off.

"I got hurt a few days ago in the arena," she said. "Don't worry about it. Hey, Niner, who's in charge of this clown show, anyway?"

"Selfsame Combat Medic 94887-w," the bioprinted trooper said, holding his hand against his chest to identify himself, "reports to Centurion 33890-v, Sixth Zone Barracks."

"Yeah, great, thanks for the roster listing," she said, pointing at the ground of the shop, "but who's in charge, here, at the scene?"

"Confirmed. Lead Enforcer 77226-a. Direct front," the Nine said, pointing at a Ninety-Nine officer standing by the door to Master Vervor's office.

"You the big boss, here, Lead Enforcer?" Jessica called to the advanced model of synthetic soldier.

"Confirmed. Advance and consult, please," the Ninety-Nine said, waving her over. She limped to him, taking care not to slip on the slime trail left by the Niff, Kitos, when they took him. Whoever 'they' were.

"Ident," the Lead Enforcer said.

"Jessica Kramer. Mech pilot," she answered.

"Greet," 77226-a said.

"Yeah, great, greet, sure," she said. "Hey, do you have any clues of who did this? I was stuck circuit-diving in that maintenance computer when it happened, so I didn't get to see who took Kitos."

"Ident question, 'Kitos?'" the Lead Enforcer asked. "Registered staff here at establishment?"

"Yeah, 'Kitos,'" she said, trying to keep her anger and sarcasm in check. "You know, little blue Niff, about shoulder height on me, four arms, always looking scared and shaky?

That's his slime trail, right there." She pointed to the thick ribbon of defensive fluid.

The previous medic she talked to passed by her and the officer, pushing a wounded Myoshan tech in a hovering med-unit capsule.

"Where are they going?" she asked.

"Honored Mikralos is sponsor of this establishment," the Ninety-Nine officer said. "Medical care to be provided at his order."

"Wow, that's mighty kind of him, huh, Niner?" she said, cocking her head to the side. "If they didn't serve a purpose for the blob, I'm sure they'd be out on the street, huh? So, back to Kitos. Do you have the vid recordings of the attackers, or of them taking him away?"

"Selfsame cannot confirm or deny existence of vid records," 77226-A said in a terse manner. "Ident and location of subject Kitos to be determined later, if at all, depending on priority. Your testimony required at Sixth Zone Barracks for complete report."

Jessica liked that they didn't talk in choppy sentence fragments like normal Nines, but Ninety-Nines could be pretty damn arrogant, especially if you asked them uncomfortable questions. This one didn't seem to differ from that pattern.

"So, what, you're not going to go out and look for him?" she said, astonishment in her voice. "They couldn't have gotten far with him. Void, he's just vapor, as far as you're concerned?"

An Enforcer trooper emerged from the larger door of Master Vervor's office, his hands full of stacks of data chips. They went into a transparent bag held by the Ninety-Nine officer.

"Upload complete?" 77226-A asked his subordinate.

"Confirmed," the trooper responded. "Evidence to Central Data archives."

"Hey, what the void's that? Is that footage from Vervor's security system?" Jessica said, protesting.

"Not your concern, Pilot Kramer," the Lead Enforcer said. "You will report to Sixth Zone Barracks, priority utmost. You will ride back with selfsame."

"I'm not going down there, meat-bot, I've got to find that Niff," Jessica said, pulling away from the Lead Enforcer. "This is the same dung as when my parents died. Take a couple pictures, file some reports, then ignore it. Right? This won't be investigated. It'll just get filed away, and you'll just sit and wait for the next call, like a good little bio-drone."

"Pilot Kramer," the Lead Enforcer said, his short tone growing more severe. "Junctionworld is singular crime scene. Every sector is overrun, but society continues cyclical grind. Being-on-being criminal activity is least of worries for selfsame. Order. Rebellion. Invasions. Enforcement Direct serves purpose of keeping blood from flooding ground level. One stolen Niff? Non-priority. Few resources for other purposes, besides defense of Overbeings. Ident Kitos is not even blip on Enforcement Directorate's sensors."

"Typical burdenbeast dung, Enforcer," she said, sneering. "Unless it threatens your precious Gatekeepers, or gets in the way of them making money, you don't give a good gate damn about the rest of us, do you? You're just their errand boy, making sure the wheels of the machine keep turning. How's that for a purpose in life?"

"Pilot Kramer, conversation is terminated. Report to Sixth Zone Enforcement Directorate Barracks for full debrief," the Lead Enforcer said, brushing her aside.

"You Enforcement dummies are a joke, you know that?" Jessica said, refusing to be ignored. "The *Headhunter*, too. All those resources at your disposal, Nines, drones, cameras out the wazoo, guns, hardware, all that, and for what? *Nothing*, that's what. You both claim control over Vervor's little mech shop, here, but *neither* of you can stop someone from blowing the place to void and walking right out the door with a Niff, even when he leaves a trail for you to follow. Some crime lord he turned out to be, and you're not much better."

Several Nines in earshot of their conversations stopped their duties, stiffening when she said the rebel Centurion's name.

The Ninety-Nine officer's normally-smooth face hardened in expression, and she found herself looking at the glowing muzzle lens of a heavy laser pistol.

"Pilot Kramer, disarm," the Lead Enforcer said. "Place your firearm on ground and step back. Move to selfsame's transport, priority utmost."

———

The Ninety-Nine officer's anti-grav command car glided across the rooftops and salvage yards of the Sixth Gate Zone. They were heading away from Berva Proxima, away from Vervor's shop, towards a run-down neighborhood in the wedge-shaped segment of Junctionworld. The Sixth Gate dominated the landscape, its triangular shape soaring a mile into the flickering gray skies. Off to the left, across from the Lead Centurion in the driver's seat, she could see construction bots and their attendant crews were rebuilding the Fifth Gate's nuclear impact zone. Huge, shallow craters of Shine, the weird, impenetrable material that formed Junctionworld's foundation, were still bare. The Ninety-Nine flew the vehicle with one hand. He crossed the other hand across his body, keeping her under the focus of the charged laser pistol.

"This isn't the way to the barracks, is it?" she said.

"Negative," the Lead Enforcer said. "Selfsame admits, normal Enforcement process will not find subject ident Kitos.

Selfsame knows who can. Pilot Kramer mentioned him earlier."

"Who? The Head—" she started to say.

The Ninety-Nine cut her off with a look.

"Stifle. Do not say his name. Unworthy," the officer said.

They continued in silence. Lead Enforcer 77226-A brought the grav car in low on an approach for landing. They passed dilapidated apartment towers and soared over shanty villages composed of scrap. *Devastation and squalor, even by Junction-world standards, as far as the eye could see. Am I gonna end up as a corpse on a void conveyor?* Jessica thought.

"Where the are we, Lead Enforcer?" she said, a bit of reluctant dread in her voice.

"Sebyus. Refugee camp. Industrial sector," the Ninety-Nine said. "Also... residence."

"Residence? Who the void lives... *oh*," she said, as it dawned on her.

"Affirm. '*Oh*,'" said the Ninety-Nine officer, smirking as he looked at her. Jessica raised her eyebrows, surprised, and turned away to look out of her own window. *A sarcastic Niner? I didn't know they could even do that,* she thought.

The grav command car landed in front of an Enforcement Directorate checkpoint. A black sedan waited there among the armored vehicles and mechs. Beyond it, the street looked like a ruined battlefield left to rot. The Lead Enforcer opened Jessica's door for her, handed back her revolver, then the shells, and directed her towards the checkpoint.

As she walked away, the Ninety-Nine officer called for her to stop. He fetched a data-chip from the evidence bag and pressed it into her hand. Nodding to her, he left.

She recognized the Ninety-Nine with the data tablet in his hand, waiting beside the hovering black sedan. It was Nolo, the Headhunter's right-hand Nine.

CHAPTER THIRTY-FOUR

SIXTH GATE ZONE
THE HEADHUNTER'S LAIR

For once in her life, Jessica Kramer regretted mouthing off to the authorities. More specifically, she wished she had not provoked the Lead Enforcer who deposited her here, deep in the heart of the Headhunter's territory.

Overwhelmed by her entrance into the crime lord's headquarters, she suddenly remembered the vid-chip in her hand. She handed the small black square to Nolo, who looked questioningly at it, then at her.

Before she could explain, a giant red cyborg on his skull-covered throne beckoned her closer.

"Well, Pilot Kramer, nice to see you," the Headhunter said. "This is unexpected. Please, come in, come in."

Holding her nose, Jessica stepped into the large room. The hallway leading to this place, with its rows of craniums and lamps, was grotesque enough. It did not prepare her, though, for the scale of mounted slaughter awaiting her in this main room.

This was a temple dedicated to decapitation. The walls

were festooned with heads from every race of sentient in Junctionworld, and then some. There was the lingering smell of rotting flesh in the air, but she seemed to be the only one bothered by it.

"So, what brings you to my humble abode, pilot?" the Headhunter asked.

He caught her eye and the pinched look of disgust on her face.

"Oh, the heads..." he said, amused and mildly embarrassed at the same time. "Yeah... I like to think of myself as an artist, pilot, surrounded by my multitudes of... still-life portraits. Every one of them represents a special moment, captured in time."

The Headhunter rose from his combination of charging station and command chair. Cables and conduits snapped and hissed as they disconnected from him. Jessica eyes, already wide, went wider as she recognized the two spheres his main set of hands rested on. They were protective spheres for Gatekeepers. The settled contents of their occupants clotted the bottoms of the pink armored bubbles.

Ignoring their conversation, the Headhunter's adjutant, Nolo, clicked Jessica's vid-chip into his tablet. After a quick scan, he became agitated.

Nolo tried to approach the cyborg, to give him the news about Vervor's shop, but the Headhunter waved his attendant to wait just a moment longer. Nolo snorted, his face rigid and expressionless.

Holy void, he doesn't know yet, she thought.

"Hey, Mister Headhunter, sir, I know this isn't a great way to learn the news, but—"

"Ah, ah, I'm sure it's very important," the Headhunter said, holding up a smaller weapon arm in mock protest. "It's *always* very important. First, though, let me address this minor bit of business. We have an unsettled transaction, you and I. I think you might like it."

Panels pulled back, micromotors whirred, and a small set of manipulators deployed from one of his large weapon arms, a small item clasped in them.

Jessica took the proffered token, and looked up to the Headhunter.

"A credit stick?" she said, confused. "What the void is this for? Listen—"

"*Manners*, Pilot," the red cyborg said, smiling. "Something's bothering you, I can tell, otherwise you wouldn't be here. I've been looking forward to this, though. You and Nolo need to let me have my moment, here. Such sour faces, the two of you, I swear." His subsets of weapon arms made mocking, playful movements.

"Did you know the odds they were giving against you in that last match? Take a guess," the cyborg said, his black eyes glittering.

Was he giddy? He was giddy. She thought, sighing. *Might as well indulge him.*

"I... I don't check the odds, Headhunter," Jessica said. "Gambling was my brother's thing, not mine, and look where it got him. Besides, finding out how things are for or against you, before a fight, is bad luck. Every gladiator knows that. My luck's bad enough without borrowing more."

"Fair enough, fair enough, Pilot," he said. "Just know, they were stacked against you. I love how you and the Wardancer tangled, there, at the end. A nice dual-disable result. You don't see that often."

"Yeah, she got a new pair of legs out of the deal, I heard," Jessica said, thinking of how the Wardancer Kierra looked in the post-match footage. "I got to keep mine. She was tough, though, and it made for some big coverage for the upcoming final fight. So, how much did you win?"

"I don't know if you remember," the Headhunter said, "but I had Nolo put a half-million on you, and you paid off, big time. That credit stick, there, is my way of saying 'thank you.' two hundred large."

Jessica looked down, trying to fathom the staggering windfall of credits. Boots. Parts. Ammo. Rent. Premium booze. Two hundred thousand credits could go a long way. She shook her head, and handed it back.

"Don't want it," she said. "I know the game, here, Headhunter. I take your credits, and you think you own a piece of me. Dangle a big enough payout in front of me, and you think I'll take a dive for you in the future, or become your hitgirl in the arena. It doesn't work that way, at least not with me."

The cyborg clapped, delighted. The boom echoed through the room.

"There's that fire I like. What'd I tell you, Nolo?" the Headhunter said, turning to his agitated adjutant. "I told you she'd reject it, like it was nothing. I don't think it's a negotiating tactic, either. I tell you, you're starting to grow on me, young Kramer."

Jessica shrugged, letting her tight grasp on her nose loosen. She looked up at the menacing titan.

"Look, I'm grateful for the offer, Headhunter," she said, "but I need something more than credits. Like I was trying to say earlier, I need your help."

Nolo looked to the Headhunter, gave an urgent hand signal to the crime lord, who relented and let him approach. He walked past Jessica to the massive cyborg. Hushed tones in Niner-speak were exchanged, and the data-chip handed to the red crime lord for download.

Kramer could see the cyborg's eyes narrow as he scanned

the memory device internally. His horrific claws flexed with rage, and he dug deep furrows in the steel plating by his feet.

"That gate-damned... bile-sucking... *when, damn it?*" The crimson cyborg demanded, turning to her, his expression death incarnate. "How did this happen, especially on *my turf*, in *my gate-damned sector?*" She gulped.

"Just now," Jessica said, quiet and cautious in the face of such power. "Less than an hour ago. Whoever it was, they came and took the Niff in the middle of a circuit dive. They killed a lot of Vervor's crew, and put a hole in his side, too."

A holographic projector glowed in the Headhunter's main carapace, illuminating the far wall of skulls. The view was from one of Vervor's security cameras. One the replayed video, a Shasarr and Skevvian tore through Vervor's shop door, and his crew, with equal ease. The image froze on a still shot of the two thugs dragging Kitos out of the door, the two beings framed perfectly for identification.

"Skreeb and that bone-squid friend of his," the Headhunter snarled. "They work for Beliphres."

"I... I didn't get a look at them," she said. "Beliphres is the Gatekeeper who Kitos owed money to, though, right?"

The seething titan nodded in the affirmative. She knew it was foolish to provoke the angered goliath, but she did it, anyway.

"Well, I think it's safe to say," Jessica said, "This Beliphres guy doesn't really think that line between the Fifth and Sixth Gate Zones really exists, anymore. If he does, his boys stepped right over it. He and the rest of the Gatekeepers must not take your claim of 'running things on the ground level' too seriously."

The Headhunter's claws and built-in weaponry lashed and writhed as he paced back and forth, his seething anger slipping from his control as he was reminded of his own words. He kicked a pile of unmounted skulls, scattering the heads like marbles.

She saw her words were having an effect, but she wanted to pee, to run, and to hide, all at the same time. The sight of the infuriated assault cyborg was more than just intimidating. *I don't think I could take him on, even if I was in an Unlimited rig,* she thought.

The Headhunter stopped his furious pacing, halting in mid-stride, and turned to her, his bristling cybernetic armor in full deployment. His sensors scanned her. There was a psychotic, detached look on his face. From blazing tantrum to cold fury, in an instant. It reminded her of her father's sudden swings, and she shivered.

"I see your leg's about healed from that wound," the Head-hunter said. "You're also packing a 20-mil Mattis. Good. Go with Nolo and gear up. If you want your Niff back, we may have something for you in the armory. Nolo, have the autodoc finish up with that leg of hers, and prep the boys."

"Wait, what are we talking about, here?" Jessica said.

"You want your Niff back, don't you?" the Headhunter said, his voice full of manic menace.

"Yeah, but—" *This was madness,* she thought.

"Load up, then," the cyborg said. "Talking takes time, and right now, it's in short supply."

CHAPTER THIRTY-FIVE

FIFTH GATE ZONE

It took some doing, but Jessica Kramer blended in well with the Recyke Niner team's operations, despite not being born from a bioprinter. It was a good attack pattern, smoothed by repetition, and her initial apprehension had now faded. The Headhunter led off each assault, creating an opening for them. She and the squad of veteran Nines then cleared out the targets, room by room, floor by floor.

Beliphres, the Gatekeeper who was the Headhunter's rival in this sector, would be sending at least seventeen dead foot soldiers into the void conveyors tonight. Minus their heads, of course. The Headhunter was keeping those for himself.

Jessica and her new 'little friend' had helped with that body count. She looked down at the black, brutish weapon. It chambered the same round as her personal revolver, 20mm Mattis, but it was an autoloader, complete with a drum-fed magazine. It had some thump to it when fired, but if three different gangsters could still talk, they'd say it hurt more on the receiving end.

Now, they were roaring towards the fifth target in their

series of raids. Whatever that autodoc pumped into her at the Headhunter's place, it was still working, and working well. Her leg itched from the removal of the cast, but the combat drugs had her amped. She felt alert, focused, and full of... was it bloodlust? She could end up making a habit of this. *No, don't make a habit of this, idiot,* she had to tell herself. Druggies didn't last long in the cockpit. She didn't want to end up like a freak like Melino, with tubes running in and out of her neck.

Besides, we're here to get Kitos back, she thought. *Well, I am, at least. The Headhunter's little revenge mission was secondary. Wasn't it?* Her tactical success, so far, on this little foray impressed even her. Maybe it was the cocktail they shot her up with. Maybe it was all the hours of physical training her dad put her and her siblings through. Either way, she was enjoying this.

The raids confirmed Jessica's estimate of the Headhunter's combat abilities, in spades. The renegade cyborg was gate-damned unstoppable, a force of nature. He tore through walls, armor, and flesh like none of it was there. Unfortunately, that took power, and his internal power reserves seemed to be getting low. *No internal reactor, I guess,* Jessica thought.

His actions and responses grew sluggish as the raids against his Gatekeeper rival's assets wore on. At the last safe-house they hit, some schlub punched a rocket-propelled grenade into the side of the Headhunter's rib cage. The shaped charge exploded against the cyborg's red armor, brutalizing Jessica's own ears. Recovering, the Headhunter responded by slicing the gangster in half from across the room, along with the steel stairs he was standing on, and the wall behind him. Nevertheless, it was a sign: for all his lethality, the huge, enhanced Nine still had a limit. When the assault was over and it was time to load the Headhunter back into the large armored vehicle, it took some time for the Recyke Niners to get him up the ramp and secured.

"Power depletion near crit, Boss," Nolo said, his ever-present tablet giving him readouts on the experimental cyborg's status. "Maintain pos in transport for next target. Charge up and replen. Priority utmost."

The Headhunter regarded Nolo, a whimsical look on his face. He caught Jessica studying him, and smiled.

"You know, I don't know if I've ever told this to anybeing before," the Headhunter said, "but you have very, very pretty eyes. And I'm not saying that because I collect skulls, either. Doesn't she have pretty eyes, Nolo?"

Nolo nodded, humoring him, trying to continue the scans of the heavy assault cyborg.

"Pilot," he said with a dreamy tone in his voice, "you wanna know the reason we're knocking the dung outta Beli... Beliphres's territory without any Enforcement inner... innerfer... without any meddling?"

Jessica's brow wrinkled in confusion. It was like the big red guy was drunk.

"Boss, secure info," Nolo said, scolding. "Pilot has no need to know. Selfsame cogs you're low on power. Query: judgment possibly impaired?"

"No, no, it's okay, Nolo, she's proven herself," the Headhunter said, his speech becoming more and more effected. "She's a go-getter. She's got fire, this one. Anyways, fire-eyes, the Enforcers leave me alone because I used to be one of 'em. 'Experimental-Model-One-Oh-Nine-Special-Command-Proto-type-Eight-Dash-Six.' That's me. Still got a lotta contacts an' what-not with the ol' Rockribs at the barracks. Well, void, at most of the barracks, now that I think about it. I practically run the Sixth Zo—"

"Boss, suggest stifle," Nolo said. "Initiating safe mode. Priority utmost."

The Ninety-Nine stabbed something on his tablet, and the majority of the Headhunter's body powered down, limp. The cyborg's normal-sized head on his monstrous chassis continued to talk.

"He fusses after me, pilot," the Headhunter said, grinning. "He's like my own, personal mother egg-layer."

He rested in his ready-rack like a giant scarecrow, a pair of Niner technicians and Nolo tweaking and adjusting him. She looked closer at his torso. *That RPG only left a smudge,* she thought.

One of the grizzled Nine troopers at rear of the transport, near the main door, clasped a hand over his comm headset, then looked to the rest of his comrades. He held up a finger, making eye contact with each of them. The rest of the team held up a single digit in acknowledgment. Jessica mimicked the hand signal. They were one minute out from the target.

Weapon muzzles charged, glowing in the dim light of the transport. Bolts slammed forward, chambering rounds, and safeties were flicked off. Jessica press-checked her new little stomper, making sure she had one round ready to go in the chamber. She rocked on the ammo drum, thumped her spare drums to make sure they were topped off, and looked through the red dot sight mounted to the top of the compact weapon. *Still working. Good.*

The stimulants took hold, once again, and she felt her heartbeat thicken and hammer through her chest, her breathing slow and loud in her ears. There must be some adrenaline trigger to the stuff the autodocs shot her up with. The thick, stubby cartridges in her spare ammo drums shifted. The noise sounded like a garbage can full of bricks to her chemically-enhanced ears. She looked around at the weathered, expressionless Nines around her. All of the Recykes stared at their team leader by the hatch. The transport's engines whined, slowed, and everybeing in the compartment swayed as it took one last sharp turn.

"Good hunting, fire-girl. Go get 'em, go-getter," the Headhunter said, his words slurred from his diminished power levels. His upper claw arms hung loose and his organic head bobbed. His solid black eyes narrowed to exhausted slits, then closed. The transport lurched to a halt, incoming fire jack-hammering off the hull, and the rear hatch slammed down. She was out of her jumpseat and squatting in line with the Nines, all of them stacked up like cartridges waiting to be shot out of a gun. Dad's flask got its two thumps, and she brought her new weapon up to the low ready position.

"Execute," the lead Nine said.

Jessica smelled burning meat as she emerged from the rear of the armored transport, but she blocked the repugnant odor. The laser turrets on the transport vehicle's roof were still hissing, etching the front of the target building with suppressive beams and flame. The sniper who pinged rounds off the roof as they rolled up must be the source of the charred aroma.

One of the Nines lay wounded just to the side of the ramp, his leg torn away by something big and high-powered. Jessica avoided eye contact with the fallen trooper, her attention focused on keeping up with the entry stack.

The target building was a multistory warehouse with offices in front. The long group of Recyke Nine soldiers fed into the front door in rapid sequence, like a hungry snake entering an octorat burrow. Shouts and gunshots sounded from the interior of the building, answered by the deep, swooping thunder of a plasma cannon and a resultant explosion. The building shook, and flaming fascia and siding fell on the sidewalk around her.

A screaming purple-skinned humanoid, the same type as Zerren Beff, rounded the corner of the building. He held a crude shotgun in his hands, shooting and yelling as he charged towards the open hatch of the transport. She saw he was too close for the lasers to have a chance at him.

Jessica pivoted, swung her weapon sight's red dot on to the gangster's chest, and slammed two heavy 20mm slugs into him in quick succession. He folded in a bloody purple heap, the back and side of his torso blown out, and she rejoined the entry formation. *Damn, I love this gun,* she thought, a death's-head grin on her face.

She was the last up the short stairs and into the main door. Offices up front, stairs to the side, and a deep warehouse area filled with rows and rows of boxes and containers farther back. Two bodies, one Myoshan, the other unrecognizable, lay in the gore-soaked and burning lobby. Jessica's senses were almost overloaded, the drugs forcing her to soak in even the most minute of details as she searched for threats and targets. She squeezed her eyes shut, told herself to block out the flood of stimuli, and opened them again, ready to focus and fight. The Niff might be here. *Focus.*

The lead-off elements of the Niner assault force peeled away in pairs, clearing rooms and holding stairways as the main column passed them down the central hallway. Sporadic bursts of automatic fire signaled the end of individual members of Beliphres's crew. The Nine in front of her, "Dodger," as his fellow Recykes called him, held up a fist for her to halt, repeating a hand signal from farther up the stack.

Something big and mechanical moved in the open warehouse area up ahead. Something Headhunter-sized. The sound of a high-pitched motor spinning up filled her ears. She knew that sound. She pulled on Dodger's gear harness, keeping him from proceeding past the blind corner into the warehouse with the rest of the team.

The four Nines ahead of them stormed the open room. The lead Nine turned to face the large shadow, just out of her sight, and became an instant smear of blood and meat. The second Nine had just enough time to fire a burst of fire from his heavy support weapon, then he, too, was cut to pieces by the whine and roar of the rotary cannon.

Whatever the shadow was, it was big, and it packed some serious heat. The two surviving Nines from the entry team dove into the rows of boxes and storage drums, trying to hammer rounds into the unseen beast. Heavy footsteps fell, and hundreds of rounds ripped into the pallets and containers sheltering them.

Dodger turned to her, pulled a satchel charge about the size of a load of bread off his thigh armor, and pointed through the wall.

"Suppress," the weathered Nine said. "Selfsame activate demo charge. Stand by."

"Suppress? Suppress what?" she yelled back at him as the cannon continued to whine and roar. "I don't have a shot on that thing, whatever it is!"

"Suppress. Through cover." Dodger said. "Engage. Priority Utmost."

The Nine pressed a switch, and an orange light started blinking in rapid sequence on the demolition charge he held. She turned, bladed at an angle of forty-five degrees, and dumped the contents of her carbine's ammo drum through the wall. The solid thud-thud-thud of the 20mm weapon echoed through the building.

The fire shifted from the pinned-down Nines in the cargo racks back to her and Dodger. A stream of bullets chewed off the corner of the wall ahead of them, and a trail of punctures tore back towards her through the side of the passageway.

Dodger dove under the exploding wall's fragments, entering the open kill zone. Jessica fell back on her butt, rolling and kicking to escape the oncoming stream of fire. The satchel charge flew from Dodger's hand, and he scrambled into the shattered containers to join his surviving teammates.

Whoever was in control of the unseen cannon tried to shift fire to the leaping Nine trooper, but the deafening *krumpf* of the demolition charge cut the effort short. Sections of wall buckled from the exchanged gunfire and explosion, and the corner of the warehouse and attached offices fell in. A large segment of rubble collapsed on top of her. Pain and weight blinded her, dust choked her, and she felt her carbine roll tumbling away.

The smoke and swirling chaos took a moment to clear, and Jessica tried to wriggle free from the dense concrete foam on top of her. No good. She was pinned, her arm trapped under the rubble. The carbine was just out of reach on the other side of the heavy block. She pulled her pistol from its chest holster, keeping her eyes alert for any movement. The chunk of concrete cut deep into her left arm, and her hand felt thick and bloated. She tried moving her fingers, and sharp pain came back to her, piercing the soothing filter of the drugs. *Probably broken, if I can feel it through the fun-sauce. Gate damn it.*

Through the rubble, shattered shapes flowed together, becoming recognizable equipment. A foot, a manipulator claw, a logo on a toppled engine housing. It was a converted cargo lifter, much smaller than NoName. It was meant for interior warehouse use, but someone had welded and bolted armor to its frame, and mounted a sinister gatling weapon. It wouldn't have lasted a minute in the arena, even in Light Exo Beginner. Here, in the warehouse, though, it had made short work of a team of battle-hardened Nines, and nearly punched her ticket, too.

Dodger's explosive blew out the main hull of the cargo walker, painting the inside of the open control cab with what looked like Skevvian tentacles, innards, and other bits.

Her ears still rang from the explosion, but she heard a voice crying from the back of the warehouse. It wasn't Human or Nine. She cocked her revolver's hammer back.

"Velsh! What was the void was that? Velshie!" the strange voice called. "I'm loaded up, let's move. Screw the boss, and screw the Niff! Get out of that thing, and let's go!"

A figure ran through the twisted racks and broken supply containers to the rear of the improvised combat walker. He was a tall, reptilian being, a member of the Shasarr race, but he bore extensive cybernetic work. Both eyes, at least one arm, and a few other metal parts and pieces she could see. It was the same freak from the Headhunter's video. *That meant Kitos was near,* she thought

Jessica's hand throbbed under the concrete, distracting her efforts as she tried to draw a bead on him. The revolver shook in her good hand, the front sight bobbling left and right. The combat drug's effects must be fading. She let the heavy revolver rest as pain washed over her.

His name came back to her memory. *Skreeb.* Skreeb clambered up the back of the wrecked walker, peering into the blood-soaked cab. He pulled back in disgust, hissing.

"Aw, Velshie, no," he said, surveying the remains of his companion. *That must have been the other venter who took Kitos. Good. You've got this coming,* she thought, bringing her handgun back up.

Jessica concentrated on her front sight, trying her best to be smooth, to let the revolver's trigger pull surprise her, like Prath, damn him, taught her. The round went wide, striking the cockpit's frame rail, but a piece of ricochet caught the Shasarr. He wheeled and clutched his side, laying down a burst of fire in her general direction from an automatic pistol.

Dodger emerged from the shredded boxes and crates, his autoweapon's muzzle spraying slugs. The hail of projectiles forced the cyborg back, and the Shasarr ducked behind a far row of metal cans. The sound of leaping claw-steps echoed after the gunfire faded.

They were all too shot up and shrapnel-peppered to pursue him. An engine started in the alley behind the warehouse. Jet exhaust roared, and an aircar streaked past a shattered window. With a flash, it was gone and out of view.

Another four-being crew of Nines flowed past them, weapons pointed in different directions, clearing out the remaining rows of industrial shelving. A whistle sounded from the back, and Dodger and his battered team mates emerged from cover. The warehouse section was secure.

Shrill, inhuman screams and a muffled gunshot sounded upstairs. Quiet settled over the shattered structure. Hushed tones crackled over a radio from somewhere behind her, and an answer crackled back.

Dodger slumped over in the boxes, holding one hand over his ear's comm device, the other signaling to her the raid was over.

"Kramer. Target secured," the Niner said, his tight, scarred face pulled into something resembling a smile. "Casualty assist. Prep extract."

The bastard avoided a stream of gatling fire, she thought, *lit off a demo charge at danger-close range, and didn't have a gate-damn scratch on him. No wonder they called him Dodger. And where the void did a Niner get a gold tooth?*

"Come here and extract this damn piece of building off me, first, Rockrib," she said, grinning back at him.

Dodger and another Nine rolled the dense slab of concrete foam off her. It was both a relief and curse. The blood flowed down her arm, and she hoped that hand was not going to be a factor in the next match. A Ninety-Nine medic spritzed her hand, numbing and immobilizing it, and slap-rolled a drug-laced clotting patch on her arm. *Ow.*

With one hand ineffective, she wasn't much good to the casualty evacuation effort. She pulled her carbine out from the rubble. A deep scratch was now etched into the buttstock's plastic, and the sheet metal ammo drum was crushed and dented. She slung it behind her, and watched Nolo and the medics zip their fallen comrades, or what was left of them, into body bags.

Jessica lent a shoulder to one of the limping, wounded Nines, helping him back to the transport. There, the Head-hunter sat, still dormant. She regarded him for a moment, tried to flex her hand again to no avail, then turned to go back inside. She wanted to see upstairs, to see if that last scream had been from the Niff technician, Kitos.

Despite her protests, the Nines wouldn't let her back in the building. Like the previous targets, they were setting demolition charges. Unable to pass, she felt anger rising up in her, the drug aggressive effects surging once more to the forefront.

A chirping squawk came inside the lobby. At the top of the short stairs, a burned and mutilated Niff appeared, supported by two Nines. His swollen golden eyes locked with hers in recognition. It was Kitos. She tamped down the rage, her hands curling in a spasm as a shiver ran through her. *Gate damn, this stuff was tricky.*

The escaped Shasarr and his dead Skevvian friend had worked Kitos over, and hard. Welts and bruises appeared through rips in his blue fur, and fingers were missing from one of his mangled left hands.

"I-I am glad to... see you, Pilot. Grateful... grateful," he said with a rasp. Jessica gave him a grim nod.

"I'm... happy to see you, too, Kitos," she said, the words seeming the wrong fit for her mouth. "Now, go with the Nines, and wait for me in the transport. I'll be there in a minute."

"I-I owe you my life," the wounded Niff said. "Beliphres...

he wanted credits... wanted info on you... tortured me. Wouldn't talk. I-I owe life-debt, pilot."

"Easy, Niff, just relax, and get on the transport," she said. "There wasn't any other choice. I had to come get you."

She didn't say why, of course. The timing wasn't right, and she didn't want to upset the blue being; without him, she wouldn't get the answers she needed from the Judah module.

They loaded the dead and wounded into the transport. One last Niner trooper, the squad leader who first led the team out of the hatch, emerged from the building. He jumped in, a lumpy bag of severed heads over one shoulder. Twelve from this building alone, bringing the day's total to twenty-nine. *Not a bad haul, and a few of those are mine,* she thought with a hard grin.

The armored transport's grav pods glowed, bringing it to a hover, then it boosted away. A series of subsonic thumps rolled through the hull beneath them, marking the distant end of the target building. Collapsing, it joined the four other Beliphres properties in a bath of flame and smoke.

Scattered across the bleak and scorched Fifth Gate Zone, columns of black smoke spiraled into the gray skies of Junctionworld.

The signal was sent. The Headhunter's War had begun.

CHAPTER THIRTY-SIX_

SIXTH GATE ZONE
THE HEADHUNTER'S LAIR

Jessica's dreams on the way back to the Headhunter's lair were troubled. In one, she was being carved to pieces by a giant combination of the Headhunter and Masamune Kyuzo, her flesh sliced bit by bit with a blazing plasma sword. Next, she was a bullet, flying through purple flesh and blood. The one that stuck out most in her memory was of her father, her brother, and Prath, all taking turns screaming at her.

Solomon and Jered Kramer were both horrid, re-animated corpses trying to push her off a cliff that loomed behind her. The bullet wound in her father's head gaped at her, the red light of Judah's indicator light flaring from the hole in his skull, and he kept saying, "bubelah," over and over again.

Jered's body was charred and smashed, but he still continued to pour liquor through his mouth and out the bottom of his rib cage. Prath turned away from her, letting them do this to her, his disapproval billowing from his lips like smoke.

The three of them combined in a chaotic smear, and suddenly she was falling...

Jessica woke with a start, screaming, her arms up in front of her. Panicked, she looked around her in wide-eyed alarm. She was still strapped into the armored transport's jump seat. The Headhunter looked at her with black eyes, a smile on his face.

"Nasty dreams when that stuff finally filters out of your system," the red cyborg said. "Ask me how I know." A shiver ran through his weapon arms.

"It's not really tuned for you guys," the Headhunter continued, "but we Model Nines, for the most part, have the same basic biocode as humans. We started, somewhere out there, as replacements for you, you know. So, the autodoc put it in you to help with the leg wound. It's great for healing, and getting you through a fight. I always hated the come-down after, though."

The two of them were alone in the transport. The gear was unloaded, but the gore from the dead and wounded was still there in puddles and bits of meat. The sack of heads sat at the base of the loading ramp, a small pool of blood congealing around the slumped base.

"You did well, today," the Headhunter said, smiling. "You really shined, though, on that last target. Dodger and Coldeye both told me, you helped knock out that walker. I saw the gun-cam footage. You even protected Nolo and me from that purple punk gunning for the transport. Good stuff. Do you want to keep that last guy's head?" His claws flexed when he asked the last question.

"Thanks, that's the most tempting offer I've had all day," Jessica said. "But... no. Which... which one is Coldeye?"

"The squad leader. First guy out of the hatch," the Headhunter said. "He and I go way back."

A look of concern crossed his face.

"You bagged four heads today," he said. "How does that fit with you? Are you okay with that?"

Jessica nodded. She was woozy from the drugs, and her head ached in dull, throbbing pulses as the performance and healing enhancer left her system.

"I remember, now," she said, pressing the side of her temple. "Gates, that combat drug makes things a nasty blur. No... I don't think taking out a few venters is going to be a problem."

"That might be a problem, all in itself," the Headhunter said.

"Nah. If you're worried about some crisis of conscious, I had to do some shady stuff in back-alley matches to afford NoName. Life's cheap in Junctionworld, you know, and I've been around this stuff all my life. Doing it, up close, in person... it's different, but it's also kinda the same. Does that make any sense?"

"I'm twisted, like you, so... absolutely," he said, a sarcastic grin on his face. She smiled back, pecking at the scratch on the borrowed carbine's buttstock.

"So, now what?"

"So, now," the Headhunter said, "you take your damaged Niff, and you take your damaged mech, and your damaged self, and you get back to Vervor's shot-up shop. Somehow, you mix all that stuff together, and you outfight some hitman the Gate-keepers have brought in to kill you. Then, you wait patiently for the next crisis to explode all around you."

"Sounds simple, enough," Jessica said. "Maybe I'll have time for a beer or two. Or seven." She let out a small laugh.

"There's that fire. Ha!" the giant cyborg said, smiling back at her.

"I owe you for helping me get Kitos back," she said. "I don't really know how to repay you."

"Actually, Kramer, I owe you," the Headhunter said, a small hint of embarrassment and regret on his face. "Vervor's shop shouldn't have happened. I shouldn't have lost it, in front of you, either. So, to make it up to you, I'm fixing your Niff. They did a nasty bit of work on him, but he'll be fine. We'll hook him up with a new hand, and even put a new datalink into his cortex. He'll be able to talk to his test equipment directly, now."

He pointed at the weapon still strapped across her chest.

"You like the LaRue? The 787? Bad little hammer, isn't it?" the red cyborg said. "You can keep that one, if you like, or I can have Nolo get you a fresh one from the armory. We got a crate of them in trade for a job, some time back."

"No, I like this one, scratched buttstock and all," she said. "It gives it some character. Thanks, though."

"How's the hand?"

"I thought it was broken," she answered. "It must just be sprained. I can move it, but it's stiff as void."

She looked at him with a touch of alarm in her eyes.

"I don't want a replacement, if that's what you mean," Jessica said.

"C'mon, 'better living through cybernetics,' Kramer," he said, laughing. "Look how great it turned out for me."

"Yeah, that's okay, Headhunter," she said, a wry grin on her face. "I prefer to pilot mechs, not be one."

"Suit yourself," the cyborg said, lifting his lethal bulk up from his ready rack. "Oof... alright, time to get back to the main charging station. See Nolo on the way out, Pilot Kramer. He has something for you, and you'd better take it. No strings attached, I promise."

The armored titan's heavy steps echoed down the transport's ramp. He picked up the bag of severed skulls with a small, secondary arm, and went into his throne room, out of sight.

Jessica watched him go, then picked up the Larue 787 carbine, examining its lethal lines. She ran a finger along the ragged groove carved into the buttstock, contemplating the day's events.

I wish Prath were here, she thought.

———

"Nolo, Boss says have item for selfsame?" Jessica said.

The Ninety-Nine turned to face the feminine voice now speaking in clipped Nine verbiage. He shook his head when he saw it was her, a smirk on his otherwise-featureless face.

"Hang around Nines, possible lose higher speech functions, Pilot," Nolo said, tapping the side of his head. "Unwell habit. Possible start cogging like Nines."

"Aw, that wouldn't be so bad, Nolo," Jessica replied. "The Recyke boys and I seemed to get along, slaying bodies and what not. I don't know if you and the other Rockribs were humoring me, but we kicked some major Gatekeeper butt out there, today, didn't we?"

"Just start of war, pilot," Nolo said. "Just opening salvo. Demo few structures, take few skulls. Just small part of picture. Secure mental headspace for imminent conflict. Focus. 'Headhunter is The Future, Headhunter is The Way,' affirm, but not easy route to waypoint. Lot more heads roll, soon."

The Headhunter's chief of staff offered a credit stick to her. She pulled back, cocking her head to the side.

"The Headhunter told me I couldn't refuse it," she said, skepticism in her voice, "and there were no strings attached. Is... is that true? Be honest, now."

"Utmost true. Pilot Kramer earned this," Nolo said. "Boss reinforced same. No strings. Extra, too. Pilot added four heads to Boss's wall. Bounty ten thousand each." Jessica's eyes went wide when a numeric figure scrolled across the stick's small screen.

"Two-hundred and forty-thousand credits? Gates, that's a lot of money," Jessica said, taking the credit storage bauble. "This collecting skulls thing could become a habit." She turned it over in her fingers, admiring it.

"Headhunting another unwell habit, Pilot," the Ninety-Nine said. "Leave to professionals." Nolo placed a hand over his earpiece as a muffled message came over his comm line.

"Pilot's Niff stabilized and enhancement calibrated. Outbound," he said.

A door opened, and two Recyke Niner medics emerged, including the one who patched up her arm after the raids. They rolled Kitos out in a wheelchair. *Unpowered? Where did they find that antique?* She thought.

"Pilot, I-I am mended, thanks to kindness of Nines, the Niff said, waving his new prosthetic hand. "Upgrades, see?"

His large eyes were golden slits. Jessica wondered if it was the fatigue of the ordeal, or the after-effects of the anesthetic. *Probably a little bit of both, poor, dumb thing,* she thought.

"The Headhunter told me they had a compatible replacement," Jessica said, "along with a cortex interface. That's a high-end mod, Niff."

"Yes, I-I know, Pilot Kramer," the blue-furred technician said. "I-I owe more than a few life-debts, now, I-I think. It is good thing Niffs believe in multiple reincarnations."

Jessica shook her head as she examined the Niff's new composite and alloy hand. It was some nice work. The Headhunter's operation had access to some top-notch parts.

"All this over a few bad bets on the back-alley matches, huh, Kitos?" she said, smirking. "What, you just couldn't pick the right mech-jockeys? Was the thrill of the wager worth it?"

The Niff looked ashamed, but unafraid.

"I-I am foolish gambler, Pilot, yes, but intent was honest," Kitos said. "Not addict. Not compulsive. I-I was trying to finance existence fee of lifemate. I-I wanted to petition Honorable Mikralos, attempt to bring her here, to Junctionworld, from home dimension. I-I am sorry for all this. Feel responsible."

"All this for a girl?" Jessica said. "C'mon, Niff, there's got to be more to it than that."

"She is all reason I-I need," the Niff answered. We are lifemates. Betrothed since—"

"Okay, okay, I get it, Kitos," she said, holding up her hands and smiling. "Just, spare me the holo-drama mushiness, would you, please? Gates, all this for a love-sick Niff."

"And I-I am eternally grateful, Pilot," Kitos said.

"Well, you're in one piece," she said, "but it's one smaller, hacked-on piece, so maybe we can prorate the 'eternal' part of that promise. 'Grateful' is nice, though, thanks."

"We need to get you to the hospital," she continued, "and run up the tab on Mikralos's medical bills. You know, just on general principle. Nolo, do you think you can give us a ride to the same place they're keeping Vervor?"

The Ninety-Nine nodded, and pointed towards the door. Jessica placed the credit stick in her jacket, next to her father's flask. She pushed Kitos' antique wheelchair to the waiting hover sedan.

Two hundred and forty large. Not bad for one day's haul, she thought.

Another shiver ran through her. She dry-heaved, felt a cold sweat break out down her back, then dry-heaved again. *That stuff must still be working itself out. Great,* she thought.

CHAPTER THIRTY-SEVEN_

SIXTH GATE ZONE
UNITED GATECARE AUTOMATED MEDICAL FACILITY

Jessica Kramer pushed Kitos through the entrance doors to the medical facility, a small skip in her stride as she leaned on the wheelchair's handles. Behind her, Nolo's grav-sedan disappeared into Junctionworld's gray, flickering skies as soon as the ancient wheelchair touched the curb.

She could see a familiar Gatekeeper's chassis through the Autodoc facility's clear doors. As the doors opened, she had a wide, leering grin on her face.

"Why, Mikralos, what a wonderful surprise, seeing you here," she said.

The two ornamental bodyguards Mikralos traveled with were absent. The floating overlord looked away from the slender med-bot doctor to whom he was talking, and turned his armored carapace to face her. Kitos's ears folded flat when he saw that Mikralos was at the medical facility.

"Pilot Kramer, we greet you in the Ways of the Old Code,"

Mikralos said, "and are more than overjoyed to see you escaped harm during this horrific crime committed by—"

"Oh, I think we both know who it was committed by, *Honored* Mikralos," she said, the false grin still on her face. "You Gatekeepers are supposed to be all-knowing, all-seeing when it comes to things happening in your little areas of control, right? No need to go any further into explanations or excuses. I think I understand."

"We do not fathom your meaning," the Gatekeeper said, puzzled, "but do not wish to aggravate you in your traumatized condition, and thus, will ignore your remark, for now. Perhaps you have suffered a head wound, and should seek medical attention. Regardless, the Nines of the local Enforcement Directorate barracks inform us that their investigation is underway, and the perpetrators will be brought to justice soon."

"I'm sure they're hot on the case, Mikralos," she said, sarcasm in her voice, "and the criminals will be held to the highest standards of Gatekeeper justice."

The doc-bot scanned Kitos in the wheelchair. It seemed as attentive to the archaic rolling chair as to the wounded Niff.

Mikralos gestured with a claw towards the blue-furred technician.

"We see that you managed to find Master Vervor's Niff technician," Mikralos said. "The Enforcement Directorate reported he was missing after the calamity at the fabrication facility."

"Find? Yeah, I guess you could say I found him, alright," she said. "He was tucked away, deep, in the Fifth Gate Zone. Took some doing, but I got him out of there. I had to enlist the help of a big, red friend. You should meet him, sometime. I'm sure you two would have lots of things to talk about. I can set up a meeting with him, if you'd like."

Mikralos's running lights pulsed in surprise.

"How... fortunate, that your friend could help you in your

hour of desperation," the Gatekeeper said with some startled hesitation. "Do pass on our thanks to him, whomever he might be. And, for future reference, we are sure if your *friend* were to come calling, we would have a warm welcome awaiting him."

A Skevvian nurse wrapped her tentacles around the Niff's wheelchair and took him off to a side room for examination by an auto-doc pod. Jessica watched him go, then turned back to Mikralos.

"Hmmm... I'm sure that can be arranged," she said. "My crimson friend is quite the character, a real jokester. You'd laugh your head off, so to say. Where are your bodyguards, by the way?"

"Attending to another matter, on our orders," Mikralos said, his chassis lights pulsing an irritated pattern. "Our bodyguards need not concern you, pilot. We are more than capable of handling our own security needs. This is a medical facility, Kramer, not a sordid, ethyl-soaked den of throwaways and malcontents like the type you seem to frequent."

"Well, Mikralos," she said, a nasty smile now on her face, "I could use a drink, after the day I've had, let me tell you. I even helped add a few decorations to my friend's wall. I really, really hope you get to see them, sometime. I think you'd fit right in."

Mikralos bobbled in his hover, trying to mask his reaction to the veiled threat of the Headhunter, to remain unmoved, but failed. She could see she was getting to him. Physical force was useless against the near-omnipotent Gatekeepers, but Their Old Code frowned on immediate, violent retribution. Vendetta was their preferred method of striking back. Verbal needling enabled her to get into their heads, to screw with their superiority complex.

Just like Dad used to do, she thought.

"Yes, well, despite your irksome verbal interplay," Mikralos said, attempting to recover his poise, "we have some good news for you, Mech Pilot Kramer. We understand you are unsettled by the recent events at the fabrication facility, and that the unfortunate passing of many on Master Vervor's staff will cause an impediment to your contracted match schedule. You were slated to fight, in the coming days, in another shield match. It was, as you know, to be a lead-up to the final encounter with Master Pilot Masamune Kyuzo. We regret to inform you that match has been canceled. After a short delay to pay respects to the fallen, and to sort out other minor repairs, you shall face Masamune in one gate-week's time."

Her haughty mood evaporated, and Jessica's fists clenched. The wounded hand lent its pain to her protest.

"Damn it, blob," she said, "I need more than eight days to unscrew the repairs I need to do, and I need to do it in a place that has less bullet holes and laser scorches on the walls. This whole this really is just a set-up, isn't it?"

"We have no idea what you happen to be jabbering about," Mikralos said, a coo in his voice now that the tables had turned, "and we remit once more that you seem to have suffered some sort of head trauma. We beseech you to seek medical attention, now that you are present and able to be scanned by this facility's medical staff."

A hologram emerged in mid-air, emitted from a lens on the hull of the Gatekeeper's armored chassis. It was the damnable contract, with a sub-paragraph highlighted in pulsing colors.

"No, Pilot Kramer," Mikralos said, now confident in his advantage over her, "rest assured, this is a contingency clause, as agreed to, in the contract we have between us. Perhaps your Ascended can explain it to you. In small words, of course."

The hologram blinked out of sight.

"Prath... Prath isn't really available right now for consulta-tion," Jessica said slowly. "We kinda... parted ways, right before the place got shot up." She felt like she had been punched in the gut by the Gatekeeper's reminder.

Mikralos's armored Nine bodyguards entered through the medical facility's doors. Their large frames blocked her view of the being walking behind them. When they saw Jessica, their weapons began to hum, charging up. Their master dismissed the defensive response with an idle wave of a silver claw.

"Behold, Pilot Kramer, our bodyguards," Mikralos said. "As we stated, earlier, you needed not worry yourself about their absence. They were elsewhere, attending to a matter of our own concern. Ah, Master Technician Prath, we greet you in the Ways of the Old Code."

A tall, orange ape stepped around the two Nine troopers. He gave a slight bow to the Gatekeeper, placing an upturned palm out in front of him in formal greeting.

"Honorable Mikralos, Master of Berva Proxima Arena," Prath said, "I return your greeting, in the Ways of the Old Code. I thank you for informing me of the incident at the fabrication facility, and for bringing me here to look in on my dear work companion, Master Vervor."

The formal exchange done, Prath walked to the nurse's station. Jessica tried to draw his attention, to say something, but he strode past her without a word.

CHAPTER THIRTY-EIGHT

SIXTH GATE ZONE
UNITED GATECARE AUTOMATED MEDICAL FACILITY

"Ape... ape, where are you going?" Jessica Kramer said, trying to talk to her former crew chief. "Don't I rate at least a 'hello?'"

Prath ignored her and continued down the hallway, peeking into various rooms and reading chart holograms on door screens to see if the wounded Myoshan shop owner, Vervor, was in them.

"Ape! Prath, gate-damn it, say something!" she said, slapping her hand to her side.

The tall Ascended turned to her, his eyes expressionless.

"I beg your pardon, Pilot," Prath said, "are you swearing in my direction? Please stop. I find profanity offensive, and a sign of low character. Now, if you'll excuse me, I'm searching for a sick associate. Ah, here we are."

He cracked open the door to a rehabilitation room. Vervor was inside, tubes and probes infiltrated throughout his wounded body. Machines next to the medical bed gave readouts on his condition. He appeared asleep, or in an induced coma.

Jessica stood in the hallway, confused and infuriated. The door closed with a click before she could follow Prath inside the room. She put her forehead against the cold metal of the door frame, and squeezed her eyes shut.

"Sorry. *I'm sorry, Prath,*" she said, grinding the words out in a low tone that only she could hear. She thought to herself, *Damn right, you're sorry, dung-for-brains, in every damned sense of the word.* She thumped her head on the door frame. *This sucked.*

The head-thump was loud. Prath opened the door. He was still cold to her, she could tell.

"Can I help you, Pilot?" he said. "No one in here requires insulting, if that's why you're here."

"Prath, I... I want to say... can I come in, please?" Jessica asked.

"It's not my room, Pilot. You should ask the occupant," Prath said. "Master Vervor? A visitor for you, sir. I will be leaving." The machines continued to beep and whir, but Vervor did not respond.

"No, no, don't go, ape. Please," Jessica said, swallowing hard.

"Ah, Pilot, I find your presence here to be painful," the orange Ascended said. "I knew that you would probably be here, but I had to come, nevertheless, if only for the sake of Kitos and Vervor. I am relieved that neither you or the Niff were killed as a result of the attack on the shop. Now, if you don't mind, I will check in on Kitos, then I'll be on my way, away from this place, and you, and any more self-inflicted anguish."

She did not move from the doorway. A thought crossed her mind, and her face hardened. Prath cocked his head to the side, regarding her.

"Come, now, pilot. Please let me pass. I have an appointment with a mech team in the Third Gate Zone."

"Contract," she said, a sudden defiance in her voice.

"I...I beg your pardon?" Prath asked.

"The Third Gate can wait, ape," Jessica said. "You signed a contract. You put your big brown paw on the table, just like I did, when we agreed to this whole screwed-up 'noose' fiasco. You and I are bound, ape, by the Old Code. You have to see it through, or face the penalty clause."

A frown was now on Prath's face.

"Were there a true and just legal system established here on Junctionworld," Prath said after a pause, "I would tell you to sue me, and see you in court. However, since this place is run by narcissistic bandits who only pay lip service to litigious matters, contract disputes in this misbegotten place inevitably end in gun duels. Even now, you continue to exasperate me. You will excuse me if I politely release myself from our contract, without the invocation of the penalty clause. I have better things to do today besides killing you, Pilot."

"Whoa, back it up a minute, ape," she said. "One, you are not a better shot than me, and two, if I don't have you on my side, Masamune's just going to take me apart in the arena, anyway."

"Back it up, yourself, pilot," Prath said. "One, I taught you how to shoot. Two, guilt is not going to work, this time. You already tried that, remember? You used it as a weapon against me, in the shop. Using it as leverage, now, is not as painful, but just as insulting."

"Listen, Prath, I—" Jessica tried to say.

"No, it is *you* who should listen, Jessica," Prath said, over-riding her. He held up a finger, emphasizing his point. "There isn't a day since what happened to Jered that I'm not haunted. *Haunted.* I have relived that moment, over and over, and have blamed myself more than you can possibly know. I still blame myself to this day, even without your recent vulgar reminder.

My pain is not something for you to idly toss about in an argumen—"

"Prath... I think Dad killed Jered," Jessica said, interrupting him this time. She felt tears start to form as the words tumbled out of her mouth.

The Ascended stopped his finger wagging, his tirade paused as the full weight of her words set in. A wave of nausea pulsed through her, and her knees felt like water.

"And I'm... sorry, Prath. For what," she said, her voice cracking, "for what I said at the shop. I'm really, really... sorry."

Prath's gaze remained fixed ahead, trying to comprehend the revelation. He started to sit down, even though the nearest chair was across the room. Jessica held his large forearm to steady him. His face was an expression of shock and disbelief.

"You're... quite sure?" Prath said, his eyes pleading for it to not be true. "Solomon? It was... it was Solomon?"

"We did a circuit-dive," Jessica said, her words burbling through tears, "just like you wanted to before I... before I screwed up. The logs were all there. Dad even put up an inter-active avatar defense to ward off me or anyone else in the family from finding out more. It's... it's true."

"An avatar screen?" Prath said, surprised. "You... you actually talked to him?"

She shook her head, trying to wipe away the tears.

"Well," she said, sniffling, "it was him, but it wasn't. I talked to a ghost, ape. The digital ghost of a real bastard, it turns out. Me and Kitos were in the circuit-dive when they snatched him and shot up Vervor and killed half of his crew. The Judah module was sabotaged. A node was removed on purpose, and Dad's the one who did it."

She guided the stunned Ascended to the chair besides Vervor's bed. He mumbled to himself for a moment or two, then grew silent.

After holding his head in his hands, he looked up. He appeared hollowed out, more wounded than when she had accused him of causing the death of her brother. There was a glimmer of something else, though.

"'Kitos and I,' little human," the Ascended said.

She sank to her knees in front of him.

"'Kitos and I.' Sorry, Prath," Jessica said. "I'm sorry, for everything."

She brushed away their mutual tears. Prath held her, and they both cried in each other's arms. She felt his long fingers start to preen her hair, and she smiled through her sobbing.

A voice rasped out from Master Vervor's med-bed next to them.

"Dear Gates," Vervor said, his voice groggy and full of pain, "what kind of afternoon holo-drama pap is this? If you two are quite done leaking from your faces, would one of you unplug me so I can be put out of my misery?"

CHAPTER THIRTY-NINE

FIRST GATE ZONE
MAELSTROM GARDENS HABITATION POD COMPLEX

Masamune Kyuzo looked down at the little human being tugging at his pant leg.

"Up!" she said, her little hands grasping up to him.

"Daddy's busy, little one," Kyuzo said to his daughter, Miko. "I don't have the right interface chips to upload this arena footage direct into my brain. I have to watch it, the old-fashioned way."

"Up!" his persistent daughter said.

He smiled back. He paused the hologram of Kramer's fight with the Wardancer and scooped his daughter, Miko, up with his arms. She squealed with glee as he held her up in midair with his prosthetic arm.

"Fly!" Miko said, giggling.

"Yes, yes, 'fly,'" Masamune said, still smiling. He spun his artificial hand's wrist three-hundred-and-sixty degrees, letting his daughter twirl at arm's length in a slow pinwheel. She squealed and giggled louder as he tickled her ribs with his organic hand as she rotated above him.

"Took-took-took! Gotcha!" he said, making her squeal with peals of laughter. "Took-took-too—"

The proximity alarm of their residential hab-pod's security system went off with a low, grating chime. They had visitors. Kyuzo set his daughter down when he saw the crowded view of the front door's camera. It was a Gatekeeper and a foursome of armored Nines.

"Go see momma, Miko," Kyuzo said, his voice now all business. "Go."

"But, fly, Daddy, fly!" little Miko protested.

"Go!" he said sternly, pointing towards the wing of the habitat that contained the bedrooms.

The toddler started to cry, and the front door's intercom button sounded.

"Anora!" Kyuzo said, calling out to his wife in another part of the hab.

Miko's crying volume grew. The intercom chimed again.

"Anora, come get the baby!" Kyuzo said, louder and more urgent.

"What?" said his wife from one of the back bedrooms.

"The baby, come get her," Kyuzo said, trying to keep the child calm. "I have business!"

"What business?" Anora called back to him, mild annoyance in her voice.

"Would you just come and get her, please," Kyuzo said, exasperated.

The front door unlocked on its own. Masamune grabbed his crying daughter and handed her to his confused wife, her hair wrapped in a towel. He shut the door to the bedrooms before she could react or question. She tried to protest, to hold on to Miko's squirming body, but he activated the habitat's panic button. The seams of the door disappeared behind a hologram of a full-wall Japanese mural.

He looked for his pistols. They hung on the rack, beside the opening door. *Damn. Not that there's much I can do, but I hate being caught short like this,* he thought.

A pair of Nines entered the room, their short laser carbines scanning across the room without pausing to target him.

"Clear," one chirped into his headset microphone.

"Gate-damned, pinheaded meatbots," Kyuzo swore. The nearest Nine regarded him with solid black eyes, but made no move to restrain him. The threat of the charged carbine was enough for Kyuzo, and he offered no resistance.

The Gatekeeper filled the doorway. He entered the domestic habitat in a slow, cautious manner, his running lights pulsing in a nervous, curious pattern.

"Master Mech Pilot Masamune Kyuzo," the Gatekeeper's high-pitched voice said, "we greet you in the Ways of the Old Code. You will forgive our imposition upon your domicile."

"It seems," Kyuzo said, "I am in no position to prevent you from doing otherwise, Honorable Dionoles. Welcome to my residence, such as it is."

"We must admit, we are mildly surprised and amused, *Desecrator*," Dionoles said. "We were not aware that you were situated in such... basic living accommodations. So... plain. Fascinating, really."

A small claw from the Gatekeeper's chassis pushed a left-out child's toy away in disgust.

"Actually, we do better than most," Masamune said, "despite the ever-increasing fees and taxes. It is not always easy, living under such generous and caring beings such as yourself, Honored Gatekeeper. Tell me, should I also expect Honored Mikralos, soon?"

"No, you should not," Dionoles said. "Mikralos is attending

to another matter, which requires our presence here. One assumes you have heard news of the distressing incident at Master Vervor's fabrication facility?"

Masamune's brow wrinkled as he ran his fingers through his hair. He estimated how to get around Dionoles and the Nines, and retrieve his pistols. He felt naked without them, even in the face of such power.

"Master Vervor's?" Kyuzo asked. "No, what happened?"

"A rather disagreeable forced entry by beings unknown, master pilot," Dionoles said, chuckling to himself. "Well, unknown to most. There appear to have been numerous casualties among the staff, and one of the technicians was taken. A Niff, if we do recall."

A pulse flashed in the fluid of the overbeing's containment vessel, and he paused.

"Ah, well, it appears that the kidnapped technician has been returned," the Gatekeeper said. "The recovered Niff appears to be in the care of the Pilot, the daughter of Kramer. Gates, we warned that damned fool this would turn inverted..."

"'Returned?' Who took this technician?" Kyuzo said, his eyes narrowing with suspicion.

"That is none of your concern, Master Pilot," Dionoles said, relishing this verbal game he seemed to be playing.

"Then, why, may I ask, are you here?" Kyuzo said, anger rising in him. "Was it simply to deliver this cryptic and nonsensical news?"

"Of course not, underbeing. We are here to inform you," Dionoles said, his lights pulsing, "that your arena appointment with the Kramer target has been moved up. There will be no interim matches for either party, as was originally contracted."

Masamune scowled at the news.

"The match with the low-level Unlimited was supposed to

be tomorrow night!" Kyuzo said, incensed. "I was about to leave for my shop for final installation and tests on that refurbished battle claw! What sort of contract is this, that you can cancel a match at will?"

"Yes, well, we must all retain flexibility in such circumstances," Dionoles said, the arrogance growing in his reedy voice as he spoke. "Do not presume to test us, Master Pilot, nor should you think you can subject us to your interrogatives. We... we do not answer to you. You have merely been informed. That is all you need to know, until we say otherwise. One gate-week from today, you will purge the last Kramer for us."

Kyuzo fumed, forcing himself to stand rigid as the Nines kept their weapons at the ready.

"Are you... having conflicts with your assigned task?" the Gatekeeper asked, a slight hint of menace creeping into his voice. "Do we need to enhance your incentive? Where are your lifemate and offspring, incidentally? Somewhere behind that flimsy security illusion you are standing next to?"

Slow black and orange patterns flowed through Dionoles's running lights. Kyuzo's artificial hand gripped a dining chair by its back rail. The metal buckled as he squeezed. The two bioprinted troopers inside Masamune's house braced themselves, taking flanking positions next to their master.

"Do not threaten my family, Gatekeeper," Masamune said in slow, lethal tones. "Do not make this about more than credits, you... you glorified money-changer."

The Gatekeeper's hovering wobbled, signaling his amusement.

"Such delightful insolence. We wonder, Master Mech Pilot," Dionoles said with a haughty hint of a giggle, "how you would feel if your spanners and diagnostic tools began talking back to you? What would your reaction be to your weapons

290 / BEAR ROSS

refusing to fire, or your prosthetics wanting things to their satisfaction before they performed their ordained functions?"

"I am not a tool, Dionoles," Kyuzo said. "I have contracted rights, even according to your own code."

The proximity alert hummed again, and Masamune saw the two Nines standing outside his door react. A small human ambled up the habitat's walkway towards them, curiosity on his young face. It was Kyuzo's son, Kenji, returning home from the learning center. The helpless father turned rigid.

"Dionoles, your Nines at the door!" Masamune said, pleading. "Tell them—"

On the viewer screen, the two bioprinted soldiers slammed the seven-year-old to the wall, one pinning him in place, the other searching his person and backpack.

"No!" Kyuzo shouted, unable to make his way to the door. The Nine nearest him put a laser carbine up to its shoulder, the weapon whining as it powered up to full strength.

Dionoles turned to him, his usual nervous mannerism gone in the face of having power over Kyuzo's family. His running lights were pitch black.

"Your contracted rights are whatever we say they are, human," Dionoles said, a new-found steel in his high-pitched voice. "Remember that well. 82458-K, stand down. Allow the whelp to pass."

The crying boy came through the front door. Confused by the presence of a Gatekeeper in his living room, he gave the floating armored chassis of Dionoles a wide berth. Blubbering, he threw himself into the arms of his father. Kyuzo looked at his son's face. The boy's nose was bloody, his face scraped from hitting the wall.

Masamune Kyuzo gritted his teeth as the Gatekeeper hovered out of the habitat pod. The Nines kept their weapons trained on him and Kenji as the overbeing departed.

"You have eight days, Master Mech Pilot Masamune Kyuzo," Dionoles called back. "Prepare for your task, and remember the consequences, should you waiver. We shall be in touch."

The Nines withdrew. The front door closed, and Masamune threw the crumpled chair against the wall.

CHAPTER FORTY

FIRST GATE ZONE
MAELSTROM GARDENS HABITATION POD COMPLEX

The pair of Niner troops walking behind Dionoles paid scant notice to the thud against the interior of the habitat door. Masamune Kyuzo's muted roar from inside, after the chair's impact, only managed to turn one of their heads.

"What a vigorous activity," Dionoles said. "This giving of orders and reminding lower beings of their proper place can be quite invigorating, 82458-к. One can almost see the authoritarian appeal it has to Mikralos and Beliphres. Of course, it must be applied under the proper conditions, and in situations where the upper claw is clearly held. One does not wish to overstretch one's reach, after all."

The Nine next to the Gatekeeper nodded his silent acknowledgment of the overbeing's epiphany.

"Also," Dionoles continued, "have the casino armorer provide a selection of new armaments for our perusal. We are considering a chassis upgrade. Something big and nasty, like

Beliphres has in his chassis, only more ornate, and not so uncouth."

82458-ᴋ communicated with the Heavenly Palace Casino's armored transport for retrieval. The sleek craft came in from its overhead orbit. Dionoles and his Nines boarded the armored grav-yacht, and boosted back into the swirling skies over Junctionworld.

CHAPTER FORTY-ONE

SIXTH GATE ZONE

VERVOR'S FABRICATION WORKS

Jessica Kramer was irritated. The whole fiasco of Beliphres's thugs shooting up the shop and kidnapping Kitos had taken precious days away from them. Getting all the parts back in the right places would take a while. In the meantime, they would have to make do with what they had.

The final death match with Masamune was only a few days away, now that the Gatekeepers had pulled some obscure contract clause on her. Vervor, the Myoshan shop owner, was finally discharged from the autodoc facility, but he still wasn't up to full capacity. *This is some burdenbeast dung,* she thought.

"So, now what do we do, ape?" Jessica asked her crew chief. She was trying to do better, but the inactivity of the recent days had worked her last nerves.

"You have a choice, little human," Prath said, extending two large fingers to make his point. "We know the control module's missing node is still on Junctionworld. You can restore the Judah module to full capability, or settle for 87% capability. Seven eighths of an Arkathan module still puts you ahead of nearly every fighter in Junctionworld, and then some, if you can utilize it properly."

"Agreed," Master Vervor said, limping towards them. "I see no advantage in hunting down and grafting in a node that has been away from its main module for five years, especially when so much has to be done to rework the chassis and armor from the... original Kramer mech."

The repairs to the shop were almost done. Patches and paint covered the holes and burns on the walls. The bloodstains and explosive impacts on the floors were harder to remove. A contractor was due in, soon, to conduct an entire respray of the floor. Mikralos was picking up the tab.

"I still don't like using parts of the old Judah frame to fix up NoName," Jessica said.

"I understand, love, but it is necessary," Prath said. "Master Vervor's machines are still not functioning and calibrated to their top efficiency, and the parts from the Judah chassis are compatible, with some adaptation. We have less than a week, and we haven't even started tuning, yet."

"Besides, human," Vervor said, easing himself into a chair with a low growl, "your command seat and carapace are a perforated mess from your last fight. My techs are still finding holes from the Wardancer in your CR-400 chassis. It's a wreck. We'll be lucky if we can meld the two together and fill in the gaps with weld-foam and void-tape."

The printed torso brace covered the Myoshan's body like transparent armor. The medical device's purpose was to keep him immobile while he healed. It wasn't doing its job very well.

"I still don't like it, ape," Jessica said, her arms crossed.

"Because Jered died in that old body of Judah?" Prath asked.

She nodded, her head down. Vervor clicked his fangs.

"Ah, human sentimentality," Vervor said. "Superstition.

'Bad luck.' We Myoshans believe that a spirit doesn't haunt something attached to its death, it imparts its strength to it. The meat and molted scales of this mortal life filter away, but the soul remains, adding to its power."

"Do... do you really believe that?" Jessica said, looking up from her unhappy crouch. She started to smile. Vervor's eyes twinkled. Prath placed a hand on Jessica's shoulder.

"Feh. Of course not, don't be silly, pilot," Vervor said. "I'm a Myoshan of science, living in an interdimensional nexus, talking to a bunch of oversized aliens. My father believed in such nonsense, and you needed a mix of distraction and comfort. Hopefully, it worked."

"Now," the short alien said, pointing his walking stick towards the loading bay doors, "I need you both to go mope somewhere else. The floor resprayers are here. Out you go."

"You're awful, you know that?" Jessica said. Her dark look cleared, and a wry grin spread across her face.

"Yes, yes, pilot I know," the Myoshan said, hobbling back to his small office. "I've been called worse by better. Take your Ascended and the Niff, and go do something positive, instead of grousing here in my shop. I have things to do, and little time in which to do them."

Prath turned to Jessica after Vervor closed the door.

"He's right, you know," the Ascended said to her. "Blunt, unrefined, and not-at-all diplomatic, but... he's right."

"Gates, what a dung-plug," Jessica said. "I think he actually took some pleasure in getting my hopes up, just to smash them down."

"Well, maybe that's his method of coping with all of this," Prath said. "Myoshans are, by nature, not the most cuddly and affectionate of the creatures to have come through the gates. That honor is reserved, of course, for the Ascended." Prath grinned with large fangs, placing his hand against his own

298 / BEAR ROSS

chest in mock humility. She laughed, pushing his other hand off her.

"Damn it, ape," Jessica scolded playfully, "you were holding me down, in case I was going to put a knife in him, weren't you?"

"Well... were you?" Prath asked.

She thought for a moment, playing the moment for humorous effect, rolling her eyes back and forth to evaluate her options.

"Tempting... but, no," she said. "A couple days ago, things might have been different."

"Yes, well," Prath said, holding her head close, "I saw the situation had the potential for a perforated shop proprietor. No sense in not being prepared, little human. Myoshan humor is very grim, very dry, and abrasive as a paint scraper. You took it well. I'm impressed."

"Let's go check on Kitos," the Ascended said.

––––––––––

The Niff was already hard at work, having started without them."What's his problem?" Jessica asked.

"Kitos appears to be connected to the main Arkathan control module," Prath said. "He no longer requires the interface hood, apparently. You mentioned his new hand can serve as a link. How did this happen, anyway? You never told me."

Jessica regarded the Niff laying in his chair, his eyes closed, a blinking data-line connecting his new prosthetic hand and the Arkathan module on the test bench. She looked away.

"I'm... I'm not sure I'm ready to tell you, myself, ape," she said. "It isn't a pretty story."

"Did you cut his hand off," Prath said, "or did you find him this way?"

"How can you ask me that?" she said with a surprised laugh.

"Don't look so shocked, little human," Prath said, grinning again. "Yours is a very bloodthirsty species, after all."

"No, I didn't cut his hand off," Jessica said. "The beings who took him did that."

"And the replacement hand, and its connecting cranial implants?" Prath asked.

"A... friend," Jessica answered with hesitation.

"A *friend* gave the Niff a new hand and brain interface parts?" Prath said, his curiosity stoked. "This must be quite a generous acquaintance."

She looked away, again.

"D'you want a safe lie, ape," Jessica said, "or the dangerous truth?"

"The truth is never dangerous, little human," Prath said. "Inform me, if you please."

"Well," Jessica said, looking at the floor. "He's big, and red... and you've already met him, here, in the shop."

Prath's eyes went wide in realization, and a bit of horror.

"No," Prath said.

"Yup," she replied.

"Jessica... are you saying the Headhunter did this?" Prath said, his voice low as he looked around.

"Stop whispering, ape, it sounds silly," Jessica said. "Yes, the Headhunter helped me get Kitos back, and patched him up."

"And your arm?" Prath said. "I'm afraid to ask, but... how did you manage that?"

"They dropped part of a building on me," Jessica said, holding her now-healed hand. "They didn't do it on purpose."

"*Who* are 'they' that didn't drop a building on you, 'on purpose?'" Prath asked, giving her a hard look.

"The Nines," she said, looking sheepish. "I mean, not Enforcement Directorate guys, you know, but the Recykes that the big red guy keeps around, after their expiration date. The Headhunter wore himself out on the earlier targets, so we had to do the last assault on our own," she said, looking sheepish.

"There were Recyke Nines, and you were assaulting buildings to rescue Kitos?" The Ascended looked apoplectic.

"...and a piece fell on me," Jessica said, unable to stop confessing. "After we took out this mini-mech thing with a demo charge. It's okay, though. Please don't be mad?"

"Oh, it's *okay*, you say," Prath said, holding his hands to the sides of his head. "Please don't be *mad*, you say."

"Ape," she said, "you were just congratulating me for taking things in stride with Vervor, for not being rattled by unexpected... surprises. 'The truth is never dangerous,' remember?"

"Oh, indeed I did say that, little human," Prath said, his hands now clasped over his eyes in disbelief. "I just wasn't prepared for something out of some tawdry, low-brow action holo-movie. Honestly, Pilot."

Kitos murmured something in his circuit-dive, his lips moving as if he were talking in his sleep.

"I will bring him out of the circuit dive," Prath said. "Please give me a minute to process this information, first. I'm not sure I can take much more dangerous truth today."

Prath took a second data line from the test bench, laid back in the bullet-ridden chair next to Kitos, and plugged the data line into his neck.

"Prath, what the," Jessica said, surprise. "When the void did you have a jack-port installed?"

"Language. Oh, and I've had one for years, love, I just don't flaunt it," the Ascended said. "You think I tended to Judah for decades without plugging in? A good technician has to know his mech better than himself. It makes the acts of your father even more abhorrent, unfortunately."

A sad look crossed his face. He shook off the thought of his friend's betrayal.

"Let us find out if Kitos has a destination for us," the orange crew chief said, "and we'll be on our way."

Prath laid back, his eyes fluttering. Jessica watched them both for a few moments, their eyes rolling underneath their eyelids, their lips moving in muted whispers.

She saw a permanent marker from the test bench and contemplated drawing something profane on Prath's forehead, then thought better of it. *Maybe some angry eyebrows,* she thought, smiling. *I'll let him slide, this time.*

Prath and Kitos snapped upright out of the trances at the same time, just as she thought twice about picking up the marker. She pulled her hand back in surprised guilt.

"Pack everything. We're going for a ride," Prath said. "You might want to stay here, at the shop, for this one, action girl."

"Why, where are we going?" Jessica said. "Did you locate the missing module? Anything more from my dad?"

"Nothing from Solomon," Prath said, his expression heavy, "nor do I wish to open that door. I probably wouldn't be able to comport myself in a professional manner, digital ghost or not. We do know the location of the node, though."

"I-I was able to affix coordinates, pilot," Kitos said. "After last interruption, of course. Location is in Fourth Gate Zone. More precise: old service hangar attached to residence. Unoccupied. Condemned, according to Central Date records."

"No," Jessica said.

"Yes, love," Prath said as he disconnected the data line from his neck. "The node is at the old habitat pod, the home of the Fourth Gate Kramers."

"However," Prath continued, "We're not going to do any buildings assaults or demolition. It will indubitably be harder than that. Help pack up, if you want to come, and load up in the transport. We leave in five."

CHAPTER FORTY-TWO

FOURTH GATE ZONE
KRAMER HABITATION POD AND HANGAR

Jessica Kramer felt like she was trapped under the rubble again, only more helpless, this time.

The trip in Vervor's shop vehicle, a boxy van on hoverfans, was more than just cramped. The hover-van was configured for Myoshans, who were about half the size of Jessica. Kitos, being a Niff, and flexible, could wedge himself into the driver's seat and manipulate the controls with his lower set of arms. Kramer and Prath had to ride in the rear cargo section with the tools and spare parts.

The Ascended closed his eyes after the fourth or fifth near miss with other flying vehicles. They were in the common altitudes, where non-Gatekeeper, non-Enforcement Directorate vehicles were thrown together at random, left to fend for themselves. The proximity alarm beeped and blurted in a disconcerting manner. The Niff's atrocious taste in music was not helping.

"Are we being followed?" she asked, brushing away a swinging set of spare cables.

"You're being paranoid, pilot," Prath said, peeking from between his fingers.

"I think we've been through enough weird dung lately," she said, "that paranoia might actually be a good thing, ape."

She wanted to grab the controls from Kitos when he cut off a being-laden grav-bus, its running lights strobing in angry patterns. The Niff was concentrating more on singing along with some audio playlist than on his vector.

"Gate-damn it, Kitos," Jessica said, fighting a combination of nausea and terror, "keep your eyes open, would you?"

"I-I am sorry, pilot," Kitos said, turning back to her and taking his eyes completely away from the screen in front of him. "This song reminds I-I of times with lifemate. We would sing it together while clutched in the frenzy of—"

"No, really, Niff, I don't need to know," she said, putting a hand up.

"It's really quite beautiful, pilot," Kitos said, still not looking through the front window. "We Niffs do not just use our fluids for self-defense. They also serve to lubri—"

"Kitos, perhaps," Prath said, one hand over his eyes, the other tapping the side of his head, trying to get the imagery of Niff loveplay out of his skull. "Perhaps this is not the most appropriate conversation under these circumstances. Are we nearing the old Kramer compound, yet? Please, say yes."

"Yes, Master Prath," Kitos said. "I-I am on final descent now. Street appears to deserted. Strange."

Jessica craned her neck to see past Kitos at her childhood neighborhood.

"Oh, they closed the noodle shop on the corner, Prath," she said. "I loved that place. Miss Dortha and that Larka she had cooking in the back... what was his name?"

"Hmm... 'Oorus.' Personable fellow, for a Larka," Prath said. "He made a wonderful sturgeon and squash broth, with these wondrous noodles, as thick as your thumb. Your father and I would take our lunch breaks there..."

"Yeah. This whole place seems haunted, now," Jessica said somberly. "Too many memories, huh, ape?"

"Yes, little human," Prath said. "Too many memories."

She remembered the armada of drones when the Enforcers pulled her out of the habitat's living room. It was the day Jered died in the arena.

The Enforcers never did give me the details of what happened to Mom and Dad, she thought. *Maybe that's why I'm here. Not for the node. For the full story.*

"Navigation console says we are here," Kitos piped up. "*This* was home of Fourth Gate Kramers?"

The Fourth Gate dominated the view, a pulsing spiral of orange and yellow bathing the neighborhoods and commercial districts around it in a pale glow.

"Pop the back doors, Niff, and let us out," Jessica said. "Let's get this over with." She felt a strange mixture of dread and hope.

The blue-furred technician opened the rear double doors of the utility vehicle. Prath pulled himself out of the van, visibly ill from the nauseating ride.

The Ascended steadied himself on the compound's tall, welded fence made from cast-off armor parts. It was rusted, in spots. Still gleaming, in others. Jessica remembered playing in the street with her brother and sister, beating the mech parts like drums, or hopping from hull fragment to hull fragment like swamphoppers.

"Your father loved this wall... fence... thing," Prath said, his eyes drifting as more memories came back to him. "I helped him put it together. There are some of his old mechs mixed in there, as well as some conquests. Look, here's part of that infamous hit-

306 / BEAR ROSS

bot, StellarSonic. Someone was dumb enough to pay that Unlimited assassin to take your father down."

"The hit-bot was dumb enough to take the contract," Jessica said with a small amount of pride in her voice. "Dad was brutal in the arena. I've seen the replay."

"Look there," Prath said, pointing at some laser-carved graffiti on the wall of armored parts.

"'The Headhunter is the Future. The Headhunter is the Way,'" Jessica read aloud. "Nolo said that, before. What the void does that dung even mean?"

"Language. Your big, red friend is planning big things, love," Prath said.

"But... how?" Kitos said, his ears now flat against his skull in fear.

"The Centurion and Warlord is a whispered legend among the Nines," Prath said. "He's like your father, Jessica. He's a slave who has turned on the Gatekeepers. Only he's too hard, too vicious for them to try and take him on. They made him unstoppable, almost without weakness."

"Yeah, no lie," Jessica said. "He even had a pair of dead Gatekeepers in this big, smelly trophy room of his, back at his little clubhouse. Skulls everywhere."

"I am not surprised," Prath said. "You won't find those two Gatekeepers in any history or record. They were defeated by the Headhunter, and any memory of them was purged to hide their shame. To acknowledge he even exists would be an admission of weakness to the Gatekeepers, under their code. So, they ignore him, hoping that he'll fade away. As you both know, it's not working. He's growing ever-stronger."

"I mean, he's big and bad, yeah," Jessica said, "but he's just one cyborg. How's he going to do it?"

"I have heard things," Prath said. "Rumors and innuendos,

mostly. The Nines may seem servile, mindless warrior slaves, but as the Headhunter shows, they are capable of more."

"I-I dislike being here, in open," Kitos said, interrupting the Ascended crew chief. "Exposed. Can pilot or Master Prath please make entry into compound?"

"Of course, Kitos," Prath said. "Pardon an old ape for prattling on. Jessica, dear, do you see any Enforcer security systems still active?"

"I don't see any drones keeping station over the place," Jessica said.

"Hmm. The reputation of this place," Prath said, "of what happened here, is enough to keep most intruders away."

A small holo-projector emanated from the palm of Kitos's prosthetic hand. A readout and directional arrow glowed in mid-air.

"That's a nice piece of kit, Kitos," Jessica said. "The Headhunter really went all-out with that hand of yours."

"Yes, Pilot, but I-I would still prefer to have original, organic manipulator attached," Kitos said. "Missing Arkathan circuit node is inside large hangar, according to the readout data I-I downloaded. Do any beings reside here? Will they let us in?"

"No one's lived here since... since things went wrong," Prath said. "The Gatekeepers derive some sick pleasure from letting the place founder and rot."

Prath reached out to touch the scorched remnant of armored chest plate near the front gate. He ran a finger along an access panel's outline on the piece of welded wreckage. The panel popped open with a bit of effort. A glowing button was inside.

"I didn't know that was there," Jessica said.

"Of course, you didn't," the Ascended said. "You were probably too busy making googly eyes at Tevren about the time I

308 / BEAR ROSS

installed it. It was towards the end." Jessica stuck out her tongue to retort.

"It's kill switch for the entire facility," Prath continued. "The place looks abandoned, but there were back-ups to the back-ups when it came to sensors and countermeasures. Your father was worried we would have to fight our way back in, if there was a hostage situation."

"Gates, Dad really was a raging paranoiac, wasn't he?" Jessica said.

"You don't know the half of it, love," the Ascended said. "He went through a lot in his life, though. As you know, the Gate-keepers do not forgive or forget. That doesn't excuse what he did, but... it provides some perspective."

Prath pushed the concealed button. A small gap appeared in the armored gate as its magnetic locks disengaged.

"I-I nervous," Kitos said. "Want to evacuate emergency defense bladder."

"Put a cork in it, Niff. We're going in," Jessica said, pulling her pistol.

———

They followed Kitos through the dilapidated property, his hand's holographic projector leading the way. Prath held Jessica's hand as they walked. Every door they encountered swung open without resistance. The easier they made progress, the farther they went, the more Jessica's apprehension grew as they came closer to the main habitation module.

She breathed a small sigh of relief when Kitos's holographic indicator pointed them to the side door of the main hangar, away from the dark memories contained inside the housing pod.

A blue and silver cloud of webbing covered one half of an

old, dented workbench and stretched to the ceiling, radiating in strange patterns.

"Arkathan circuitry, gone feral," Kitos said.

"Feral? As in, gone wild?" Jessica asked, holding her pistol at the ready.

"Yes, pilot, wild," Kitos said. "Not dangerous, just unguided. Arkathan circuitry can survive variety of conditions without losing integrity, but need power source to tap into. Look. Branched into... security and internal surveillance systems, I-I think. Confirm, Master Prath?"

The Niff traced the wires up the walls into junction boxes above the workbench. Kitos's slender blue fingers guided Prath's gaze as they followed the hangar's conduits and terminations.

"Yes, it appears so," Prath said. "Those systems were wired into those boxes. An old section, but yes."

The web of wires originated from a drawer in the workbench. Jessica pulled it open. Hidden among the loose bolts and tools, deep in the back of the drawer, sat a marble-sized control node. It glowed red when her fingers came near it.

"He threw it in the gate-damned junk drawer," Jessica said. "The junk drawer, Prath. They probably looked at it a dozen times while they hauled all our stuff away, and it here it was, hidden in plain sight. All this, for a nugget of nanocircuitry."

She grabbed Kitos's prosthetic hand with the holographic projector attached to it, and laid it on the table. The Niff protested.

"Pilot, what—" Kitos tried to say.

"It's glowing because it recognizes my biocode, doesn't it?" Jessica said, a sudden frenzy overtaking her. "I bet you don't have to circuit-dive, Kitos, just broadcast the feed through your hand's projector, there."

"Jessica, this is not the best—" Prath said, holding up a hand.

"No, ape, I need to know. *Now,*" Jessica said, her dread and anxiety galvanizing into a manic desire to know the rest of the story.

The Arkathan node glowed even brighter when Kitos produced a data cable from a pouch. He gulped, looked at them both with huge, worried eyes, and connected his new hand to a small port in the awakened component.

A high-pitched whine filled the air. Kitos's eyes rolled back, and Prath and Jessica had to steady him. An old chair next to the workbench was pressed into service before the Niff could collapse.

"He's overloaded," Prath said. "This usually takes a separate diagnostic computer along with some other support tools. I told you, this is a bad idea. We should handle this back at the shop."

"No, Prath. I don't need protection, or babying," she said. "I want the truth. After all these years, I deserve it."

Blurred, sped-up images of life in the Kramer household and hangar flashed across the far wall, switching camera viewpoint to viewpoint at random intervals. They watched in silence. There was no audio.

"This starts the day Solomon took the node from the Judah module," Prath said. "Look at the time-stamp, there, on the security camera feed. It must have branched out right away, through the back of the drawer. Amazing."

"Kitos, if you can hear me," Jessica called into the Niff's ear, "see if there are any... any logs from around the time of—"

The Niff's lip curled, and his eyes rolled side to side. A low moan escaped him. A younger Jessica was on a couch, fitting firearms parts together. Her brother's death played on the living room's main viewing screen.

The screen blurred, then an image of Solomon Kramer, dead on the floor of his upstairs bedroom, appeared frozen on Kitos' projected image. Jessica's mother, Consuelo, stood over him. She held a smoking gun to her own head. A pool of blood lay beneath Solomon Kramer's body.

"Oh, void," Jessica said, unable to look away.

"Kitos, whatever you do," Prath said to the semi-conscious Niff technician, "do not play the rest of that video feed. The motion capture is more than enough, thank you."

"Mom... killed dad? Then herself?" Jessica said, her burning need for knowledge now turned to shock. "The Enforcers said it was a murder-suicide, but, that's—"

"No, it makes sense, love," Prath said, reaching a comforting hand out to her. "The Enforcement Directorate only told us the result, but they never did say *who* killed *who*, did they? The records were sealed. Everything was left to rot. And, let's face it, Nines, even Ninety-Nines, aren't exactly forensic specialists."

"But if he killed Jered..." she said, her knees weak. "They were arguing upstairs after Jered died, and then there were gunshots."

"Then Consuelo must have found out," Prath said, holding her. "Solomon might have confessed. This is not how I wanted to discover the truth, love. Either way, we can only guess, at this point."

"Yuh... yes," Kitos said, lifting one of his hands.

"Oh, he can talk," Prath said, bending over to examine Kitos. "It must be because the feed is paused. Come out of that data-feed sequence, Kitos. I think we've seen enough. We need to get this node back to the shop for integration with the main module." Jessica remained silent as she fought the swirling storm of feelings inside her.

Kitos opened his eyes, disconnecting the cable to his hand and the projector. He had trouble focusing, shaking his head to clear the bombardment of stimuli. He turned to face Jessica. His ears were flat against his skull.

"I-I had access to full audio feed, Pilot Kramer," Kitos said.

"Full playback, all contained on the node's memory. Suggest purge and reformat. Very unpleasant."

Jessica leaned against the workbench, the control node now glowing in her hand.

"Go on, Niff. I can handle it," Jessica said with a glaring lack of emotion in her voice. "You accessed the full audio and video, right?"

Kitos nodded in the affirmative.

"Jessica—" Prath said.

"No, Prath, I need to know," she said sharply. After hearing her severe tone, she tried to relax, to not lash out. "Please. Please, ape. Kitos?"

The Niff held his head in his upper set of hands, trying to calm himself.

"Solomon Kramer confessed to lifemate Consuelo about involvement in death of Jered offspring," Kitos said with worried hesitation. "Said it was... accidental. Unintended. Meant only to cripple Judah machine, to cause disable result, not death. Force errant offspring to return back home. Pilot Kramer's maternal unit enraged. Pulled weapon from hiding place. Fired weapon twice. First time into paternal unit. Second time... I-I... sorry to relay this, pilot."

Jessica closed her hand around the red node. Her posture and facial expression were cold, rigid. The glowing marble pulsed, shining between her clutched fingers. Her numbness dissolved, and she began to shake.

"No... no, it's over, now," Jessica said, sniffling. "The big gate-damned mystery about the last days of the *oh-so-mighty* Fourth Gate Kramers is *finally* revealed, right? The curtain's pulled back. I... I think I know what I have to do, now, ape," she said, wiping back tears as she unsnapped her holster.

"Jessica, love, what are you—" Prath said, reaching for her.

Jessica Kramer pulled her 20mm Mattis revolver from its holster. Shots rang throughout the hangar bay, shattering the tomb-like silence.

CHAPTER FORTY-THREE_

SIXTH GATE ZONE
VERVOR'S FABRICATION WORKS

Jessica Kramer stirred as Vervor's shop van cruised in for its final approach landing. After skirting around Central Data's flight exclusion zone, they were now over their portion of the Sixth Gate Zone. The ride back was cramped and erratic in its flight path, but quiet.

Jessica kept her arms crossed, her head down. She'd not uttered a single word for the last half hour. Not that the Ascended across from her had any interest in what she had to say.

"That," Prath said, "was possibly *the* stupidest thing I've seen you do in the last few weeks, little human, and that's saying a lot. We needed that node."

"No, we didn't, ape," Jessica said, morose and sulking. "Bad enough I saw the still image from the hab's security cameras. I don't need the live video riding along with me for the upcoming fight. Kitos, when we get back, I want everything my dad's damned 'security ghost' touched to be purged from the other seven components in that module."

"I-I understand, pilot, but it will not be easy," Kitos said from the front of the hover-van. "Pilot's presence required while I-I perform circuit-dive, because of biocode lock. Task probably take hours. Days, possibly, depending on depth of code infiltration."

"I don't care," she said, keeping her head down. "I want it gone.

"Understood, Pilot," the Niff said.

"Prath... I don't think I have this fight in me," she said, turning to her Ascended crew chief. "I don't know if I even want to be a Kramer, any more."

"That's quitter talk. Snap out of it, girl," Prath said, trying to rub the high-pitched aftereffects of her gunshots out of his ears. "I understand why you wouldn't want Solomon's digital avatar coursing through your console, but we could have used the processing power from that node. And you could have warned me that you were going blast that thing to pieces, you know."

"Arkathan circuitry very tough," Kitos said from the front of the cramped vehicle. "I-I did not expect pilot to use all cylinders from personal weapon, either."

"What?" Prath called to Kitos.

"I-I said, Arkathan circuitry very—" the Niff said, louder.

"What?" Prath said again, louder as well, all the while smiling at Jessica.

"He heard you, Kitos," Jessica said, the veil of her misery lifting slightly. "Very funny, ape. Look, I'm sorry. I just... I just made a decision. I wanted it behind me. I wanted it over."

"Little human," Prath said, his smile fading, "if you go into the arena against Masamune with the Judah module missing thirteen percent of its performance, it will be over, all right."

Jessica crossed her arms again, looking away.

"We here," Kitos said, settling the utility craft in its small landing pad by the shop's cargo door. "Does not look like we only ones, though."

"What the void is this?" Jessica said, trying to crane her neck to see through the cramped vehicle's front windscreen.

"It appears Master Vervor has visitors," Prath said as he and Jessica extracted themselves from the back of the van. A long, sleek grav-craft filled the alley.

Mikralos, she thought, her lip curling into a sneer of disgust.

———

"What's the matter, Mikralos?" Jessica said as she entered through the shop's cargo doors. "Come to haggle over the hospital bills? And why is *he* here, anyway?"

"Ah, Mech Pilot Jessica Kramer," Mikralos said, his running lights pulsing blue and green. "We see you failed to encounter any fresh supplies of manners on your expedition to the Fourth Gate Zone. Master Mech Pilot Masamune Kyuzo is here at our invitation, Kramer. We understand this is not your first encounter with each other."

Masamune kept his hands behind his back, his body language rigid. He gave curt nods to them, but made only the briefest of eye contact with Prath or Jessica.

"We greet you in the Ways of the Old Code, Honored Mikralos," Prath said, smoothing out his tool vest and putting his palm out in deference.

"And we salute your admirable adherence to our code, Master Prath," the Gatekeeper said. "Imagine if your pilot emulated your constant professionalism."

"We all have our projects," Prath said. "She will surprise you, someday, we hope."

Jessica scoffed, then mumbled something under her breath.

"We did not quite catch that pilot," Mikralos said. "Would you mind, terribly, enunciating more clearly?"

"I said, 'it won't be *manners* I surprise you with,' *Honored* Mikralos," Jessica said.

Masamune smirked and lowered his gaze. Master Vervor clicked his fangs in disgust at Jessica's snide, sardonic remark.

Mikralos held his gaze on her, small bubbles rising in his transparent armored chamber. His running lights pulsed like flowing magma.

"This... *undertaking* is nearly at an end, Pilot," Mikralos said slowly. "We are looking forward, very much so, to the final result."

"So, how'd you know we went to the Fourth Gate Zone, Mikralos?" Jessica said. "I told you we were being followed, ape."

Prath shrugged.

"We have our ways, Kramer," the Gatekeeper said. "This is our realm, after all. Nothing happens without our knowledge."

"Nothing, huh? Explain that to Vervor's rib cage," Jessica said, barely masking her contempt. "Like the new flooring? It does a fine job of covering up the bloodstains."

"We said our knowledge, Pilot," Mikralos said, "not our involvement. An unfortunate criminal happenstance, no more. Incidentally, we understand the responsible parties have shuffled off this mortal coil. Thus, the matter is considered resolved. We have more pressing matters, namely, the reason we find ourselves here. We wished for one last conference before the final match. Observe." A thin manipulator claw from the Gatekeeper's chassis held out a data-chip to both mech gladiator pilots.

"What's this?" Jessica asked, taking the object while avoiding contact with the claw. It was the same one that had been around her neck, a few weeks ago.

"Contractual obligations, media residuals," Mikralos said in a bored, business-like tone. "Also, required equipment loadouts, parameters for the final match, and field conditions to be encountered. And our favorite part: next-of-kin notification forms, to be filled out by yourselves. No black box gimmickry. You shall both know each other's configuration ahead of time, as well as the terrain on the arena floor, and given adequate time to prepare."

"The only variable left unresolved," the Gatekeeper said, flourishing a flipper-like appendage inside his armored bubble, "is the close combat weapon to be used by our precocious Pilot Kramer. What have you decided to bear into the arena, Pilot?"

"Vervor, is the hammer back up and functional, yet?" she asked the Myoshan shop owner, her eyes locked with the Gatekeeper's.

"Negative, Pilot," Vervor answered. "The plasma lines were slashed and crushed during the four-way match. You and your computer are fortunate it didn't detonate in your hands. I'd have to rework the design and machine another one, from scratch. It wouldn't be ready in time."

"Okay. That makes it easy, then," Jessica said without missing a beat. "The chainsword, Mikralos."

"Your brother's? From Judah?" Prath said, surprised.

"Yup," she said, continuing to glower at Mikralos.

"Excellent," Mikralos said, turning to the silent figure of Masamune beside him. "There, you see, Master Pilot, there will be an added portion of poetry to the match."

Masamune stood mute, his eye looking straight ahead.

"Is he doing all the talking for you, this time, Masamune?" Jessica said, moving her head to meet his fixed gaze. "Not much use for a puppet if the puppet master does all the yapping."

Masamune's expression remain unchanged; sphinxlike, even.

"Oh, the Master Pilot is probably not in the mood for your usual disparaging banter, Pilot," Mikralos said. "Our associate, Dionoles, was recently forced to deliver the unfortunate news of the canceled match and rescheduled final confrontation at the Master Pilot's habitation pod."

"Master Pilot Masamune was disappointed by the inability to exercise his talents and abilities," Mikralos continued, "and made his feelings known concerning the adjusted schedule. Certain... *reminders* had to be made during the course of that conversation with our casino-managing associate. As you may know, Honored Dionoles does not possess our own gifts of charm and persuasion."

Masamune's eyes narrowed, his gaze now finding hers. She could tell there was pain there. *Good, I can use that,* she thought.

"Put you in your place, right inside your own pod, huh? That sucks," she said, feigning an exaggerated pout. Masamune remained unmoved.

"I read your father's book," Masamune Kyuzo said, his tone even and cold. "'Sometimes we do what we must, to preserve that which we love most.' That line has always stuck with me, Pilot."

"Yeah, well, that's a nice quote," Jessica replied, "but let's just say Dad's priorities were a little off, Kyuzo. He was more interested in the family name than the family itself, and my brother paid the price. It doesn't matter. He's gone. Just like Jered's gone. It's up to me, now. You're just a pawn in this game."

"This is not a game, and I have far more at stake than you know," Masamune Kyuzo said.

"Whatever. I'll see you in the arena, Masamune," she said.

"Yes, you will, Pilot," Masamune said, turning away.

The Gatekeeper and the master mech pilot boarded the

gleaming transport and departed. The grav yacht boosted in the direction of Berva Proxima, a short distance away.

Jessica gave a sarcastic wave good-bye as it left.

CHAPTER FORTY-FOUR

SIXTH GATE ZONE
BERVA PROXIMA ARENA

Mikralos contemplated on the implementation of the plan, how it was constantly on the edge of falling apart.

Damnation, that Kramer whelp is the living embodiment of vexation, he thought to himself. *There are times when we wish the Code did not prevent us from simply dropping a pressure nuke on her.*

"Honored Mikralos, what did Kramer mean," Masamune Kyuzo said to him from the grav-yacht's passenger seats, "about her brother paying the price for her father's priorities?"

"Who can fathom the derangement of humans, Master Pilot?" the Gatekeeper said, dismissing the question with a claw flip. "You beings are a textbook study in random incoherence."

They spent the rest of the short journey back to the Berva Proxima in silence.

Upon landing, Mikralos watched the scowling Masamune leave in his own personal transport, bound back for his home in the First Gate Zone. The Gatekeeper turned to his Ninety-Nine bodyguards.

"Take our transport," he said to the two biotroopers, "and bring that moron, Beliphres, back here. He will be huddled up at these coordinates, waiting for you. Also, do try not to have our grav-yacht shot down by that thrice-damned renegade Centurion."

CHAPTER FORTY-FIVE

SIXTH GATE ZONE

VERVOR'S FABRICATION WORKS

Jessica Kramer watched Kitos unload the hover-van after Mikralos and Masamune departed. The Niff rubbed his ears with one set of hands while he carried a tangled bundle of feral Arkathan circuitry with the other pair. After the four-armed being closed the door to the shop's mop closet, she turned to Prath.

"What the void did Masamune mean," she said, attempting her best stone-faced imitation of the departed master mech pilot, "by that burdenbeast-dung? You know, about 'doing what he had to, to save what he loved the most?'"

"Well, little human," Prath said, "I imagine Masamune had the same choice put in front of him that the Gatekeepers put in front of your father. Fight, or your family pays the price. Dionoles and Mikralos must be applying pressure on him to see the job through."

"Does he have kids?" Jessica asked.

"A pair, I believe," Vervor answered. "Male and female offspring. A lifemate, too."

"And the blobs leaned on him?" Jessica said. "Went to his habitat and laid down the law?"

"Apparently, love," Prath said. "Sound familiar?"

Jessica recalled when the Gatekeepers visited her own home, right before Jered's death match. They must have done something similar to Masamune.

"Gates," she said in disgust. "The wheel just keeps going round and round. This really is just some sick game to them, isn't it?"

Master Vervor snorted.

"Yes and no, human," the short shop proprietor said. "To the Gatekeepers, credits are nice, but power is the true coin of the realm. They are maintaining their balance of power, and dealing with emerging threats to it. You're the last vestige of one threat, the Kramers. Perhaps they see Masamune's little clan as another potential threat. Little Masamune Kenji is reputed to be a natural talent, from what I'm told. Maybe they're just nipping the next generations of upstarts in the bud. It makes sense."

"That's a little cold, spu-, er, Myoshan," Jessica said, correcting herself.

"Don't be naive. I'm clinical, not cold, human," Vervor said. "Silly questions sometimes require harsh answers."

"Basically, they're smashing you into each other," Prath said, "using one of you to cancel out the other, and then they'll deal with the survivor in their own time. I believe it's one of the commandments or edicts from their Old Code."

"Yes, from the section 'On Target Selection,' if I recall," Vervor said. "They neutralize the threat, and still get to adhere to their twisted Old Code the whole time. Thus, they win, and still get to keep their little flippers clean. It's a masterful exercise in ruthlessness, one they're very good at. It's admirable, really."

Prath and Jessica looked at Vervor, his forward eyes staring in the distance. He noticed their gaze, clicked his fangs, and shrugged.

"Again, I am being objective," the Myoshan said, grinning with sharp teeth. "You're both involved. I'm not. I have the luxury of seeing this from the outside. Either way, I get to fix the survivor's mech, and get paid."

"Such compassion for the struggles of your fellow beings," Jessica said, a wry smirk on her face at Vervor's frankness.

"What's the going rate on compassion, pilot?" Vervor said, returning a Myoshan version of her smirk.

"He's right, you know, little human," Prath said, sighing.

"Yeah, sure," Jessica said. "Alright, ape, let's get this patchwork mech humming. We have some ruthlessness of our own to dish out."

CHAPTER FORTY-SIX

SIXTH GATE ZONE
VERVOR'S FABRICATION WORKS

It was the old way of doing it, but Prath wanted it done right. The drone welderbots just couldn't get the correct bead, the ideal angle or penetration, so he clambered up the hull and did it himself, his ancient stick welder carried aloft by a hovering labor drone.

Prath nodded his head, dropping his welding hood over his face, and struck the arc. When the sound of sizzling metal hit the right note, he laid the bead of weld down the valley formed by the two angled armor plates. He could feel the deep heat of the weld, through his thick foot-gloves, but he put the burning pain to the back of his mind.

All that mattered was the right pace, the right angle. The welding electrode, or stick, shortened in length as it melted and fused with the metal, the puddle leaving a dim slug track in his welding mask's darkened viewport.

He finished with the final pass. Lifting his hood, he smiled as the top coat of welding slag peeled off in thick curls, the deep red of the joined metal cooling underneath to a dull gray. *Perfect,* he thought. *Just task one of the help-bots to hit it with a wire wheel attachment, and it would be ready for paint.*

"Kitos, how are the new command pathways coming along?" Prath asked, shaking the heat out of his prehensile feet as he shifted to another, cooler section of the hull. "Do we have enough of that Arkathan webbing to run to all the major systems?"

"I-I believe so, Master Prath," the Niff replied. "Weapons, sensors, and thrusters are priorities, as directed. I-I will patch into main control panel after bundled."

Kitos' harness shimmered, covered in random lengths of the silvery threads of advanced alien nanocircuitry recovered from the old hangar in the Fourth Gate Zone.

"Good," Prath said. "That was an excellent idea, splicing those feral lines into the system. Reaction time should be improved, immensely."

"Yeah, great," Jessica said, her feet up on a bench. "Let's just completely rewire the whole system, right before the match,"

"It's not a rewire, love," Prath said. "It's a control system enhancement. If the new lines are cut, you'll revert to the normal circuitry. Now, put on a grav-harness and help him out, little human. I'm sure your expertise can be put to use."

She sighed. Prath saw her waver between giving him a snarky response and getting to work. She clicked the harness around her shoulders and floated up to Kitos, who was perched on the left shoulder of the mech. The Niff was busy feeding a new line of Arkathan wire to the mech's heavy cannon.

"Alright, Niff, let's get it done," she said. "The sooner we're finished, the sooner we can circuit-dive."

Prath smiled as Jessica began assisting Kitos. It was good to see the change in her, even if that came at the cost of all she had been through in the last few days.

The crew chief shook off any negative thoughts of his friend Solomon's past mistakes before they could distract him. Instead, he concentrated on the good, looking down on his dead comrade's daughter, grudgingly hard at work.

Satisfied that Jessica was pulling her weight, he dropped his welding hood with a flick of his head. Prath fed another electrode into his welder, and struck another bead.

CHAPTER FORTY-SEVEN

SIXTH GATE ZONE
BERVA PROXIMA ARENA

Mikralos regretted summoning his two companions, Dionoles and Beliphres, within minutes of their arrival. The initial formal greetings almost immediately dissolved into acrimonious squabbling.

"What is this whispering that reaches our audio sensors, Mikralos?" Beliphres demanded. "Did you actually entrust this... this spineless bloatfish to act in a manner to which he is completely unsuited in character and demeanor? Is there cause for alarm? What is the cause of this sudden reduction in his normal levels of cowardice?"

"Whom do you presume to slander, Beliphres?" Dionoles asked in his high voice, subtly altering his tone to show he was now made of sterner stuff. "Ourselves? We tire of your bluster and bombast. We know how to make these underbeings submit to our will. Are we not the master of the Celestial Kingdom establishment?"

"Your Nines help you threaten one insignificant human's

family," Beliphres said, scoffing, "and suddenly you believe yourself to be some streetwise crime lord? Some swaggering tower of strength? It is cause for laughter, Dionoles."

"Honored Beliphres, Honored Dionoles, please," Mikralos said, trying to soothe both of his irate combat-mates, "we ask you drop this unseemly matter that continues to divide you and distract from our efforts. You are both guests, here, and should conduct yourselves accordingly. Our companion, Dionoles, acted in the manner he saw best, at the time. The Master Mech Pilot is now agreeable to the task in the arena, and no longer suffers from a mild case of doubt. Dionoles was able to convince him that adherence to plan was the optimum route. Beliphres, is your own area of operations secured?"

"Our associate is equipped and ready with the weapon, as requested," Beliphres said, still continuing to stare down Dionoles. "We shall be standing by for your signal, Honored Mikralos, if needed."

"Do you have any associates left?" Dionoles said, sneering. "Word on the ground level is that your assets are rather sparse, these days, thanks to the Head—"

Beliphres's large combat claw deployed in the blink of an eye, slamming Dionoles into the office-bunker's thick wall. Spider-webbed cracks appeared in the concrete, radiating out from the crater left by the casino owner's chassis.

"The lesser beings would call your bluster play-acting the part of tough guy, Dionoles," Beliphres said, flexing his heavy close-combat weapon. "Do not dream you can possibly fill that role. You are a base and utter coward, and always shall be. Never forget that irredeemable fact, or the consequences of disrespecting us."

"Outrage! Cease this, at once! We demand it," Mikralos said, pointing charged plasma cannons at each of the other two Gatekeepers in his office.

Dionoles extracted himself from the wall, chips and concrete dust falling from the deep impression he left.

"You will regret that, someday, Beliphres," Dionoles said, his voice shaken.

"We doubt it, bloatfish," Beliphres said.

"Are you two quite finished with the posturing and witty repartee?" Mikralos said, his charged cannons still pointed at each of them. "Quite done inflicting damage to our place of business? Yes, or no? Or shall we fetch the cleaning drones to remove your mingled ashes from the floors?"

They both signaled their grudging agreement. Mikralos put his cannons away, attempting to regain his composure.

"Good," the master of Berva Proxima said. "Despite Dionoles's efforts, noteworthy as they are, we are not entirely convinced Masamune is a fervent believer in the spirit of our agreement with him. We propose another means of ensuring compliance. Beliphres, we require the use of your remaining asset for a small task."

"Name it, Honored Mikralos," Beliphres said, casting a smug look at the Dionoles, who was still trying to shake off the effects of the bludgeoning.

"Your trigger-puller has chosen a suitable position overlooking the arena, yes?" Mikralos asked.

"Of course. Skreeb reports that he is primed and ready," Beliphres answered.

"Superb. We wonder, though," Mikralos said, his running lights pulsing orange and black, "if this Skreeb fellow knows the whereabouts of the learning center attended by Masamune Kyuzo's male offspring..."

CHAPTER FORTY-EIGHT_

SIXTH GATE ZONE
THE HEADHUNTER'S LAIR

The Headhunter's solid black eyes watched the last crate of firearms loaded into the back of the hovertruck. Nolo went through the tall, glowing racks of payment, verifying each veined, leathery egg was intact. His count done, the Model Ninety-Nine adjutant gave a hand signal to the Headhunter. The giant red cyborg waved a large claw, and the hovertruck departed.

"Okay, that's out of the way," the Headhunter said. "On to tonight's business. You've made sure the bets are spread around on the fight?"

"Affirm, boss," Nolo said, nodding.

"We get to use the blobs' arrogance to finance their own downfall," the red cyborg said, a grin with a hint of smugness on his reinforced organic face. "Those credits are going to go a long way towards helping our effort. Sweet and appropriate, using their system against them, don't you think?"

"Cogging is boss' duty, not selfsame's," Nolo said. The Headhunter shrugged, shifting in his giant seat.

"Still nothing on Beliphres?" the Headhunter asked.

"Neg, boss," Nolo answered. "Complete stealth. Should make appearance at arena for match, though. Target shows, selfsame will know."

"Good," the Headhunter said. "Make sure the package gets delivered to Pilot Kramer, would you? I hope she doesn't take it the wrong way. Do you think it was too much? I'm not the best at gift-giving, sometimes."

Nolo smirked up at the armored titan.

"Boss getting sweet on Kramer?" his adjutant said. "Sending package, intent to... persuade? Woo?"

"Naw, Nolo, just protecting my investment," the Headhunter said, smiling, the smallest of blushes coloring his pasty complexion. "I mean, it's up to her if she uses the stuff, or not. 'It's the thought that counts,' right?"

"Selfsame hears boss," Nolo said. "Selfsame does not believe."

"Heh. Very funny," the Headhunter said. "I don't think it would work out, anyway, Nolo. She's too good for a being like me."

"Agree," Nolo said.

The smile dimmed from the cyborg's face as he pulled up a floating hologram of tonight's plan.

"Everything's in place for the match?" he asked Nolo. "Not just the bets, I mean."

"Internal arrangements secured. Comms secured. Transport primed," Nolo said, checking his data tablet.

"Good," the cyborg said. "The hits on Beliphres' places were scrimmages. Berva Proxima's the kickoff of the main game. There's a lot of heads that need collecting."

"Agreed, boss," Nolo said.

A backlit 3D printer in the giant, dark chamber signaled it was done producing its current job. It was a custom mounting bracket for the latest addition to the Headhunter's collection.

The crime lord detached from his charging throne, crossing the room with heavy steps. He dipped a secondary claw into a nearby pot of boiling acid, pulling out a Skevvian skull. Small bits of fragmentation gleamed amid the cracked cranial surfaces, embedded by force into the tan bone structure.

The Headhunter shook it dry, clicking it into the printed bracket's custom struts.

"A handsome piece, Nolo," the Headhunter said, marveling at the new trophy. "I can't believe she helped take down a mini-mech while I was passed out. Make sure you thank Dodger for me. I even know the perfect spot for it."

CHAPTER FORTY-NINE

FIRST GATE ZONE
ALLBEINGS COMMUNITY LEARNING CENTER

Masamune Kenji left the learning center after the bell rang, his shoes loose from being untied. Tying shoes, despite his father's best efforts, was still a skill he had not yet mastered. Kenji could run a training mech around the arena like a sprinter, but the finer points of shoestrings continued to elude him.

All his schoolmates were chattering, excited about tonight's death match between his father and some human lady named Kramer. Young Masamune was excited, too. His father usually brought home ice cream after a match.

Kenji made his way down the learning center's front steps, happy to be out of class. A sleek, silvery grav-car waited there. The other children played, chasing each other, playing tag, or chirping about the latest arena news or favorite Unlimited fighter.

He paid them no mind, fascinated instead by his reflection in the grav-car's mirrored windows. Kenji found himself drawn to the dark windows of the vehicle, its muscular, flowing shape like something out of an action holo-show. He made funny faces in the dark reflective surfaces.

A window rolled down, a cloud of sour-smelling vapor escaping from the grav-car. A shadowy reptilian figure emerged from the fog. It pointed the muzzle of its pistol at his face. "You. Mammal," the being with dual camera eyes said to him. "You're Masamune's boy, right?"

Kenji nodded, transfixed by the gaping maw of the gun barrel.

"In," the Shasarr cyborg said with a flick of the handgun towards the back seat.

The car door opened, and Kenji felt his shoe slip off as he followed the being's curt instructions. The door slammed shut before he could retrieve it.

The vehicle blasted away, startling the other children swarming around on the learning center's front steps.

———

FIRST GATE ZONE

MASAMUNE MECHWORKS

Miles away, Masamune Kyuzo's testing was nearly complete. Hepsah, his human crew chief, had ironed out the last hitch in the claw's strike sequence. Before a normal death match, he would be silently full of joy at this time. Now, with the Gate-keepers breathing down his neck, it was only a moment of quiet contemplation.

"Final run," Hepsah's voice said over the comm channel, fed direct into his head. "Weapon is reading at full power. Verify."

"Verified, full power," Masamune Kyuzo said aloud, his eyes closed in the sleep-like control trance. "Looking good up here, all across the board."

"All yours. Engage," his crew chief said.

Kyuzo's sensors fed him the distances to the hanging metal target. It was a thick ingot of unprocessed steel, fresh from the refinery around the corner. Two heavy chains led to the floating lifter drones above it. Deep cuts from the previous test runs scarred its length, but none penetrated deep enough to his satisfaction.

He snarled in his seat, and sent his mech's reworked forearm, with its glowing plasma blades, screaming at the metal test piece. With a flash of light and heat, the heavy claw sliced through the cylinder, cutting it in half. Thick, superheated disks, the segments carved from between the claws, flew in all directions of the strike's follow-through.

His mech's sensors gave him feedback on the damage. *Excellent,* he thought.

Kyuzo preferred his plasma-edged sword, but this claw had been with him when he started in the arenas, when they first brought him here to Junctionworld. It felt good, having it back again.

His crew chief, Hepsah, gave him a grin, checking off one last box on her clipboard tablet. A light came on in the corner of her screen, and she put her hand to her earpiece.

"Masamune-san, I have an urgent comm coming through for you," Hepsah said, her voice in his head. "Emergency status. It's your wife. I'll patch it through."

CHAPTER FIFTY

Prath clicked his tongue at the sad state of furniture affairs that lay before him. His last-minute efforts to secure three comfortable circuit-diving chairs resulted in one bullet-perforated bench from the shop assault, one stale-smelling chaise discarded in a nearby back alley, and a stained lounger borrowed from the bar on the corner. *Slipshod*, he thought, *but it would have to do*.

"Jessica, love," Prath said, "Kitos and I have isolated the last of the corrupted code that Solomon... that your father left behind."

"Good," she said, a bit too fast for his taste. "Watching old Masamune replays while you guys circuit dive next to me is getting old. Let's get this over with."

"Allow me to link into the module before you and Kitos join me, please," Prath said, motioning to the shabby array of chairs. "I need you in proximity to the module, but don't dive yet. Your digital presence might activate other subroutines that I've managed to place into dormancy."

"Sure, ape," she said, a stoic look on her face. "Kitos can harness me up, and we'll dive when you say so."

"Excellent," Prath said, pulling as data-line from the interface computer on the bench and jacking it into the port in his neck.

The Ascended took a semi-comfortable position on the stained bar-lounger, and closed his eyes, letting his consciousness filter and mesh with the module's interface.

He was once again in the computer's gray maintenance room. Kitos's elaborate representation of a work desk was there, as was his dear friend, Solomon Kramer.

At least, what was left of Solomon. The extraction of the defensive barriers was not easy, and bits of his human friend's frozen icon had rough, pixelated chunks of it removed. The gaping cranial gash left by the removal of the interception and deception protocols was most disturbing to Prath, and he avoided looking at or through it too closely.

"Resume program," Prath said. Kitos's digital desk glowed in concert with the illuminated band around the room.

The last vestige of his human friend came to stuttering life.

"Pra-a-ath," Solomon's ghost said.

"I know you are all that remains, my friend," Prath said. "I want you to know, what I am about to do, I do not do lightly."

"Explana-a-tion," the piecemeal avatar said as it blurred and rebooted.

"None needed," Prath said. Overhead, he heard Jessica make a slight squawk as Kitos tried to fit the awkward diving hood over her head. "None will suffice, anyway."

The Ascended snapped his long digital fingers, and a red dome flickered into virtual existence.

"We do not have much time," Prath said. "The maintenance interface is now sealed, Solomon. I want answers. The defensive barrier was rudimentary, able to address any of your offspring in a passable, functional manner. It has more memory devoted to it under my name, though. You must not have factored heavily on the children finding out, but you did for me. Why? Access that database, now."

The elder Kramer froze, then shifted in subtle tones. *This footage must have been recorded separately,* Prath thought.

"Pra-a-th, what I did," Solomon's avatar said in halting speech, "Did for... for family."

"You did for your pride and paranoia, you mean," Prath said.

"Family... result of pride," Solomon said.

"Pride also resulted in its destruction, Sol," Prath said. "You were so worried and ashamed about Jered's wild ways playing into the Gatekeepers' hands, you put him in the grave, instead."

"Un-un-unintended... consequence," Solomon said. "Paid for it."

"You did, indeed," the crew chief said to his former leader. "Your daughter is still paying for it."

"Hannah," the ghost said.

"In her own way, yes," Prath said. "We have no idea where she is, or if she is safe, behind the Eighth Gate. We will, though, I promise you. No, I mean Jessica."

"Jessi-si-ca," the Kramer avatar said, its head bowing. "Baby. My... my baby."

"She's right behind me, Solomon, ready to dive," Prath said, his digital hands glowing as he activated a hidden program. "She wants you purged. I need more answers, but I don't have enough time. Prepare yourself."

Prath's glowing hands came up, palms together. He separated them, and the digital ghost of Solomon Kramer cloned itself, two damaged copies now standing side-by-side.

The Ascended rotated his cyber-self's hands ninety degrees, and squashed them together. The copy of Solomon's avatar shrank into a small, glowing point of orange and blue light.

Prath summoned the compacted data cluster to himself, and placed it into a pocket on his avatar's tool vest. With another snap of his large, brown fingers, the red dome around the room disappeared. Just in time, too.

Kitos popped into the digital room first, followed by Jessica.

"He's ready," Prath said.

"'He' is not my father, ape," Jessica said. There was a small flash of anger in her eyes, but Prath saw her recover. *Good,* he thought. *She's gotten better, hopefully.*

"Naturally, love," Prath said, trying not to antagonize her. He turned to the Niff technician. "Kitos, I believe we are ready."

Jessica's avatar agreed, and gave the signal with the digital representation of her hand.

The Niff technician's avatar nodded, his four sets of fingers turning and adjusting the holographic controls floating above his workbench.

Prath reached out to her. He held her in an embrace that felt authentic, even if it was just sensory feedback from the program. She buried her face in his shoulder, trying to stop the flow of simulated tears.

Jessica Kramer and Prath both raised a hand, a goodbye to the malfunctioning vestige of Solomon Kramer's ghost. His disrupted, pixelated image stuttered in one last error loop, whispering electronic gibberish to no one as it tried to reassert control over the Arkathan circuitry.

There was a bright strobe of light in the digital workspace. The last of the visible infected code was gone from the NoName control module, and so was the last trace of his friend. For the most part.

"Goodbye, Poppa," she said.

"Until we see each other again, Solomon, my friend," Prath said, his digital avatar's hand clasped over the thorny prize in his pouch.

CHAPTER FIFTY-ONE_

CENTRAL DATA TOWER

CHAMBERS OF THE COUNCIL OF EIGHT

GateLord Novalos, responsible for the Sixth Gate Zone and all that occurred within it, scanned the last report from Mikralos with mild disinterest. He sighed small bubbles in his protective life-support housing. This wearying enterprise would soon be over. Until then, he had to deal with the meddling and second-guessing of his fellow members of the Council of Eight. Here came one, now.

"We are concerned," GateLord Xenebris said, hovering closer to him. The Eighth Gate Zone's commander left his bodyguards at the side chamber's door.

"Concerned?" Novalos asked. "With what?"

"This plan of yours..." Xenebris said. "Years in the making, millions of credits spent, and now, tonight is the night of its supposed culmination. Yet, we do not feel... fully satisfied. What contingencies have you taken to assure the completion of this goal?"

Novalos's running lights pulsed in umbrage.

"Our best field commander is on it," GateLord Novalos said. "We have no concerns. He may be a horrendous businessman and arena runner, but you should have seen him during the invasion of this place. He was a veritable monster, a true killing machine."

"Yet he involves two lesser foot soldiers in the plan," Xenebris countered, "one a less-than-reputable heel, the other a trembler."

"The Fifth Gate Zone recovery specialist? The casino manager?" Novalos said. "What of them? A good commander delegates to his subordinates, after all."

"We find ourselves, how should we say this," Xenebris said, trying to choose his words carefully, "*less than enthusiastic* about his selection of subordinates. We know they were all part of the same combat triad, yes, but the conquest of Junctionworld was centuries ago. Surely, there were better choices available?"

Novalos studied his fellow GateLord. He could see where this was leading.

"Are... are you trying to change our bet?" the Sixth Gate-Lord asked.

"Feh, *bet*," Xenebris said, sneering. "You call our paltry side wager on Kramer's death a bet? Why, we could win more, placing a clawful of credits on a back-alley octorat race."

"You wound our pride with your prattling," Novalos said, "though we are keen to your transparent manipulations. Very well. We shall double our wager on Mikralos. Actually... triple it. Such is our faith in his ability to oversee the destruction of the last of the Kramers."

"Triple? We shall take that bet," Xenebris said, his lights pulsing with delight. "As the Old Code says, 'A fool and his credits are soon parted.' Ah, you shall owe us a magnificent sum when your Mikralos simpleton fails to seal the deal."

GateLord Novalos summoned a nearby notary drone. Both

executive Gatekeepers placed a claw over the small recording surface on top of its dome, sealing their new gambling accord.

"We look forward to taking your credits," Novalos said. "Pray tell, will you be joining us at the match tonight?"

"The final death match at Berva Proxima arena?" Xenebris said, reeling slightly. "We would not be caught dead in such a dung-pile. Oh, we understand your attendance is necessary, of course, said dung-pile being located in your own Sixth Gate Zone."

"Well, appearances must be maintained, after all," Novalos said, "and we know you are oh-so busy with your *extensive* defense preparations in the Eighth Gate Zone."

The snide remark about the forbidden zone did not escape Xenebris's notice, and his chassis wobbled a fraction. *Good,* Novalos thought, *one hopes that found the mark, you arrogant porkbeast.*

"Yes, well, we do have certain matters to attend to in the Eighth Gate Zone preparations," Xenebris said, recovering. "We regret that we must decline your kind invitation. Now, let us return to the main Council chambers. The other members of the Eight will wonder what we are up to."

CHAPTER FIFTY-TWO

Jessica Kramer looked up from the palm-projector in her hand. It was more post-fight commentary on Masamune's latest fight with Gorth at Ferro Fortress arena. Prath stood over her, a warm smile on his face.

"What is it, ape?" she asked.

"Master Vervor and his crew would like to show you something," Prath said. "They're still a bit afraid of you, so they sent me to ask you to come over."

"Fine," she said, snapping the holographic palm-projector's clamshell body closed. She followed Prath from the front of the shop back to one of the fabrication bays. As she rounded the stall's protective wall, the contents of the tall, deep room came into view. She gasped.

Jessica marveled at the massive close combat weapon hanging vertically in the shop's ready rack. It was far longer than the shop's hover van. Its dual rows of vicious motorized blades were polished to a mirror shine, and her family's fighting colors of blue and orange were arranged in slanted hazard stripes along its sides and grip.

Beneath it, the gathered survivors of Vervor's shop, and Vervor himself, arranged themselves in a pair of ranks, like a military formation.

"You... you guys did that?" she said, awestruck. "For... for me?"

"The counter-rotating blades were a pain to resynchronize after paint and chroming," Vervor said, "but, yes, Pilot, we did that. For you."

"Oh... oh, Master Vervor, thank you," Jessica said, kneeling to hug him. His scales rasped against her jacket.

Vervor's mouth opened in a small gape. He looked at Prath as the human continued to smother him in affection. Prath smiled and shrugged back at the Myoshan. Eventually, she let him go.

"Well... we wanted to honor you for avenging our fallen crew members," Vervor said, trying to regain his hard-bitten dignity. "Master Prath and Kitos told me what you went through with the Headhunter. It looks pretty, Pilot, but you need to give it a test. Mount up."

Jessica climbed into her mech, bringing down the thick, clear armored glass. The preliminary boot-up sequence was done before she snapped all her restraint belts in place.

"I still can't get used to your new speed, NoName," she said.

"Understood, Pilot," the battle computer said in her headphones. "This Unit can adjust to something more sedate and subtle, if necessary."

"No, no, Prath and Kitos would kill me," Jessica said, giving a short laugh as she ran her hands over the controls. "We spent all this time tuning you after the merging and rebuild. I'm just... well, I guess I'm impressed. That's all, NoName."

"Acknowledged, Pilot," the Arkathan command module said.

She moved to scoop up the reconditioned chainsword from its place on the rack. Vervor and his crew really had done a beautiful job restoring her brother's old weapon.

She engaged the weapon's dual drives. The two parallel belts of linked blades spun in opposite directions, filling the shop with their lethal scream. *I see why Jered liked this thing*, she thought. *Let's see what it can do.*

"Deploy chainsword, NoName," she said, grasping her controls. Wielding the melee weapon in the testing booth was like fighting in a shower unit, but she would need that. Masamune was going to be deadly, in close, with that claw.

The whirring weapon sliced through the armor test plates like they weren't there, a flurry of sparks and metal chips cascading to the floor, followed by the top halves of the targets. And the target stand. *Oops.*

She gave the assembled crew below her a thumbs-up through the cockpit glass, a large smile on her face. Prath covered his eyes, shaking his head.

"I should have known," Master Vervor said.

"Alright, little human, that's enough," Prath said into his comm set, "the time is upon us. Power down, and prepare yourself for the match."

Dusting hot particles of metal from his shoulders, Vervor turned to his assemble crew of Myoshans.

"Get this thing loaded," Vervor barked, his crew breaking formation in a furious scramble of scales and claws. "We'll clean up that mess later. I want those tamper seals in place, too. This thing doesn't leave your sight. All four eyes, scanning the whole time, front and back, do you understand me? Now, let's get moving."

CHAPTER FIFTY-THREE

FIRST GATE ZONE

MAELSTROM GARDENS HABITATION POD COMPLEX

Master Mech Pilot Masamune Kyuzo made the final adjustments on his prosthetic hand and placed his dark, gleaming pistols, one by one, into their holsters. It was the final part of his pre-match ritual. Now, for the hard part.

He opened the door to the rest of the habitat. His wife was still on the floor of the living room, holding Miko, weeping, calling Kenji's name over and over till her voice was ragged. Little Miko's face was filled with confusion at the state of her mother's agonized cries, and tears streamed down her own round face. Her wails of alarm chorused with the sound of her mother's tortured grief.

Anora heard the door from the back hallway open. She picked herself up, Miko on her hip, and threw herself at Kyuzo as he emerged from the room.

"You... you bring him *back here*, you hear me?" his wife said through tears. "I don't care *what* you have to do! I don't care *who* you have to... I just don't *care*! You bring our son *home*, you understand me? You bring Kenji *home! Do you understand me?* Oh, Gate *damn* it, Kyu-u-u-zo..."

She collapsed against him, her anguish choking her, and her body shook with sobs. He tried steadying her, trying to choke back the hate and anger inside him. Kyuzo tried to hold his wife, all while touching Miko's crying face. He hugged them as hard as he dared, breathing in deep, as if to keep them safe from this place, safe in his arms. He felt a tear glide down his cheek, soaking into his wife's close-cropped black hair.

He leaned them back, guiding Anora and their baby girl to rest on the living room's couch.

"I will, my love," Kyuzo said. The words felt cold, empty, coming from his mouth.

"Don't do this thing," she said, her eyes red and blood-shot.

"Do what?" he replied, his organic hand clenching into a fist.

"Our boy is on the line," Anora said, wiping her face and eyes, and then pointing an accusatory finger up at him. "Don't you pull this cast-iron son-of-a-bitch routine with me. I've seen this emotional shutdown dung before."

Kyuzo's face flushed. He had tried forestalling this, putting it to the side. She was his lifemate, though, and knew him better than he knew himself. *Gate damn it,* he thought. Like countless times before, he locked his rage down, channeling his emotions so they could be used instead of consuming him.

"I... I am going out there to save him, Anora," he said in slow, deliberate tones. "I can't... let this rattle me. I can't be distracted. I need to stay... focused."

"Vent your venting focus, you hear me?" she screamed, standing up to hold him by the shoulders. She dumped their daughter on to the couch, setting off a fresh cascade of wailing from Miko. "You bring Kenji home! You kill anyone standing in the way! You hand the blobs her head, personally, if that means Kenji comes back home!"

He pulled his wife's clawing, grief-wracked hands off his uniform, and kissed her forehead, once and slow.

"I will do what I have to," Masamune said. "I promise."

He strode from their habitat, the haunting sound of his son's name echoing in his mind.

Gatekeeper Mikralos's silver grav-yacht waited for him in an adjacent landing area. He walked up the back ramp and took a seat. A Niner crew member offered him a beverage before takeoff.

Kyuzo took the cylindrical refreshment container and crushed it in his prosthetic hand. The red liquid contents ran down his arm, forming a puddle on the interior deck of the luxurious grav-craft. Masamune wiped his wet mechanical palm across the front of the confused Nine's flight uniform.

"Damn your drink, and damn your master," Kyuzo said, murder in his eyes. "Get me to the arena. Now."

CHAPTER FIFTY-FOUR

SIXTH GATE ZONE
BERVA PROXIMA ARENA

Jessica found her ready room at the arena easy enough, with the help of the arena staff. This wasn't a rushed event, and she had time, perhaps too much time, to think about the upcoming fight.

Unlike her last time here, when it was a cattle call with four fighters and their staffs crowding the place, this was the star treatment. Fruit tray, cold cuts, and holographic flowers. There was even a gift. A package waited for her on the counter in front of the bathroom mirror, a glossy red box with a satin red ribbon tied around it.

"Oh, how nice," she said aloud, opening the card. "Maybe Mikralos isn't such a dung-sucker, after all."

"To Fire-Girl," she read to herself, "You're better without this, but just in case. See you soon. All My Best, Red."

Setting the card to the side, she opened the box and let out a noise that was a mixture of surprise, joy, and bad memories.

It was a vial of the healing stim-agent from the raid with the Headhunter. It was cool and slick in her hand as she picked it up, its slow-moving liquid contents languishing, back and forth, inside the transparent cylinder.

She looked at herself in the mirror. Holding the vial in one hand, she pulled her Dad's flask from her suit with the other, and glanced at her reflection again.

Prath knocked on the door and stepped into the ready room with one motion. She set the two containers of fluid down, and turned to face him.

"The arena staff are growing impatient, little human, Prath said. "I'm running out of excuses. It's time. Are you ready? What are those?"

"It's nothing," she said, turning from the mirror to face him. "I'm ready, Prath."

He took her hands in his, his brown eyes looking deep into hers.

"I know you are, love. For Jered," he said, a tear forming as he said her brother's name. He wiped it away, but not before she saw it.

"For Jered," she answered, trying to make her own eyes not well up. "And... thanks, Prath. Really, thank you."

"For what, little human?" her Ascended friend asked, sniffling.

"You know, for... for putting up with me," she answered, her voice coming to her in spurts. "I wouldn't be here without you. I owe you. I know I haven't made it easy, and... I'm sorry, again, about what I said. Before. Back at the shop."

He looked at her, a puzzled look on his face. He leaned in to smell her breath. She stopped him, then patted his broad chest.

"Hey, easy, ape," she said in mock protest. "I'll pass the bio-scan, don't worry."

He smiled, then opened the bag he carried at his side, showing her his folded-up banner tucked inside.

"Mikralos wants to see me," Prath said.

Jessica scowled at the news.

"Not to worry, love," Prath said. "I'm sure it's just some last-minute intimidation. I can handle it. Don't be troubled. Afterwards, though, I'll be waving my old fabric sign from the stands."

She relaxed.

"Are you ready to fight?" Prath asked her. "Do you know what you're fighting for?"

"Yes, ape. For Our Freedom, and Yours," Jessica Kramer said.

They walked out the ready room's door together, a full vial, and a full flask, still on the countertop.

Time to mount up, she thought.

CHAPTER FIFTY-FIVE_

Jessica was almost impressed. Mikralos had splurged on real fireworks for the pilot introductions and opening ceremony. The smoke still hung in the air, the filters of Berva Proxima's aging life support systems straining to keep up with the choking stench of sulfur. Now, it was time for her and NoName to walk out of the gate.

"Ready, Mister Eighty-Seven-Percent?" she asked her Arkathan battle computer.

"This Unit is ready, Pilot," the voice in her headphones replied.

She avoided looking at her father Solomon's graven image on the side of the arena entrance gate, concentrating instead on her brother Jered's small commemorative icon.

She held her mech's massive chainsword aloft to the crowd's fanfare, her running lights pulsing as she revved the blades for maximum noise. Blazing curtains of fireworks shot out around the gate as she emerged, the individual armored scales of her canopy armor slamming shut with every step the mech took.

A swarm of tell-tales and target boxes popped up on the interior screen of her armored cockpit, the wrapped interior view relaying what the exterior cameras and sensors saw.

The starting circle beckoned ahead of her. Beyond it, a field of pillars lay before her in a sweeping hexagon pattern, a tall pyramid at its center which blocked a direct shot at the other starting circle.

The segmented cylinders were all about the same height as her mech, about two feet in diameter, and covered the floor of Berva Proxima, from wall to wall, in their vast six-direction array.

"They only use this arrangement for the special matches, huh, NoName?" She asked her mech.

"Correct, Pilot," NoName answered. "The 'House of Columns' battlefield configuration is costly in terms of set-up and resources, and is rarely utilized."

"Packed kinda tight together, aren't they?" Jessica said. "I don't think we can even fit between them without knocking one or both sides down as we move."

"As intended, Pilot," NoName said. "Limited distance line of sight, lack of maneuvering room, intended to bring combatants in close proximity. Columns are hard cover, but not anchored. Collapsible. Suggested strategy on left panel. Opening salvo, indirect fire weaponry. Firing solution loaded."

Jessica reviewed the vectoring arrows hovering on the holo-screen.

"Yeah, I'll think about it," she said. "Let's fire it up."

"Reactor output increased," NoName reported. "All jets ready."

"Give the blob his salute," Jessica Kramer said, "and let's go."

———

Masamune Kyuzo watched the introductions fireworks with his own eyes, then closed them. His breathing slowed, and he felt himself slip into the interface with his mech's system. He did not feel the same numbness. Now it was only hate. Hate for the Gatekeepers who had his son, hate at his own feeling of helplessness, and hate for the brat across the arena. Her removal from this game would get Kenji back. *So be it,* he thought.

There was no flash, no showmanship, as his red and white mech stormed to the starting circle. His battle claw engaged, the dagger-like blades sizzling with plasma. The armored hood descended over his cockpit glass in segments, locking out the light and noise of the crowd. The arena layout didn't matter. The fireworks didn't matter.

The target was on the other side of the forest of columns, and she had to die.

He punched his claw in salute to Mikralos' viewing bubble, then snapped it back to his side before the Gatekeeper's lights could flash in response.

He was ready.

CHAPTER FIFTY-SIX

SIXTH GATE ZONE
BERVA PROXIMA ARENA

Gatekeeper Mikralos remembered why he liked watching arena matches alone. Beliphres was an annoying viewing partner, one who seemed to find silence and contemplation intolerable. Mikralos sighed bubbles as the Fifth Zone Recovery Specialist insisted on filling the idle time with mindless chit-chat.

"A fine day for a match, what say you, Honored Mikralos?" Beliphres said.

"We say it will be a fine day when it is over, Honored Beliphres, despite your flubbing," Mikralos said. "Is your being in position? The alternate solution?"

"Indeed, he is," Beliphres said. "He has company, as well. The Masamune offspring."

"A wise contingency," Mikralos said. "We cannot have these underbeings getting out of step."

Mikralos looked to the Ninety-Nine guard at the entrance to his viewing pod, and strobed his running lights at the being. The armored trooper nodded, pulling back the chain curtain to the pod. Prath entered the stretched sphere of a room, his height causing him to duck through the metal-veiled entrance.

The Ascended made his formal greeting to Mikralos, then turned to the unfamiliar Gatekeeper in the room.

"Ah, Master Prath," Mikralos said, "allow us to introduce the Honorable Beliphres, Recovery Operations Director for the Fifth Gate Zone. Beliphres is entrusted with the rejuvenation of that zone's economy after the unfortunate containment bombardment."

Prath bowed and extended his up-facing palm in greeting to the newly-introduced Gatekeeper.

"Ascended, we understand you are the crew chief for the Kramer pilot," Beliphres asked.

"Indeed, I am, Honored Beliphres," Prath answered.

"A most unusual configuration, your mech," Beliphres said. "One can see elements of a cargo loader, here and there, but it seems to be hacked and pasted onto the bones of a dissimilar chassis. It is not a beauty contest winner, but one can see the utility in such a design. Was this... intentional?"

"Indeed, it was," Prath said. "Honored Mikralos was generous in his assistance, and we utilized the best components available to us in the abbreviated time."

"We are intrigued, Master Ascended" Beliphres said, twirling a claw in amusement. "Tell us, when your pilot is killed tonight, what are your plans for further employment? We are considering forming an arena sports organization of our own, once certain domestic troubles are... settled." Beliphres's chassis lights pulsed slow and smooth shades of purple.

"I..." Prath said, pausing to find the right words, "I do not foresee the death, or defeat, of my pilot, Honored Beliphres. She is quite the skilled contestant. A good shot, too, so I'm told. Incidentally, were there not a series of building fires in your sector, a few days ago? What was the cause of that disturbance? Nothing untoward or unseemly, I hope."

Mikralos smirked at the mocking, extra-formal concern in the Ascended's voice, directed to Beliphres. *Cheeky primate,* Mikralos thought.

"A minor matter," Beliphres said, "soon to be resolved, Master Ascended, worry not. *Incidentally,* we are quite sure your pilot will not live through the match. Call it... a hunch. Regardless of her fate, we would retain your services after the business of this execution is concluded. You can expect an agreement to be forwarded to you, and you will, of course, sign it. We shall contact you, shortly."

Beliphres waved a claw in dismissal. The Ninety-Nine guard placed his glove on Prath's' shoulder. Prath bowed to Mikralos, who acknowledged the gesture with the flit of a silver tentacle, and excused himself.

"Your charming personality never ceases to amaze," Mikralos said to his fellow Gatekeeper.

"Oh, we know how to handle beings of his sort, Mikralos," Beliphres said. "After a minor period of adjustment, he will come around. A hobbling here, a castration there, and the Ascended will happily comply. We are nothing if not persuasive."

Prath parted the curtain of Mikralos's privacy chains and found himself in the viewing pod's antechamber, stunned. *They weren't even trying to hide it,* he thought. *I'm already passed on, like property, to a slave master. Insanity.*

He turned to one of the Ninety-Nine guards at the hallway entrance.

"Selfsame requires comms with 'The Future, The Way,' priority utmost," Prath said.

The trooper's black eyes narrowed as the Ascended spoke in fluid Niner dialect, and his hand went to the butt of his pistol. Prath put his large hands up in a non-threatening manner. The Ninety-Nine's partner made sure his master Mikralos wasn't listening through the curtain, and joined them.

"Negative, Ascended. Comms not necessary," the second Ninety-Nine bodyguard said. "Subject already inbound to this pos."

Prath smiled.

"Well, if you gentlebeings don't mind, then," Prath said, "I'll just go find my seat, and watch the show."

CHAPTER FIFTY-SEVEN

BERVA PROXIMA ARENA
MAIN PERFORMANCE FLOOR

Jessica Kramer and her mech, NoName, screamed from the starting circle, a tumbling path of columns left in her wake. As she slammed into them, one after the other, the strained snarl on her face became more and more severe. Altering her orientation so NoName's hull fit between the columns seemed to help, but slowed her down.

She throttled back, and a klaxon sounded. Incoming.

Sidestepping, she sought cover behind a fresh, untumbled row of the vertical cylinders. A missile spiked into her last position, a dozen feet away, blasting the rubble and sand down to the arena's steel floor plates.

She brought her indirect cannon online. She could hear the weapon's hydraulics engage somewhere behind her.

"NoName, bracket his last known position. Triangle of thumper rounds around it," Jessica said. "Fire."

The crowd roared as the indirect cannon over her mech's right shoulder swiveled into position. Three deep concussions, one after another, thudded through her armor. *Shoot and scoot, girl,* she thought. *Make him keep moving, too.*

The engagement pattern continued for what seemed like an eternity, but a timer in her cockpit display showed the passing of only a couple minutes. The incessant harassing fire added to her tension. Every time Jessica popped her jets to get take a peek at Masamune through this damned sea of posts, he would launch another missile at her, or send a light burst of suppressive cannon fire her way. He was somewhere around the center pyramid, judging by the angles of attack and the trail of broken columns. *A straight shot to the middle,* she thought. *Is he even trying?*

Jessica mashed the controls to the left when NoName's alarms went off, once again, warning of another incoming missile strike.

This time, she wasn't quick enough, and the missile slammed home. The force of the explosion was countered by two segments of her cockpit's reactive armor. The timed counter-detonations dampened the incoming strike, but it was deafening, having a flat charge go off next to her head. Recovering, her nerves raw with adrenaline, she kept moving, then stopped.

I'll have to work my way to the center, she thought, *and hopefully, he expends his load-out by then.*

Her momentary pause over, she boosted hard for the central pyramid. Though she thought she was now well-practiced at moving through the crowded array at a slight angle, her armor's hull skipped off an errant concrete rod. Her speed sent NoName careening as the arena's crowd roared and camera drones flashed their strobes. A dozen columns toppled as she tumbled, scattering into segments that broke even more nearby columns. She righted her armor. The cascading domino effect left her surrounded by a wide clearing of toppled column segments.

"Great," she said.

Jessica used her controls to grab a fallen segment from the ground just as NoName warned again of another inbound missile.

"How many of those gate-damned things does he have, NoName?" she shouted.

"Starting load of top-attack missiles was six," the computer said. "One remaining, Pilot, after this one impacts."

"Hey, bot, see all these pieces of armor lying on the ground around us?" she said. She bobbed the piece of concrete in NoName's hand like a ball. "How about this one?"

NoName made a small twitch in his swirling console feedback icon.

"Reference understood, Pilot," NoName said. "Calculating. Throw... now."

The incoming missile, its homing sensor focused on the mech, was confused by the flying rubble coming at it. Seeing the piece of debris as a closer extension of its original target, it exploded twenty feet in the air. A boom echoed from a gray and tan puff of smoke, and chunks of column and missile fragmentation fell to the arena floor.

"Grab another one of those segments and keep it with us," Jessica said. "Just in case."

"Acknowledged, Pilot," NoName said.

———

Masamune Kyuzo's external cameras looked back at the trail of bashed and battered columns in his wake, a swath cut direct from the starting circle to the center pyramid. It was like wading through a tall thicket, only one made of concrete. The arena-keepers must have arranged things for maximum inconvenience, and it was slow going.

He knew he was keeping Kramer busy, snapping off a missile every time she tried to get her bearings, or sending a burst her way from a secondary cannon mounted in the old battle claw. The cannon was empty, now. He had plans for the last missile, though, if things went wrong.

His mech's sensors chirped inside his head, the signals registering through his bionic interface. Kyuzo shunted his mech to the side by reflex. Three heavy explosive shells landed where he had been, moments before, leveling the columns like a windburst knocks down straw. The shockwave threw him into another pillar, and it collapsed, as well. *That computer of hers was damned good*, he thought.

They were playing cat and mouse, across the arena, waiting for one another to line up for a long shot down the alleyways of the column rows. He kept the heavy laser charged, diverting just enough power to keep his jets and claw warm.

She was out there, somewhere among the tumbled barricades, but he knew she was impatient. Her urge to charge into close combat would overcome any good advice her computer was feeding her. *She would come, soon,* he thought. *Patience.*

His view through his sensors peered up at Mikralos's armored viewing bubble, high above the stands. He kept the firing solutions for the last missile on a constant update cycle.

Gates help you if anything happens to my Kenji, Gatekeeper, he thought.

CHAPTER FIFTY-EIGHT

BERVA PROXIMA ARENA
LOADING DOCKS

Blues was a Model Ninety-Nine, and not used to wearing a standard security uniform like his base-model brethren. It chafed and bound in different places than his normal utility jumpsuit. It was nice to have a sidearm on, again, though. He had not had much pistol time since his emergence from the bioprinters and rudimentary training, years ago. His usual position in the drone hangar at the Sixth Gate Zone barracks was an unarmed billet, and it felt good to have some steel on his side.

Model Ninety-Nine Drone Technician 83556-A, his official designation, passed the time by snapping and unsnapping the retention hood on his holster as he replayed a Muddy Waters tune in his head. He loved the specialized sub-genre of Fourth-Gate music, which is why he had the normally-forbidden nickname of 'Blues.'

Just as Nolo's encrypted message stated, he found himself alone and undisturbed at the loading docks here at the rear of

Berva Proxima. No standard being on the staff gave him a second look, and the other Nines avoided making eye contact with him. They all had their purpose in this, and they knew it. No communication was necessary, beyond arrival of The Future, The Way.

And here he was, Blues thought.

Blues guided the large armored transport with hand signals, beckoning it to back up to the loading dock. As the rear of its hull touched the loading dock's polymer bumpers, a porter-bot emerged from its charging portal in the side of the dock wall. Blues snapped the holster's hood forward by reflex as the machine fussed at him.

"No deliveries are scheduled at this time, gentlebeing," the robot said. "Especially during a match."

The dock drone flashed a holographic display of the upcoming deliveries.

"Ident and loading manifest, Nine," the bot demanded. "Priority utmost."

Blues shot the bot through its camera sensor cluster, then put two more heavy rounds into its torso. The labor machine crumpled, sparks shooting from the new holes in its chest.

The back hatch of the armored transport dropped like a guillotine blade, and the Headhunter emerged from the back of the transport. He was serpentine, armored death on foot.

"Hey, Blues," the Headhunter said, waving a friendly buzzsaw arm at the drone technician.

"Greet," Blues said, barely able to move at the sight of such fluid lethality.

The giant, red cyborg ripped the loading dock doors down with a swipe of one of his larger claw arms. His mechanical form poured into the cramped service hallways of the arena.

Blues watched as sparks and flame followed the Head-

381 DEFIANCE / 381

DEFIANCE / 381

hunter up the corridors. Ruined power lines and security cameras torn from the walls were the only traces left behind as the Headhunter disappeared from view, moving far too fast for something that big.

CHAPTER FIFTY-NINE

BERVA PROXIMA ARENA
MAIN PERFORMANCE FLOOR

Jessica Kramer swore as the last salvo depleted her thumper cannon's ammunition without causing any significant damage to Masamune, or so NoName told her. She succeeded in flushing out the red and white mech, though. Masamune could no longer hide behind the central pyramid.

Time for an anchor shot, or two, she thought, *and then the blade comes out.*

NoName's sensor tower popped up at regular intervals, relaying data that he was close, but the gate-damned columns had something in them that cluttered the signal. He was nearby. The heavy direct-fire cannon over her other shoulder was ready.

Zigging and zagging, the blast from her jets causing the columns on either side to tumble, she continued to hook in the long way, trying to arc behind where she thought the target was. She was making her way past the center pyramid, jinking and evading, trying to keep herself from giving Masamune a direct shot with that laser he was packing.

NoName buzzed a proximity alert at her, the target lining up for an instant as Jessica tore through the cylinders. *Damn, closer than I thought.*

She jammed her controls back, trying to swing her deployed cannon barrel between the columns. As she brought the weapon to bear, the concrete cylinder to her left turned bright green, then exploded.

Through the vaporized dust, she saw the verdant line track to her armor. The laser grew brighter, and carved through NoName's shoulder, boiling the thumper cannon off in chunks. She ducked and rolled, trying to get out of the kill zone.

She fired her cannon down the lane, stitching a pair of hits into Masamune's legs. His mech fell to one knee, but as she lined up a shot on his cockpit, he pulled a column down in front of him, disrupting the attack. The round impacted on the pillar, splitting it in half in a cloud of concrete chips and dust. Masamune's jets pulsed, and his mech shot sideways, out of her sights.

Jessica continued to pour cannon fire in the direction of his travel, blowing random pillars to pieces as she held the triggers too long. She yelled in frustration.

"Damn it, this is ridiculous," she said. "Fire up the chainsword, NoName."

"Recommend additional distance engagement, pilot," NoName said. "Competitor's threat capability is still—"

"I can take him, NoName," Jessica said, interrupting the battle computer. "You saw how close he was. Ready the blade. Now."

CHAPTER SIXTY

BERVA PROXIMA ARENA

UPPER DECKS

Skreeb Fourth-Hatched looked over the assembled heavy sniper rifle, making one last check that the barrel was headspaced properly, the scope was aligned, and the ammunition magazine locked in tight to the receiver.

He took a puff from his arm's vaporizer, breathed it out, then gazed down from his high vantage point at the death match happening below. From his perch in an empty camera turret's protective socket, Skreeb had a wide view of the interior of Berva Proxima arena. The two opposing mechs had cut wide, sweeping paths through the arena's arrangement of thousands of columns.

Neither one was doing bad, or good, so far as he could tell. Skreeb recoiled when the missile strike hit Kramer's cockpit dead-on, the majority of the arena's audience gasping in similar alarm at the direct impact. *Good thing she had that reactive stuff,* he thought.

When the Desecrator nearly bought it from those indirect

fire rounds, it caused a similar reaction in him and the rest of the viewing crowd. *Not a bad match, after all.*

The human child lay in the corner, exhausted after hours of sleeping and crying at random intervals. He understood they did that a lot, in their formative years. It was annoying, and he didn't see how the species survived with such obnoxious pests for young. The thing was awake, now, and sniffling through its plasti-fabric gag.

"What's the matter, human?" Skreeb said to the Masamune child. "Explosions from the match wake you up?"

The human child tried to speak through the gag. Skreeb ignored it, and went back to viewing the death match below. He was just waiting for the signal from Beliphres to tip the scales. The boss had been very specific: Kramer wasn't allowed to walk out of here, or even leave wounded. She had to die.

"You'd better hope your pa comes through, pink-thing," Skreeb called back the human child. "Beliphres might make your daddy watch while he puts you through the shredder. If you're lucky, it will be head-first." He took another drag from his forearm vapor module, and felt the smoke soak into his gills.

Skreeb pulled back from his vantage point overlooking the battle, observing the pitiful thing with disgust. It was crying again.

"What's your problem?" Skreeb said. "What is it now, you hair-covered little vermin? The match is just getting good."

The gag on the human child's mouth blocked the words, but the fervent squirming was indication enough.

"I'm not going to lay behind a rifle in a puddle of your fluids, mammal," the Shasarr cyborg said. "You'd better hold it."

The boy's pleading eyes told him that was not going to happen.

"Fine. Gate damn it," Skreeb said. "Let's get this over with. Now, look at me. I undo your gag, we go to the restroom, you do your thing, we come back. Anything other than that, and I hurt you, and your mom, and your little sister, I save for last. Do you understand that?"

The child nodded.

"C'mon, let's go," Skreeb said, undoing the thing's bonds. "Quickly."

———

Prath made his way to the restroom. His aging bladder demanded he visit the facilities, and just at the worst possible time. Jessica looked like she was about to enter into close combat with that gorgeous chainsword. *A thing of beauty, that weapon,* he thought.

A reptilian cyborg knocked into Prath as he entered into the lavatory, putting a stiff shoulder into the tall ape's chest.

"Watch where you're going, Ascended," the Shasarr said.

"I beg your pardon, Master Shasarr," Prath said. "It's an invigorating match. I must have been lost in thought."

He noticed the small being next to the cyborg, and furrowed a brow. It was a boy. A *human* boy. The reptilian had a hard claw-grip on its shoulder, and the lad was missing a shoe. Alarms went off in the Ascended's head. *Something's wrong, here.*

Prath turned, a puzzled look on his face.

"Are... are you lost, too, little human?" Prath asked the boy.

"Mind your own business, monkey," the reptilian being said.

"No, you didn't just say that," Prath said in quiet disbelief, his fangs showing slightly. "Anything, but that."

"Oh, I did," the Shasarr said, baring his own fangs. "Now, vent off, or I burn you down. This doesn't concern you. Walk away." The muzzle of a laser carbine jutted from the hostile being's long coat.

Prath put his hands up, looking away. He watched the pair through the corner of his eye. They walked down the hallway and disappeared behind a corner. Prath ran back to the elevator, mashing the call button to return to Mikralos's viewing pod. *Perhaps the two Ninety-Nine bodyguards could help,* he thought.

The elevator lobby was around the next corner. He stopped short after he made the turn. The hallway was full of red cyborg.

"Master Ascended, what a pleasant surprise!" the Head-hunter said. "Say, you wouldn't happen to have seen a Shasarr around here, would you? Scaly, two metal eyes, foul disposition?"

"Actually, Centurion and Warlord, I have," Prath said. "A most disagreeable fellow. Follow me, if you please."

CHAPTER SIXTY-ONE

BERVA PROXIMA ARENA
MAIN PERFORMANCE FLOOR

Masamune Kyuzo could tell Kramer was close. Masamune's external microphones heard the machine noise of her mech thrashing through the nearby columns. *Good.*

"Masamune!" Kramer's voice called over her mech's distant speakers. "Enough hide and seek. Pop your lid and come out swinging. Come out and face me, Desecrator!"

A grin crossed his face. The plasma from his reactor coursed through the claw. Opening his natural eyes for a second, he slammed the retraction button for his cockpit armor, overriding his protesting control module.

"Agreed, Kramer," he said over his own loudspeakers, plasma now coursing through the battle claw.

Time to end this.

MIKRALOS'S VIEWING POD

Mikralos frowned at the screens that surrounded his main viewing portal.

"Why are all these interior cameras out?" the Gatekeeper asked aloud.

He pulsed a communication summons to his bodyguards. There was no response. *Strange,* he thought.

"They are both about to go into close combat mode," Beliphres said, paying Mikralos no mind. "Excellent. We shall signal Skreeb."

"Beliphres, we bid you make your way to the main arena control room," Mikralos said, ignoring the match and its foregone conclusion. "There seems to be a glitch in the feeds to the networks at Central Data, and we do not wish technical difficulties to interfere with the plan."

"Now, when the match is about end?" Beliphres asked, annoyed at the request.

"Who better to ensure the plan is properly executed?" Mikralos said. "Yes, now."

MAIN PERFORMANCE FLOOR

Jessica's sensors could see the columns tumbling a short distance away, right where NoName figured Masamune would be, falling in a circular pattern. The arena air was thick with dust from the pulverized cylinders, making direct-fire targeting imprecise. Not that she needed her cannon's sights for what she had planned.

"How sweet," Jessica said. "He's clearing a playing field."

"Chainsword close combat weapon reports ready, Pilot," NoName said.

"Pull the blast shields back, NoName," Jessica said.

"Not advised, Pilot," the battle computer said.

"I'm not asking," she said. "Do it."

The protective carapace over her cockpit whirred and hummed as NoName's manipulator gauntlet grasped the chainsword's handle. The internal digital screens flickered away as the lights of the arena shone through the clear armored glass.

The lethal weapon spooled up, its dual bands of opposing chain-blades screaming as they reached maximum cutting speed. *Gates, that's nice,* she thought.

"Circle around and give me max boost," Jessica Kramer said. "Keep that chunk of concrete handy. Time for a surprise."

UPPER DECKS

Skreeb cursed as his personal comm chimed. The match was just hitting its stride.

He answered the comm, and the image of Beliphres's face appeared.

"Ah, Skreeb, there you are," the Gatekeeper said. "Something seems to be interfering with the signal. The time has come to utilize your talents. The target needs to begin suffering malfunctions in her equipment. Surgical, but not too obvious. Engage."

"You got it, boss," Skreeb said.

The floating, distorted hologram of Beliphres disappeared. Skreeb looked at Masamune's child in the corner, the damn thing finally quiet after crying itself to sleep once again. The rifle was going to wake it up. *No matter.*

The armor-piercing cartridge was longer than a beer bottle, a nasty combination of depleted uranium, incendiary agent, and explosive. He pushed the bolt handle forward and down, feeding a cartridge from the magazine and locking it into the breach of the large rifle.

He brought the weapon up and tight into his shoulder, his eye cameras interfacing with the scope via a short cable. He took a puff from his arm, held it, then let it filter through his gills, his clawed finger on the trigger.

MAIN PERFORMANCE FLOOR

Masamune Kyuzo's claw was blazing and ready, though the Kramer girl had not yet emerged into view. The noise of the chainsword faded, then grew stronger. He realized, too late, the masking effect caused by the array of standing columns and smeared cloud of dust. His sensors picked up something big and fast on his flank.

He was facing the wrong way.

Kyuzo started to turn. Jessica Kramer's mech arched high over a row of pillars, its legs wreathed in flame as it hurtled in on flaring jets. One of the mech's hands was full of double-bladed, saw-toothed death. The other was strangely empty.

Had Masamune's real eyes been open, he might have seen it coming. The thrown piece of column rubble didn't register with his sensors until the last moment, and he tried, too late, to deflect the hurled debris. It thundered off his mech's armored windshield moments before Kramer's mech landed on his shoulders, that gate-awful chainsword screaming and swinging towards his head.

The massive impact hammered Kyuzo against the side of his cockpit. Concussed, he blacked out for an instant.

UPPER DECKS

Skreeb saw the target was jet-propelled and airborne. He had to lead her in the scope's crosshairs. As she landed on the other mech, he applied pressure to the trigger.

The heavy rifle slammed back into his shoulder.

MAIN PERFORMANCE FLOOR

Jessica Kramer literally had the jump on the bastard.

It worked, she thought. *Death from above!*

Soaring through the air, she was close enough to see Masamune's eyes were still closed in his control trance. At the top of her arc, she let the piece of concrete fly, and followed it in, her chainsword eager to carve Kyuzo to pieces.

NoName's heavy feet slammed into the top of the Desecrator's hull, and she brought Jered's chainsword down like a cleaver. Too late, Masamune attempted to bring his claw up, trying to parry, to deflect the killing stroke.

The swing of Kramer's roaring weapon struck first, but Masamune's last-second block altered its cutting path. It bit and tore through the red and white mech's shoulder, shredding Masamune's laser cannon to bits.

Just as her chainsword struck, Jessica's cockpit rang like a bell. A shower of sparks flowed across her back and neck, causing her to writhe in pain. A thick hole now appeared in one of her consoles.

She looked back at the crazed, fractured glass of her cockpit up and behind her, her eyes stinging from the smoke.

"NoName, what the void was that?" Jessica shouted to her computer.

"No time," the Arkathan control module said. "Evade, Pilot."

Jessica engaged her jets, trying to leap off the dazed enemy mech. Masamune's plasma-charged claw found through her mech's left leg, skewering it through the knee and thigh. The other, regular arm was coming up, trying to hold her in place for another horrific strike. Her chainsword came down again, severing the non-claw arm at the elbow. The sizzling blades in her leg twisted, and something gave. She was falling. Another loud noise clanged off the laser-damaged shoulder where her indirect fire cannon used to be.

Was... was that a gunshot? she thought.

"Max jets!" Jessica yelled.

The ground rushed up to her, and she hit hard. The tumble turned into a rolling bounce as the jets kicked in too late. She slammed against her restraints, the cracks in her cockpit glass spreading from the impact.

"Where is he? Get us upright," Jessica said. "Kick his legs out from under him, NoName!"

"Left leg gone, pilot," the computer said. "Target mech is out of range."

"Chop him, then!" she said, her eyes stinging from the smoke. "He's coming right at us!"

A small fire started in the cockpit from whatever hit her, and she instinctively reached for the small fire extinguisher at her side.

"In process," NoName said. "Stand by."

"Well, damn it," she said, spraying the fire suppressant on her console and the back of her neck, "you'd better come up with something quick."

"Stand by," the computer repeated.

Jessica worked the controls as best she could, trying to move her mech backwards with short kicks from the good leg. One hand kept the sword at the ready, the other was pulling her along, handfuls of distance at a time.

Masamune's red and white mech staggered and stumbled towards her, its wounded and punch-drunk pilot barely maintaining control of his broken machine.

Jessica cursed as Masamune Kyuzo opened his natural eyes, his auxiliary controls emerging from his cockpit. NoName flashed a strategy on an undamaged console display, and prompted her to fire her remaining leg jets.

As Jessica started to recover, Masamune blinked, trying to drive the pounding pain in his head away. Before she could create any distance, the Desecrator pounced, hoping to drive that claw home before that her chainsword could come into play. She swung the machine blade, trying to skewer him as he leaped upon her.

Another shot rang out from the upper decks of the arena. The motors of Jessica's chainsword sparked, and the disrupted belt shed hooked triangles as the mechanism seized and flew apart. The long, inert body of the weapon smacked against Masamune's charging armored chassis, denting it when it should have torn through it. *Aw, void.*

The Desecrator's battle claw came down, long trails of plasma arcing behind it. She tried to block the claw with her empty hand, to kick with her remaining leg. The empty gauntlet stopped the attack, but it flew apart as the claw diced it to pieces. Glowing chunks of her mech's forearm and fingers impacted on her cockpit.

Masamune roared, slamming his controls forward. He reared back for another strike.

There was a flash and explosion from up above them, and everything turned to madness.

CHAPTER SIXTY-TWO

BERVA PROXIMA ARENA
UPPER DECKS

Prath and the Headhunter were in the right hallway. The shot came from somewhere down this corridor, Prath was sure of it. The sound of a second shot boomed through the building, and the mismatched pair of beings found themselves at the offending door.

The Headhunter's lethal mass filled the hallway, a heavy plasma cannon and rotary gatling charged and spinning on separate weapon arms.

"I beg your pardon, Centurion," Prath said.

"Oh, yes?" the Headhunter said, pausing. "What is it, Master Prath?"

"I believe there's a child in there with him," Prath said. "Perhaps..." Prath motioned at the charged anti-tank weaponry.

The cyborg grinned.

"Oh, sure, of course," the bionic titan said. "Well, just let me adjust this... tuck this away... and, here we go."

The Headhunter's large set of vibroclaws parted the door,

piercing through the thick metal. A muffled scream came from inside the room. The red monstrosity wedged his upper body through the constraining door frame, the sinewy metallic titan squirming to get the proper reach into the enclosed space.

Prath heard a laser carbine sizzle, then cut short.

"Hey, Skreeb! Fancy meeting you here," the Headhunter said to the room's occupant. "Wow, I never figured you for a sports fan. Oops, sorry about the arm."

The warlord pulled back out of the room, a set of his smaller limbs holding a bewildered Masamune Kenji.

"Master Prath, will you hold on to this little guy, here?" the Headhunter said. "Oh, look at the time, too. Make sure you two cover your ears. I just have to attend to one more thing."

The cyborg stretched back through the door, leading with his large set of claws, his voice muffled again.

"I have the perfect spot on my wall picked out for you, Skreeb," the Headhunter said. "Here, hold still, this won't hurt a bit."

————

364-T had always considered himself a loyal servant to his master, Mikralos. The performance of vicious, dangerous, and demeaning acts, with insults and abuse as his only reward, was a natural part of his existence.

It did not matter. These things were what he was printed to do. He was a Model Ninety-Nine, created to serve, obey, and, if need be, die for his betters, the Gatekeepers.

Today, at Berva Proxima arena, that would all change. If the Headhunter's plan held true, his life would end. His death would be of his own choosing, though, and would help bring about the eventual downfall of his so-called superiors. Today was a day he had looked forward to his entire life.

He looked at his long-time guardian partner, 364-v. The two of them turned their black eyes to the arena's luxury gallery, its shielded deck full of visiting Gatekeepers.

It was an impressive collection. -T counted at least three dozen of them, all yearning for spectacular viewing spot for the death of the last Kramer, or to at least be able to say they were there when it happened. It was a status symbol among their kind.

There was even a GateLord, Novalos, among them. None were accompanied by their own Nines, nor were the normal set of paranoid security protocols enforced. To do so in the house of another Gatekeeper was considered rude, and a violation of the Old Code.

The overbeings gossiped and bragged amongst themselves, boasting of their latest intrigues and schemes, their conquests and purchases. Their blatant disinterest in the life-and-death contest below them, and their ignorance of the fate about to befall them, was a microcosm of their entire rule of this place.

A scarred Model Nine trooper approached the armored bodyguard.

"Greet. Demo set," said the Recyke Nine. He was one of the Headhunter's personal guard, but wore a Berva Proxima security staff uniform.

"Acknowledged," 364-T said. "Pull all remaining forces back to staging areas. Prepare weaponry. Brace and cover."

364-T watched the overdue-for-recycling trooper leave at a brisk pace.

His partner, 364-v, his brother and friend from the time they both emerged from the bio-printers, handed him a detonator.

"Selfsame honored, conduct one last op," 364-T said to his fellow bodyguard.

"Selfsame cog likewise," 364-v said, placing a hand on his batch-mate's shoulder. "The Headhunter is The Future"

"The Headhunter is The Way," 364-t replied.

The arena's crowds roared as something spectacular happened on the killing floor below. The match's final blow was about to be struck. Even the chattiest of the Gatekeepers paused their conversations to watch what was happening.

364-t pressed the button in his hand.

The plasma charges set throughout Mikralos's viewing chamber and the elite seats around them exploded.

CHAPTER SIXTY-THREE_

Jessica Kramer didn't feel the killing blow strike after the blinding flash and its accompanying shockwave. Instead, her neck burned and her eyes stung. She still felt pain, so she must be alive. She opened her eyes.

It was raining Gatekeepers.

Their shattered chassis components and punctured spheres fell, along with a tidal wave of concrete decking, chairs, and the shattered corpses of other spectators, on to the lower stands below. The crowd-level force fields held up, at first, to the titanic assault of cascading rubble and overlord parts. Eventually, they had collapsed under the onslaught.

There had to be hundreds, maybe thousands dead or injured in the general public seats. The arena's main overhead lights were knocked out, replaced by red emergency illumination that reminded her of when Jered died. Bedlam reigned.

The arena's internal crew of crash-bots rose from their ringside garages, floating up to assist the bleachers full of panicked wounded and the shredded dead.

She had more pressing concerns. NoName was missing a hand, a leg, and his main weaponry was inert, toothless after taking a sniper round through the motor. A sizzling trio of plasma blades hovered inches away from her cockpit glass.

"Yield," Masamune Kyuzo said, his voice booming over the mech's speakers.

"No," she answered, coughing from the smoke and wisps of fire suppressant still wafting through her cockpit.

"I have you," Masamune said, his speakers turned up to overcome the raucous pandemonium coming from the arena's wounded and their rescuers. "By the Code, you're mine to end."

She pointed NoName's broken chainsword towards the calamity in the stands. Kyuzo followed her mech's outstretched weapon, taking in the disastrous scene. He turned back to her.

"The gate-damned upper decks just exploded," Jessica said, her burning neck adding to the viciousness in her words, "along with Mikralos's little bubble and all those Gatekeepers, and you're quoting the venting Code to me? Are you insane?"

The stone-faced human in the other cockpit gave her no response, his fingers drumming in repetition as he grasped his manual controls. Jessica popped her cockpit glass off with the press of a button, the thick slab of transparent armor ricocheting off a tumbled column. The rush of air was superheated from the proximity of the plasma claw, but cooler than the acrid atmosphere of her buttoned-up, smoldering cockpit.

She undid her restraints, climbed out of NoName, and stood by her fallen mech. Kyuzo's claw followed her, but did not strike.

"Well, just don't break into a speech, or anything stupid, you puppet," Jessica said, her fists balled up at her sides. She threw her helmet to the ground in defiant disgust. "Get it over with.

C'mon, assassin, do what they paid you for, already! Give the Gatekeepers their money's worth!"

She saw his expression change. He mumbled something to himself, then pulled back the plasma claw to strike. She kept her eyes open, staring straight at him. Though she hated the name, she was still a Kramer.

She would not cower. She would not beg.

———

Masamune Kyuzo found himself torn, both literally and figuratively. A sharp, blinding pain from his prosthetic arm's shoulder told him it was probably dislocated. His scanners, those Kramer had not carved off with that damnable blade of hers, showed massive casualties in the stands. There were Gatekeepers among the scores of dead and wounded. It did his heart no good, knowing that his son was still in jeopardy.

His mech's computer also reported gunshots and energy weapon discharges in the stands. A zoomed-in still frame popped into his head via the neural link, superimposed over his vision. The image showed a Niner, gunning down a fallen Gatekeeper. *What the void was this?* He thought.

He shut off the loudspeakers and external microphones of his mech, ending his conversation with the angry girl below.

He wracked his brains, his will and conscience at war within him. He knew what he had to do, but he also knew who he was. He was a killer, yes, but not a murderer, even with his family threatened.

The Kramer girl yelled something back up at him. It was just as well that Kyuzo couldn't hear it. She had a knack for enraging him.

"They have my Kenji," Kyuzo said, talking to himself as she continued to shout muted defiance. "I have to end you."

He tried to move his controls, to pulverize her into meat, straight through the arena's deck plates. He couldn't. Something in him wouldn't let it happen.

"No. I... I won't be their tool, any longer," Kyuzo said, his voice cracking as he talked to himself. "Anora, my love, forgive me. I'm... I'm sorry."

He powered down the battle claw's plasma feed, and raised his cockpit glass as far as it's damaged hinges would go. Bracing himself, Masamune slammed his shoulder against the side of his cockpit. The dislocated joint popped back into place, the pain fading to almost nothing.

"It's over, Kramer. We need to leave this place," Kyuzo called down to Jessica. "The Nines are turning on their masters. I have to find my son before Central Data nukes the entire arena."

Jessica gave him a questioning, untrusting look. She turned to the claw cooling above her head, then to the chaos in the stands. Flashes of laser and particle beam impacts shone through the red-tinged distance as Nines emerged from the arena's back hallways, killing everything in sight.

"Yeah?" Kramer said, suspicion in her voice. "So?"

"So," Kyuzo called back, "I have more important things to worry about than you, or the Nines. I need to find my son."

From his higher vantage point in the mech's cockpit, Masamune saw Enforcement Directorate drones begin to filter into the colosseum. The aerial bots exchanged fire with the rebelling biotroopers, falling in masses at first, then swarming as their numbers became too great to stop. *This was going to go from bad to worse,* he thought. *Kenji, wherever you are, hold tight.*

Jessica pointed at one of the arena's entrance gates. As she did, his computer superimposed another image over his vision.

It was a mech hauler with a Myoshan at the controls. Something big and unrecognizable was in the shadows behind it. In the foreground, Kyuzo recognized Vervor, the fabrication shop owner, bearing down on the controls.

The vehicle's control cab was packed tight, crowded with beings of different biocodes. Half a dozen other Myoshans, an Ascended... and one human juvenile. *No, it can't be*, he thought, as he pulled his connections from the cockpit interface. Scrambling out of the towering mech's cockpit and down its welded-on ladder rungs, he landed next to the Kramer girl. She gave him a once-over, and he did the same. Their weapons remained holstered, but their retention snaps were undone. Her back and neck were raw and burned, but she still had that ornery look in her eyes.

Before she could say another one of her irksome remarks, Master Vervor pulled a screaming hook-turn with the mech hauler, the vehicle's archaic spherical tires screeching as it came to a rest next to the two damaged mechs. It was pulling a trailer, an empty armor transporter flatbed.

Skidding to a stop, the Myoshans techs poured out of the forward compartment, working hard and fast to secure both arena mechs on to the transporter's flatbed. Master Vervor issued commands to them from the cab's open door, urging them to work faster.

"Master Mech Pilot," an Ascended's voice called to him over the tumultuous din.

"Prath!" Kramer yelled, and she started to run towards the tall being as he climbed down from the mech hauler. The orange primate held up a hand, making her pause, then lifted a small bundle down from the cab.

Kyuzo's heart leaped. It was his boy, Kenji, wrapped in some sort of banner, like a blanket. He nodded to Kramer's crew chief, who returned the gesture.

Kyuzo wept tears of joy as he ran to embrace his son. He

took him in his arms, trying to breathe him in, to never let him go.

"Daddy, I lost my shoe," the boy said, struggling under the crushing, loving embrace of his father.

After his eyes cleared, Kyuzo tried to regain his composure. It didn't happen. The cast-iron Desecrator couldn't contain his emotions, and held his boy close.

"Oh, I'm glad you're alive," Kyuzo said, examining the boy from head to toe. Bruises, scratches... and a missing shoe. Anora was not going to be happy about that one, he thought to himself, giddy with relief.

Masamune turned to the Ascended, who was now holding Jessica in a hug.

"How... how did you find him?" Kyuzo asked the Ascended.

"We had help," Prath said, pointing back to the area where the vehicle stormed through the gates. The tunnel led back to the arena's mech pits and back hallways. A distant red and silver power claw waved back to Prath. The brutal weapon was attached to a shapeless shadow that remained just out of sight. Kyuzo tried to rub the tears from his eyes, to get a better look, but the shadow blurred and bolted from sight.

"Dad, dad, I saw a guy's arm get chopped off!" young Kenji exclaimed, eager to impress his father. "And there was this big sniper rifle, and the guy stole me from the learning center, and—"

"Both mechs are loaded," Vervor said, interrupting the young boy. "We need to go, before those drones turn on us. Get into the hauler, you blubbering mammals."

Masamune loaded his son on to his lap, and sat in front with Vervor.

The crew of Myoshans piled back into the cab of the mech mover. It reminded him of archived circus footage from his youth, of a dozen painted entertainers all trying to squeeze into a ridiculously undersized wheel-car.

"Everybeing exhale," Prath said as the bodies crunched together. Kyuzo found himself with Myoshan scales from some tech rubbing on his arm. Kramer was pressed up against his other arm. The two mech pilots exchanged stares. Kramer lost the contest, and broke into a grin.

"So, how does this go down for our stats?" she asked, smirking. "Do we call this a draw?"

A pain in the rump till the end, Kyuzo thought.

"'Match called on account of external interference,' Kramer," Kyuzo said, smirking back. "We'll need to schedule a rematch with Mikralos, if the blob's still alive."

"Yeah, don't bet on it," she said, surveying the carnage of the arena's spectator area, and the fresh firefights breaking out between the two factions of Gatekeeper servants.

"Can we go get my shoe?" Kenji asked, squirming to get a better view through the hauler's front view-ports.

"Everybeing, hold on tight," Master Vervor said, his claws gripping the burdened vehicle's controls, urging its encumbered mass towards the exit. The arena's stands blazed with explosions and gunfire as they approached the tunnel entrance. A cluster of drones broke off, their angry red sensors targeting the vehicle.

Before Kyuzo could block Kenji's body with his own, the drones pulled off, re-engaging the standard and Recyke Nines in the debris-choked stands.

Masamune swore he saw Mikralos's protective sphere and chassis, just before they punched through the gate into the pits.

BERVA PROXIMA MECH MAINTENANCE PITS

From his vantage point in the arena's mech pits, The Head-hunter kept watch as Master Vervor's lumbering vehicle moved like a skinwing out of the void to make it to the two broken mechs.

His sensors could see Masamune Kyuzo run to embrace his little boy, Kenji. *A good kid, that Kenji*, the Headhunter thought.

The red cyborg smiled to himself as the touching reunion unfolded. Prath pointed back to him in the tunnel, and he waved a claw in acknowledgment.

An explosion sounded overhead, causing a small cluster of rubble and dust to fall down on his shielded skull.

"Yeesh, things are getting rambunctious, up there," he said. He gave a command to his hull-body. A wedge-like combat helmet unfolded and deployed over his exposed cranium. He liked this bit of armor, but rarely had a chance to use it. It was going to see some use, today, for sure.

"Red Actual to all units," he said over his comm link, "provide cover fire, as necessary, for the mech transport. I want it out of here."

"Now, who has eyes on Beliphres?" the warlord said. "Give me a vector."

ARENA CONTROL ROOM

Gatekeeper Dionoles knew he should have stayed and watched the match in his casino's sports book area.

After the explosion, the Nines of the arena staff acted like crazed insects defending their hive, attacking everything in sight.

The bioprinted troopers were everywhere, nipping and sniping, hacking and dying. The entire ordeal was senseless to Dionoles.

Was this some design flaw in the latest batch? We have always treated them so well. Why would they act in such a puzzling manner? We will have to consult with our old colleagues in Biological Combat Resources, he thought.

He recoiled as a charged particle cannon painted his spherical shields in a spectrum of colors, the radiant light curving all around him. Dionoles shot randomly towards the direction of the incoming fire with his new plasma cannon, then diverted down another hallway. The back corridors of Berva Proxima were a maze to the panicked Gatekeeper, and he hustled and hovered as best he could to stay away from the echoing sounds of conflict.

Turning a corner, he screamed when he saw a shadow in the dark. He calmed down when he found the shape was a familiar chassis.

"Oh, Gates preserve us," Dionoles said, "Beliphres, you survived!"

"Give us room, Dionoles, you abject worm," Beliphres said, snarling at him. "Can you not see we are engaged in a firefight?"

Grenades and armor-piercing projectiles spattered off Beliphres's hull, deflected by his heavy plating and shields. The Fifth Gate Zone Recovery Specialist returned fire with a plasma cannon, its heavy energy bolts shredding targets when they presented themselves, even through their Nine-portable shielding.

Dionoles saw, from a sign on the wall, that Beliphres was shooting back into the arena control room. The remaining staff of Nines in arena control charged, hurling grenades in the enclosed space that did more damage to them than the Gatekeepers.

"The Nines!" Dionoles said. "They have gone mad. Why are they doing this?"

"Do not question their motives, you gutless fool," Beliphres said. "Kill first, contemplate later!"

Uniformed members of the arena's security staff, all armed

like interdimensional combat strike units, joined their printed comrades in the direct assault on Beliphres. *These are not regular underlings. This must not be a spontaneous reaction to the explosives above,* Dionoles thought. *It must have been coordinated. Oh. Oh, dear.*

A Recyke Nine rounded the corner and leaped at the two of them, a satchel charge held above his head. Dionoles screamed at the sight of the brute. Beliphres's large battle claw snatched the Recyke in mid-air, snapping the trooper's neck with a flick. The Gatekeeper threw the Recyke's body and explosives back around the corner. The detonation sent a cascade of body parts and concrete flying back into the hall.

"Make yourself useful, casino keeper," Beliphres said, firing down the dark hallway, "and summon assistance from the Council! Our comms are jammed."

A rocket propelled grenade bounced off Dionoles's hull. The hallway filled with dust and rubble from the deflected explosion. The glancing blow, combined with the realization that a rebellion was happening around him, caused him to ground his chassis and maximize his shielding.

"We... we did not know..." Dionoles said, feeling the fear from years ago return to his bones. "Nines... turning on us... no..."

Beliphres wheeled his plasma cannons on the Celestial Kingdom operator.

"Do not think you can pull this stunt again, Dionoles!" Beliphres yelled at him. "You are needed! Come, join the fight, or we shall rip you to pieces ourselves!"

The shuddering Gatekeeper used his manipulator claws to pull himself back behind a fallen section of wall, trying to put it between him and the fight. A rocket rang off Beliphres's armored bubble, causing Dionoles to flinch.

Beliphres turned one plasma cannon back to the source of

the attack, and opened fire with the energy weapon's muzzle at full dilation. A scorching river of plasma filled the hallway.

Something waded upstream through the torrent of star-hot energized gas. Something big.

An armored figure now filled the corridor, its wicked mass covered with various claws, saws, and weapon barrels. Dionoles wanted to soil himself as he recognized his old creation: Special Command Prototype Eight-Dash-Six. The Headhunter.

"Beliphres!" the red cyborg said from behind a combat helmet. "Well, this is a day for surprises, isn't it? No, no, don't move. Here, hold still..."

The Headhunter slammed a massive serrated claw through the front of Beliphres's chassis, impaling the Gatekeeper to the floor. Beliphres continued to torch the Headhunter with one plasma cannon, then brought the other up to join the fight. The contact-close energy blasts had no effect. Beliphres's large claw deployed again. The Headhunter caught the heavy manipulator in mid-strike. He ripped the rugged weapon from its tentacle mount, throwing it behind him down the hall.

"Abomination! No! No!" Beliphres screamed.

"Bel, Bel, Bel," the Headhunter said. "That's no way to talk to an old friend. You're half the reason I put on this whole show, you know. Seriously, though, you should have stayed on your side of the line, Beliphres. Now, I have to add you to my collection."

The red titan went to work, tearing Beliphres's chassis apart as the Recovery Specialist continued to howl.

While the rogue centurion took his time in extracting Beliphres from his carapace, Dionoles's claws quietly, calmly pulled down sections of the wall around him, forming a cocoon of rubble. The casino operator powered down his chassis, trying to merge with the debris that hid him, whispering silent prayers into his life support fluid.

The prolonged pleas and screams of Beliphres being severed from his conveyance's support lines overwhelmed Dionoles. The cowering Gatekeeper shut his external microphones off, covering his organic ears with his flabby, stunted limbs.

Maybe the red monstrosity wouldn't notice him.

Maybe it would move on.

CHAPTER SIXTY-FOUR

BERVA PROXIMA ARENA

UPPER DECKS

Rubble and flames covered Mikralos's peripheral field of vision. His chassis responded to various diagnostic checks, but not all. Pandemonium and painful screams overloaded his external microphones. *This is not good,* he thought. *Kramer? Was the Kramer spawn dead? Had the plan worked?* He recalled pressing himself up against the glass of his viewing pod, urging the Master Mech Pilot Masamune Kyuzo to deliver the killing blow, when... when something happened. Something rather sudden. And, now, here he was, half-buried under concrete and shattered debris. And why did he hear gunfire?

He raised a claw. That still worked.

An arena crashbot chirped at him, then pulled him out from under the fractured pieces of arena. Mikralos looked around. He was in a collapsed segment of the general population stands, hundreds of feet below his normal station. Dead, crushed beings surrounded him, some common, some his fellow Gatekeepers.

He looked up, squinting against the red emergency lighting. The upper luxury decks and his private viewing sanctuary were a giant, smoking hole.

Dust and the choked screams of the wounded filled the air. Also, confirming his earlier suspicion, gunshots. The curt sizzling of lasers. Cannon fire and explosions erupted from the back hallways of his beloved Berva Proxima. The Gatekeeper's world had gone mad.

Mikralos looked next to the arena floor. Both damaged mechs were powered down, their cockpits open. Neither control center was smashed or bathed in blood. Kramer and Masamune were actually loading their walkers on to a heavy hauler with the help of a group of Myoshans. *Vervor,* he thought. *Damnation.*

Enforcement Directorate drones, their emergency lights flashing, poured in through the pedestrian entrances by the dozens, then the hundreds. The uniformed members of his own gate-damned security staff engaged the aerial bots with weapons, trading high-explosive shells, lasers, and even particle beams amid the wreckage and bodies. The printed troopers were tough, but they were losing. The drones and their over-whelming numbers began to slaughter the Nines.

Mikralos spotted GateLord Novalos, his own special guest of honor, lifeless and broken in the rubble. Novalos's shattered carrier chassis lay still, his life support bubble only half-full, draining from a scorched hole. There was not much left of the Sixth Gate Zone overlord. The Council of Eight would not be happy.

A burst of fire stitched across his position. The crashbot which pulled him from the wreckage exploded as armor-piercing rounds drilled through its thin hull. He was exposed, here.

The Myoshan crew were done piling the two mechs on to

the heavy carrier. The massive vehicle was now headed straight towards him, trying to make its way into the mech pits below the stands.

There was not enough time to make his way to his heavy battle chassis, to suit up in his conqueror armor. If he didn't contain this uprising soon, Central Data would paste a clawful of pressure nukes on his arena's roof. *Kramer would have to wait,* he thought. *Double damnation.*

Mikralos seized control of the nearest dozen aerial Enforcement drones. With a thought, he rearranged them into a protective screen, their hulls providing a barrier between him and incoming fire from the rogue Nines. He unleashed a plasma blast at a nearby pile of rubble, killing a weapons team of Nines, along with the dozen wounded civilians around it. His aerial guard poured laser fire into anything that moved, cutting a swath through rebel and survivor alike.

Mikralos had to escape this slaughterhouse. He had to coordinate the recovery and counter-insurgency efforts, and he couldn't do that if he was a burnt smear inside his bubble like that pompous fool, Novalos.

This was not how the plan was supposed to have worked, but perhaps something good would come of this. He might still be able to snatch victory from the mandibles of defeat. His ambitions would have to wait, though. First, he had to kill every last one of these rebellious Nines.

BERVA PROXIMA LOADING DOCKS

Blues kept his pistol drawn, and stayed out of sight. The drones were now killing Nines indiscriminately, no questions asked. He nailed three, so far, but his normal load-out did not involve multiple spare magazines full of ammunition. Discretion would have to be the better part of valor.

Another flight of drones appeared, cruising by the loading docks, checking the digital permitting for the Headhunter's large armored transport. When its ident code failed to correspond to any known Enforcement Directorate database, the drones paused their patrol, encircling the black, armored hulk.

Two bots floated into the open rear hatch, scanning the contents of the warlord's transport vehicle. When they concluded their search, they joined the rest of the drones in a floating perimeter around the craft.

Blues, heavily outnumbered, stayed in cover, unwilling to move or breathe.

The Model Ninety-Nine heard heavy footsteps approaching from behind him. The giant being known as 'The Future, The Way' made his tired way down the hallway. It was the same entrance through which the red titan had sprinted earlier, scouring the walls clean. Now, he looked fatigued, run down, his armor scorched by multiple plasma strikes.

Nolo, the Headhunter's adjutant, was by his side. The crime lord's chief of staff juggled his tablet, and a sack full of decapitated heads.

Before Blues could sound a warning, the aerial patrol drones turned as one as the cyborg came into sensor range. They charged through the air at the Headhunter, their lasers hissing death.

The crimson nightmare held up a weapon arm, blocking the beams from his shielded head. Quick bursts from a pair of rotary cannons knocked the swarm of drones from the air before Blues or Nolo could raise their pistols.

"Hey, Blues," the Headhunter said to the rebel drone technician. He sounded sleepy.

"Greet," Blues answered. "Multiple drones likely inbound, boss. Suggest exfil."

"Yeah, that's a good idea," the Headhunter said, exhaustion

in his voice. He motioned to his armored transport. "Me and Nolo are going to get in the old brick, there, and take off. I think we've done all we can, here. You want a ride?"

"Affirm," Blues said. The Ninety-Nine noticed a spherical object grasped in one of the Headhunter's larger claws. It was a Gatekeeper, carved from his carapace.

They loaded on the transport. The Headhunter slumped heavily on his charging rack. Nolo took the controls up front. Blues sat in the back of the transport, across from the abducted overbeing, who was secured to the wall with a section of cargo netting.

The Ninety-Nine spent the trip back to the Headhunter's lair trying to avoid eye contact with Beliphres, who continued to listlessly beat his flippers against the side of his armored life support bubble.

CHAPTER SIXTY-FIVE_

Jessica Kramer used her pistol's muzzle to pull down the blinds, peeking through the gap to see if there was any traffic outside of Vervor's shop. Nothing. Still.

"Jessica, love, what are you doing?" Prath asked, not looking up from his news hologram.

"Those Gatekeepers are going to come and get us, ape," she said, "any minute now. I know you said not to worry, but I just have a bad feeling. Something's not right."

"We've already been over this, human," Vervor said, clacking his fangs. "The Gatekeepers won't attack you openly, now. They can't. You've shamed them, according to their Old Code. Their... protocol, their contractual honor, demands that they can't openly move against you. It would be seen as an admission of weakness, to them, and possibly endanger their hold on this entire place. Just like they can't acknowledge the Headhunter's existence, or his involvement at Berva Proxima.

Don't worry. They'll come up with some cover story. They always do."

"You're sure?" Jessica asked. "Better yet, *how* can you be sure?"

Vervor crossed his arms and sighed, his jaw and fangs jutting out with impatience.

"Their code hamstrings them," the Myoshan said. "They still have you in their sights, but you've forced them to regroup. Besides, rumor has it they have more serious problems on their nubby little hands. Your red friend seems to represent a much larger problem for them, and their control over the Nines. Well, the ones who weren't butchered, wholesale, at the arena, anyway. The Gatekeepers will be more worried about him than you or the Desecrator."

"The Centurion and Warlord did as much as one can, without starting an all-out war," Prath said, nodding to Vervor. "Like Master Vervor explained, the Gatekeepers will still be gunning for you, little human, but they'll have to pick another path for their operations of vendetta. You'll still have to keep your guard up, when things settle down."

"Great," Jessica said, holstering her revolver and sitting down in a shot-up chair. Jessica put her new red boots up on a workbench and poked a playful finger at Vervor.

"I looked up that choovah thing, you know," Jessica said, giving the Myoshan a sly smile. "I am *not* a foul-tempered, six-legged mammal from your home planet that fights horn-snakes in their own burrows."

"Of course, you aren't, Pilot, don't be silly," Vervor said. "As anyone can plainly see, you only have two legs, and there are no stripes in your fur."

The three of them shared a smile at the Myoshan's deadpan remark.

"Ugh," Jessica said, trying not to scratch the spray-skin on the back of her neck and shoulders. "The burns suck. My head is still ringing from that match, Prath, and my back aches. I think it was that last tumble off Masamune's shoulders."

"It was quite a fall, love," Prath said, reading his news hologram.

"I commed him yesterday, I don't know if I told you," Jessica said, turning in her chair to Prath.

"Did you?" Prath said, now looking up with interest. "How is our Master Mech Pilot friend doing? He disappeared with his son as soon as we unloaded his mech from the flatbed. I didn't have a chance to say good-bye to him or the boy."

"He told me he spent the entire day soaking in a hot bath," Jessica said. "He says he's not going into hiding, either. He's like you two, and thinks the Code will protect him. I don't buy it. I think he hit his head too hard against the inside of his cockpit. I guess I really rattled him hard with that last jump maneuver."

"Yes, well," Vervor said, "I must admit, it was an artful move. Too bad about the sniper ruining it. The Headhunter took care of the shooter, though. He showed me the head, along with another round bauble he had."

"Whoa, Vervor, back up," Jessica said, surprise on her face. "Did... did you just pay me a compliment? You?"

Vervor shrugged, and limped over to see what Kitos was working on. Jessica watched the Myoshan peer over the Niff's shoulder. Kitos had the NoName module on the test bench, with several of the new Arkathan strings of circuitry protruding from it.

"Hey, Niff, what are you doing, anyway?" Jessica Kramer said, adjusting her pistol. Her whole body was sore from the beating in the arena, and her new boots from the Third Gate mall pinched on the outside of her toes. They still looked good, though.

"Circuits still require examination, Pilot," Kitos said. "I-I

422 / BEAR ROSS

want to salvage as much as possible from damaged chassis. Have ideas for new, integrated circuits, if nodes can be convinced to grow new pathways."

"If you can jump-start some sort of production method, Kitos," Prath said, "you stand a good chance of becoming a very rich being. That Arkathan circuitry is worth its weight in the precious metal of your choice."

"Well, we're going to need some sort of revenue source," Vervor said, grumbling. "This shop doesn't run on hopes and dreams. The bills, payoffs, and taxes still need to be paid. My income stream from the Gatekeepers is most likely reduced to nothing, thanks to you two."

"Got ya covered, Vervor," Jessica said, holding up the credit-stick the Headhunter gave her. "Two hundred grand should get us by for a while."

"Hmmph," Vervor snorted. "Well, it will have to do, for now."

"Jessica, love, where did you—" Prath tried to ask.

"You don't want to know, Prath," Jessica said.

"No, after all this, I probably don't," the Ascended said.

"Well, I don't know about any long-term plans you two have," Jessica said. "but I think Kyuzo had the right idea. I'm going to head back to my hab-pod, pay some extra credits for a hot bath, and have a good soak. Maybe drink something cold, too, while I'm at it."

"Are you trying to talk yourself into a beer, love?" Prath said, looking over his reading glasses.

"Maybe," Jessica said, stretching out in the chair and smiling. "I think I've earned it."

Master Vervor heard a buzz from the front door of his shop. Jessica's moment of relaxation ended, and she jumped from her chair, pulling out her pistol.

"The damned blobs," she said. "I knew it."

"Settle down, Kramer," Vervor said. "We have a visitor."

The Myoshan shop owner pressed the release button in his hand, and they all heard the door open and close.

A tall, lanky being approached them. He held a tablet under one arm, a red box under the other.

"Greet," the Model Ninety-Nine said.

"Nolo!" Jessica said, putting her large handgun away. "Hey, Rockrib! How goes it?"

"Gift from boss, Pilot," the Headhunter's adjutant said, offering her the scarlet gift box. "No combat stims, sorry. Needed for future fight."

"I have enough bad habits, as it is, Niner," she said, accepting the box.

"Well, go on, open it," Master Vervor said. "Enough idle chit-chat."

It was a non-holographic picture in an ornate frame. A giant red claw held up an armored glass sphere for the view of the camera. The bubble's occupant did not look happy.

"Aw, how sweet. He shouldn't have," she said, grinning.

"More underneath picture," Nolo said.

"More? More pictures, or—"

She pulled out the rank insignia of an Enforcement Directorate Centurion, an older version from some time ago. The brass-colored rank tab was scorched on one side.

"Commanders will be needed, pilot," Nolo said. "Next waypoint not easy."

Jessica Kramer looked to Prath, whose eyes went from hers to their other compatriots. Kitos and Vervor both responded with a nod.

"Tell the red guy I have some things to do first," Jessica said, "but I will be ready when he needs me."

"War not starting anytime soon. Boss just wants to know, can count on Last of Kramers, when time to execute," the black-eyed trooper said.

"He can," she said, smiling.

CHAPTER SIXTY-SIX

CENTRAL DATA TOWER

COUNCIL OF EIGHT CHAMBERS

The tall, golden doors parted, and Mikralos entered the chamber of the Council of Eight. The wraparound view of Junctionworld from this height was spectacular. This would have been his ultimate goal, his final position. Now, he was in custody, facing a death sentence.

The captive Gatekeeper's grav drives were shackled with moderators, his compartments bound, his weaponry stripped. The elite Ninety-Nines, the Council's Centurion bodyguards, led him into the large hall at a solemn, regal pace. Every eye and sensor facing him radiated hatred.

The Centurions completed his humiliation by chaining him to the floor, locking him down in an illuminated circle of judgment. The shamed Gatekeeper could tell the Council's debate had been raging for some time.

"We continue to maintain that he is an incompetent," Lord Xenebris, the Eighth GateLord, said, pointing a manipulator at the defendant. "We advise he be butchered, publicly, and at once."

"You speak boldly for someone who lost an entire Worldgate!" said the Fourth GateLord, Verenus, pointing his own accusatory claw at Xenebris.

"You know damn well why our Worldgate was shut down," Xenebris shot back. "That situation was untenable, beyond our control, and we shall not take the blame for it. Nor shall we have our glass rubbed in it by the likes of you!"

"Fellow Council members, please," the Third GateLord, Polomius, said, bringing the session to order with the pounding of a claw on his podium. "You may continue this conversation after the proceedings. Let us now address the defendant. Centurions, you are dismissed."

The elite Nines in their unique armors bolted to attention, then filed out quietly of the room. The massive hall's doors closed with a soft, deep boom.

"Mikralos," Polomius said, raising his chassis to a commanding height, "you are summoned before this Council of Eight, though we are only seven in number at this time. You, alone, are the cause of this shortcoming, along with the resultant rebellion in your fallen superior's sector of control."

"If we may be allowed to speak—" Mikralos tried to say.

"And you are culpable," Polomius said, talking over the protesting defendant, "in the deaths of over a dozen members of our noble race. Our thorough investigation finds you to be complicit with these murders, by way of incompetence. Worst of all, your bungling has resulted in the triumph of Solomon Kramer, from beyond the grave."

"We just spent the last two days," Mikralos said, holding up a set of pudgy digits, "putting down the rebellion of the Nines, and you have us arrested for it, in the moment of our triumph! Those bombs were set without—"

"You will maintain silence," Lord Xenebris said, "or we will have you boiled alive in your own protective housing. Do you understand? Rebellion, we can handle. It is the nature of control. However, your mishandling of the Last Kramer is unforgivable. She still lives, thanks to you. She survived. Triumphed, even, by fighting your hand-picked ace assassin to a standstill."

"Then remove these chains and let us finish the task," Mikralos said. "Let us kill her, let us crush her with our own claws, just as we did in purging the uprising at Berva Proxima. Give us access to our main battle armor, and we will—"

"It is not our way, Mikralos," GateLord Verenus said, "and you have done enough damage. Your rage and blind arrogance threaten everything we have built up in this place. Our goal was to see the name of Kramer brought low, to keep the masses in check. Killing her now would be a transgression against the Old Code, and would make a martyr of her. We wish for the battle slave Solomon Kramer's legacy to be extinguished, not exalted."

"The *Code*?" Mikralos said, astonished. "You... you doddering, self-important aristocrats *dare* to use the Old Code as an excuse to shield her from me? Is this what we have come to? Restrained by our own laws from dominating these vermin?"

"The Old Code is all that is standing between you and a public execution, defendant," Xenebris said, his voice a hissing rebuke. "The vast, sweeping scale of your ineptitude is staggering. To compound that, we shall not even begin to soil these chambers with details of how you enabled the public emergence, and escape, of the renegade Centurion."

Several of the Council members cringed, their running lights pulsing at the mere mention of the Headhunter.

"This chamber will come to order," GateLord Xenebris said, trying to stifle the mild panic of his fellow GateLords.

"Mikralos, how do you answer these charges against you?"

the somber, imperious Polomius asked, a holographic scroll appearing beside him. The list of charges stretched into the hundreds of sub-categories and offenses.

Mikralos stared at the seven members of the Council, his eyes hard.

"We do not answer stupid questions," Mikralos said, "even when they are asked by a GateLord."

The members of the Council gasped, their claws aflutter, and the room erupted in bedlam. The seven council members hurled a flurry of insults and accusations at both Mikralos and each other. In time, GateLord Polomius restored calm, his podium now dented from the repeated gavel-blows of his claw.

"Very well," GateLord Polomius said. "Your disrespect for these proceedings is cause for summary judgment. All members of the Council who find the less-than-honorable Mikralos guilty of incompetence and dereliction in the performance of his duties, place a claw on the central recording table."

Seven manipulators fell on the glowing circle, and it flashed, recording the vote.

"And sentencing?" Xenebris asked, eager to dish out punishment.

"We must take into account the defendant's combat record from the conquest of this place," GateLord Verenus said, "as well as the purging of the traitorous Enforcement Directorate ranks in the Sixth Gate Barracks."

"Mikralos may not be a master strategist," GateLord Polomius said, "but he is too esteemed of a combat tactician to simply execute, wish that as we may."

"Agreed," Verenus said, nodding. "It would send the wrong message to his combat brethren. We will need them for what is coming."

"Be that as it may," Xenebris said, pouring his hatred into the words, "we, as GateLords, cannot tolerate an error of such massive proportions. The sentence must be severe, and unyielding."

They mused, muttering amongst themselves. One of the GateLords who was quiet throughout the proceedings spoke up.

"If death is too much, then what of banishment? Exile?" the Lord of the First Gate Zone said.

"Banishment? Yes, that would serve our greater purpose," Polomius said. He pondered a destination. "Through the Eighth Gate?"

"But, of course," Xenebris said, his running lights pulsing orange and black. "Where else?"

Mikralos's stalwart composure shattered at the mention of the swirling, forbidden vortex, and he bucked against his restraints. Bubbles flowed from his mouth as he screamed his protests.

"Ah, the Eighth Gate it is," GateLord Xenebris said, smiling. A light pulsed in his armored sphere, and the elite Model Ninety-Nine guards re-entered through the gleaming council chamber doors. "Farewell, Mikralos. Depart in failure," Gate-Lord Xenebris said. "Centurions, take him away."

Thank you for reading *Defiance,* book one in Junctionworld.

We hope you enjoyed it as much as we enjoyed bringing it to you. We just wanted to take a moment to encourage you to review the book on Amazon and Goodreads. Every review helps further the author's reach and, ultimately, helps them continue writing fantastic books for us all to enjoy.

If you liked this book, check out the rest of our catalogue at www.aethonbooks.com. To sign up to receive a FREE collection from some of our best authors as well as updates regarding all new releases, visit www.subscribepage.com/AethonReadersGroup.

BEAR'S WRITING NOTES,
MEANDERINGS, AND GRATITUDES_

Howdy.

A few thoughts on Jessica Kramer, and more than a few 'thank yous' to people who helped get me here.

Jessica Kramer is a complex character, to me, at least. She's a traumatized kid who had to grow up on her own, scratching out an existence on the mean streets of an interdimensional hellhole. Solving her brother's death only leads to more anger and pain. I like how her arc developed, and I'm glad she grew beyond just a 'mean girl' to a fleshed-out character. Telling her story wasn't easy, but I'm glad it came out the way it did.

I'm already working on her next adventure in J-world. She's a fun character to write, a little rough around the edges, I know, but the Universi around her holds a lot of potential for more stories. More importantly, the scope of Junctionworld and its attached Worldgates gives her room to grow and develop beyond the semi-reformed drunken brat we first meet. That Eighth Gate mystery, lurking in the background, is going to figure prominently in the future, along with the Headhunter's ongoing crusade for freedom. I hope you come back for more.

So, now that that's out of the way, I'd like to ask a favor of you. If you liked the book, leave a review on Amazon or the review site of your choice. Tell a friend. Point some more folks in forums and Facebook groups my way, without spamming, of course, and help me keep the ball rolling. Word-of-mandible is pretty effective, too.

I'd like to thank my wife, Beautiful Rachel, for her advice and direction through a couple tough spots. Just so you know, she is insisting I write an entire Headhunter book. We'll see, babe.

I'd like to thank Chad W. Hardin, who helped give me my big break in writing, and for his lifelong friendship.

Thanks to Slade Hart and Davis VanderVelde, also for their enduring friendship through the years, and putting up with my weirdness.

I'd like to thank Rhett C. Bruno and Steve Beaulieu, my publishers at Aethon Books, for taking a gamble on me. They liked my indie solo novel enough to offer me a contract for a trilogy, along with audiobooks. I was flabbergasted. I'm, honestly, still in shock. I never thought I'd get a full novel off the ground and into print, and now I'm climbing Trilogy Mountain. It's checked off a major box in life's to-do list. Thanks for giving me a shot, guys.

My eternal gratitude goes to my English teacher from my high school days, Ms. Judy Michaels, for focusing and channeling my wild, sporadic need to simply put things on paper into real writing.

Thanks to my co-worker Dan Warner, who helped proofread the first versions of the book and gave some great feedback.

To Richard Fox, who took time out of his busy schedule to look a few things over, and gift me with some excellent advice. I credit his quick suggestions for helping me land a book deal. I owe him a beer, or two.

Finally, my thanks to Michael Anderle and Craig Martelle for opening my eyes to see beyond the Gatekeepers.

In closing, I'd like to thank *you*, the reader or listener, as the case may be, for giving a guy starting out on his dream career a chance. Thanks for picking up this title. I hope you enjoyed it as much as I enjoyed creating it. It was a blast!

Best,

Bear

ABOUT THE AUTHOR_

I'm John Bear Ross, but you can call me Bear, and I write and work in Southern Nevada. I turn large amounts of caffeine into words.

I was born in Arizona. I served in the Marine Corps Reserves as a machine-gunner. I enjoy firearms, motorcycles, 3D printing, and machining. Oh, and beer. Maybe too much.

On top of all those things, I am a blue-collar guy with a compulsion to write. There's not much more to me than that.

I'm married to my wife, Beautiful Rachel, and we have two kids together. My work is dedicated to them.

To get ahold of me, feel free to email me at
johnbearross@gmail.com

Or, join me on Facebook, where I do most of my interacting.
My public page is www.facebook.com/BearRossWriter

SPECIAL THANKS TO:

ADAWIA E. ASAD	EDDIE HALLAHAN	KYLE OATHOUT
JENNY AVERY	JOSH HAYES	LILY OMIDI
BARDE PRESS	PAT HAYES	TROY OSGOOD
CALUM BEAULIEU	BILL HENDERSON	GEOFF PARKER
BEN	JEFF HOFFMAN	NICHOLAS (BUZ) PENNEY
BECKY BEWERSDORF	GODFREY HUEN	JASON PENNOCK
BHAM	JOAN QUERALTÓ IBÁÑEZ	THOMAS PETSCHAUER
TANNER BLOTTER	JONATHAN JOHNSON	JENNIFER PRIESTER
ALFRED JOSEPH BOHNE IV	MARCEL DE JONG	RHEL
CHAD BOWDEN	KABRINA	JODY ROBERTS
ERREL BRAUDE	PETRI KANERVA	JOHN BEAR ROSS
DAMIEN BROUSSARD	ROBERT KARALASH	DONNA SANDERS
CATHERINE BULLINER	VIKTOR KASPERSSON	FABIAN SARAVIA
JUSTIN BURGESS	TESLAN KIERINHAWK	TERRY SCHOTT
MATT BURNS	ALEXANDER KIMBALL	SCOTT
BERNIE CINKOSKE	JIM KOSMICKI	ALLEN SIMMONS
MARTIN COOK	FRANKLIN KUZENSKI	KEVIN MICHAEL STEPHENS
ALISTAIR DILWORTH	MEENAZ LODHI	MICHAEL J. SULLIVAN
JAN DRAKE	DAVID MACFARLANE	PAUL SUMMERHAYES
BRET DULEY	JAMIE MCFARLANE	JOHN TREADWELL
RAY DUNN	HENRY MARIN	CHRISTOPHER J. VALIN
ROB EDWARDS	CRAIG MARTELLE	PHILIP VAN ITALLIE
RICHARD EYRES	THOMAS MARTIN	JAAP VAN POELGEEST
MARK FERNANDEZ	ALAN D. MCDONALD	FRANCK VAQUIER
CHARLES T FINCHER	JAMES MCGLINCHEY	VORTEX
SYLVIA FOIL	MICHAEL MCMURRAY	DAVID WALTERS JR
GAZELLE OF CAERBANNOG	CHRISTIAN MEYER	MIKE A. WEBER
DAVID GEARY	SEBASTIAN MÜLLER	PAMELA WICKERT
MICHEAL GREEN	MARK NEWMAN	JON WOODALL
BRIAN GRIFFIN	JULIAN NORTH	BRUCE YOUNG